THE DELICATE STORM

ALSO BY GILES BLUNT

Forty Words for Sorrow

GILES BLUNT

THE DELICATE STORM

A MARIAN WOOD BOOK

Published by G. P. Putnam's Sons · a member of Penguin Group (USA) Inc. · New York

A Marian Wood Book
Published by G. P. Putnam's Sons
Publishers Since 1838
a member of
Penguin Group (USA) Inc.
375 Hudson Street
New York, NY 10014

Grateful acknowledgment is made to Donald Lorimer for permission
to quote lines from his poem "The Delicate Storm," published
in *Tendencies* (Toronto, 1975).

Library of Congress Cataloging-in-Publication Data

Blunt, Giles.
The delicate storm / Giles Blunt.
p.   cm.
"A Marian Wood book."
ISBN 0-399-14865-5
1. Police—Ontario—Fiction.   2. Ontario—Fiction.
I. Title.
PS3552.L887D4   2003   2002036817
813'.54—dc21

Printed in the United States of America
1   3   5   7   9   10   8   6   4   2

This book is printed on acid-free paper. ⊗

Book design by Victoria Kuskowski

FOR JANNA

ACKNOWLEDGMENTS

I owe a debt of thanks to the following people, who read troublesome early drafts of *The Delicate Storm* and made crucial suggestions for cuts and improvements: Anne Collins, my editor at Random House of Canada; my agent, Helen Heller; my editor at HarperCollins, Julia Wisdom; and my editor at Putnam, Marian Wood.

Thanks are also due to Staff Sergeant Rick Sapinski of the North Bay Police, who was generous with information on police methods; to Daniel Johnson, who did extensive research; and to The Writers Room in New York.

It is that these distant pawns
Breach this human wish.
Crashing as they do
Upon so particular a heaven.

—DONALD LORIMER
"The Delicate Storm"

THE DELICATE STORM

1

FIRST CAME THE WARMTH. Three weeks after New Year's, and the thermometer did what it never does in January in Algonquin Bay: it rose above the freezing mark. Within a matter of hours the streets were shiny and black with melted snow.

There wasn't a trace of sun. A ceiling of cloud installed itself above the cathedral spire and gave every appearance of permanence. The warm days that followed passed in an oppressive twilight that lasted from breakfast to late afternoon. Everywhere there were dark mutterings about global warming.

Then came the fog.

At first it moved in fine tendrils among the trees and forests that surround Algonquin Bay. By Saturday afternoon, it was rolling in thick clouds along the highways. The wide expanse of Lake Nipissing dwindled to a faint outline, then vanished utterly. Slowly the fog squeezed its way into town and pressed itself up against the stores and the churches. One by one the red-brick houses retired behind the grubby gray curtain.

By Monday morning, Ivan Bergeron couldn't even see his own hand. He had slept late, having drunk an unwise amount of beer while watching the hockey game the night before. Now, he was making his way from the house to his garage, which was less than twenty yards away but totally obscured by fog. The stuff clung in webs to Bergeron's face and hands; he could feel it trailing through his fingers. And it played tricks with sound. The yellow bloom of headlights glided by, dead slow, followed—only after an otherworldly delay—by the sound of tires on wet road.

Somewhere his dog was barking. Normally, Shep was a quiet, self-sufficient kind of mutt. But for some reason—maybe the fog—he was out in the woods and barking maniacally. The sound pierced Bergeron's hung-over skull like needles.

"Shep! Come here, Shep!" He waited for a few moments in the murk, but the dog didn't come.

Bergeron opened up the garage and went to work on the battered Ski-Doo he had promised to fix by the previous Thursday. The owner was coming for it at noon, and the thing was still in bits and pieces around the shop.

Bergeron switched on the radio, and the voices of the CBC filled the garage. Usually, when it was warm enough, he worked with the garage door open, but the fog lay in the driveway like some creature out of a nightmare, and he found it depressing. He was just about to pull the door down when the dog's barking got louder.

"Shep!" It sounded like the dog was in the backyard now.

Bergeron waded through the fog, moving with one hand out before him like a blind man. "Shep! For God's sake, can it, willya?"

The barking changed to growling, interrupted by peculiar canine whines. A tremor of unease passed through Bergeron's outsize frame. Last time this had happened, the dog had been playing with a snake.

"Shep. Take it easy, boy. I'm coming."

Bergeron moved with small steps now, edging his way forward. He squinted into the fog.

"Shep?"

He could just make the dog out, six feet away, down on his forepaws, clawing at something on the ground. Bergeron edged closer and took hold of the dog's collar.

"Easy, boy."

The dog whined a little and licked his hand, calmer now. Bergeron bent lower to see what was on the ground.

"Oh, my God."

It lay there, fishbelly white, hair curling along one side. Toward the wrist end, the flesh still bore the zigzag impression of a watch with an expandable bracelet. Even though there was no hand attached, there was no doubt that the thing lying in Ivan Bergeron's backyard was a human arm.

.   .   .

IF IT HADN'T BEEN for Ray Choquette's decision to retire, John Cardinal would not have been sitting in the waiting room with his father, when he could have been down at headquarters catching up on phone calls, or—better yet—out on the street making life a misery for one of Algonquin Bay's bad guys. But no. Here he was, stuck in a waiting room with his father, waiting to see a doctor neither of them had ever met. A female doctor, at that—as if Stan Cardinal was going to take advice from a woman. Ray Choquette, Cardinal thought, I could wring your lazy, inconsiderate neck.

The senior Cardinal was eighty-three—physically. Even the hair on his forearms was white now, and he had the watery eyes of a very old man. In other ways, his son was thinking, the guy never got past the age of four.

"How much longer is she gonna make us wait?" Stan said for the third time. "Forty-five minutes we've been sitting here. What kind of respect does that show for other people's time? How can she possibly be a good doctor?"

"It's like anything else, Dad. A good doctor's a busy doctor."

"Nonsense. It's greed. A hundred-percent pure, capitalist greed. You know, I was happy making thirty-five thousand dollars a year on the railroad. We had to fight like hell to get that kind of money, and by God we fought for it. But nobody goes to medical school because they want to make thirty-five thousand dollars."

Here we go, Cardinal thought. Rant number 27 D. It was like his father's brain consisted of a collection of cassettes.

"And then you've got the government playing Scrooge with these guys," Stan went on. "So they become stockbrokers or lawyers where they can make the kind of money they want. And then we end up with no damn doctors."

"Talk to Geoff Mantis. He's the one who took the chainsaw to medicare."

"They'd make you wait anyways. No matter how many of them there were," Stan said. "It's a class thing. Class not only must exist, it must be seen to exist. Making you wait is their way of saying 'I'm important, and you're not.'"

"Dad, there's a shortage of doctors. That's why we have to wait."

"What I want to know is, what kind of young woman spends her day looking down people's throats and up their anuses? I'd never do it."

"Mr. Cardinal?"

Stan Cardinal got to his feet with difficulty. The young receptionist came round from behind her desk, clutching a file folder.

"Do you need some help?"

"I'm fine, I'm fine." Stan turned to Cardinal. "You coming, or what?"

"I don't need to go in with you," Cardinal said.

"No, you come too. I want you to hear this. You think I'm not fit to drive, I want you to hear the truth."

The receptionist opened the door to the consulting room and they went in.

"Mr. Cardinal? Winter Cates." The doctor couldn't have been much more than thirty, but she rose from behind her desk and came round to shake hands with the brisk efficiency of an old pro. She had fine, pale skin that contrasted sharply with her black hair. Dark eyebrows knit themselves in a quizzical look now, aimed at Cardinal.

"I'm his son. He asked me to come in with him."

"He thinks I can't drive," Stan said. "But I know my feet are better, and I want him to hear it from the horse's mouth. How old are you, anyway?"

"I'm thirty-two. How old are you?"

Stan emitted a quack of surprise. "I'm eighty-three."

Dr. Cates gestured at a chair facing the desk.

"That's okay. I'll stand for now."

The three of them stood there in the middle of the room, Dr. Cates flipping through Stan's chart. Her hair was held in place by a clip; without it, Cardinal noted, it would be springing out all over the place, wild and black. She radiated energy, and Cardinal had the sense of enormous vitality held in check by the seriousness of her profession.

"Well, you've been a healthy guy up until recently," she said.

"Never smoked. Never drank more than a beer with dinner."

"Smart guy, too, then."

"Some people might not think so." This with a glance at Cardinal that Cardinal ignored.

"And you have diabetes, which you keep under control with Glucophage. You're self-monitoring?"

"Oh, yeah. Can't say I enjoy pricking my finger every five minutes, but yeah. I keep my blood sugar right in the normal range. You're welcome to check it."

"I plan to," she said.

Stan looked at Cardinal. His expression said, "Is this woman being rude to me? By God, if this woman's being rude to me . . ."

"And Dr. Choquette notes you had considerable neuropathy in your feet."

"Had. It's better now."

"You were having trouble walking. Standing, even. Driving must have been out of the question, right?"

"Well, I wouldn't say that. My feet just felt—not numb, exactly—but like they had sponges on 'em. It didn't slow me up much."

Please don't let him drive, Cardinal was thinking. He'll kill himself or somebody else, and I don't want to get that phone call.

Dr. Cates led Stan to a door off to the right. "Just take a seat in the examining room. Remove your shoes and socks and shirt."

"My shirt?"

"I want to listen to your heart. Dr. Choquette noted some arrhythmia—six months ago. He referred you to a cardiologist. I don't see any results here."

"Yeah, well. I never got to see that cardiologist."

"That's not good," Dr. Cates said. There was a note of flint in her voice.

"He was busy, I was busy. You know how it is. It just never happened."

"You have heart failure in your family history, Mr. Cardinal. That is not something you ignore." Dr. Cates turned to Cardinal; she had the kind of cool gaze that he found sexy in a woman, no doubt because it was meant not to be. "I think you'd better wait out here."

"Fine with me." Cardinal took a seat.

There was a rap on the door and the receptionist came in. "Sorry. Craig Simmons is here. He insists I tell you he's still waiting."

"Melissa, I'm with a patient. I have patients lined up all day. He can't just drop in like this."

"I know that. I keep telling him. I've told him fifty times. He won't listen."

"All right. Tell him I can see him for five minutes after this patient. But this is the last time."

"Sorry about that," Dr. Cates said when her receptionist had gone, dark eyes no longer cool. "Some people can't take no for an answer."

She went into the examining room and closed the door. Cardinal could hear their voices but not what they said. He looked around at the consulting room. In Ray Choquette's day it had been all chrome and vinyl. Now, there were leather chairs, a ceiling fan, and two glass-fronted bookcases crammed with medical texts. A deep red Persian rug gave the place a warm, inviting feel, more like a study than an office.

Fifteen minutes later Dr. Cates came out of the examining room, followed by Cardinal's father, who was looking thunderous.

Dr. Cates pulled out her prescription pad and spoke while she wrote. "I'm giving you two prescriptions. The first one is a diuretic; that should help keep your chest clear. And the other one is a blood-thinner, to keep your blood pressure down." She tore off the scrips and handed them to Stan. "I'm going to call the cardiologist myself. That way we'll be sure to get you in. My assistant will call you later to let you know what time."

"What about the driving?" Cardinal said.

Dr. Cates shook her head. A strand of black hair came loose and curled around her neck. "No driving."

That did it for Stan. "God damn it. How would you like it if you had to call someone every time you wanted to go out? Thirty years old, what do you know about anything? How do you know what I can or can't feel—in my feet or any other damn place? I was driving twenty years before you were born. Never had an accident. Never had so much as a speeding ticket. And now you're telling me I can't drive? What am I supposed to do? Call *him* every five minutes?"

"I know it's upsetting, Mr. Cardinal. And you're right: I wouldn't like it at all. But there're a couple of things you might want to keep in mind."

"Oh, sure. Now you can tell me what to think, too."

"Let me finish."

"What did you say to me?"

"I said let me finish."

Good for you, Cardinal thought. A lot of people were cowed by Stan's bluster—including Cardinal himself sometimes—but this young woman was holding her own.

"A couple of things to keep in mind: First, this neuropathy will probably get better. You've been looking after your blood sugar, and that's the best thing you can do. Three or four more months might make all the difference. Second, everybody depends on other people. We all have to learn to ask for what we need."

"It's like being crippled, for God's sake."

"It's not the end of the world. Frankly, I'm far more worried about your heart. I'm hearing a lot of fluid in your chest. Let's get that looked after, and then we'll worry about your driving, all right?"

When Cardinal and his father stepped back into the waiting room, a man got out of his chair and brushed by them. Something about him was familiar—the combination of blond hair and the gym-rat physique—but he had entered the consulting room and closed the door before Cardinal could place him.

Cardinal waited while the receptionist explained a referral form to his father. Angry voices issued from the consulting room.

"Dr. Cates get many patients like that?" Cardinal said to the receptionist.

"He's not a patient," she said. "He's a—well, I don't know what you'd call him."

"Can we please get out of here?" said Stan. "Believe it or not, I don't want to spend the rest of my life in a doctor's office."

. . .

CARDINAL HAD TO TAKE it slow up Algonquin. The fog that had been blanketing the region for the past few days was thickest at the bottom of Airport Hill. Third week of January and it was as warm as April. Normally this time of year you'd expect blinding blue skies and temperatures so far below zero it didn't bear thinking about. But the fog was beginning to have a permanent look.

"Of course, there's no such thing as global warming," Cardinal said, trying to shake his father out of his mood.

"She talked to me like I was six years old," Stan said.

"She told you the truth. Telling someone the truth is a mark of respect."

"Like you don't have better things to do than drive me all over hell's half acre."

"Well, you're always telling me I'm in a lousy line of work."

"Which is true. Why you want to spend your time chasing lunatics and vagabonds is beyond me. Or those domestics you get? Husbands so drunk they can't stand up? You and I both know the only reason anyone ever gets caught is because the crooks are even dumber than the— Where are you going, John? That was my driveway back there."

"Sorry. Can't see a thing with this fog."

"Look, you can just make out the squirrel there."

Stan Cardinal had a huge copper squirrel in his front yard, an ancient weather vane covered with verdigris, that he'd salvaged years before. The fog lent it a certain creepiness. Cardinal made a careful U-turn and pulled into the drive.

"Give me a call tomorrow and we'll get you to the cardiologist. If I can't do it, Catherine will be happy to—hold on." His cell phone was buzzing.

"Cardinal, where are you?" It was Duty Sergeant Mary Flower. "We got a 10-47 at Main and MacPherson, and we need everyone we've got."

"I'm on it." He clicked off the phone. "Gotta run," he said to Stan. "Call Catherine later and let her know what time tomorrow."

"Major crisis, is it? Another one of your domestics, I bet."

"Actually, it's a bank robbery."

. . .

THE FEDERAL TRUST was right downtown on Main Street—a low red-brick structure that made no attempt to blend in with the century-old buildings surrounding it. Cardinal didn't bank there, but he remembered going inside with his father as a kid. By the time he pulled up in front there were already three black-and-whites parked at crazy angles in the street and on the sidewalk.

Ken Szelagy, the size of a grizzly bear and by his own description a mad Hungarian, was at the door, jabbering into his cell phone. He raised a hand as Cardinal approached. "Guy's long gone. We're trying to get access to the security tape right now. Gonna be fun looking for him in this pea soup, eh?"

"Anybody hurt?"

"Nope. Shaken up some, though."

"Delorme inside?"

"Yeah. She's got things pretty much under control."

Lise Delorme, in addition to being a first-class detective, had a calm, reasonable manner that was a real asset in dealing with the public. She had compelling physical qualities, too, but right now it was that reasonable manner that counted. Cardinal had handled several bank robberies, and usually it meant a scene of excitement verging on hysteria. But Delorme had got all the employees sitting quietly at their desks, waiting to be interviewed. Cardinal found her talking to the manager in his glass-fronted office.

The manager himself hadn't seen anything of the robbery, but led them to the young teller who just minutes before had been looking at the barrel of a gun. Cardinal let Delorme ask the questions, but the teller could recall very little about the man behind it.

"He was wearing a scarf over his face," she said. "A plaid scarf. He had it pulled up like an outlaw, you know, in a Western. It all happened so fast."

"What about his voice?" Delorme said. "What did he sound like?"

"I never heard his voice. He didn't say anything—at least, I don't think so. He just stood there staring at me and passed a note over the counter. It was terrifying."

"Do you still have that note?"

She shook her head. "He took it with him."

Cardinal glanced around. There was a balled-up piece of paper at his feet. He picked it up and opened it by the edges, trying to preserve any fingerprints. There was typing on one side, and on the other, printed in pencil with idiosyncratic spelling: *Don't make a sound or I'll shot. Don't press any alarms or I'll shot. Hand over all the money in your droor.*

"I emptied the top drawer and put it in a manila envelope. That's what we're supposed to do in this situation, we're just supposed to do what they ask. He shoved the money in his knapsack."

"What color was the knapsack?"

"Red."

"Are you certain he said nothing at all?" Delorme said. "I'm sure it happened very quickly, but try and think back."

"He said, 'Just do it.' Something like that. Oh, and 'hurry up.' "

"Did he have an accent?" Delorme asked. "English? French Canadian?" Her own accent was light French Canadian. The only time Cardinal noticed it was when she was angry.

"I was so terrified he was going to shoot me. I didn't notice."

"Oh, my God," Cardinal said, staring at the other side of the note. "It's Wudky." He stepped away from the counter and gestured for Delorme to follow.

"What the hell is a Wudky?" she wanted to know. Delorme had worked the mostly white-collar arena of Special Investigations for six years before moving to the Criminal Investigation Division. There were gaps in her knowledge of the local fauna.

"WDC—or Wudky—short for World's Dumbest Criminal. Wudky is Robert Henry Hewitt."

"You're saying you know this Hewitt's the guy?"

Cardinal handed her the note. "Hold it by the edge, there."

Delorme peered at both sides of the note, then caught her breath. "It's an old arrest warrant. The guy writes a holdup note on the back of his own arrest warrant? I don't believe it."

"You don't win the title of World's Dumbest Criminal by half-measures. Robert Henry Hewitt is a real champ, and I happen to know where he lives."

"Well, so do I. It's right here on his holdup note."

ROBERT HENRY HEWITT lived in the basement apartment of a miniature, run-down house tucked into the crevasse of a rock-cut behind Ojibwa Secondary School. Cardinal stopped the car in a gray swirl of fog. They could just make out the row of dented garbage cans at the end of the driveway. "Looks like we beat him home."

"If he isn't home by now, what makes you think he's coming?"

Cardinal shrugged. "It's the dumbest thing I can think of."

"What kind of car does he drive?"

"Orange Toyota, about a hundred years old. Even the spackling is rusty."

They heard the car approach before they saw it—a disembodied collection of sound effects for the Tin Man. Then it clattered past them, a dangling exhaust pipe scraping the sidewalk as it pulled into the driveway.

"Open your door," Cardinal said. "Let's be ready to move."

"But he's armed," Delorme said. "Shouldn't we call for backup?" She looked at him, those earnest brown eyes sizing him up. Cardinal thought about Delorme's eyes more often than he would have liked.

"Technically, yes. On the other hand, I know Robert. We're not in a hell of a lot of danger."

The Toyota's one good taillight dimmed and went out.

Cardinal and Delorme got out of the car and left the doors open so as not to make a sound. Stepping carefully on the wet pavement, they moved in on the Toyota.

The driver, a small man with frizzy ginger hair and a plaid scarf around his neck, got out and opened the trunk. He pulled out a bulging plastic FoodMart bag, slung a red knapsack over his shoulder, and slammed the trunk shut with his elbow.

"Robert Henry Hewitt?"

He dropped the knapsack and the groceries and started to run, but Cardinal caught hold of his jacket and the two of them fell to the ground in a tangle of arms and legs. Then Cardinal hauled him up, and Algonquin Bay's master thief was facedown against the trunk of the Toyota, feet spread wide behind him.

"If he moves, spank him," Cardinal said, and patted him down. He pulled a pistol from a jacket pocket. "Goodness me. A firearm."

"That there is a toy," Hewitt said. "I wasn't gonna hurt nobody."

"Wasn't gonna hurt nobody where?"

"At the bank, for Christ's sake."

"Robert, what do I say to you every time I see you?"

Wudky turned to look over his shoulder. When he recognized Cardinal he grinned, showing splayed front teeth in appalling condition. "Oh, hi! How you doing? I was just thinking about you, eh?"

"Robert? What do I say to you? Every time I see you."

Wudky thought for a moment. "You say, 'Stay out of trouble, Robert.'"

"Nobody listens to me, Sergeant Delorme," Cardinal said. "It's a real problem. Check the knapsack, there. I'd say we have probable cause."

Delorme unzipped the knapsack and pulled out a plump manila envelope with Federal Trust stenciled in one corner. She opened it wide and showed the contents to Cardinal.

Cardinal gave a low whistle of appreciation. "Quite a haul, there, Robert. Why, it looks like you made off with tens of dollars."

2

AFTER WUDKY WAS SAFELY booked and in his cell, Cardinal went back to his desk to type up his supplementary reports.

The amount of money Wudky had made off with was minuscule. If he'd stolen it from a cash register, he wouldn't be likely to get more than probation, but Cardinal knew the Crown would insist on a charge of bank robbery and wrote his report accordingly.

He was almost finished when Duty Sergeant Mary Flower called out to him, "Hey, Cardinal, I think you better talk to Wudky." She was coming out of the doorway that led from the cells to the front desk.

"Wudky," Cardinal said. "How important can it be?"

"He says he has information on some murder."

Cardinal looked over at Delorme, several desks away. She rolled her eyes.

"Do you know how unlikely that is?" Cardinal said.

Flower shrugged. "Tell him. Don't tell me."

Cardinal and Delorme went back to the holding area. There were eight cells that formed an L between booking and the garage. Wudky was in the second-last cell, the only one occupied at the moment.

"I ain't telling nothing for free," Wudky said, trying to sound tough. He looked as forlorn a creature as Cardinal had ever seen, with his frizzed-out hair and his hangdog eyes and his smelly sweatshirt. "I want to, like, make a deal. Like, so's I can get out on bail maybe?"

"Chances aren't great on that score," Cardinal said. "But it depends what you have to tell us. I can't make any promises."

"But you'd put in a good word for me? Tell them I did my duty as a citizen? I helped the police?"

"If you give us some valuable information, I will tell the prosecutor that you have been helpful."

"And apologetic, too, eh? Tell him I'm sorry about the bank. I don't know what I was thinking."

"I'll tell him. What have you got, Robert?"

"I mean, I feel bad, you know—especially since you're always telling me to stay out of trouble—and I appreciate that. I don't want you to think I don't listen. I do listen. I just forget. You know, an idea gets in my head and it kinda worlds around in there like a clothes dryer."

"Robert?"

"What?"

"Just tell us what you've got."

"Okay. Day before I pretended to rob the bank?"

"You took money," Delorme said. "That isn't pretending."

"Okay, okay. Day before. I'm down in Toronto visiting my girlfriend."

Cardinal made a mental note—when he had a lot of time—to hear more about this girlfriend. She would have to be either a lunatic or a saint.

"I'm down in T.O. to see my girlfriend, and I decides to go out one night to a bar. You know, just a night out on my own. So I goes over to Spadina—you know the Penny Wheel?"

"All too well." Before Algonquin Bay, Cardinal had spent ten years on the Toronto force. Every Toronto cop knew the Penny Wheel. It was a dank basement on Spadina, the kind of red-vinyl dive that only a criminal could love. The remarkable thing was that, unlike practically every other square foot of Toronto, this particular dive had managed to remain utterly unchanged.

"So, I'm over at the Penny Wheel, when who comes in but Thierry Ferand. You know Thierry—he's like a trapper and shit."

"I know Thierry." Ferand was indeed one of the local fur trappers. Twice a year he came in out of the woods to sell his wares at the fur auction. Every time he did, he was arrested for drunk and disorderly, and often some variation of assault. There were rumors he occasionally did some work for the local version of the mafia, but nothing had ever been proved. He was a small guy, but mean with it, and sneaky. When he was upset, his filthy little hand would sprout brass knuckles.

"Well, me and Thierry go way back."

"To Kingston Pen if I recall correctly."

"Wow! How'd you know that? You guys're amazing. Anyways, I see Thierry sitting in a corner by himself so I go over and we start shooting the breeze. And Thierry is really drunk, eh? I mean really drunk. And he starts telling me things." Wudky stepped right up to the bars of his cell and peered both ways along the corridor. Then, in a tone implying information of national import, he added, "Big things."

"Such as?"

"Oh, nothing. Just a little murder. Would you be interested in that?" Whatever else Robert Henry Hewitt may have been, he was easily the world's worst actor; Cardinal had difficulty keeping a straight face. He was afraid to even glance at Delorme, in case they both broke up.

"Why, yes, Robert. We would be interested in murder."

"And you'll tell the Crown guy I helped you out?"

"That's it, I'm leaving." Cardinal started for the door.

"Wait! Wait! Okay, okay! I'll tell you. You're such a hardass. I've met guys in stir that're more calmer." As if to clear Cardinal's impatience from his brain, Wudky inserted a finger into his own ear and reamed it out. "So, what I was saying: Thierry is really drunk and he starts telling me this stuff he knew about, that, like, really scared him, you know? He finishes like his tenth beer or so, and he's leaning all over the table, and he tells me what happened to a friend of his. Guy named Paul Bressard. He's another trapper, eh? Turns out Paul Bressard got himself murdered. Some guy from out of town he owed money to. Could be mafia, maybe, a godfather or something. You ever rent that movie?"

"Could we just stick with the story here, Robert?" Bressard had indeed, though long ago, been charged with aggravated assault after half-killing a man who owed money to Leon Petrucci. Perhaps it was the chilling sound on the tapes from the wiretap of Petrucci's voice synthesizer (legacy of a fondness for Cuban cigars) telling Bressard he'd be well rewarded for "explaining their position," but the jury had gotten cold feet and neither Bressard nor Petrucci had served a day. It was just possible his mob connections had somehow come back to bite Bressard.

"I'm telling you. This guy—some bad guy—comes up to Algonquin Bay from out of town and kills Bressard, and Thierry says he knows where the body is."

Cardinal turned to Delorme. "We receive any missing persons report on Paul Bressard?"

"Not that I know of. I'll go check the board."

"Okay, Robert, where's the body?"

"Do I have to know that before you help me out?"

"Let's just say it would add to your chances. And how did Thierry Ferand happen to know where the so-called body was buried in the first place?"

"I don't know! I didn't ask!" Wudky cocked his head to one side like the RCA dog and scratched his scalp. "Well, maybe he did tell me, only I can't remember. I had a few beers myself. But I'm telling you about a murder you didn't know about, right? The Crown'll like take that under consignment, right?"

"I'll check it out," Cardinal said. "But I hope you're not wasting my time."

"Oh, no. I would never do a thing like that, eh?"

3

CARDINAL DROVE OUT PAST his father's place to the northern limit of Algonquin Bay, where he made a left onto Ojibwa Road. There were only three houses on Ojibwa—two decrepit bungalows and Bressard's brick split-level. Even in the mist it looked like any other middle-class suburban residence; there was nothing about it to tell the passerby that the owner made his living the way generations of his forefathers had, by trapping animals for their fur.

Paul Bressard himself was another matter. He was just coming out of the house as Cardinal swung into the drive, and he looked anything but suburban. Fur trappers are a breed apart, with a tendency to eccentricity, even wildness, that makes them stand out in a place as conservative as Algonquin Bay. But even among that flamboyant species, Bressard was a man who made an impression. He swept down the front steps now in a wide-brimmed beaver hat and a floor-length raccoon coat, even though it was too warm for either. He had a handlebar mustache that drooped past his chin, and deep-set brown eyes that were so dark as to be almost black. He turned those eyes on Cardinal now, and recognizing him, broke into a grin that would have done credit to a movie star.

"You working for Natural Resources now? Coming to nail me for some out-of-season crap?"

"No, I heard you were dead, that's all," Cardinal said. "Figured I'd stop by to make sure."

Bressard frowned. Eyebrows the size of squirrel tails met in mid-brow.

"I hate to alarm you," Cardinal went on. "It's just that there's this rumor going round that you're deceased. Guess it could be the start of an urban legend."

Bressard blinked exactly twice, taking this in. Then once again flashed his movie-star grin. "You came all the way out here just to see if I was okay? I'm touched, man. I'm really, really touched. How was I supposed to be dead?"

"Story is, some guy from out of town—maybe one of those nasty tourists you take hunting—took it into his head to kill you and bury you in the woods."

"Well, I don't see too many tourists this time of year. And as you can see, I'm still alive."

"I know—you're not even missing. It's disappointing."

Bressard laughed.

"These rumors happen to all the greats," Cardinal said. "At least now you can say you have something in common with Paul McCartney."

"You kidding? I'm way better-looking than that guy. Sing better, too." Bressard got into his Ford Explorer and rolled down the window. "You should come out to the Chinook on karaoke night. You'll be begging for my autograph."

Cardinal watched the Explorer drive away toward town, past the edge of the woods where Bressard made his more-than-adequate living.

CARDINAL REACHED THE INTERSECTION of Algonquin and the Highway 11 bypass only to find his way blocked by a traffic accident. The back end of a tractor-trailer had swung round into the oncoming lane. Nobody had been killed, but the traffic moved in fits and starts while the truck was sorted out. Cardinal listened to the news while he waited. The provincial NDP leader outlined the party's platform for the upcoming election: health-care reform, day-care subsidies for working mothers, and a higher minimum wage. Unfortunately, Cardinal didn't like the guy, even though he agreed with everything he said. Then came Geoff Mantis's rejoinder, in which he referred to his opposition as "the champions of Tax and Spend." There was no doubt about it: The Tories had better slogan writers; they just didn't seem to think the government should do anything for anybody. Close the hospitals, shutter the schools, and voilà—everybody's happy.

Then there was the weather. Fog was expected to continue over most of Northern Ontario, and then they'd be in for a little rain. An expert explained why this weird warmth was not necessarily a sign of global warming but more likely just a statistical anomaly.

Cardinal's cell phone rang.

"Cardinal."

It was Mary Flower. She sounded excited. "Cardinal, you have to head out to Sackville Road right away—Skyway Service Center. Delorme's already on her way."

"Why? What's up?"

"They've found a body. Sort of."

CARDINAL TURNED AROUND and headed west to Sackville Road. The fog was thinner on this side of town, not much more than a mist. Eventually he came to a bedraggled gas station. Skyway Service Center, Snowmobile & Outboard Repairs. Dented shells of snowmobiles were stacked against the side of the building like multicolored cordwood.

As he stepped out of the car, Lise Delorme was just pulling to a stop behind him.

"We can tell Wudky thanks a million, Lise. We should ask the judge to tack on an extra week to whatever damn sentence he gets."

"Paul Bressard is not dead?"

"Paul Bressard is not only not dead. Paul Bressard is prospering."

"Well, this should be a little more interesting."

A big man came out of the garage in filthy overalls. He was wide at the shoulders, narrow at the hips, and at one time would have been an imposing figure. But the overalls were distended in front, as if they concealed a basketball. His face was submerged in the bushy beard of a cartoon woodsman, black shot through with gray. Ivan Bergeron was one half of the Bergeron brothers, a pair of identical twins who had dominated team sports at Algonquin High for the entire six years they had attended it. That had been a little before Cardinal's time, but he still remembered Ivan and his brother Carl as a dynamite combination on both the hockey and football teams back when he had been a freshman.

"Tell us what you found," Cardinal said. "Then we'll go take a look."

"I'm in the shop," Bergeron told them, "trying to resuscitate a '74 Ski-Doo that should have been tossed on the junk heap twenty years ago. The dog starts barking. This is a very quiet dog, not usually a problem, and suddenly he's barking like a maniac. I yell at him to shut up, but he keeps on yapping. Finally I come outside, and there he is in the backyard and— Why don't you follow me? I'll show you."

Around the side, a two-story house slumped against the garage as if it had lost consciousness. Bergeron led them past it to the backyard. "That's it, right there," he said, pointing. "I dragged the dumb-ass dog straight into the house when I saw what it was. He was expecting me to congratulate him or something, but I was like 'this is unreal.'"

"What time was this?" Cardinal asked.

"I don't know— round ten, maybe?"

"And you waited till now to call us?"

"Well, how'm I supposed to know what to do? It didn't seem like exactly an emergency. And to tell you the truth, I didn't really want to think about it."

Cardinal had seen a lot of unpleasant things in his twenty years as a cop, but he had never seen a human arm completely detached from its owner. They were standing maybe ten feet away. Ivan Bergeron showed no inclination to go closer. He planted his feet wide apart and folded his arms across his vast, maternal belly.

Cardinal and Delorme approached the thing.

"You guys are taking it with you, I hope."

"Not right away," Cardinal said. "Are you certain the dog brought it here? You didn't actually see him, right? You came out and found him barking at it?"

"He must have dragged it in from the bush. He was rompin' around out there for quite a while before he brung it back."

Cardinal's stomach was making odd maneuvers. There was something unsettling about a part of a human being so absolutely out of place. It lay on a grubby crust of snow, pale white except for the black hair that curled thickly toward the elbow end, thinner toward the wrist. There were deep claw marks, but very little blood.

"Looks like someone had an argument with a bear," Cardinal said.

"A bear?" Delorme said. "Aren't bears hibernating this time of year?"

"They can get confused by a warm patch," Cardinal said. "It's not unusual for them to wake up. And when they do, they tend to be peckish. Gonna be fun trying to ID this guy."

"Look at the hair on the forearm," Delorme said, pointing. "It's gray."

"Yeah. We'll have to run through Missing Persons for older men. In the meantime, we're going to have to find whatever's left of the guy."

"You're gonna get that thing out of here, right?" Bergeron said again. "I find I can't work too good with an arm on my lawn."

IN THE END, Ivan Bergeron had to work with an arm on his lawn for the entire afternoon. Cardinal got on the phone and ordered up as many off-duty constables as Mary Flower could muster. Then he called the Ontario Provincial Police and arranged for thirty officers. Last, he called the Fire Marshall and brought another thirty firemen to help—and most important, they brought with them three cadaver dogs. Cadaver dogs have nothing to do with the Dalmatians associated with firehouses. These are German shepherds trained to sniff out corpses in burned-out buildings that are too dangerous to send a human being into.

Within an hour Cardinal had a squad of constables, augmented by firemen and OPP cops, searching the woods, a small army of men and women in blue uniforms moving slowly among glistening pines and birches. No one spoke. It was as if they were in a movie with the sound turned off.

They tramped through sodden underbrush, the earth releasing rich smells of pine and rotting leaves. Branches stung their cheeks and clung to their hair. After about ten minutes, constable Larry Bourke made the next discovery, this time a leg. Once again, Cardinal experienced that weird tumbling sensation. What they were looking at was a man's leg torn at the hip, whole at the foot, with tremendous rips in the flesh of the thigh.

"Jesus," Delorme said.

"Definitely a bear." Cardinal pointed to the wounds. "You can see there. And there. Thing must have teeth the size of your hand."

The fog kept things slow. It was another two hours before they found more pieces of the body: another partially eaten leg and a lower torso so chewed as to be barely recognizable—one of the cadaver dogs had growled at it underneath the trunk of a fallen tree. Presumably the bear or bears had hidden it there to finish it off later.

Later Cardinal found a bit of ear and scalp with a pair of tinted aviator glasses still attached. "Does this distribution look random to you?" he asked Paul Arsenault, who was photographing the glasses. "Or do you think somebody could have spread the parts around?"

"You mean somebody not a bear?"

"Somebody not a bear."

Arsenault sat back on his haunches, chewing one end of his mustache. "If there's a pattern, I don't think we're going to see it from here. We need an aerial view."

"But even with the fog thinning, we're not going to be able to see anything through the trees. Not even with red markers."

Arsenault chewed the other end of his mustache. "We could put up helium balloons. My daughter had a birthday last week, and we've got a bunch of 'em at home."

A constable was duly dispatched to Arsenault's house and returned twenty minutes later with the balloons. They attached thirty yards of fishing line to each balloon, tied to a weight on the ground near each piece of evidence. Then the OPP took pictures from the air.

CARDINAL AND DELORME were back at Skyway Service Center redeploying searchers when a black Lexus pulled up. Cardinal recognized it and sagged inwardly. Dr. Alex Barnhouse was the kind of irritant an investigation didn't need. A good coroner, true, but he ruffled feathers, and not just Cardinal's.

Barnhouse rolled down his window. "Let's get a move on, shall we. I haven't got all day."

Cardinal waved cheerily. "Hi there, Doc! How are you?"

"Can we get moving, please?"

"Isn't this the most gorgeous day you've ever seen? The trees? The mist? Right out of a storybook, don't you think?"

"I can't imagine anything less relevant."

"You're right. Better park that beautiful Buick of yours over there, and we'll get started."

Barnhouse got out of the car, carrying his bag. "God help us," he said, "when the local constabulary can't tell the difference between a Buick and a Lexus."

"You're being naughty," Delorme said quietly.

"He does tend to bring out my immature side," Cardinal said.

Barnhouse examined the severed arm, then followed them into the woods, black bag in hand. He barely glanced at the various body parts.

"Detective Cardinal," he said. "It is my professional opinion that this unidentified male met with his fate in an unnatural manner. There being no clothes near the body is one such indicator. The small amount of blood is another—given the severity of the injuries inflicted by the animal or animals, these trees and leaves should be covered in blood. They are not."

"But that could just mean the bears killed him someplace else and dragged the body all over hell's half acre."

Barnhouse shook his head. "The bear or bears ate him. They didn't kill him. You can see it in the major bones. It is my opinion that some of the injuries were inflicted not by an animal but by a man or men wielding an axe or other sharp object. The bones appear to be chopped through, not yanked out. I am no expert in such matters and no doubt you will be availing yourself of the services of the Forensic Center in Toronto."

"What can you give us on time of death?"

"Great God, man. How can I give you anything on time of death? We haven't even got a stomach to measure contents."

"Well, what about this axe business? Was that inflicted after death, or before?"

"After. There's no bleeding into the bones, which means the heart had stopped before the chopping up. And for that, I'm sure we're all grateful." Barnhouse scribbled on a form, tore off the top sheet, and handed it to Cardinal. "Give my regards to the Forensic Center. Now, if someone will be good enough to show me the way out of here, I'll bid you good day."

Cardinal motioned to Larry Bourke.

"This way, Doc," Bourke said. And Cardinal watched the two of them head off into the mist.

"I should be used to him by now," Delorme said. "But I'm not."

Cardinal's walkie-talkie squawked, and a voice said something unintelligible.

"Cardinal. Could you repeat that?"

"I said we've got a structure down here." It was Arsenault's voice. "I think you should take a look."

"Where are you?"

"Downhill from the service center. Follow the creek west."

Delorme looked off into the woods, the webs of pale gray. "West? It would be nice if there was a trail."

THEY FOUND THE CREEK and followed it, and eventually they heard voices. The dim outline of a cabin took shape. They found Arsenault on his knees beside a bush, doing something with a penknife and a test tube.

"What have you got?" Cardinal asked.

"Paint scrapings. Looks like someone drove in here recently." He jerked his thumb in the direction behind him, the faint outline of tire tracks. "This could be where it went down," he added. "I mean before the bears got to him."

Cardinal took a closer look at the tire tracks. "You think we can get a mold out of these?"

"Nope," Arsenault said. "Too many leaves."

"That's what I figured. What is this, an old logging road?"

"Yeah. Must be from eighty years ago. You can see it's been used, though. Probably by whoever owned that wreck of a place."

Arsenault's ident partner, Bob Collingwood, was inside the shack.

"Gah," Delorme said. "The smell."

The cabin was hardly more than twelve feet square, constructed of rough-hewn lumber that did little to keep out the cold and nothing to keep out the damp. There was a fridge, a rusted cot with a stained mattress rolled up at one end, a metal counter with two sinks, and an ancient cast-iron woodstove with the door hanging open on a broken hinge. The whole place, as Delorme had noted, smelled of decay—mildew, mold, and rotting wood.

"There was no lock on it," Arsenault said from behind her. "The door was just hanging open."

"Hasn't been used for a long time." Delorme pointed at the giant cobwebs around the doorway. "Is it a trapper's shack?"

"Totally illegal, of course," Cardinal said. "They build them wherever they damn well want. The question is, whose trapper's shack. There must be at least a dozen guys make their living out here."

Collingwood was young, jug-eared, thorough, and silent. Cardinal could count on one hand the number of complete sentences he had uttered in his entire career, because he tended to speak, when he spoke at all, in single words. He was pointing silently to the sinks. They were the kind with a pump handle where the faucets should be. Wearing a latex glove, Collingwood stuck his finger in the drain and brought it up again, stained.

"Is that rust or blood?" Cardinal asked.

"Blood."

"So he could have been killed here. On the other hand, it may just be animal blood."

Delorme was kneeling in front of the woodstove. "Looks like somebody tried to burn clothes in this thing. Collingwood, have you got a drop sheet?"

Collingwood wordlessly opened a leather case that contained all the tools of his craft, and together they spread a thin plastic drop cloth, white so that evidence would be visible against it. They used a pair of tongs to extract the blackened mass from inside the stove. There was a pair of denims, reduced to little more than the waistband, a shirt collar, several buttons, most of a pair of shoe soles, and a mass of burned, unidentifiable material.

Collingwood took an instrument from his case and measured the shoe soles. This provoked exactly one word from him: "Elevens."

"All right," Cardinal said. "We'll need sizes from the waistband and the shirt collar, too, if there's enough left to measure."

Delorme, ever so gently, was stirring the burned matter with the tongs. "What's this?" She said it more to herself than to the others.

She held a small lump of fused metal in the tongs. She turned it over on the drop sheet. The other side was shinier, and there was part of an incised outline of an animal.

"Looks like a loon," she said. She looked at the two men.

Cardinal leaned over her shoulder to get a better view. "I think I know exactly what that is."

4

THE NORTHERN SHORE of Lake Nipissing
is one of the prettiest places in Ontario, but Lakeshore Drive, which runs
along the top of the inlet that gives Algonquin Bay its name, could have
been designed for the sole purpose of keeping this fact from the public. It
has been a magnet for eyesores for as long as anybody can remember. On
the lake side there are fast-food joints, gas stations, and quaintly named
but charm-free motels. Across from these, car dealerships and shopping
malls.

Loon Lodge was at the western edge of this ugliness. It was not actually a lodge; it was a dozen miniature white cabins with green shutters and
country-style curtains, having been built in the fifties before the log-cabin
look became the fashion in the sixties. Many people in Algonquin Bay
imagine such businesses are closed in winter, but in fact they have two
sources of winter income. One is from ice fishermen, the dentists and insurance salesmen who take a few days off to come up north with their
buddies and drink themselves into oblivion. The other is from people who
want a dirt-cheap place to live, and nothing is cheaper, off-season, than a
cabin on Lakeshore Drive.

Cardinal had been to Loon Lodge a few times. Every so often one of
the winter residents would knock his wife's teeth out. Or the wife would
tire of her husband's drinking and insert a steak knife neatly into his ribs.
Occasionally there were drug dealers. Then in summer it was all sunburnt
Americans, families on a tight budget, taking advantage of the reliably
frail Canadian dollar.

Cardinal and Delorme were in the first of Loon Lodge's white clap-
board cabins, the one marked OFFICE. It was four times bigger than the

rental units, and the proprietor lived in it with his wife and kids. He was an egg-shaped man named Wallace. His face was puffy, with a wounded expression, as if he suffered from toothache. An equally egg-shaped and disconsolate four-year-old boy was watching cartoons in the next room. Smells of supper hung in the air, and Cardinal suddenly realized that he was hungry.

Wallace pulled out a guest register, found the name, and turned the book around on the counter.

"Howard Matlock," Delorme read aloud. "312 East 91st Street, New York City."

"I wish I'd never set eyes on the guy, now," Wallace said. "Was a really slow week last week. So I was glad as hell to see him, even though he only wanted to stay a few days."

"Ford Escort," Delorme read, and copied down the license number.

"Yeah," Wallace said. "Bright red one. Not that I've seen that car for a couple of days."

"What day did he arrive?" Cardinal asked.

"Thursday, I think. Yeah, Thursday. I'd just turned away a couple of Indians who wanted to rent a place. Sorry, but I don't care how many vacancies I've got, I won't rent to those people. I just got tired of cleaning up the blood and the puke. I have a reputation to maintain."

"You better hope none of them lays a discrimination complaint on you," Delorme said.

"People don't understand about Indians: Put two or three of them together with a bottle of Four Aces and you got a unit that's unrentable."

"And what have you got now?"

"You say you took this key ring off a dead body?" He pointed to the melted mass in the Baggie Cardinal had put on the counter.

"More or less."

"Then I guess I got a bill that's not paid and a tenant that's not alive." Wallace shook his head and cursed under his breath. "Do you have any idea how long it takes to build a reputation like Loon Lodge? It doesn't happen overnight."

"I'm sure it doesn't," Cardinal said. "Did Mr. Matlock say why he was in Algonquin Bay?"

"I'm telling you, something like this comes along, and all that effort—all those extra little touches that make a motel a special place, the kind of place people want to come back to—all of it comes to nothing. I might as well take down my shingle and declare bankruptcy."

Cardinal wondered how anyone as gloomy as Mr. Wallace would have had the optimism to open a motel in the first place, but he stuck to his original question. "Did Mr. Matlock say why he was in Algonquin Bay?"

"Ice fishing's what he told me."

"Little early in the year for ice fishing. Even without the warm spell."

"That's exactly what I said. I told him no one's going out on that lake for at least another two weeks, even without the warm snap. He said he was well aware of that fact. Said he was only up here scoping the place out for a bunch of buddies planning to come up with him late February."

"From New York?" Delorme said. "New York seems like a long way to come just to check out the ice fishing."

Wallace shrugged. "Americans."

He plucked a key from the rack behind the counter, and they followed him outside, past several cabins.

"Never seemed like much of a sport to me," Cardinal said to Delorme. "The fish are stunned with cold. They're starving. Where's the skill? Sitting over a hole in a dingy little shack."

"You're leaving out the beer," Delorme pointed out.

"Oh, don't leave out the beer," Wallace said. "You wouldn't believe the cases these guys haul out there. I keep a toboggan in each unit, supposedly for the kiddies, but do you see any hills around here? They use 'em to haul their two-fours out on the lake."

"You say Mr. Matlock arrived on Thursday. When did you notice the car wasn't here?"

"I guess that'd be Saturday. Two days ago. Yeah, that's right. Because I asked him to move it Friday morning. Had it parked in the spot for number four. Not that there was anybody in number four. Anyways, it definitely wasn't there Saturday morning. Which made me think something was up. Car's gone, and I haven't seen any smoke coming from the stovepipe. Knocked on the door this morning, got no answer, and figured I'd give him another few hours before I started to worry I'd been stiffed."

"Did he make any phone calls?" Cardinal asked. "Would you know if he had?"

"Long-distance I'd know about—he didn't make any of those. I don't keep track of local."

"Thanks, Mr. Wallace. We'll take it from here."

"Fine with me." Wallace opened the door for them. "If there's any cash in there, I figure I'm due a hundred and forty."

The inside of a Loon Lodge cabin hadn't changed since the last time Cardinal had seen one. Double bed tucked in an alcove, a floral couch, and a kitchenette in the corner: mini-fridge, hot plate, aluminum sink. A memory assailed Cardinal. A shrieking woman hurling a frying pan at him when he had come to arrest her husband.

There was a table covered with yellow oilcloth beside one window. A copy of *The New York Times* lay on it. Dated five days previously, Cardinal noted, and probably acquired on the airplane.

The bed (slightly tattered chenille cover complete with the same Loon Lodge emblem that was on the key ring) was neatly made. Beside it lay a small wheeled suitcase containing enough clothes for a weekend and a paperback novel by Tom Clancy.

"Here's his wallet," Delorme said. She retrieved it from under the kitchen table, nearly toppling a lamp (loon emblem on the shade) in the process.

"Well, here's a question," Cardinal said. "The car's gone. Why would you go out in your car and not take your wallet with you? You go out in the car, you take your license, right?"

"Maybe whoever killed him showed up at his door."

"Possible. And he loses his wallet in the struggle—although there isn't much sign of a struggle in here."

Delorme opened the wallet. "In any case, I think we can rule out robbery as a motive. There's eighty-seven dollars here, all American. Maybe he just went out to buy a pack of cigarettes. Didn't need his wallet."

"He's got cigarettes." Cardinal pointed to a half-empty pack of Marlboros on the nightstand.

"Howard Matlock," Delorme read from one of the wallet cards in a formal voice, "is chartered to practice accountancy in the state of New York."

"Ice fishermen. I swear they're all accountants."

"He is also a member of the New York Public Library, Blockbuster Video, and carries a New York driver's license."

She showed Cardinal. The dead man stared out at him from the license photo. He was wearing the same aviator glasses they had found in the woods.

They both glanced around the room.

"Except for the wallet on the floor, everything looks undisturbed," Cardinal said. "And his room key was still in his pocket, but not his car key. Which makes me think the killer or killers made off with his car."

"If you're going to steal a car, why pick a Ford Escort? And if you're covering up a car theft, chopping the body up in the woods seems a little extreme."

"Maybe there was something incriminating in the car."

They went through the contents of the suitcase: three store-label shirts, three pairs of Hanes underwear, three pairs of socks, two with holes in them.

"I thought accountants made decent money," Delorme said. "But this guy looks like he wasn't doing so well."

On the bathroom shelf they found a roll of Tums, and travel packets of Imodium and Ex-Lax. "Obviously a Boy Scout," Delorme said. "Prepared for anything."

"Anything except hunting or fishing, you notice. No rod, no reel, no tackle. Nothing. I know he said he was just scoping the place out, but still."

"Maybe he kept it in the car. When we find the car . . ."

They stood facing each other in the middle of the cabin. Waiting for an idea to descend, Cardinal thought. A theory.

"This is a strange one," Delorme said. "As far as we know, Howard Matlock, visiting CPA, came up here to check out the ice fishing. While here, he goes out for a drive—without his wallet—and gets himself killed. Maybe someone tried to rob him and killed him out of frustration because he wasn't carrying his wallet."

"Thank you, Detective Delorme. That explains everything. Obviously, we can close this case right now."

"All right. So it has a few holes."

"I think we both find the ice-fishing business a little thin. And . . ."

"And what? You look worried."

"I'm getting a bad feeling about this. My guru on the Toronto force used to say it takes three things to solve any case where the perpetrator isn't readily apparent: talent, persistence, and luck. Any one of those is missing, you don't make your case. Call me egotistical, but I'm not worried about the first two."

"Come on, Cardinal. We've barely started."

"I know. The problem is, if we don't believe Matlock came up here to check out the ice fishing, then we don't have the first clue what he was doing here—or who he came to see—let alone who wanted to kill him."

THE CALL WENT OUT to search for Matlock's red Ford Escort, a rental from the Avis counter at Toronto Pearson Airport. The search in the woods went on until dark. All the body parts that could be found were gathered together and shipped to the Forensic Center in Toronto. The aerial photographs were developed and tacked up on the bulletin board in the ident room. The Mylar balloons glittered amid the mist and trees, but there was no pattern visible in their distribution.

By the time Arsenault and Collingwood were finished going over the shack, and then the cabin at Loon Lodge, the day was long gone. There were no prints of interest at the motel, and they were still running down the ones from the trapper's shack. Cardinal had been writing reports for a good two hours. He was tired and hungry and looking forward to being with Catherine, but he didn't want to go home feeling that the case was at a dead end. He needed some time alone, some time away from the reports and the noise of his colleagues shouting to one another, to think about Howard Matlock and why this American had ended up dead in Algonquin Bay.

DOWN BY THE LAKE, the fog was still thick, wedged like gray batting among the cabins and the trees. The Loon Lodge vacancy sign glowed dull red. The parking lot was empty.

Cardinal opened the cabin that had been Howard Matlock's and ducked under the yellow police tape. Inside, he flipped a switch, but the light didn't come on—the proprietor would have turned off the power until he had another paying tenant. No heat, either. Cardinal switched on his flashlight and shone it over the bed, the chair, the nightstand. Ident had been so busy with the scene in the woods that they would not be finished here until the next day at least. Howard Matlock's personal effects were still here, right down to the half-smoked pack of Marlboros beside the loon lamp.

In the dark and the silence Cardinal tried once more to visualize what had happened here. He imagined the American sitting in the white wicker chair, watching the tiny television, when there was a knock at the door. But who would come to him, and kill him, and drive him away in his own car? Did someone follow him here from New York?

Cardinal sat on the edge of the bed. Trying to figure out this case was like trying to catch smoke. Half the time—at least in a place the size of Algonquin Bay—it was the killer himself who called cops to the scene of the crime. Now, here was a genuine mystery and Cardinal didn't have a single lead. An American citizen had come up to his town and—if he hadn't been followed—had managed in a very short time to upset somebody enough to get himself murdered. And whoever it was didn't just kill him, but also fed him to the bears. Why?

A thought was beginning to take shape inside Cardinal's head; he could feel the fine end of a theory in his mind but couldn't quite grasp it. He stared at the closet door. It had been open earlier; now it was closed, dotted with powder where ident had gone over it for prints.

Cardinal stood up and slid back the closet door, and before it was half open a hand shot out from the darkness and fixed itself around his neck. A fist plunged into his gut and doubled him over.

Cardinal staggered back, gasping. An expert kick swept his legs out from under him, and then he was facedown on the floor, one arm pulled up behind his back. The cold barrel of a gun was pressed into the back of his head. His own holstered Beretta was digging painfully into his ribs.

"You wouldn't happen to be armed, would you?" The voice was young, male, unfamiliar—WASP, at a guess.

"No."

"Uh-huh. And what's this?" Cardinal's jacket was yanked up and his Beretta removed.

"You're making a mistake," Cardinal managed to say before his head was forced down again.

A hand went for his inner pocket and removed his wallet. "You're a cop?"

"In my spare time. When I'm not getting beaten up in tourist cabins."

The man's weight shifted on Cardinal's back. "I can't believe you walked into this," he said. "On your own? In the middle of the night? I could have been anybody."

"Yes. I've been meaning to ask you about that."

"All right. Here's what I'm gonna do. I'm going to get off you. I'm going to hang on to your gun, but I'm going to get off you. So let's be civilized, okay? Don't try anything, or I'll have to put you down again."

"Fine."

"You're going to get up and put your hands against the wall. I'll stand over by the door."

The man got off him, and Cardinal took a deep breath before he stood up and dusted himself off. Jesus, the indignity.

Behind the snubnose .38 that was pointed at him stood the youngest gunman Cardinal had ever seen—blond hair cropped close to the skull, pale fuzz on the cheeks and chin. He wore a houndstooth sports jacket, as if trying to impersonate an older man. He opened the door slightly and peered out at the parking lot.

"You really did come alone." When he spoke, the kid's mouth gleamed with too many teeth. "All right, turn around and put your hands against the wall. You know the position—feet spread, on your toes."

The .38 glinted in the light from the window. Cardinal did as he was told and stared at the wall. "What are you?" he said. "About eighteen?"

"You're way off. And we've got more important things to talk about." The kid patted him down, looking for an ankle holster. Cardinal didn't carry one. "For starters, how do we get out of this?"

"What do you mean 'we'? You're the one who just assaulted a police officer. And I have a feeling that—unless you're RCMP—you're not licensed to carry that thirty-eight, junior."

"And you're the cop who just let his gun be taken away. I don't think we want word of that getting around town, do we?"

"That would be embarrassing. Give it back and I'll shoot myself right now."

"What do you know about Howard Matlock?"

"Did Malcolm Musgrave send you? He always had a roundabout way of making a point, even for a Mountie."

"I asked you a question," the kid said. "What do you know about Howard Matlock?"

"He's an American. He's a chartered accountant. He's dead. Why are you so interested?"

"I have the guns, so I think it's more appropriate if I ask the questions. Why did you come back here? Your scene work must be done."

"Look, clearly you're RCMP. Why don't you tell me who you are and what you're up to?"

"I asked why you came back to the cabin."

"Obviously for the same reason you're here—to find out more about Howard Matlock. A tourist comes to visit my town and gets fed to the bears, it doesn't look good. It also bothers me that he probably wasn't a tourist. I came back because I wanted to get a better sense of the guy. I came back because a lot of things aren't clear to me. I came back because at the moment there's no way to go forward. Now, if you don't mind, I'd like to get on with my job." Cardinal waited for a moment, listening. There wasn't a sound from the doorway. He turned to look.

The doorway was empty. Cardinal's Beretta was lying on the kitchen table, minus the clip. He got to the doorway too late to see anything. He cursed under his breath. The most upsetting thing was the missing clip; that would be difficult to explain.

He closed the closet door and took one last look around the cabin before locking it up. The kid was good, he had to admit. Catches him by surprise, lifts his gun, and melts away like a wisp of fog. On the way up to the parking lot, Cardinal thought about putting out an all-points on blond WASPs. But when he got to his car he found his Beretta clip sitting on the roof above the driver-side door.

WHEN CARDINAL GOT HOME, Catherine was sitting in the lotus position, absolutely motionless. A candle flickered in the breeze from Cardinal's entry. Smoke spiraled up from a stick of incense on top of the television.

"You're home late," Catherine said.

"Smells like Shangri-la in here." Cardinal always made a comment about her incense, and she always ignored it. "How's my swami?"

"More like a Buddha than a swami. I'm never going to get rid of this hospital fat."

"You're not fat."

"All that bread and potatoes they fed me in the O.H. I can't fit into any of my clothes."

It was true Catherine had put on a few pounds in the Ontario Psychiatric Hospital, she always did, but on the whole Cardinal thought his wife looked great. A little heavier in the hips, a slight increase in belly, maybe, but for a woman with a twenty-six-year-old kid, she looked damn good.

As she untangled her legs, Catherine let out a long sigh. Cardinal was always glad to see her doing yoga, even late at night; she rarely got sick when she was taking care of herself.

"Your dad called. He has an appointment with the cardiologist tomorrow morning. I'll drive him over."

"That's excellent. His new doctor really knows how to get things done."

"You look a little upset," Catherine said. "Are you all right?"

"Bad day at work, that's all. Nothing to worry about."

"You want to tell me about it?"

"Nope." He rarely did. None of the detectives on the squad talked to their wives about what happened at work. "Misguided chivalry," a friend had told Cardinal once, and maybe he was right, but he probably didn't live with a manic depressive. Cardinal was not about to add to his wife's burdens. Besides, he was still too embarrassed about having given up his gun. He flopped down on the couch and breathed in the scent of sandalwood. Very high vibrations, Catherine had assured him.

The house was beautifully quiet. His refuge. The last embers of a fire in the woodstove cast a warm glow.

"This came for you," Catherine said, handing him a square envelope. "Very messy handwriting."

No return address, either, Cardinal noticed. He tore it open and pulled out a card decorated with a big red heart. Embossed on the front: "*It's been twelve years, honey . . .*" And on the inside, "*. . . but I still love you like the day we met!*" Underneath this, someone had written, "*See you soon.*"

It was unsigned, of course, they always were, but Cardinal knew who it was from. Twelve years ago he had helped put a man in prison; that man would be out soon. But the crucial message was not on the card, it was on the envelope between the lines of Cardinal's home address: We know where you live.

Catherine was saying something to him, but Cardinal couldn't quite focus. His mind was fixed on the events of more than a decade before, the single biggest mistake of his career—of his life, really. It had cast a pall over every moment of his career since, and now, even though he had tried to rectify it, it was presenting a threat to his home. His refuge, yes. But between his wife's emotional fragility and the demands of his profession, not an impregnable one.

"I'm sorry," he said. "What were you saying?"

"I said Kelly called a while ago. Are you sure you're all right? What was that card about?"

Cardinal stuffed it in his pocket. "Nothing. Garbage. Funny how Kelly always manages to call when I'm out. She must have someone watching the house."

"Don't say that, John. She asked after you. I really don't think Kelly's capable of holding a grudge. Not against you, anyway."

"Uh-huh."

"She's found a new place. Sharing an apartment in the East Village. She says it's very funky but very livable."

"God knows why she wants to live in New York in the first place. You couldn't pay me enough money to live there. Toronto was bad enough."

Cardinal went into the bathroom and ran the shower as hot as he could stand it, then turned it gradually colder. The sting of the water restored his spirits a little, but his mind still kept going back to the events of a dozen years before. He had crossed a line, and when he tried to go back—back to the last point where he had been his real self, his full self—it turned out not to be a line at all but a chasm.

Cardinal forced himself to think of the present, of the farce at Loon Lodge. He remembered that just before he had been attacked, a thought had been forming in his mind. Then, as he was rinsing off, the thought came back to him. It had been about Wudky.

He dried off, wrapped himself in a thick dressing gown, and went out into the living room to use the phone.

"Delorme? It's Cardinal."

"Cardinal, do you know what time it is? Believe it or not, I do have a life."

"No, you don't. I've been thinking about Wudky. You know he told us Paul Bressard got himself murdered and buried in the woods?"

"Wudky is retarded. Everybody knows he's retarded. I'm surprised you bothered to check his story out."

"But look at what we've got. We've got an American chewed up in the woods, right? Near an old trapper's shack, right? And Paul Bressard is a trapper."

"Right. And Wudky said Paul Bressard got murdered, and Wudky was wrong."

"And why? Because Wudky is the world's dumbest criminal. And why else? Because Wudky had had a lot to drink the night he heard that story. But suppose Wudky got it backwards? Suppose Paul Bressard killed a tourist and did away with him in the woods? That would make more sense, wouldn't it? Maybe he even killed him accidentally and tried to cover it up."

"Me, I don't think feeding a guy to the bears is accidental. Even just to cover up."

"But it's the sort of thing that would occur to a trapper. Someone who knows exactly where the bears are."

"I guess. Yeah, you could be on to something."

"Are you just saying that to get me off the phone?"

"No. But I thought you already talked to Bressard."

"I did. And he seemed completely innocent. But then I was just checking to see if he was alive."

"Maybe we should talk to him again. Oh, sorry—maybe you and Malcolm Musgrave should talk to him. Matlock was American. That means working with the Horsemen."

"Don't remind me."

Cardinal went back to the bathroom and dried his hair. He had an idea now. A direction. When he went into the bedroom, Catherine was under the covers, fast asleep. Beside her, an oversize library book called *New York and New Yorkers* lay open to a picture of the East Village.

Cardinal got into bed beside her and turned out the light. He listened to the rhythm of her breathing, the sound of peace, love, and security. And then he thought again about the card.

5

was still trying to rid his office of his predecessor's ghost. D.S. Dyson, aside from being a crook, had been a supernaturally neat man, and so Chouinard felt it necessary to keep his office in a state of turmoil. Half-installed blinds hung from the windows at an alarming angle, law books and procedural manuals tilted in precarious towers on the floor, and the bookshelves formed a lean-to against the wall. On his desk lay a hammer, a variety of screwdrivers, and a tablet of white foolscap on which it was his habit to take illegible notes.

When the position of detective sergeant had become available, it had been offered to Cardinal. He was one of the more senior detectives, after all, and had cleared some of the highest-profile cases in Algonquin Bay's history. But Cardinal had turned the job down, even though it would have meant more money and regular hours. At the time, he had been on the brink of quitting the force—Delorme had stopped him at the last minute—and felt he didn't deserve any promotion. Also, there was the undeniable fact that being Detective Sergeant was a desk job. Cardinal just couldn't see it. Being out on the street, dealing with real people, was the best thing about police work, the single thing that made him feel useful.

The only factor that made Cardinal hesitate at all was the fear that the job would go to Ian McLeod. McLeod, who was away on vacation at the moment, had a knack for sowing discord that would have made him an out-and-out disaster. In the end Chief Kendall had offered the job to Daniel Chouinard, who had been a detective long enough to understand the needs of the CID staff. He had suffered along with the rest of the squad under the unpredictable D.S. Dyson, and he had solid organizational skills. Most important of all, he knew every one of the eight detectives well enough to know whose strengths would balance out whose weaknesses.

When he'd heard about the appointment, McLeod had declared it was simply because Chouinard was French Canadian: It made the department look strongly bilingual, which it was not. But nobody else found any reason to be upset with the appointment of Daniel Chouinard. The worst that could be said of him was that he was bland—especially for a French Canadian. All right, he was boring. He was so boring that really you could only define him by what he lacked—such as any sense of irony, or for that matter any sense of humor. He had no axe to grind, no political ambitions, and no major psychological problems. He was given neither to tantrums nor to vendettas. The man didn't even have an accent. D.S. Daniel Chouinard, despite the messy office, was just, well, reasonable. Sometimes unbearably reasonable.

"Let me sum things up," Chouinard said. Delorme and Cardinal were on their feet in the at-ease position, owing to Chouinard's chairs being covered with stacks of acoustic tile. "We have an American male in his late fifties or early sixties found in the woods where he was eaten by a bear."

"Murdered by persons unknown and then eaten by a bear," Delorme corrected him.

"The fact that he's American means we have to bring in the Mounties. Anything international is their turf. Which means we'll be working with Malcolm Musgrave. So, I don't think we need Delorme on this just now."

"Actually," Cardinal said. "Delorme's the best possible person to work with Musgrave. They've worked together before and they get along fine. That's bound to speed things up."

"Maybe," Chouinard said. "But I don't want too many cooks on this."

"D.S., I want to be in on it," Delorme said. "I'd be happy to work with Musgrave."

"Sorry. Besides, Cardinal, you're the more senior officer and you should be the one to coordinate with the esteemed sergeant."

"Really, D.S., I don't think I should be working with Musgrave right now."

"Why? Is he annoyed with you? Why would a Mountie stationed in Sudbury be annoyed with a detective in Algonquin Bay?"

"You're forgetting he sicced the entire department on me last year."

"Oh, now that's not fair," Chouinard said in his reasonable way. "He had good grounds to think there was a leak in our department, and it turned out he was right. He just had the wrong man, that's all."

"A minor detail," Cardinal said. "Can't imagine why it bothered me." What was bothering him even more, just then, was that a young Mountie had snatched his gun away the night before.

Chouinard was silent for a few moments, his soft features moving ever so slightly, as if he was working out several equations. Then, as if the calculations had become a physical problem, he swiveled around in his chair and shifted several law books from one windowsill to another, carefully examining the spine of each before setting it down. When he turned around again, his expression was more cheerful.

"So there's bad blood between you and the Horsemen," he said. "That's a shame. But the truth of the matter is that we're never going to have a better opportunity to smooth things out with our colleagues in scarlet. So you work with the Mounties—make sure you give them everything, understand—and you and Musgrave will be on excellent terms in no time. That'll be good for the case, and also for the long-term interests of the department."

"But D.S., I don't think you realize how bad the communication problem is between Musgrave and me."

"All the more reason. You're the one who has the problem. Therefore, there's no one better qualified to repair it, is there?"

ALTHOUGH IT SHOULD HAVE been first on his agenda, Cardinal put off calling Musgrave. Instead he called the Toronto Center for Forensic Sciences, where he spoke to Vlatko Setevic in Chemistry. Two things about Vlatko you could count on: He was an absolute workaholic, first into the office, last out, and never happy unless he had cleared his desk; and he was prone to unpredictable moods. Vlatko had been in Canada since the sixties and had always been an even-tempered sort until Yugoslavia came apart in the nineties. He didn't talk about it, but since that time his disposition had taken a decided turn toward the stormy. Sometimes he could be funny, other times he could be a bastard; you just never knew what you were going to get. Cardinal asked him about the paint sample they had sent, and braced himself for heavy weather.

"Paint sample? I didn't get any paint sample. Not from Algonquin Bay."

"You better have, or there's going to be serious trouble. Are you telling me you guys never—"

A big Slavic laugh blew over the line from Toronto. "Relax, Detective. I was joking. I got your precious paint sample right here."

"Hilarious, Vlatko. Sense of humor like that, you could be on *Royal Canadian Air Farce.*"

"So tense, you northern guys. Take up yoga, maybe—you'll get centered, feel calmer, be one with the universe."

"My wife says the same thing. What have you got for us?"

"It's kind of lucky, actually. The paint matches so-called walnut brown that Ford started using on its Explorers last year. New batch. So you're looking for this year's Explorer—Explorer with bad scratch."

"You're doing my heart good, Vlatko. Keep going."

"In another way, you're also unlucky. In Canada alone? Ford sold thirty-five thousand Explorers, give or take."

"Let me guess. The most popular color?"

"Of course. Walnut brown."

When it couldn't be put off any longer, Cardinal put in a phone call to Malcolm Musgrave at the Sudbury detachment. The civilian who answered informed him that Musgrave was out of town. Cardinal put down the phone with relief, only to have it ring in his hand. It was Musgrave.

"You and I have to talk," the sergeant said without preliminaries. "About a certain individual named Howard Matlock."

It turned out Musgrave was already in Algonquin Bay, at the Federal Building a few blocks away on MacPherson. At one time the RCMP had maintained a detachment there, but the Mounties lived in the age of cutbacks like everyone else, and now their closest presence was in Sudbury, eighty miles away.

Cardinal drove over to the Federal Building and parked in a space marked POST OFFICE VEHICLES ONLY. He found Musgrave in an office furnished with nothing but a metal desk, a phone, and three plastic chairs in primary colors.

Musgrave had the self-confidence of a man who can rely on always being the biggest, toughest male in the room. He was V-shaped, and looked like he'd been carved out of the Precambrian shield. Throw a rock at him, Cardinal figured, and there was a good chance the rock would shatter.

"Sit," Musgrave said, gesturing at the chairs. "I want you to know I have no bad feelings about last year."

"That's big of you. Considering you nearly screwed me out of my job."

"Look at it objectively. I was just following procedure."

"I'll tell you something about procedure," Cardinal said. He had been rehearsing in the car. "The murder of a foreign citizen on Canadian soil may fall under the jurisdiction of the RCMP, but that doesn't give you carte blanche to trample over a local investigation. If you want to examine a crime scene in my bailiwick, you call me. If you want background on the case, ask me. Don't send your flunkies unannounced into my turf, or next time they'll end up in my jail."

Musgrave regarded him with a cool blue gaze. "I don't have the slightest idea what you're talking about."

"I think you do."

"Listen, Cardinal. You have a dead American citizen. An American. As you say, that makes it an RCMP matter. How long were you going to wait before you told me about it?"

"If I had my way, I'd never tell you. You're an unpleasant person. But the law being what it is, I called you this morning just before you called me."

"Uh-huh. Then why do I hear about it from our Ottawa division first?" Musgrave threw a copy of the fax at him. It was just a small item, one of a number in a bulleted list. American Howard Matlock found murdered in Algonquin Bay.

Cardinal stared at the page. How could Mountie headquarters have got hold of it so fast? And if the kid who had taken his gun away wasn't with Musgrave, who was he?

There was a rap on the door.

Musgrave nodded at it. "Someone you're going to want to meet."

Cardinal looked up from the fax.

"Detective John Cardinal, this is Calvin Squier. Detective Cardinal is with Algonquin Bay police. Mr. Squier is an intelligence agent with CSIS."

CSIS (pronounced see-sis) was not an agency that came up a lot in Algonquin Bay, and Cardinal did not expect to see anyone he knew.

Standing in the doorway in a sport coat and tie, the blond young man looked like a teenager trying on his father's clothes. Nothing about him indicated he could take your gun away from you in a darkened cabin.

"Pleased to meet you," Squier said and put out a hand that was pale as a veal chop.

"Likewise," Cardinal managed to say. He felt a blush rising from under his collar and traveling up his neck.

"Great job you did on the Windigo killer," Squier said. "Read up on you this morning."

"You're with CSIS?"

"Canadian Security Intelligence Service," Musgrave said.

"I know who they are, thanks."

"That's right. I've been with them five years."

"They must have hired you when you were nine." Cardinal sat down on a sky-blue chair that creaked like a new shoe. He turned to Musgrave. "What's the deal here?"

"I'll let him tell you."

Squier opened his briefcase and set a silvery laptop on the desk. He unfolded it so that the screen was visible to all of them and pushed a button; it sprang to life with a chime. He pulled a small object the size of a lipstick from his pocket and pointed. A graphic appeared, showing the command structure of NORAD—North American Aerospace Defense.

"As you may know," Squier said. "NORAD is a joint operation of the U.S. and Canada that was developed during the cold war to keep us safe from Russian invaders." He clicked his remote and the graphic changed to Joint Command Installations. "Each country built what they called a ground environment—basically a three-story office building inside a mountain. The Americans have theirs at Cheyenne Mountain in Colorado. We have ours in Algonquin Bay, out by Trout Lake."

"I grew up here," Cardinal said. "You really don't need to be telling me this."

"I'd like to do this right, if you'll just be patient," Squier said. "Besides, Sergeant Musgrave didn't grow up here."

"Sergeant Musgrave would like to get on with it," Musgrave said. "Assume we know about the CADS base."

"Okay. The cold war may be over, but the Canadian Air Defense System is still in place. There are still a hundred and fifty people inside that mountain. They still have their eyes on radar screens. And those radar screens still light up with any object coming into Canadian airspace."

"They're closing the place down, I heard," Cardinal put in. "Algonquin Bay doesn't even have an air base anymore."

"They may move it. But it's not going to close, believe me." A muffled twitter interrupted them. "Sorry," Squier said, and reached into his jacket pocket. "Forgot to turn it off." He aimed the remote at the screen again and it changed to a radar readout. White objects shaped like planes throbbed in the upper right corner. "CADS monitors all incoming traffic. This is just a simulation, of course, showing regular commercial traffic. With the end of the cold war, the CADS base has found new things to do. They keep an eye out for drug flights, for example. Recently they were instrumental in stopping twenty million dollars' worth of heroin, simply by relaying data on a suspicious Cessna to an RCMP drug squad."

A click of the remote, and the screen changed again. An object that did not look like a plane entered the screen from the upper left side. It glowed red and began to flash with a throaty beep.

"Post–September Eleven, the most important part of the CADS mandate—at least as far as my outfit is concerned—is antiterrorism. This could be anything from a hijacked aircraft to a rogue missile. That's what we have on the screen now."

"Simulated, of course," Musgrave said pointedly.

"Oh, yes," Squier said. "There's no way on God's green earth I could be walking around with a real CADS readout. Now I know you're wondering why I'm here, so I'll get right to it. Friday morning CSIS got a call from the CADS base. Their security unit caught a man with a pair of binoculars up on the hill. Apparently, he didn't seem to be doing anything much. They questioned him, and he said he was a tourist, a bird watcher. It's not like he's wearing a turban. They didn't have enough to hold him or even to call in you guys." He nodded at Cardinal. "So they checked his ID and told him to vamoose, basically.

"They phoned the info down to us. Completely routine procedure. We run a check on Howard Matlock. Nothing against. Then—and this is the same day I'm talking about—the guy turns up again in the middle of the night. Night-shift security catches him on the perimeter, with those binoculars practically glued to his face."

"On the perimeter," Cardinal said. "If he was a spy, he must be the most inept spy the world has ever seen. I've been up to that base, and there's absolutely nothing to see until you get two miles inside the mountain. It's trees and rock. Period."

"True enough. But his objective may not have been the installation hardware. It may have been the security itself. The whole point may have been to check out their strength by getting himself caught. We just don't know. The worst thing is, security screwed up. Screwed up big time. They neglected to check the day ledger when they caught the guy, so they didn't know he'd already been nicked earlier. Unbelievable as it seems, they let him go. By the time security realized their mistake, it was too late. That's when they called us for the second time, and believe me there were some red faces there."

Squier clicked his remote, and the laptop went dark. He folded it up with a snap. "My superior called me at six in the morning," he said. "Told me to be on the seven o'clock flight to Algonquin Bay. Security had taken down Matlock's license plate number—a rental car from Toronto airport—and the Loon Lodge address. But I got here too late. I never even caught sight of him, and then suddenly you guys were all over his cabin."

"What would you have done if you had found him?"

"Followed him, of course. Not me personally—we use surveillants for that sort of thing."

"Really," Musgrave said. "We use cops."

"It's unfortunate I didn't catch up with this individual before he got killed, really. Personally, I suspect he isn't anything to worry about. No links to al-Qaeda or anyone like that. But not having cleared him, and him being dead after two hits on NORAD security, well let's just say it raises red flags. And that's what puts us in the ball game."

"Well, maybe we could get the OPP in on this, too," Cardinal said.

"Oh, I don't think the provincial police have any jurisdiction here."

"He was joking," Musgrave said.

"We could get the Knights of Columbus and the Ladies Auxiliary," Cardinal went on. "And the Elks might be interested, too. I mean, we've practically got enough for a curling team already."

"Yes, I thought you might not be pleased," Squier said. "Home turf and all that. I just want you to know that I'm here—and CSIS is here—to give you every possible assistance. You'll probably want to see my ID." He pulled out an embossed employment card with his picture on it. "You can call that number for confirmation of everything I've said."

"Believe me," Musgrave said to Cardinal, "I've done that. He's for real, and so is CSIS, and that's just the way things are. Make whatever calls you have to make, and then why don't you bring us up to date on where you're at with the investigation?"

Cardinal considered calling Chouinard and raising bloody hell, but he had a strong sense that it would get him nowhere. He was also grateful that Squier was pretending they'd never met.

"Basically, there's nothing to tell," he began. "Forensics doesn't have a lot to work with—an arm, an ear, pieces of leg, scalp, bits of pelvis. The guy was killed, then he was hacked up, then he was fed to the bears. The story Matlock gave the owner of Loon Lodge is that he was here to check out the ice fishing. There were no other guests, and so far the only lead we have is a paint scraping taken from where the body was chopped up. We're looking for a late-model Ford Explorer, walnut brown. We've got an ad coming out in tonight's *Lode* asking for help from anyone who may have talked to Matlock."

"Tell me if I'm being rude," Musgrave said. "But have you examined his car? CSIS here says he rented a red Escort."

"We're looking for the car. Are we done here? I'd like to get on with it."

"What about the American end?" Squier asked. "What's first on the agenda down there?"

Musgrave stared out the grimy window at the traffic on MacPherson, as if the question had nothing to do with him.

"First thing we have to do with New York is notify next of kin, if there are any, and interview them. We'll have to ask the usual questions—any enemies etcetera, recent altercations . . ."

"I can do that," Squier said with childlike eagerness. "Why don't you let me do that? I have to handle a lot of American stuff, anyway, liaising with the FBI and so on."

Musgrave whirled on him. "Do us all a favor, will you?" he said. "Put one of your former Mounties on it. What the hell do you CSIS infants know about investigating a murder? Or investigating anything for that matter?"

"The top brass at CSIS may still be former Mounties from the old security service days," Squier said, "but among the rank and file there's hardly any of them left. And frankly, I don't think my superior is going to want them on this case."

"You little dorks with your laptops and your cell phones. You think you run the universe, don't you."

"Sergeant Musgrave, I'm sure you know that the former Mounties on CSIS staff were never criminal investigators; they were security officers, same as I am."

"Oh, really? And I'm sure you know—or would know, if you took the trouble to look back a little further—that a lot of those security men put

in ten or fifteen years in the criminal divisions before moving on to security. Unfortunately, when the media went Mountie-hunting, a little window dressing was in order, so Ottawa passes a new law and abracadabra:
you jerks do exactly what the Mounties were doing, only now it's legal.
Oh, yes, and dear me, so sorry, I hope you don't mind—a lot of damned
good men were forced out."

There was a slight tremor in Musgrave's voice that spoke of emotions
more complicated than anger. Cardinal had never seen him so upset, and
felt the beginnings of something like sympathy.

Squier started to speak, then apparently thought better of it, and
started again. "I can't control ancient history. And believe it or not I'm not
here to make trouble. But we need your cooperation, and the fact is, I'm
not asking. If you want to dispute that, either of you can take it up with
my superior in Toronto or with CSIS Ottawa. You have the number.
When you're ready to cooperate, give me a call. I'm at the Hilltop Motel."
He tucked his laptop under his arm and left the room.

When he was gone, Cardinal gave a low whistle.

"My God," Musgrave said. "Somebody shoot me."

6

CARDINAL DROVE TO THE Trianon Hotel out on the bypass. If Algonquin Bay could be said to have a scene for power lunches, the Trianon would be it—not that anyone would give the food anything more than two stars—simply because, of the few higher-class places in town, it was by far the most expensive.

And the Trianon had, Cardinal had to admit, a certain Old World charm that was hard to find in Algonquin Bay. As he stepped inside, he could see it gleaming in the silver, twinkling in the chandeliers and candelabra. Cardinal could only afford the place on special occasions: the last had been Kelly's graduation.

"Which party?" the maitre d' inquired, with a passable imitation of Parisian hauteur.

"I'm meeting R. J. Kendall."

The maitre d' led him across the crowded dining room. Cardinal recognized an assistant Crown Attorney and nodded to a provincial court justice. Police Chief Kendall was ensconced in a plush side room that Cardinal had never seen before.

"It's the Windigo man himself," Kendall said, as Cardinal entered. The chief's face was florid, not from embarrassment or drink but from high blood pressure. "Do you know Paul Laroche, here? Of Laroche Real Estate?"

"Of course. I mean I know who you are," Cardinal said, shaking hands with the man who stood to greet him. Laroche was no taller than Cardinal, but he gave the impression of size—massive chest, wide shoulders—a man who could take care of himself. His grip was strong without being showy.

"Haven't I seen you out at the club?" Laroche said.

"Blue Heron Club," R. J. explained. "Paul owns it."

"With partners," Laroche said. "Are you a golfer?"

"Not me," Cardinal said. "Haven't got the patience. I want to just carry the ball right over to the pocket."

"Not a golfer. Are you a hunting man, then? A skier?"

"None of the above. In summer I like to go out in the boat. Watching the hockey game's about as close to any sport as I get. Unless you consider woodworking a sport."

Laroche smiled. His dark hair had flecks of gray in it, but it was close-cut, in a clinging style that flattered his well-shaped head. He was wearing a beautifully cut chalkstripe that must have cost four times the highest sum Cardinal had ever paid for a suit. He looked like an investment banker.

"You said you're impatient. But I would have thought patience was a necessary virtue in your line of work," he said, sitting down again.

"Actually, Detective Cardinal is one of our stars," R. J. said. "The Windigo case?"

"Really? That must have been something," Laroche said. "To take down two serial killers in one case. Quite a victory. And you probably saved a lot of lives."

"I had help. Lise Delorme was the one who actually—"

Laroche raised his hand. "Lise Delorme," he said. "I know that name. . . ."

"Well, she was in the papers a lot with the Windigo thing. She—"

"No," Laroche said. "She's the one who brought Mayor Wells to grief."

"Yes, she did. Performed a real service to the city that time."

"Oh? You think so?"

"Excuse me, gentlemen," R. J. said. "I don't mean to be rude, but we'd better get our orders in. What's good, Paul?"

"The maple-glazed venison is your best bet. But you must let me order the wine."

The Trianon mostly succeeds in its efforts to ape European elegance, but the one area in which it falls down is the staff. Instead of old professionals, diners are waited on by charming but not necessarily competent young women. Laroche was polite but firm with the knock-kneed, freck-led creature who served them.

Real estate was obviously a paying proposition. Laroche's whole being glowed with money the way an athlete's body glows with health. It shone in the gold cufflinks, glinting against the snowy perfection of French cuffs. It shone in the just-right shade of tan in Laroche's face—a skier, Cardinal surmised.

After they had ordered, Kendall said, "You mustn't get Paul onto politics, Detective Cardinal. He's one of the key men behind Premier Mantis."

"Of course. You ran his local campaign," Cardinal said.

"Which is the reason for this meeting," Kendall said. "The Conservatives are having a major fund-raiser this coming weekend, and Paul is asking for extra police presence."

"Plainclothes? Shouldn't you be talking to Chouinard about this?"

"Chouinard's already agreed. We're thinking two detectives, one man and one woman, which means Delorme and you."

"This will not be too onerous," Laroche said. "It's going to be at our new ski club—the Highlands?—and the dinner will be sumptuous, I assure you. Except for being on watch for suspicious individuals, I think you'll manage to enjoy yourselves."

"You'll need more than two detectives to secure an event like that."

"We'll have our own private security, of course. They will be on the doors and backstage and so on. But frankly—in the wake of September 11—I don't think private security's enough. I'll be much more comfortable if we have a couple of professionals right in among the tables. Premier Mantis is a very prominent figure."

"We'll put three or four patrolmen outside as well," R. J. said.

"Are we going to be doing this for the Liberals and the NDP, too?" Cardinal said to Kendall.

"Certainly. If they ask us."

"They won't," Laroche said. "Their political fortunes are such, these days, any fund-raiser they hold is likely to be a low-profile affair. We are, after all, the only party with a provincial premier as its candidate."

The food arrived, and the venison was as good as any Cardinal had ever tasted. He was tempted to try the Bordeaux with it—the chief wouldn't have minded—but he wanted to be absolutely clearheaded for the afternoon.

They discussed various angles of security for the fund-raiser. Cardinal tried not to let his impatience show. Security detail was the last thing he wanted to be thinking about while investigating a murder. Laroche had brought a floor plan of the new club, and they talked about deployment of the security personnel inside, patrol officers outside, and the two detectives among the guests.

When they were having their coffee, Laroche said to Cardinal. "So you didn't care for Mayor Wells, I take it? You know he was a wonderful mayor."

"Well, yes—if you ignore the fact that he was stuffing ballot boxes," Cardinal said. "You don't think he deserved what he got?"

Laroche looked Cardinal up and down—taking his time about it. "People in our society have decided it is a crime to stuff ballot boxes. That makes it a crime. In other places it's not a crime, or it's overlooked. It's not inherently evil. And one shouldn't forget all the things Mayor Wells did for this city."

"He built the airport. He built the overpass. Then he stole an election."

"Let's not make him out to be Richard Nixon," Kendall said.

"There's good and bad mixed in every man, don't you think?" Laroche said. "For example, you saved the city from a murderous rampage, but I'm willing to bet there are things in your life that might not look so heroic on page one of the *Toronto Star*."

"You're right, there," Cardinal said. He thought of Bouchard's anniversary card. *We know where you live.*

"And Wells was a character. People underestimate how important that is in a leader. That's why I could never run for office myself, much as I'd love to. Too colorless."

"But you're very impressive," Cardinal said. "We've just been introduced, and I'm sitting here, impressed. That's half the battle, isn't it?"

Laroche laughed, showing perfect teeth.

"I'm a behind-the-scenes man, born and bred, Detective. Give me a candidate like Geoff Mantis, I'll do everything I can to get him elected—I'll call in the debts, twist the arms, you name it. But run for office myself? Not a chance."

Laroche spoke as if he were laying out his points in a seminar, his modulation highly educated. Cardinal wondered if he had lived abroad. Laroche gripped Cardinal's arm lightly. "Forgive me for being so earnest. These questions are on my mind, what with the election coming up."

"Is Geoff Mantis going to win again?"

"Oh, yes. I'm going to make sure of it."

After the luxurious interior of the Trianon, the parking lot felt even more cold and damp. Disembodied headlights glided through the mist along the bypass, and rain felt imminent.

Laroche climbed behind the wheel of a Lincoln Navigator that was parked by the restaurant entrance. He rolled down the window, and said, "R. J., I forgot to ask. How are things progressing with your body in the woods?"

Kendall shrugged. "It's Detective Cardinal's case. We have some leads. We're moving along. Right, Detective?"

"Not as fast as I'd like. But I always feel that way."

"Don't worry," Laroche said. "If your record on the Windigo case is anything to go by, you'll have this matter wrapped up in no time." He drove off into the fog, his turn signal winking toward town.

"Smooth character," Cardinal said.

"Rich character. Not bad for a guy who grew up in an orphanage. I mean, running the premier's campaign?"

"I voted against Mantis."

"Luckily," Kendall said, "most people had better sense."

ON HIS WAY DOWNTOWN AGAIN, Cardinal called his father on the cell phone. "Hold on a second. I'm just pulling some chocolate chip out of the oven."

Since his wife had died ten years previously, Stan had taken up an interest in cooking. It still gave Cardinal a kick to see his father—tough, sinewy Stan Cardinal, with his muscley forearms and his powerful chest—wearing an apron and wiping flour from his hands. Cookies were his specialty.

"Did you see the cardiologist?"

"Catherine drove me up this morning. Dr. Cates irritated hell out of me, but she knows how to get things done, I'll say that for her."

"What's the cardiologist say?"

"He's scheduling me for a bunch of tests up at the hospital. He thinks I have congestive heart failure."

"What? Dad, why didn't you get this taken care of six months ago?"

"It's not a big deal, John. It's just some tests. And he's giving me tons of drugs. They're working already. I feel better than I've felt in months."

"Heart failure, though. I wish you weren't living out to hell and gone."

"Nonsense. Whole reason I moved in here was so you wouldn't have to worry about me. Why the hell do you think I got a bungalow? No damn stairs to break my neck on, that's why. This is the easiest place in the world to keep clean and get around in. I've got peace and quiet and fresh air. I've got my stereo and my VCR and the best microwave on the market. I'm telling you, I'm king of the castle here."

"Well, if the fog gets any worse, you might want to think about moving in with us for the duration."

"Drop it, John."

Cardinal turned onto MacPherson, skirting a messy construction site.

"They said on the news you found a chewed-up body in the woods?" Stan said. "Sounds a little more interesting than the usual crap you get. Those stupid domestics."

Great, Cardinal thought. Here we go.

"These trailer trash constantly shooting each other. Drug dealers. Robbers. Fat-assed drunkards. I don't know why you didn't go into a more interesting line of work. It's not like you didn't have the education. Your ma and I saw to it you and your brother got to college. You could have gone into any profession you wanted."

"That's exactly what I did, Dad. I went into the profession I wanted. A line of work that can actually make a difference in people's lives. A lot of my colleagues didn't go to university—that doesn't mean they're stupid. Look at the people you worked with."

"Fools! Morons! The bunch of them! Except for Mark McCabe. Mark was the smartest guy I ever knew. Read more books than most college professors. Did long division in his head, Mark did. But he was a union man through and through. And it was guys like you—your oh-so-brainy colleagues—that saw fit to bust his head open for having the guts to call a strike against the fat bastards that run this country. That nightstick came down on his head—and I heard it. It sounded like a plank dropping on a cement floor. That nightstick came down on Mark's head, and for the next three years he did nothing but drool, and then he died. A good, good man."

The phone went quiet. Cardinal heard his father sniff and knew that he was crying. Stan Cardinal, who had for most of his long life displayed few emotions other than irritation, now became teary when he talked of the past. It didn't seem to be self-pity, but some deeper, long-abiding sorrow. The tears would flow for a minute, then gone.

"You okay, Dad?"

There was a loud sniff from the other end of the line.

"Fog's turning to rain," Stan said. "Maybe I'll plant some zinnias in the spring."

7

"LISTEN," MUSGRAVE SAID. "I've gone over it with my regional commander. I'm not working with that laptop-toting twerp from CSIS. What we do is, I deal with you, you deal with him."

"Squier didn't seem all that bad to me," Cardinal said.

"You haven't worked with CSIS before, have you?"

"No."

"You poor bastard. Anyway," Musgrave said, looking at his watch, "this is forty-five minutes of my life we've wasted. Tell me again what we're doing here?"

They were parked in an unmarked on Main East. The fog had finally condensed into actual rain that was drumming on the roof.

The moment Cardinal had hung up with his father, the cell phone had rung in his hand and Paul Arsenault was on the line telling him they'd matched a print at the trapper's shack to a name: Paul Bressard. Cardinal had driven straight out to Bressard's house. Mrs. Bressard, who was already reeking of scotch at one thirty in the afternoon, told him her husband would probably be at Duane's Billiard Emporium. Cardinal didn't mention that he was a cop, and she wasn't sober enough to notice.

Which was how he and Musgrave came to be sitting in the unmarked on Main East watching the decayed entrance to Duane's Billiard Emporium.

"Duane's is a hangout for the guys who can't quite make it to big-time crime," Cardinal said. "Bikers that failed the entrance exam to Satan's Choice, Italian guys too dumb for the mob."

"And the wife just handed you this information. Why'd she take a shine to you?"

"In Cutty Sark veritas."

"In Cutty Sark bullshit, it looks like."

"Tell me something, Musgrave. Does your wife know your every move?"

"You could fill a mountain of CD-ROMs with what my wife doesn't know. It's a point of pride with her."

"Fine. So let's give it another half hour."

They listened to the rain hammering down for another ten minutes, and then the Explorer came into view.

"That's him with the mustache?"

"That's him. The guy with him is Thierry Ferand, another trapper."

Bressard parked half a block away, then he and Ferand came slouching back toward the pool hall through the rain. Ferand was half the other man's size and had to scuttle along beside him like a dachshund.

"Bressard's a dresser," Musgrave said. "Get a load of the coat."

"He better hope the antifur movement never hits Algonquin Bay."

Bressard and Ferand entered the building. Cardinal and Musgrave left the unmarked and went to examine the Explorer. A jagged line ran across two doors on the passenger side. "We'll have to get our ident guys on it," Cardinal said, "but for now, I'd say that looks fresh, wouldn't you?"

"I would. Is this guy going to be a problem?"

"Bressard? No way. Bressard will come along voluntarily."

Musgrave laughed. "Christ, Cardinal. I'd never have pegged you for an optimist."

As they stepped into the dark stairwell that led down to Duane's, Cardinal said: "Watch out for Ferand. He's got a mean streak a mile wide, and he's fond of brass knuckles."

"Let me handle him," Musgrave hitched up his belt. "It's always the small guys."

When Cardinal was a teenager, the pool room had been like a secret society. Cardinal and his friends would play endless games of Boston,

High-Low, or Snooker, chain-smoking their Players and DuMauriers like thirties gangsters. Smoke used to hang like storm clouds over a landscape of green felt. So he was a little surprised to step into Duane's and find that the air was not even visible; even pool players had become more health-conscious.

Duane himself was behind the counter from which he served easily the worst hamburger in town, for twice the going price. He was a great fat stoat of a man, who, without ever having been convicted of anything more than the odd traffic offense, radiated an air of sleaze.

Most of the clientele were in their late teens or early twenties, all male, all trying with varying degrees of success to look tough. With a single glance around the room, Cardinal recognized two drug dealers and one car thief. Bressard and Ferand had started up a game at a corner table. Bressard was bent over the table, lining up a shot. Without straightening, he looked up along the cue at Cardinal as they approached. Ferand was drinking a Dr Pepper and spilled a good deal of it over his shirt when he caught sight of them. Cardinal had arrested him twice for assault, though only one charge had stuck. Ferand cursed, placed his cue in the wall rack, and grabbed his coat.

"Relax, Thierry," Cardinal said, flashing his badge. "We just need to talk to your buddy here."

"Don't tell me," Bressard said. "You've come to make sure I'm not dead."

"Oh, no, I can see you're not dead, Paul. I just need some help clearing up a few things with that story I mentioned to you yesterday."

Ferand said, "What are you looking at?"

Musgrave was standing in front of the rear exit, arms folded across his massive chest, and staring at Ferand with a funny little grin, a barely perceptible uptilt in the corner of his mouth.

"See, we still have this story about a murder in the woods," Cardinal said to Bressard. "We've even got a body, now—not yours, obviously— but maybe you heard about it on the news."

"What if I have?"

"Well, you're the only person whose name's come up in this whole deal. So I was hoping you'd come down to the station and help us clear it up."

"What the fuck are you looking at?" Ferand said again. "You a faggot or something?"

Musgrave was still planted like a sphinx in the doorway, still doing that funny little Mona Lisa thing at Ferand.

"Tell him to stop looking at me."

"Shut up, Thierry," Bressard said. "He's just trying to psych you out. And you're letting him do it."

"So, what do you say, Paul? Come on downtown with us, we'll have a chat about how your name got mixed up in this. I'm sure it's nothing we can't—"

A small blur launched itself past Cardinal in Musgrave's direction. Before he could even turn to look, the small blur came flying back over his head and landed on the pool table. Balls went flying; the overhead lamp swung crazily back and forth. In the flashing light something gold or brass glittered in Ferand's hand as he lay groaning on the table, and then it slid to the floor with a clunk.

"Assaulting a police officer," Musgrave said. "He's even dumber than he looks."

8

FERAND WAS BOOKED and placed in the cells. Wudky had been transferred to the jail for his own protection, in case Ferand should happen to remember who it was he had mentioned the murder to.

Musgrave was all for going at Bressard full-force, which was one reason Cardinal insisted that he do the interview alone.

Musgrave shrugged. "Suit yourself. I'm heading back to Sudbury. Let me know what the *habitant* has to say for himself."

Cardinal sat Bressard down in the interview room. The trapper tried to appear calm, slouching back in his seat, but he kept playing with the straw in his can of Coke. Cardinal's manner was inquisitive but not unfriendly—just two colleagues out to solve this peculiar set of events together.

"I'm hoping you can help me out here, Paul, because right now I have to say it looks pretty bad. How's it happen that we find a dead body near your old shack in the woods? Can you help me clear that up?"

Bressard took a sip of his Coke, stared at the wall a moment, and went back to twirling his straw.

"We know it was chopped up at your old shack, by the way. There's no doubt about that. Blood everywhere. All sorts of evidence."

Bressard took a deep breath, sighed, shook his head.

"You know, I might be inclined to think it had nothing to do with you. Somebody had an argument and got rid of the body in your old neck of the woods, maybe. But there's one thing bothers me, and I hope you can explain it." He waited, but Bressard didn't look at him. "Just tell me this, Paul. How'd you get the scratch on your passenger doors?"

No answer.

"You might want to respond to that one, Paul. Because our scene man, and the Forensic Center, and Ford Motors all say the paint we found on a stump in the woods matches the paint on your Explorer."

Bressard sucked on the straw of his Coke until the contents rattled.

"You may think I don't know anything about you, Paul, but in fact I have a very good idea how you make your living. Number one, there's the trapping—you have good years and bad years with that, like everything else. Number two, there's the odd job for Leon Petrucci."

The corner of Bressard's mouth lifted in the beginning of a smile, but he didn't take the bait.

"Leon Petrucci. It's been a while, maybe, but we know you've worked for him in the past. Number three, there's the guiding. I know that a good part of your income comes from taking novice hunters out into the woods and finding a bear or two for them to shoot. And I also know that you don't rely on luck for that. Put a few steaks out on the trail at the right time of year, you're going to see a bear—especially if you know where they live, which I'm sure a longtime professional like you does.

"Howard Matlock told the Loon Lodge people he was interested in ice fishing. He didn't bring any guns or knives with him. Didn't show the slightest interest in hunting. Now, I don't mean to sound unpleasant, but how does Mr. Matlock come to be eaten by bears near your old shack, Paul?"

Bressard burped quietly, picked up the Coke can, and read the French side of the label. Cardinal had been at this game long enough to know when he was getting nowhere, and he could see he was getting nowhere with Bressard. One more shot, he thought. I'll just give it one more shot.

"You had a fight about something. Maybe he came after you first. Maybe you shot him accidentally—I won't even pretend to know how—and then you decided to get rid of the body. I have to give you credit for originality there. But however it happened, unless you give me some kind of explanation, there's a good chance you'll go down for second-degree murder on this. It may take us a while to make the case, but we have a good beginning."

Bressard set his Coke can on the table, turning it slowly. Cardinal grabbed it and tossed it into the wastebasket, where it landed with an enormous racket.

"All right," Cardinal said, rising. "I was trying to help you, but you're just making things worse for yourself. Unless you give me some reason not to, we're going to have to charge you with murder. The Crown already has the paperwork; he's just waiting to hear how cooperative you were."

Bressard didn't move a muscle.

"Oh, for Christ's sake," Cardinal said. "Let's go."

He reached for Bressard's elbow, but before he could take hold, Bressard swung mournful eyes his way and said, "I got a serious problem."

That's a world-class understatement, Cardinal thought, but he didn't say so. He sat back down and all he said was, "Tell me."

"If I don't say anything, you take these bits and pieces you have and put me away for life—maybe or maybe not."

"You fed him to the bears, Paul. I don't think there's a lot of maybe here."

"So, me, I have a question."

"Shoot."

"What exactly can you offer in terms of witness protection? Would I get a new name, resettle somewhere?"

Cardinal sighed. Since Canada inaugurated its witness-protection program in 1996, every thug with even the most tangential connection to organized crime had fantasies that, should the day come when the gang gets rounded up, he'd turn "state's evidence" in return for a new identity and a nice cottage on a distant lake.

"I have no control over witness protection, Paul. The Mounties decide who qualifies, and it's seriously underfunded. I wouldn't hold my breath."

"Then why the hell should I give you Petrucci?"

"Are you saying you killed this guy for Leon Petrucci?"

"I didn't kill nobody. Me, I'm just asking a question. If I go to prison at least I get life. With Petrucci I get a nice view of the bottom of Trout Lake."

"So you're going to go down for him? You want to do his time for him? You're a nicer guy than I thought, Paul. Lot of guys wouldn't sacrifice their entire lives for a guy like Petrucci. It's very thoughtful of you, and I have to wonder how much he'll appreciate it."

"So you, you keep talking, Cardinal. You got nothing to lose. Me, I got everything to lose."

"You're making a mistake about Petrucci. I'm not an organized-crime expert—that's an RCMP job, thank God—but I can tell you this: Leon Petrucci is not Don Corleone. Leon Petrucci has a distant, and I emphasize distant, connection with the Carbone family in Hamilton. They back him on a few enterprises up here in return for their cut, but they do not whack people for him, and I don't think they're going to miss him a whole lot if he gets put away."

"So, what do I get if I do this?"

"Concentrate on what's going to happen if you don't. You will go down for murder. A murder you say you didn't commit. If you can help us nail Leon Petrucci, you're still an accessory after the fact, but I will ask the Crown to reduce your charges to something like interfering with a dead body or whatever the hell the statute is."

"Interfering? 'Ostie, I'm no pervert."

"I just mean you disposed of the damn thing. You fed it to the bears, right?"

"Okay, I fed it to the bears. But I don't want no stories getting around I interfered with it."

"Depending what you can give us on Petrucci, I'm prepared to ask the Crown to push for protective custody. And I'll talk to Musgrave about witness protection."

Bressard stared down at the floor and cursed. "Like I say, I didn't kill nobody. Last Sunday, it's like nine in the morning, me and the wife are having breakfast. The doorbell rings. My wife goes to answer it, and there's no one there, just a fat envelope stuck between the doors. The envelope is marked personal for me, nothing else on it. I open it up and there's five thousand dollars cash along with a note."

"What'd the note say?"

"The note says, 'At your shack you'll find a fresh supply of bait. There's another five thousand when the bears have had their dinner.' "

"Was it signed?"

"Just P. Initial P. Petrucci, he has to write everything. He's got no voice box."

"I know that. Was it handwritten or typed?"

"Typed. First I was gonna toss it, but you never know how things are gonna turn out. I thought maybe I might need it." Bressard reached into his pocket and pulled out a wallet.

"Wait," Cardinal said. "Don't touch it anymore than we have to. Just dump it on the table there."

Bressard held his wallet upside down so that a square-folded piece of paper fell to the table, along with some coins and half a dozen Lotto tickets.

Carefully, using just his fingernails, Cardinal unfolded the paper without smoothing it out. The wording was pretty much as Bressard had said: *There's a fresh supply of bait at your old shack. There's another five when the bears have had their dinner.* It was signed simply, *P.* It looked like it was from a computer printer; they wouldn't be tracing any typewriters here.

"It could be from anybody," Cardinal observed. "And the last I heard, Leon Petrucci moved down to Toronto to be close to Mount Sinai."

"Yeah, sure. And you think that's gonna get in the way of business? Not too many people are gonna drop five grand in my mailbox and leave me a dead fucking body to get rid of. I told you. Petrucci don't talk. He's got no goddamn voice box. Who the fuck else you think it's going to be from?"

"How do I know you didn't type this up to cover your ass?"

"Jesus, Cardinal. You're so fucking skeptical."

"I'm paid to be skeptical."

"How do you get around in life? How do you cross the street? I mean, how do you know the street isn't going to cave in the minute you step on it? Some things you just got to believe, you know what I mean, or there's no point in living."

"Fine. So what did you do?"

"I go out to my shack—the old one that I haven't used for like seven, eight years. That's how I met Petrucci years ago, by the way. I took him on a bear hunt must be ten years ago. Anyways, I find this big sack on the ground outside. Like a duffel bag. Right away I knew what was in it. I didn't even have to open it. It's a dead guy, right? This is the first I know for sure it's a body. So, what am I gonna do, call the Sanitation Department?"

"You could have called the Police Department."

"Obviously you know Leon Petrucci really well. Besides, I figured the guy's already dead, I'm not hurting him any."

"We know you took the body into your shack. Did Ferand help you?"

"No."

"Was he involved in this in any way? You're not helping yourself if he was and you don't mention it."

"Thierry had nothing to do with this. I never told him about it till after." It was true the ident guys hadn't found any evidence linking Ferand to the crime.

"Did you cut the body up yourself, or did you have help?"

"Myself. There was quite a bit of blood. To tell you the truth, the first thing I did when I got in there was throw up. I don't know, I've seen a million dead animals, doesn't bother me. But there's something about a dead person, even if you don't know them. Know what I mean?"

"Oh, yes."

"Anyway, I didn't want to get blood all over me. I bundled up the pieces and attached a rope so I could drag it to the bear trail. I knew they were awake and I knew they'd be hungry. I didn't figure there'd be too much left of the guy."

"Was the body stripped when you found it?"

"No, I did that. Didn't want to be sawing through clothes. Didn't figure the bears'd be interested in polyester or whatever, either."

"We found some material in the stove. Was there anything else with the body—any kind of ID or personal effects you might have kept?"

"I didn't keep nothing. There was nothing to keep. I slung everything into the stove."

"Did you recognize the victim?"

"Never seen him before in my life."

"Frankly, I'm still a long way from buying the godfather angle. Do you have any idea why Petrucci would have wanted this guy dead?"

"No. And I wasn't about to ask, either."

"You have a good business, Paul. A wife. Nice house. Why'd you do this to a guy you didn't even know?"

"Why?" Bressard looked away at the far wall of the interview room. After a few moments of reflection he turned back to Cardinal. "Two reasons. One: Leon Petrucci. And two: Leon Petrucci. What do you think he's going to do if I tell him thanks but I can't do it? You think he's just going to let me walk away from this? I don't think so."

"And there was the ten thousand."

"Five. I'm still waiting for the other five."

CARDINAL HAD BRESSARD SIGN a brief statement, then led him back to the cells. He would be formally charged that afternoon and let go on his own recognizance, mostly so he could be watched.

Cardinal called Musgrave, who was still on the road.

"You think it's the mob?" Musgrave said. "You think that note means the order came from Petrucci?"

"Well, Bressard has worked for Petrucci before. I think the case was before your time—about eight years ago?"

"Yeah, I was in Montreal back then."

"We had a case where Bressard beat a guy pretty bad on orders from Petrucci. We could never nail Petrucci for it because Bressard was too scared to involve him. But when we were making the case, lots of characters did mention him—and one of them had a note, initialed P. Petrucci had his larynx out years ago—it wasn't unusual for him to write notes. On the other hand, Bressard could be lying through his teeth."

"I'm impressed that you got him to talk at all, considering. But you know Leon Petrucci moved down to Toronto."

"Yeah, I heard."

"Which leaves it barely in the realm of the possible. Tell you what. Why don't you let me handle the Petrucci angle? I'll get someone from our Toronto detachment on it. They work organized crime all the time."

"Sounds good to me."

Musgrave let out a curse.

"What's the matter? You all right?"

"Goddamn truck driver just cut me off. I'm telling you, there's never any cops around when you need one."

9

THE CROWN ATTORNEY'S OFFICE was on MacIntosh Street in an aggressively ugly building of poured concrete that also housed local offices for the Ministry of Community and Social Services. It was right across the street from *The Algonquin Lode*, a location that came in handy when Reginald Rose, Q.C., wanted to make his opinions known to the public, which he often did.

Everything about Reginald Rose was long. He was tall and thin with a slight stoop that gave him the look of a scholar. He had long fingers that handled documents and evidence and even the knot of his tie with grace. He was given to red neckties and starched white shirts and red suspenders that—when he wasn't wearing his habitual blue blazer—gave him the look of a crisp new Canadian flag.

He was just now addressing himself to a group gathered around a long oak table—an odd-looking group, Cardinal thought. Aside from the elongated Rose himself, there was Robert Henry Hewitt, a.k.a. Wudky, who kept drooping over the table like a dormouse. There was Bob Brackett, his pro-bono attorney—a plump but decidedly lethal criminal lawyer. And there was Cardinal himself, who was sure he must look as uncomfortable as he felt, because although he was usually perfectly clear what side he was on, just now he had his doubts.

"I must tell you right from the start," Rose said, "that I am not of a mind to make a deal in this case. Why should I? According to all the evidence—and there's a mountain of evidence—Robert Henry Hewitt is guilty of armed robbery. And not just a little guilty, but absolutely, positively, deadbang guilty. We have his admission of guilt—"

"Of course you do. Obtained without benefit of counsel."

"Mr. Brackett, let me finish. We have your client's admission of guilt. We have the cash from his knapsack. We have the plaid scarf he wore over his face. We have the holdup note written in his appalling but distinctive penmanship—written on the back of his previous arrest warrant, which coincidentally provides his name and address. Why should we make any deal?"

Bob Brackett leaned forward against the conference table. He was dressed in impeccable pinstripes—he always was, perhaps because it lent an edge to his portly figure that otherwise had no edges at all. Pinstripes were nothing unusual in the legal trade, of course, but the gold hoop gleaming in Bob Brackett's left earlobe most definitely was—especially on a half-bald, tubby man in his mid-fifties. He had never married, and in a place the size of Algonquin Bay that alone was enough to feed rumors. Toss in one gold earring, and the whispers rose a good deal higher in volume. Not that it mattered; as far as his clients were concerned, Bob Brackett could show up in a tutu, as long as he was in their corner.

"Come now, Mr. Rose," he said. His voice was soft, reasonable, friendly. "Don't you take any pride in your work? Are you really so desperate for victories that you have to corner a mentally impaired young man and put him away for fifteen years?"

"Have him plead guilty. I'll ask for ten."

Brackett turned to Cardinal. Cardinal was ready to give his views on the Matlock case and how Wudky had tried to help them out. Unfortunately, Brackett had something else in mind. "Detective Cardinal, I believe you have a nickname for my client down at police headquarters."

Cardinal coughed, partly from surprise, partly as a stall. "I don't think we need to go into that, do we? I thought we were just going to . . ."

"Do you or do you not have a nickname for my client down at headquarters?" Brackett's voice never wavered from its note of pleasant inquiry.

"Detective Cardinal is not in the witness box," Rose said. "You don't get to cross-examine him."

"I'm not cross-examining him. He'll know when I'm cross-examining him. I'm asking a simple question."

"We have nicknames for a lot of our customers," Cardinal said. "They're not intended for public consumption."

"I'm not interested in your other customers, as you call them. What is my client's nickname, please?"

"Wudky."

"Wudky. An unusual cognomen. Could you spell that for us, please?"

"W-D-C."

"W-D-C. An unusual spelling, too. What do the letters stand for?"

"I'd really rather not say with Robert in the room."

Brackett smiled. It was a smile of great benevolence and gave not one inch of ground. "Nevertheless, Detective, we await your answer."

"It stands for World's Dumbest Criminal. Sorry, Robert."

"That's okay." Hewitt was slumped over the conference table, his chin resting on both folded hands. Speech made his head bob up and down.

"World's Dumbest Criminal. And you call him that why, exactly?" Brackett's round face was devoid of guile, just asking for information, please.

"I thought we were going to discuss this just the three of us."

"Oh, no, that was never on the table," Brackett said. "Please tell us why you call my client the World's Dumbest Criminal."

"Because he's just not competent. He makes dumb mistakes."

"Well, yes. Mr. Rose has the holdup note as exhibit A."

Rose tapped his legal pad with the eraser end of his pencil. "Your client has been found in previous trials to be mentally competent to contribute to his legal defense and to understand the nature of his crimes. Do you expect that to suddenly change?"

Brackett's smile was cherubic. "You're so ferocious in the pursuit of the retarded, Mr. Rose. Perhaps you'd prefer to ship my client to the United States. They execute them down there."

"Not for robbery, last I heard."

"May I continue?"

"I wish you would."

"Detective Cardinal, despite my client's intellectual limitations, I believe he has recently been extremely helpful to the police, is that correct?"

At last, Cardinal thought. "He was a little off on the details. He told us of a conversation he'd had with a known felon named Thierry Ferand. And Ferand told him that a man from down south somewhere had killed Paul Bressard and got rid of the body in the woods."

The Crown tossed his pencil onto his pad so hard it bounced onto the floor. "Paul Bressard is alive and kicking. I saw him this morning. You can't miss him in that raccoon coat, for God's sake."

"Like I say, Robert was wrong on the details."

"The details? It's a completely false statement."

Mr. Brackett twiddled pudgy fingers in the air. "Stop. Could we stop, please, and just move on to how much of Mr. Hewitt's information turned out to be correct?"

"Well, once we figured out that he had some names mixed up, it turned out he was right. That is to say, Paul Bressard wasn't murdered and buried in the woods, but Bressard does admit to disposing of a body in the woods. And the body is indeed from down south—an American named Howard Matlock. So, you see, Robert just kind of had things reversed."

"Thank you, Detective. That's extraordinarily helpful." Brackett removed his glasses and polished them with the back of his tie, another gesture that emphasized his pure harmlessness. "Would it also be fair to say you wouldn't have known about this murder without my client's help?"

"Not exactly. It's true he told us about it before we knew about it for ourselves, but we did hear of it from the person who found the body—part of it, anyway. But Robert also gave us the name of Paul Bressard, which made him a suspect sooner than he might have been, otherwise. So, all in all, yes, I would say he was very helpful and cooperative."

"Thank you, Detective." Brackett turned to the Crown. "So, Mr. Rose. It would appear the Crown Attorney's office has a choice. It can throw the book at a mentally challenged young man, or it can offer a deal to an extraordinarily helpful citizen."

Rose turned to Cardinal. "Do you have a suspect in the Matlock case?"

"We have several individuals on the radar screen. But I couldn't say any arrests are imminent."

Rose raised his arms in a gesture of helplessness to Brackett. "You see? How helpful is that?"

"Let's not play games, Mr. Rose. I didn't come here to waste your time or the detective's. Does this Crown Attorney's office want to encourage cooperation from defendants or not?"

"He pleads guilty to bank robbery, he does ten years."

"Ten years for a toy gun and an IQ of seventy-eight? I'd rather take my chances at trial." Brackett tossed his papers into his briefcase and snapped it shut. "He pleads to carrying a concealed weapon—even that's a gift, since we're talking about a toy. Two years less a day."

Rose shook his head. "Let's stay in the real world, counselor. Bank robbery, he does six years."

Brackett turned to his client and shook his shoulder gently. "Robert?"

Hewitt sat up, blinking. "Oh, hi. I was just resting."

"The Crown is offering six years. With good behavior you'd be out in four."

"Okay. That sounds good. Wow, I was having the most incredible dream, eh?"

As he was leaving, Cardinal had to endure a mini-lecture from Rose about the responsibility the police shared with the Crown to make sure criminals were adequately punished. "The police department," he said, "is not a place for bleeding hearts. If you want to empathize, I suggest you become a social worker."

Bob Brackett twiddled his fat fingers at Cardinal in the parking lot. Raindrops glistened on his scalp. Two uniformed cops were putting Robert Henry Hewitt into the backseat of a squad car. "Did Rose give you a lecture?"

"Sort of."

"It hurts the poor fellow to give up such an easy case. Some people's self-esteem depends on how many years they get. It's sad, in a way."

The squad car pulled to a stop beside them, and the rookie at the wheel said, "Customer wants to talk to you."

"What's up, Robert?"

"I just wanted to, like, thank you, eh? Thank you, thank you, thank you, Officer Cardinal. Mr. Brackett says you saved me like ten years off my life and I won't never forget it. Like never, never, never, eh? I don't forget my buddies. No way."

"Robert, the best way you can thank me is to stay out of trouble."

"Oh, I will, eh? I'm gonna be so good they'll have to send me back before I get there. Really, thank you, thank you, thank you."

The last Cardinal saw of Robert Henry Hewitt he was turned around in the back seat of the squad car, still mouthing multiple thank yous as the car turned right on MacIntosh and headed north for the trip back to the Algonquin Bay jail.

10

LISE DELORME WAS annoyed to be shunted aside on the Matlock case. What Cardinal had said was quite true: she had worked with Musgrave before and they got along fine, even though he was a chauvinist nightmare. But, no, D.S. Chouinard had wanted Cardinal on Matlock, and Cardinal it would be—which meant while Cardinal was deep in the juiciest case to come along in at least a year, Delorme was left to handle whatever run-of-the-mill stuff might happen to be phoned in.

She had been eating at her desk when the call came in from St. Francis hospital about a missing person. Delorme had taken down a few particulars and promised to be there in twenty minutes.

Missing persons. The trouble with missing persons is, they're usually not missing at all. Not the adults. In most cases, they're simply fed up— with their mate, their job, their life—and they've decided to take a powder. A spontaneous sabbatical. But there were elements in this particular "misper" that warranted immediate investigation, even though the subject—a single female in her thirties—had not yet been gone for even twenty-four hours.

"I'm here to see Dr. Nita Perry," Delorme said to the duty nurse. "Could you page her for me?"

Delorme went to wait in the sun room. On the television in the corner, Geoffrey Mantis, premier of Ontario, was explaining why teachers would have to work longer hours.

"Oh, yeah," Delorme said to the screen. "As if you're going to work longer hours." All Mantis seemed to do was vote himself pay raises and go on vacations; Delorme had never thought of golf as a year-round sport before. But she had learned to keep her political opinions to herself around the station. Definitely Tory turf, except for Cardinal. As far as she could tell, they were the only two cops on the force who didn't consider Mantis a hometown hero.

A young woman in surgical scrubs came into the sun room. She was small—a good two inches shorter than Delorme—and her red hair was held back from her face with two severe-looking clips. "I only have a few moments," Dr. Perry said. "I'm just on my way into surgery."

"You're a surgeon?" Delorme asked.

"Anesthetist. They can't start till I get there."

"You called in a missing person report on Dr. Winter Cates?"

"That's right. I have the picture you asked for. I managed to scrounge it up from our security people."

The photograph showed a pretty woman in her early thirties, with curly black hair and a crooked smile that gave her a faintly sardonic expression.

"It doesn't do her justice, believe me."

"When was the last time you spoke to Dr. Cates?"

"Last night, about eleven-thirty. I called her to tell her *Road Warrior* was on the late show. She's a real Mel Gibson fan—well, we both are. But she had rented a movie to watch. She certainly sounded fine then. Not a care in the world."

"Eleven-thirty seems late to be calling someone. Even a good friend."

"Oh, no. Winter's a real night owl, like me. I don't think I'd call her after one A.M., but any time up to then. We often speak late at night. We were joking about 'going to the farm'—that's our code for watching TV and scarfing down a bag of Pepperidge Farm cookies. Winter was just opening the bag when I called."

"When did you first become concerned about her?"

"This morning. We had a procedure scheduled for eight o'clock, and she didn't show. That would make you worry about anyone, but particularly someone as conscientious as Winter. She's just someone you can count on—the way you can't count on most people." A shadow crossed Dr. Perry's vivid blue eyes, as if she were recalling the myriad people who couldn't be counted on. "And Winter and I have become good friends, you know. Close friends. It's just totally out of character for her not to let me know what's up. I phoned a couple of times, but she hasn't called back. She hasn't even picked up the messages, as far as I can tell. Also out of character."

"Have you made any other efforts to find her?"

"After the surgery, I called her office, but her assistant hadn't heard from her. And I called her parents. They live in Sudbury, and Winter often goes to see them on weekends, but they hadn't heard from her, either. I didn't know who else to contact. She's only been in town about six months. She doesn't know a lot of people here. I was going to call her office again, but I didn't want to be a pest."

"Actually, her assistant called us just after you."

"Oh, no." Dr. Perry covered her mouth with her hand.

"Let's not get too worked up just yet. So far there's no reason to suspect foul play."

"Well, I'll tell you what really scares me," Dr. Perry said. "I drove over to her place at lunchtime, and her car's still there. So if she isn't at home, where did she go? And how did she get there? And why didn't she let anyone know?"

"Do you have any reason to suspect anyone would harm her? Did she have any enemies that you know of?"

"I can't believe anyone would want to hurt Winter. She didn't have an enemy in the world. She's just the nicest person you could hope to meet. Smart, funny, dependable—terrific doctor. Ask anybody who works with her. There's just no one you'd rather have in the O.R. with you."

"We'll certainly talk to her other colleagues," Delorme said. "But what about boyfriends? Is she seeing anyone that you know of?"

Dr. Perry looked down at the floor. Her surgical cap began to slip, and she pulled it back absently. "Winter does have an old boyfriend who is, um, problematic. From Sudbury. Craig something. I met him once. I don't think she ever told me his last name. I was over at her place one night—we were on our way out to dinner and a movie—and this Craig character shows up at her door. 'I can't see you now,' Winter tells him. 'I'm going out.' 'That's okay,' he says, 'I'll drive you!' She had a hard time getting rid of him."

"Did he seem dangerous to you?"

"Oh, no. I thought his showing up like that was a little weird. Winter said it was typical. Apparently she told him long ago that it was all over, but he insists on acting like nothing had happened. He always expected her to come back to Sudbury after she finished med school, but she really didn't want to go back there."

"Because of him?" Delorme asked.

"Oh, I don't know. I don't want to make the guy out to be a villain. I think she just didn't want to stay in her hometown. I'm sure you can understand that."

Actually, Delorme had never wanted to live anywhere other than her hometown. Even when she had gone away to university in Ottawa—and later at the police academy in Aylmer—she had missed Algonquin Bay. She had liked both cities, but there was something about living in the place that formed you—the sense of comfort and continuity—that no other town, no matter how charming or cosmopolitan, could replace. But she also knew that other people didn't feel that way.

"Is there anyone else Dr. Cates is having problems with? Did she mention anything?"

"Well, she was having some sort of dispute with Dr. Choquette, but nothing serious."

"What kind of dispute? Over what?"

"Winter took over Ray Choquette's practice when he retired. And there was some kind of misunderstanding over the arrangements."

"He sold his practice to her?"

"No. You can't sell a medical practice—not in Ontario. It was probably over equipment or something like that. Anyway, she was upset about it." Dr. Perry looked at her watch and stood up. "I've really got to go. Listen, Winter is a good person. I mean, really special. She makes people happy. I couldn't stand it if anything's happened to her."

"It hasn't even been twenty-four hours," Delorme said in her best bed-side manner. "Let's not jump to conclusions just yet."

DR. CATES'S APARTMENT was in Twickenham Mews, an expensive group of low-rises at the end of a short street behind the Algonquin Mall. Delorme still remembered the row of whitewashed bungalows that had been razed a dozen years ago to make way for it. With its red brick and cedar trim, Twickenham Mews was one of the most attractive places in the neighbor-hood. It looked homey—for an apartment building—and made you want to step inside, particularly now as the fog turned to rain.

Delorme rang the super's bell, a Mrs. Yvonne Lefebvre. She ap-peared—a spindly woman in her forties with red-rimmed eyes, clutching a handkerchief to her face. "Allergies," she said. "Winter, summer, spring, and fall. I don't know if it's mold or what. I just know they never stop." She concluded with a sneeze, as if for proof.

When Delorme had explained who she was and why she was there, it took Mrs. Lefebvre a good two minutes, stopping twice to sneeze and blow her nose, to make the journey to the end of her hallway, where she dug out a set of keys, and back to the door where Delorme waited—an ex-cursion that left her leaning against the wall, exhausted.

"How do you manage such a large building on your own?" Delorme asked.

"Oh, I don't, dear. My brother does all the repairs and maintenance. I just collect the rent. Listen, do you mind if I don't come upstairs with you? I'm not exactly feeling a hundred percent."

"Sorry. I need you to come with me. If Dr. Cates returns and there's something missing, I don't want her to think the police took it."

Walking down the hall, getting into the elevator, and reaching the doc-tor's apartment all took about five times longer than it should have. For much of it, Mrs. Lefebvre supported herself against the wall.

"What kind of car does Dr. Cates drive?"

"A PT Cruiser. Normally I wouldn't know that off the top of my head. Only reason I do is that it's just such a cute little thing, I asked her one day when I saw her hauling groceries out of it. It's still in her space out back."

Dr. Perry had pointed that out too, Delorme thought. So wherever the missing woman had gone, she didn't get there under her own steam.

Mrs. Lefebvre, red-faced and puffing, leaned against the doorframe as she opened the apartment. She sat down on a wooden chair just inside the door. "Damn antihistamines. I'm going to plunk myself down right here. Just let me know when you're done."

The lights were on, Delorme noted the moment she stepped inside. The curtains weren't drawn, either. A vast plate-glass window looked out over Lake Nipissing, a somber gray presence under the slanting rain.

The apartment had an overall look of comfortable mess. The furniture was new, the kind of country style that Delorme had seen mostly in catalogues. A colorful afghan lay in a tangled heap at one end of the couch. Stacks of movie videos tottered on the coffee table. Magazines—*The New Yorker, Maclean's, Scientific American*—fell out of an overstuffed basket. The bookshelves were jammed, mostly with paperback thrillers shoved in at all angles. Half-empty coffee cups and wine glasses were scattered about and extraneous objects were everywhere—an iron on the coffee table, a squash racquet in the dining area, a bra hanging over the back of a chair.

Not exactly a neat freak, Delorme thought. But then, neither was Delorme. The essential point was, there was nothing broken, nothing overturned, no sign of a struggle.

She moved slowly around the living room, hands in pockets to avoid touching anything. She paused over the coffee table; Mel Gibson stared up at her from the cover of a video: *Conspiracy Theory*. There were two remotes, one for the television and one for the VCR, on the couch. The TV screen was dark, but the power light was on.

There was a plate of cookies on the table, two cookies to be exact, next to an almost-full mug of tea.

In the kitchen, the sink was a rickety mountain of pots and pans. Delorme lifted the lid from a small brown teapot. The pot was half full. There was a bag of Pepperidge Farm cookies nearby, the first section of four cookies missing. Delorme herself had a similar ritual: video, glass of milk, plate of cookies—the perfect tranquilizer. Apparently, the doctor was in mid-snack when something or someone called her away. A patient? Relative? Boyfriend?

"Did you see any strangers in the building over the past few days?"

"Nope. Just the usual. Not that I keep tabs. Truth is, I'm the least nosy person I know—not to mention the fact that my unit's in the middle of the building. Doesn't look out on the front or the parking lot."

"Who were Dr. Cates's regular visitors?"

Mrs. Lefebvre sniffed and dabbed at her eyes. "Couldn't tell you. She's only been here a few months. Pays her rent on time, doesn't complain. That's all I care about. Don't get me wrong—I care about my tenants. But generally I only get to know the ones on my floor. You know, bump into them getting their mail and so on."

"Did you ever see her with anyone at all?"

"Her parents come to visit one time. And I seen her a couple of times with a woman with red hair."

"Short woman? Bright blue eyes?"

"Could be."

That would be Dr. Perry.

"Did you ever see her with any man?"

"I did, now that you mention it. Not a big guy. Real short hair and very polite. Held the door open for me. I remember 'cause I figured, Honey, you should marry this guy. She's so pretty I wondered why she didn't have a fella. 'Course, doctors are so busy. . . ."

Delorme went into the bedroom. There was a phone on the night-stand, and an answering machine flashing a bright red numeral four. Delorme pressed the play button with the tip of a ballpoint pen. The wheezy electronic voice of a computer chip announced the first message, ten-fifteen that morning. It was followed by the voice of Dr. Perry, asking Winter where she was and if she'd somehow forgotten about her O.R. schedule.

Second message, also Dr. Perry.

Third message, someone named Melissa—presumably Dr. Cates's assistant—wanting to know where she was, the waiting room was filling up. The fourth message was also Melissa.

Delorme hit the button for old messages. These were not date- or time-stamped. The voice of a young man came on: *Winter, it's me. I'm sorry for the way I was the other day, I was just so upset. I need to see you. I can't go for month after month the way you can. Weekends are the worst. Please call— God, I sound like I'm begging. I am begging. Please call me. I love you.*

Next message, same voice: *I know you're there, Winter. I know you're screening your calls. Why can't you just call me back? You know, sometimes I return twenty or thirty calls in a single afternoon—a lot of them from strangers—and I return all of them. You treat me worse than I would treat a stranger. I wouldn't treat anyone the way you treat me.*

Third message. A note of despair in the voice now. *I don't know what to say, Winter. I'm going crazy here. I'm just going out of my mind. I don't know what I'm going to do. I can't eat, I can't think, I can hardly breathe. That's what you do to me. I just—I don't know what to say. Please call. Use the cell number.*

Dr. Perry had mentioned the ex-boyfriend's name, Craig something. "Sounds like Craig Something's got it bad," Delorme muttered to herself. "Sounds like Craig Something's losing it."

But why would any woman keep such messages? Why not just erase them? Was she keeping them for evidence of some kind of harassment? Or of a stalker? Then again, sometimes you just didn't bother.

The bed was a tangled heap of duvet, pillows, and quilt. Delorme gingerly lifted them aside; there were no signs of sex.

She turned to the closet. Apparently the doctor was no clotheshorse. Half the items on hangers seemed to be jeans, and the shelves were full of sweaters. There was a pleasant scent of some light cologne and shoe leather.

She pulled a framed photograph from underneath the sweaters. It showed a young couple—a younger version of Dr. Cates in the arms of a young man. She was wearing a formal dress, but it was the man's outfit that made Delorme catch her breath: the high collar, the epaulettes, the tunic of red serge.

Delorme went into the living room and showed the picture to Mrs. Lefebvre. "Is this the man you saw with Dr. Cates?"

"Jeepers," Mrs. Lefebvre said, and paused to blow her nose. "That's him all right. But I woulda never known he was a Mountie."

11

THE HEALING ARTS BUILDING is a yellow brick box of the sort favored in the 1960s. It sits at the top of Algonquin Avenue just beyond the Highway 11 bypass. The biggest thing on the ground floor is the Shopper's Drug Mart, surrounded by a laundromat, a dry cleaner, and several other small stores. Above this, there are five floors of doctors, dentists, and chiropractors.

Delorme had often visited the place as a little girl. Her parents had taken her to a dentist whom she later recognized, when all her fillings had to be replaced, as incompetence personified.

The building directory listed Dr. W. Cates on the second floor.

A sign taped to the door said CLOSED DUE TO EMERGENCY. PLEASE CALL TO RESCHEDULE YOUR APPOINTMENT. Delorme knocked sharply and was admitted by a small woman with blond hair cut boyishly short and five earrings in each ear. This was Melissa Gale, Dr. Cates's assistant.

"Are you the detective I spoke to on the phone?" There was a quaver in the small voice.

"Yes, I'm Detective Delorme."

"Come in and let me shut the door. I can't face any more patients. I've been turning them away since lunchtime."

"What time did you expect Dr. Cates to show up?"

"Her first appointment was for eleven o'clock. By eleven-thirty I was starting to get worried. I mean, she's never late.

"I called her place a couple of times. I even called the hospital. When they said she hadn't shown up there, either, I began to panic. That's when I called you."

"Did you see her yesterday?"

"Yes, she was here all day. We finished up about seven o'clock."

"That was the last time you spoke with her?"

"Last night. Yes."

"How was she then? Did she seem worried or under any abnormal amount of stress?"

"Not at all. But, then, Winter is a very cheerful person. People can do stuff that makes me scream, and she's just totally unruffled. She seemed fine. This is so unlike her. I just don't know where she can be."

"Were there any calls out of the ordinary?"

Ms. Gale tipped her head to one side and thought for a moment. "Nothing."

"And what about this morning, when you opened up? Were there any messages that seemed . . ."

"There were half a dozen or so. You know, just people calling to make appointments, or find out about lab results, that kind of thing."

Delorme looked around. The waiting room was a small, plain space, somewhat enlivened by an old leather couch and some large, leafy plants. The empty chairs looked in order, the magazines were stacked neatly on the end tables. "When you opened up, did you notice anything unusual about the office? Anything out of place?"

"No, it's always the same. I closed up last night, and when I came in this morning everything was exactly as I left it."

Delorme nodded toward Ms. Gale's computer, where an insurance form flickered on the screen. "What about the computer? Any weird e-mail?"

"Nothing. Just the usual medicare stuff, ads from drug companies and insurance people. We get tons of junk mail."

"You mind if I look around?"

"No. Please—this way."

Adjoining the waiting room was a consulting room: large oak desk, glassed-in bookshelves, and an oriental rug. Delorme examined the desktop: telephone, scratch pad, yellow legal pad, pen and pencil set, Rolodex, no photographs. The neatness was quite a contrast to Dr. Cates's apartment.

"Her desk is always this neat?" Delorme pointed to the notepads. "Not even any notes out? Lists of things to do?"

"Winter's the kind of person who doesn't go home until everything's done. Also, she likes to start fresh in the morning—so, when we close up, this is pretty much how it looks."

The door to the adjoining treatment room was open.

"Now that I think of it," Ms. Gale said, "there was one thing unusual. In the examining room."

"Show me. Don't touch anything, though."

"Oh, God. This isn't a murder investigation, is it?"

"Just a precaution."

Ms. Gale led her into the treatment room, which looked the same as doctors' treatment rooms everywhere: bright fluorescent lights, jars of cotton swabs and tongue depressors, a nutrition poster on one wall, an anatomy chart on another, and a little brass clock labeled PROZAC.

Ms. Gale pointed at the examining table. "You see the paper covering on that? After each patient, Winter rolls down the paper and tears it off and stuffs it in the trash. That way, each new patient gets a fresh, clean surface."

"That's how it looks now," Delorme said.

"It wasn't like that when I came in this morning. It was crumpled, and actually quite torn. So I rolled it down and tore it off and put it in the trash."

"This trash?" Delorme indicated a tall, open garbage can under the counter.

"Uh-huh. That's it there."

"And there was nothing else out of place?" Delorme gestured at the jars of cotton swabs and tongue depressors.

"Well, just tiny things. There was a bandage roll on the counter that would normally be in a cupboard, and a jar of disinfectant."

"And they weren't out when you closed up last night?"

Ms. Gale winced a little. "I'm not a hundred percent sure. Mondays tend to run pretty long, and sometimes I just want to get out of here as fast as possible. Sorry."

Delorme went over to a small chrome wastebasket and depressed the pedal with her foot. "When does this get emptied?"

"Every evening. Sometimes during the day, as well."

"And the stuff that's in here now?"

"There shouldn't be anything in there now." Ms. Gale stepped closer and squinted at the canister. It contained a bandage wrapper. "That wasn't in there last night, I'm sure of it."

"How sure? Do you remember emptying this last night?"

"Yes, I do. I was carrying it out the door when Winter said goodnight."

"What if a patient had some kind of emergency later at night? Around midnight, say. What would happen then?"

"If they contacted Winter, you mean? She would just tell them to go to emerg. A doctor's office isn't set up for emergencies."

"Suppose someone calls her and says they've run out of their medication. Something like that."

"Well, they wouldn't call her at home, because her number's unlisted. And if they called here, they'd get a message telling them to go to emerg."

"All right," Delorme said. "Let's just step back to the waiting room. We don't want to disturb things too much."

"So you do think something happened to her."

"It might turn out to be nothing. But I'm going to ask our crime-scene people to come in here and take a look. Is there another office you can wait in until they get here?"

"Sure, I can sit in Dr. Bisson's office, next door."

Delorme led her out into the hallway and watched her lock up.

"Were any of her patients upset with Dr. Cates, do you know?"

"Oh, there's always patients upset. People have no idea how many wackos there are out there. Winter says they're just lonely and the moment they have someone's attention they can't bear to let it go, even if it means acting like a jerk. You know, like they'll take twice as much medication as they're supposed to, then get angry when the doctor doesn't want to refill the prescription every five days or whatever. Or they want the doctor to sign a form saying they can't work—you know, to cheat on workman's comp? I mean, I saw one guy go bananas about that. He was screaming and yelling and pounding the desk, and he even kicked over a plant. I thought we were going to have to call the police."

"What was his name?"

"Glenn Freemont." Melissa's hand went to her mouth. "Oh, I'm gonna get in trouble for telling you. This stuff's confidential."

"When did this happen?"

"A couple of weeks ago. I can look it up for you."

"Was there anyone else who was a problem for the doctor? Friend? Relative?"

"Well, she does have an old boyfriend. Craig Simmons. He's not violent or anything, far as I know. But he calls here all the time. Mostly I have to tell him she's with a patient and she'll call him back. But she doesn't always have time to get back to him, and then he gets pretty hyper. Sometimes he even shows up here. He did that yesterday, in fact. Winter was pretty steamed. I could hear them yelling at each other."

Delorme showed her the picture of Dr. Cates and the young Mountie. "Is this the guy?"

"That's him. I would've never known he was a Mountie, though. He's more like an actor or something."

"Why do you say that?"

"I don't know. He's smallish, and kinda muscley the way actors are these days. And so high-strung."

Delorme left Ms. Gale in the doctor's office next door with instructions to wait there for the ident team. She called Arsenault and Collingwood on her cell phone, then went down to her car to put in two more calls. The first was to Dr. Cates's parents. Delorme insisted the call was just routine, no evidence of foul play. She kept it brisk and to the point: Who would Dr. Cates be likely to visit suddenly, out of the blue (no one); did she have any friends or associates who worried them (yes, Craig Simmons). She tried to reassure them, but Mr. and Mrs. Cates knew that a detective would not be calling them unless there were grounds for concern, and by the time she hung up, both parents were distraught.

Her next call was to Malcolm Musgrave.

"Craig Simmons," he informed her, "is one of the best damn cops I have ever known, and I have been in this business for longer than you care to know."

"I'm sure he is. But I have a missing doctor here—a doctor who is his former girlfriend—and I have reason to believe he was upset with her."

Musgrave's tone changed. "That wouldn't be Winter Cates, would it?"

"Yes, it would. Why? Were you already worried about her?"

"Naw. But Simmons has been talking about her for as long as I can remember. When he first joined our detachment I figured they were going to get married. Didn't take long to figure out that was all in his head. You see them together, it's obvious she sees him as a friend, or maybe as a brother."

"And he sees her . . . ?

"Not as friend and not as a sister."

"Are you going to give me his address, then?"

"Yeah, I'll give you his address. He's not at home right now, though, he's out at the family cottage in Mattawa. You won't believe this place. Looks like a dollhouse. But the fishing is great."

"Why's he at the cottage in the middle of winter?"

"Because that's when cottages get broken into. You got a pen?"

Musgrave gave her detailed directions. "But listen," he said. "You're barking up the wrong tree with Simmons. Go to Mattawa if it's going to satisfy your curiosity. Interview him all you want. But the sooner you clear him off your list, the better."

THE OLD TOWN OF MATTAWA is about forty miles east of Algonquin Bay, at the junction of the Mattawa and Ottawa Rivers. That location made it a prime canoe route in the days of Samuel de Champlain and it still is—the July canoe race is a popular event, and as for fishing, the bass practically jump out of the water and beg to be taken home. It's a small community, mostly devoted to serving the thousands of tourists who head there in summer to enjoy the rivers, the high hills, and the tiny log cabins tucked among the streams and forests. Prime cottage country.

Delorme was not all that sensitive to scenery, but she had to admit the surroundings had a certain atmospheric power. The green hills loomed through the rain, and the smell of pine was thick in the car. Scarves of mist trailed from the spruce and jack pine close to the road, and the highway gleamed like a ribbon of black silk.

On the way, she listened to the news. The new mayor was talking up the winter Carnival even though it was still a month away and the warm spell had dissolved all the snow; Geoff Mantis was denouncing a Liberal proposal to raise the capital gains tax; and there was a profile of the new leader of the Parti Quebecois, along with a not-too-subtle analysis of "the Quebec problem." For as long as Delorme could remember, Quebec had been the central issue in her country, and the papers and the pundits never tired of discussing this weather pattern that refused to lift, the delicate storm of French-English relations.

"You don't actually go into the town," Musgrave had told her. "You want to make a right on LaFramboise. Just past the Chevy dealership."

"If I could see the Chevy dealership," Delorme said to herself now. It appeared half a mile later, on the right.

Delorme made the turn and passed a lumberyard, a siding warehouse, and a dog kennel—prosaic, ugly places, made even drearier by the rain. A Jiffy Lube came up on the left, and then beyond it a battered sign for Sandy Point with an arrow. Delorme squinted into the rain, trying to catch glimpses of the cottages among the pines.

A few minutes later she came to what looked like the end of the road and pulled to a stop. A few yards on she saw a mailbox marked SIMMONS. She inched the car down the driveway. There was a Jeep Wrangler at the bottom of the slope; Delorme made a note of the license number. The Jeep was parked beside a cottage that looked like something out of "Hansel and Gretel," a miniaturized Victorian gingerbread composed predominantly of mauve vinyl siding. A steeply pitched roof gleamed with the damp, and the upper half of each window was stained glass. The chimney emitted picturesque curlicues of fragrant smoke.

Delorme stepped up onto a lilac verandah of scrolled woodwork. Musgrave had called the Simmons cottage a dollhouse, and he was dead-on. There was a cast-iron boot-scraper at the top of the steps, and on the front door a brass lion's-head knocker. The door opened, and a young man in T-shirt and jeans looked her over. Muscley, as Ms. Gale had said, a man who spent a lot of time in the gym.

"Can I help you?"

His hair was longer than in the photo at Dr. Cates's house; it hung in a wheat-colored fringe over his brow. And he looked much smaller out of the Mountie uniform. But despite the casual dress, he was neat, contained: the jeans and the T-shirt were pressed.

"Craig Simmons?" Delorme held up her shield. "I'm Detective Lise Delorme, Algonquin Bay police."

"You're a little far out of your jurisdiction, aren't you?"

"Mind if I come in for a minute? It's kind of damp out here."

Simmons held the door open.

Northern Ontario has two schools of cottage owners. The first uses the cottage as a sort of attic and fills it with cast-offs—spavined sofas, cat-shredded armchairs, VCRs past their prime—any item no longer wanted at home. The second school sees the cottage as an alternate house and does everything to make it handsome, comfortable, and inviting, sometimes spending more money than on the residence.

To these two schools Delorme now added a third: dwellers in the realm of fantasy. The Simmons place was dedicated to the preservation of a Victorian era that never was. It called out from the brass candlesticks, the etched-glass cupboards, the lace curtains. It winked and shone from the beaded lampshades, the silver sugar bowl, and the grandfather clock that was off by a good half-hour. Above a massive oak dining table, a foxed photograph of Queen Victoria brooded in a beveled frame.

"My mother's place," Simmons said, gesturing at the frippery. "And someday, I swear, it's all going to change. Have a seat." He indicated a set of dining chairs, each one elaborately flounced.

Delorme chose not to waste time cozying up. "Corporal Simmons. I know you're with the Sudbury RCMP detachment. What are you doing down here in Mattawa this time of year?"

"I got a call from the OPP there was a break-in. They had a whole series of them out here."

"But the place looks in great shape."

"They broke into the boathouse. Took a pair of twin ninety-five Merc outboards."

"And where were you last night?"

"Last night? I was here the whole time. Why?"

"The whole time? What were you doing?"

"I was painting the bedroom. I thought, since I was out here, I may as well take care of it. That took most of the time. Then I watched the hockey game. Is this in reference to an investigation?"

"Who won?" Delorme asked.

As a Mountie, the corporal was no doubt more used to asking questions than answering them. He seemed thrown by the question, opening his mouth for a moment, then closing it, then looking away.

"The game," Delorme added. "You said you watched the hockey game."

"Detroit won. Five-four."

True, Delorme knew, but it was the sort of alibi guilty people cooked up all the time. "You sure you weren't visiting Winter Cates?"

"Visiting Winter? No, I wasn't, as a matter of fact. I saw her earlier in the day."

"Yes, I know. And you had words with her."

"I had a conversation with her. Look, Detective, this is my private life you're prying into. How do you even know about me and Winter? What's this all about?"

"At least one witness says your voices were raised. Angry. Are you saying that's not the case?"

"Winter was annoyed that I showed up at her office."

"But you had to, didn't you. She didn't give you any choice. She wasn't answering your calls."

Simmons's face changed, his features shifting from budding anger to fear. "Has something happened to Winter? Has she been hurt?"

"You tell me, Mr. Simmons."

"I don't know what you're talking about. Just tell me, is Winter all right?"

"Winter Cates hasn't been seen since last night. Not by the hospital, not by her patients, not by her parents."

"She is a doctor, you know. Probably she got called away on some emergency."

"What type of emergency would that be? Her car is still at home."

Simmons seemed to flinch, registering this fact.

"'You make me feel like I'm begging,'" Delorme quoted from memory. "'You treat me worse than I would treat a stranger. Worse than I would treat a dog.' Pretty strong words, no?"

Simmons's face was turning scarlet; Delorme had a feeling it wasn't from embarrassment.

"You're implying that I would hurt Winter?"

"Where is she, Corporal Simmons? I'm thinking maybe you showed up unannounced again. It seems to be a habit of yours. She wasn't answering your phone calls, she tossed you out of her office, and you were going to make her listen. It's over for her, and you just can't accept it."

"Who do you think you are?" Simmons said. "You don't know anything about me."

"Where is she, Mr. Simmons?"

Simmons was a small man; he must have only just made the RCMP height restrictions, but he gripped the edge of the oak table and with a sudden motion flipped it over, flipped it so hard that it landed not on its side but completely upside down, lion's-paw feet clawing the air.

"Take it easy," Delorme said, more rattled than she let on. "Just answer the question."

"Who do you think you are?" Simmons said again. "Some little frog

bitch fresh off the farm. That's how you got your job right? The old bilingual free pass? Tell me something: How'd you do in hand-to-hand down
at Aylmer?"

"We're not talking about me, Mr. Simmons. It's your girlfriend who's
missing. Former girlfriend. And you don't have an alibi."

The truth was, Delorme had had to repeat the hand-to-hand training,
and even then she'd only squeaked by. Since then, she had spent a lot of
hours with a personal trainer, but she was not in a rush to take on an en-
raged Mountie. She wondered whether to pull her gun. Is this guy faking
it? Or is he really going berserk?

"Corporal Simmons," she said, "a simple yes or no will do. Do you
know where Winter Cates is right now?"

Simmons took a step closer.

"Just answer the question. You can leave out the macho theatrics."

"Maybe I'm an emotional person," Simmons said. His voice had gone
very quiet. "A passionate person."

"Maybe a violent person," Delorme said. "Maybe homicidal."

Simmons glared at her for a moment, then shook his head. "You don't
know anything about me," he said. "And frankly I'm pretty disgusted that
you don't give a fellow officer the benefit of the doubt."

He went over to the door and held it open. "I don't have any idea
where Winter might be. You may not like that answer, Detective, but it's
the truth. If she's really missing, then I'm far more worried about her than
you'll ever be. And if you have any more questions, you're going to have
to wait until I get a lawyer."

"Corporal, we have your messages on Winter's phone machine, we
have a one-sided love affair, we have your explosive temperament, and we
have your uncorroborated alibi. If Dr. Cates doesn't show up very soon,
for sure you may need a lawyer."

Simmons held the door wider.

Delorme nodded at the overturned table. "Might be a good time to re-
decorate, too," she said.

Ms. Gale was right, she thought, back in the car: The guy's an actor.
Oh, I'm so tough. So passionate. Give me a break.

As she drove back toward the highway—the dim green forest passing by, rain blurring the hills—she began to have second thoughts. What if Simmons were a genuine berserker? Would it matter either way? If he was faking, it looked like he was covering up a guilty conscience. If he was not faking, then it made him look capable of—well, she hoped it wouldn't turn out to be murder.

12

DELORME TOLD CARDINAL about her missing doctor the next morning. They were in the squad room, sipping coffee from Tim Hortons cups.

"She can't have been gone long," Cardinal said. "I just saw her on Monday."

"You know Winter Cates?" Delorme said. "I wish you'd told me that yesterday."

"You didn't ask," Cardinal said. "I hope she's all right."

"It's not looking good, unfortunately. She's been gone nearly thirty-six hours, but her car's still at home."

Cardinal recalled the young woman's brisk manner, the way she had handled his father, stern but friendly. He remembered the dark eyes, the barely controlled hair. "I only met her for the first time on Monday," he said, "when she was treating my dad. But there was a guy in her office—young, muscley guy with blond hair who seemed to be having an argument with her."

"Craig Simmons. I've already talked to him. He's an ex-boyfriend, not to mention a Mountie."

Cardinal snapped his fingers. "That's where I've seen him before. Doesn't he work for Musgrave? What's his story?"

"Let's just say, if Cates doesn't show up, I'll be talking to Corporal Simmons again soon. This guy's all attitude and no alibi."

Delorme wandered over to Chouinard's office and rapped on the door.

Cardinal's phone rang. He picked it up, and the voice on the other end eradicated all thoughts of the missing doctor.

Few men can say exactly what is the worst thing they have ever done, but Cardinal knew to the hour. It had been thirteen years previously, his last year on the Toronto narcotics squad.

The squad had raided the house of one of Ontario's top three drug dealers, a violent pig named Rick Bouchard. While Cardinal's fellow officers had been dealing with Bouchard and his henchmen—including a malevolent troll named Kiki B.—Cardinal had found a gym bag full of cash in a bedroom closet. To his everlasting shame he had walked off with nearly two hundred grand. The other five hundred thousand was used as evidence, and it, along with the drugs, had been enough to convict everyone they hauled in.

Kiki B. was on the line now.

"I hope you got Rick's card. I wouldn't want you to think we'd forgotten about you."

"Kiki, I'm only going to say this once: if you—or anybody connected with you—ever shows up at my home, I will make you pay for the rest of your life. Do you understand that?"

"Twelve years, Cardinal. Do you understand *that*? Bouchard's been in Kingston Pen for twelve years. He's got another six months to go and then he's out, and he wants his money now. He sees it as his nest egg that you've been holding for him."

"Tell him not to expect interest. The market's been bad lately."

"He wants his two hundred grand, Cardinal. He knows you took it and he's going to get it back or you may as well start making out your will."

"I don't have his money, Kiki. This may be hard for you to imagine, but it's the truth." Cardinal wished he felt as calm as he managed to sound.

"Uh-huh. What'd you do—give it to charity?"

"Actually, did you ever hear of Sunrise?"

"The Sunrise Foundation? You gave it to a drug rehab outfit? Oh, man. Rick's gonna really appreciate the humor in that one, Cardinal. He's gonna laugh really hard."

It was true that was where the last of the money had gone, but before that Cardinal had used it to cover Catherine's hospital bills in the States, where her parents had insisted she get treatment, and Kelly's tuition at Yale. He had revealed the whole story to his wife and daughter the previous year, when he could no longer live with his conscience. With her tuition pulled out from under her, Kelly had been forced to leave Yale before her final semester, and Cardinal was certain she had not forgiven him. He had even attempted to resign from the force, but Delorme had intercepted his resignation letter on its way to the chief. "You're a good cop," she had said to him. "Why damage the department by quitting?" Cardinal had been in the hospital with two bullet wounds at the time and hadn't had the strength to resist.

"Kiki, why don't you find yourself a new employer?" he said now. "Put a resumé together. You're not getting any younger."

"This is your last warning, Cardinal. You think Bouchard's gonna come out of prison broke? He won't stand for it."

"Oh, he won't stand for it. Well, in that case . . ."

"Okay, I've tried to help you here. You choose not to be a good listener, that's your problem. And don't think Bouchard can't have you dealt with from prison, he can. Next time it won't be a card or a phone call."

Cardinal hung up. He held his hand out above his desk and watched it tremble. Shame welled up inside him, that something he had done—even though it had been so long ago—could jeopardize his home. For the thousandth time, he cursed his own stupidity.

His intercom buzzed, Duty Sergeant Mary Flower telling him that Calvin Squier had arrived. Cardinal went out to the desk area.

"Great to see you again, John," Squier said, putting out a hand to shake. "How you doing?" Only Americans shake hands that much, Cardinal thought. Americans and con men and Calvin Squier of the Canadian Security Intelligence Service.

"You're back from New York already? You just left yesterday."

"Couldn't wait to get back. New York's not a town I want to spend a lot of time in."

Cardinal brought him back into the CID area. The squad room was a considerable improvement over the previous headquarters with its dented file cabinets and its smells of smoke and sweat and other less palatable odors. But Cardinal was sure that Squier, with his boy-scout smile and his too many teeth, worked in the finest office a federal budget—and a hidden budget at that—could buy.

"Hey, nice space you have here," Squier said. He made a sweeping gesture at the desks and dividers, the wall of windows, the sheets of plastic sagging overhead. Delorme was just coming in from somewhere. She glanced at them a moment, then went over to her own desk. Squier's head turned.

Cardinal pulled a chair out from McLeod's cubicle—McLeod was still on vacation in Florida or some other warm place.

"Have a seat."

"New York, I'm telling you," Squier said. "Too big, too dirty, and just too darn American. I fully understand they had that awful nine-eleven thing, but I wasn't even near that area. There's no trees in that city. Nothing green. No air. Mind you, it's kind of impressive to look at. It's Toronto times a hundred. You ever been?"

Cardinal shook his head. "You spoke to Matlock's next of kin?"

Squier nodded. "Spoke to the wife. She was pretty broken up, of course."

"What did you find out?"

"According to her, Howard Matlock didn't have a single enemy in the world."

"That's what she told you?"

"Oh, not just the wife. I spoke to neighbors, local church, couple of clients—he was a chartered accountant, remember. Clients had nothing but good things to say about him: thorough, saves you money, but honest. That's not what I get from the FBI, however."

"Really? What did the feds have to say?"

"They're keeping very close tabs on a homegrown antigovernment outfit called WARR—short for Waco and Ruby Ridge, two places where the

Feds killed American citizens. Anyway, WARR is a bunch of angry white men whose first priority, it seems, is what they call 'blinding the enemy.' They want to hamper America's ability to surveil its own people. So they've been sending pipe bombs to the NSA, that kind of thing."

"Which would explain an interest in the CADS base, but not who killed him."

"The bureau had connected Matlock to an explosive device that got sent to their Washington headquarters. Luckily it didn't explode. Anyway, Matlock was working out a deal to turn state's evidence, and apparently his fellow members of WARR got wind of it."

"Solid motive for murder, in other words."

A high-speed drill started up overhead, and they had to shout at each other to be heard.

"Very solid."

"And what about the wife? She a member of this nut group?"

"Nope. That was strictly Matlock's personal hobby, far as we can tell."

"How'd they get along?"

"About average, I'd say. His own folks're dead, but I talked to his in-laws. In-laws say they had their ups and downs like anybody, but no knock-down, drag-out fights. Neighbors never heard them screaming at each other or anything like that. Why? You think the wife wanted him done for?"

The drilling stopped, and the sudden quiet seemed exaggerated.

"I only know what you tell me."

"Well, I can tell you there was no huge insurance policy on him, if that's what you're thinking. I checked that out first thing. Besides, I think this WARR angle looks a lot more promising, don't you?"

"Maybe. But tell me this, Squier: Why would they kill him in Canada?"

"Because it would be that much harder to make the connection to them. And, please. Call me Calvin."

"But I like Squier. It has a knights-in-armor ring to it."

Squier regarded him thoughtfully. Then he leaned forward in his chair and spoke confidentially. "You're not still upset about the other night, are you? I must be nearly twenty years younger than you and I had the advantage of surprise, big time."

"Squier, did anyone ever tell you you talk too much?"

Squier nodded. "People have told me that," he said. "I have to be honest. Not a good thing in my game, either."

"No, indeed," Cardinal said solemnly. "Loose lips sink ships."

Squier looked around at the squad room, his gaze settling a little longer than necessary on Delorme. "So, did you and Corporal Musgrave make any headway?"

Cardinal told him the tale of Bressard and the bears. Squier took notes on a palmtop device with a tiny metal pencil.

"And he says he was paid to get rid of the body by who?"

"A gangster named Leon Petrucci."

Squier noted the name on his palmtop. "Why would a local mafia guy have any interest in an American terrorist? I don't understand."

"Neither do I. You asked where we'd got to; that's where we are."

"I suppose they could have just contracted it out."

"Petrucci's not Al Capone. I'd be surprised if anyone in the States had ever heard of him."

"In any case, there may not be much more for you to do. All the answers are going to come from the American end and this WARR angle. Don't worry, I'll keep you fully informed." Squier fitted his palmtop into a smart leather case and put it in his pocket. "Let me know if there's anything else I can do. I've already spoken to the Forensic Center about arrangements to ship the remains back to the U.S. In the meantime, you can find me at the Hilltop."

"Well, you've certainly been busy. If I can ever return the favor, I hope you'll let me know."

"Oh, you can count on that, John." Squier reinforced his all-Canadian grin with a thumbs-up. "You can take that to the bank."

As Cardinal was showing him out, Squier said, "Was that Lise Delorme? That woman a couple of desks over?"

"Detective Delorme. She'll break your arm for you, Squier."

"Why would she do that? She's not wearing a wedding ring."

"She's a very serious person."

"Well, so am I John. So am I."

When he was gone, Cardinal went straight back to his desk and dialed New York information. They gave him the phone number for Howard Matlock at 312 East 91st Street.

Cardinal began to think what he would say to the bereaved wife, if she was at home.

"Hello?" It was a man who answered.

"Hello, is this the residence of Howard Matlock?"

"Yes."

A relative, Cardinal thought. An in-law come to comfort the wife.

But then the voice said, "I'm Howard Matlock."

DETECTIVE SERGEANT DANIEL CHOUINARD was looking for something under a stack of yet-to-be-installed shelves and banged his head when Cardinal announced that he wanted to go to New York.

"There's no reason to go to New York. CSIS is going to New York."

"CSIS has already come back. Calvin Squier just laid out a very plausible scenario for Matlock's murder. According to Squier, Howard Matlock was caught spying on the CADS base, right?"

"Right. So?"

"I just called the CADS base. Their head of security has never heard of Howard Matlock. He has no record of any such incident."

"Well, maybe CSIS told him to deep-six the records of it for some reason."

"Calvin Squier also neglected to mention one little detail." He told Chouinard about his call to New York.

"You're telling me Howard Matlock is alive?"

"Howard Matlock is alive, and Howard Matlock has never heard of Algonquin Bay."

"Meaning we have no idea who the dead man is."

"Not a clue."

Chouinard retrieved a Sony Walkman from under the shelves and dropped it into his briefcase.

"Well, you have to go to New York. No question. We won't have any trouble selling R. J. on this one."

13

CARDINAL CAUGHT A FLIGHT out of Algon-
quin Bay that morning. He had an hour wait between planes in Toronto,
and landed in New York City a couple of hours later. He had never been to
New York, and on the cab ride into town from La Guardia, he dimly registered the immensity of the city, the brutal grandeur of its skyline, not to
mention the alarming habits of its drivers. But he kept his mind fixed on
what he had to do, resolving to take no more notice of New York than was
strictly necessary.

Howard Matlock—the real Howard Matlock—had never heard of
Loon Lodge. For that matter, as Cardinal had noted the day before,
Howard Matlock had never heard of Algonquin Bay. In fact, Howard
Matlock had not so much as set foot in Canadian territory since 1996
when he had spent a weekend in Quebec City (so charming! so European!
so cheap for Americans!) and Howard Matlock had no interest whatever
in ice fishing. The only thing Cardinal had had right about Howard Matlock was his name, address, and occupation.

Matlock lived on the second floor of a small apartment building in
Manhattan's Upper East Side. "Far too upper to be classy," he informed
Cardinal at the door, "but until I make my first million, it will have to do."

Matlock was a slim man in his mid-fifties with hair very close-cropped
to hide its scarcity. His first million did not appear imminent. The apartment was a two-room affair sparsely furnished with chrome and glass. It
looked more like an office than a home.

"Obviously, your peculiar quest calls for a coffee," Matlock said. "Will
you have some?"

Cardinal said yes. Then, as Matlock busied himself at a tiny kitchenette, he put in a call to Malcolm Musgrave. He had filled the sergeant in on Squier's bogus investigation the night before.

Musgrave had responded with characteristic eloquence: "That little shit. Let's nail him to the floor."

Cardinal had asked Musgrave to make use of his contacts with the Mountie dinosaurs at CSIS and find out "Matlock's" real name and address. Obviously, CSIS was hiding this information for reasons known only to them.

"I got a guy working on it since last night," Musgrave told him now. "Give me another hour or so."

As Cardinal hung up, Matlock presented him with a steaming cup of coffee and a small plate of cookies, a napkin tucked neatly under a spoon.

"I don't suppose you're a Mountie by any chance?"

"No. I'm with the city police in Algonquin Bay."

"I have a friend who would just die with envy if I could tell him I'd met a Mountie. Try one of those, I made them myself."

The cookie was oatmeal raisin. "You make a mean cookie. There may be a chain store in these."

"You know, I've actually considered it. Except I hate chain stores."

"Listen, Howard. Can you check your wallet and see if you're missing any credit cards or ID?"

"I checked while you were on the phone. Nothing's missing. I might not notice the license—I mean, nobody drives in Manhattan. But my credit cards? Oh, no, no, no. My credit cards and I have a very close relationship."

So either the dead man had ordered up new ID using Matlock's basic information or he had access to fakes. Very good fakes.

"The man who used your identity picked you because you're roughly his age. Can you think of anyone who might have had access to your personal information within the past year?"

"Well, anyone who has me do their taxes has my Social Security number at the bottom of their tax return. But I have a lot of clients."

"You have their birth dates, right? Can you check your records for males who are within three years of your age?"

"Sit tight, and I'll take a peek at my database. Help yourself to more cookies."

A few minutes later, Howard Matlock was standing in the doorway with a computer printout in one hand, a cookie in the other. "I have three male clients in their late fifties—names, addresses, and phone numbers— but I really shouldn't give them to you; it would be very unseemly."

"I have no jurisdiction in New York; I can't force you to give them to me. And in any case, it's very unlikely he would give you his real name and address. Are any of the three well-known to you—clients of long standing?"

"Two of them, yes. One's a documentary filmmaker, the other is a lo- cation scout—my practice is mostly people in the performing arts. Both of these fellows have been coming to me for over ten years."

"And the third?"

"Well, that depends," Matlock said with a smile. "Do you have any plans for dinner?"

Cardinal didn't know what to say. He felt a blush creeping up the line of his jaw.

"Honestly, you Canadians. Here you are, you don't know a soul in town, and I offer you a chance to have dinner at a lovely restaurant with a charming professional like myself. Good Lord, man, I'm fifty-eight, I'm completely harmless."

"It's very kind of you," Cardinal managed. "But I'm on an extremely tight schedule just now."

"Oh, well. It was worth a shot."

"Are you going to give me that third name?"

"Just a pathetic ploy, I'm afraid. There were only two."

CARDINAL STOPPED IN AT a Starbucks by the 86th Street subway and called Musgrave on the cell phone.

"I got an old friend at CSIS Ottawa," Musgrave told him. "Must be sixty-five or close to. Been in the security game forever. Frog, name of Tourelle. If it wasn't for the MacDonald commission, he'd have made inspector years ago. Instead he's flying a cubbyhole in the mother of all bureaucracies.

"Anyway," Musgrave went on. "Uncle Tourelle has a nice little tale to tell. CSIS, as you may or may not know, keeps a close eye on the major airports. They have a full-time office at Pearson, same as Customs and Immigration."

"What, a couple of guys?"

"Try six. Tourelle doesn't know if they were tipped off or not. Probably were. Would have to be a hell of a coincidence otherwise. Anyway, they're taking a gander at the happy passengers disembarking from this New York flight.

"They have Immigration hold this so-called Matlock up for a minute. He's protesting the whole time, he's gotta catch a connector flight, the whole deal. To make a long story short they basically ignore the driver's license they're looking at, but they don't ignore the prints on it."

"CSIS has their own records?"

"Criminal records they get through us or locals, same as you. But they have their own files—they're not records because they're usually about suspicions, not actual crimes. We're talking security here, we're talking paranoia, we're talking deep murk, all right?"

"And they got a match."

"Oh, boy, did they get a match. Name: Miles Shackley. Current occupation: Unknown. Former occupation, get this: CIA operative in Quebec."

"Where in Quebec? When? How long ago was this?"

"Tourelle says thirty years ago. Well, nineteen seventy, actually. Montreal."

"Thirty-two years ago. So his former occupation probably has nothing to do with his murder in Algonquin Bay, right?"

"Probably not."

"When did he leave the CIA?"

"Nineteen seventy-one, according to his jacket."

Cardinal had a sudden sensation of defeat. "This has all the earmarks of a dead end."

"I agree. Thirty years is a long time. You're due for a change of luck on this one."

"So, why did Squier lie about who he was? Why did CSIS want to keep Shackley's identity a big secret?"

"Because Calvin Squier is a pretentious little twerp with a laptop. Because he works for the most useless agency on the planet. I don't know. All Tourelle told me was what he pulled off the header. He didn't have access to the actual file. It tells you affiliation, location, last known date of activity, and what Tourelle called a temperature level. Miles Shackley was coded Red. That's why they watched the guy's every move. Why Shackley is Code Red, Tourelle doesn't know, nor does he have the clearance to find out. He's working on that, though. Believe me, he'd love to bust one of these Palmtop Pinheads."

"So you think CSIS killed our guy?"

"CSIS is in the incompetence business, not the murder business. Even if they did want someone killed, they aren't going to put an agent like Squier onto it, an actual employee. They'd want at least three levels of removal. No, I think they tracked Shackley up here, and being who they are, he got killed under their noses by someone else and fed to the bears."

"Then why wouldn't CSIS make use of people like us who are investigating his murder? Why would they actively mislead us?"

"That's a very good question, and I suggest we put it to Laptop Larry at your earliest convenience."

"What about a record on Shackley? Criminal or otherwise."

"Cardinal, what do you think I do for a living? I've got calls in to my U.S. contacts. I'll let you know as soon as I hear back."

"Thanks."

"Also, while you're broadening your cultural horizons in the capital of global degeneration, I've managed to procure a useful piece of information."

"Shackley's real address?"

"Bingo. New York City—514 East 6th Street."

Cardinal scribbled it down. "That's great. I already spoke to the NYPD. They don't seem to care what I do."

"Gotta be careful how you deal with those guys. They can be touchy about turf."

"Naturally, I was completely charming."

"Cardinal, I've worked with you. You're not charming."

HECTOR ROBLES, the superintendent of 514, was a pleasant, fortyish Hispanic man who seemed to know remarkably little about Mr. Shackley. He spoke to Cardinal as they walked up a dizzying stairwell, pausing every so often to emphasize a point with a jab of the finger, a chop of the hand.

"He never complain, you know, not like some guys. I mean, he complain all the time—about the neighborhood, the punks, the noise, the housing project. He complain about the city but he never complain about the building, you know. He was not a problem for me, so I didn't pay him a lotta attention. Other people, man, I'm telling you. Every five minutes they got a problem—the tap, the toilet, the plaster—like I'm their personal servant or something."

"How'd he get along with his neighbors? Anybody ever complain about him?"

"Not complain exactly. But he had a couple of fights—not with neighbors, with delivery people. You know, every time they make a delivery they push menus under every door in the building. Nobody likes it, but Shackley, he gets really crazy out of his mind about it. He have a sign on his door says No Menu, but a lotta the delivery guys don't speak any English. And the restaurants they work for make them do it. Anyway, twice he comes charging out of his apartment, really pissed off—red in the face, face all crazy—yelling at these little Chinese guys. Shoving them hard, you know. I told him I didn't go for that. I don't like violence in my building."

"What'd he say to that?"

"He told me to mind my own business. I was very angry. But next day he come and apologize. He say he just gets so sick of the menus on the floor and littering up the streets. They are a problem, everybody knows that, but, still, he overreact.

"Second time it happen, I didn't see it. One of the other tenants told me he chased a guy right outside and then started punching him and choking him, until the tenant pull him off. If I had seen that I would have call the police. Anyway, what happen to Mr. Shackley?"

"He got eaten by bears."

"You kidding me. In New York?"

"In Canada. Don't worry, you're safe."

"Bears. *Madre*, I thought cockroaches were bad."

"How long did Shackley live here?"

"He was here when I took the job, and I been here twelve years."

They had reached the third floor. Cardinal followed Robles to the end of the hall. The super was pulling keys out of his pocket as he walked, and peering at them nearsightedly. The door to 3B had a two-foot-square hand-lettered sign on it that said NO MENUS. Robles found the right key and opened the door. "You need anything else, you know where to find me."

Cardinal pushed open the door and stood just inside. The air smelled of dirty carpet. All places abandoned by the recently dead have a sad, de-spairing feel to them. Cardinal had been in many, and none of them made you feel good. But Shackley's one-room apartment was one of the most depressing places he'd ever seen.

He examined the cheap, painted pine desk on which stood a phone, a cracked mug full of pens and pencils, and a calendar with the previous Thursday circled, the day he had flown to Toronto. The desk, indeed the entire room, was neat but dirty; grit crunched underfoot. There was a clean patch by the desk lamp about the size of a laptop. Either Shackley had taken it with him and it was now missing or Squier had got here first.

Cardinal opened the middle drawer of the desk: more pens and pen-cils, bits and pieces of office supplies. He pulled out a side drawer, finding nothing but cheap envelopes and a roll of stamps, a half-empty pad of paper. He held the pad up to the light, but there were no traces of writing on the top sheet. The wastebasket under the desk was empty. He lifted the desk lamp, lifted the phone, lifted the mug full of pens. Nothing. A search of the underside of the desk and its drawer also yielded nothing.

A quick search of the bathroom also yielded nothing, as did the cupboard in the kitchenette. Shackley appeared to live primarily on cereal. The cupboard contained four different boxes, the corners nibbled and frayed by mice.

Cardinal had rarely come across a life so colorless. Of course, it could have been intentional—the kind of deep cover one reads about in spy novels—but he didn't really think so; the despair was too convincing. He stood still and listened. Footsteps from an upstairs neighbor, high heels it sounded like. Down the hall, Van Morrison was singing hysterically. Farther off a small dog yapped.

Cardinal went to the file cabinet. Two drawers, mostly empty. There were a few hanging files—taxes (not done by Howard Matlock, he noted), social security forms, banking. Shackley's only income seemed to be from Social Security—a few hundred dollars a month. Bills: cable TV, electricity, telephone. Cardinal pulled out the last three months' phone bills. There were calls to three different numbers in the Montreal area code. Shackley's old stomping ground. Cardinal put the phone bills in his briefcase.

He spent the next hour going through every book, note, and piece of mail he could find. Nothing. He opened the back of the television, the back of a radio, and even checked the freezer. Then he stood in the middle of the room and tried to spot the one thing that didn't belong. It took a while, but eventually his gaze fell on the grille of the ventilator shaft. It was a small rectangle just above the stove and, unlike everything else in the place, it was spotlessly clean. Old building like this, Cardinal thought, you'd expect the ventilator shaft to be pretty grungy.

He found a screwdriver, removed several screws, and lifted the grille from the wall. As it came away, a clear plastic envelope trailed after it, attached by a short length of fishing line. It contained a small envelope. Cardinal opened it and extracted a curling photographic negative. He switched on the desk lamp and held the negative up to the light. He couldn't discern much other than that it showed a group of people, three men and one woman. He put it into his briefcase along with the phone bills.

Afterward, he stood outside on 6th Street. He had finished what he had come here to do much more quickly than he had anticipated. He thought about calling Kelly; he even held the phone in his hand, ready to dial. But he had hurt his daughter so much with his crisis of conscience the previous year. He had thought he was doing the right thing, deciding not to keep the rest of the Bouchard money, but it had necessitated Kelly's abrupt departure from Yale. The thought of sitting across from her in a heavy silence made his heart ache.

He called Catherine. He had been operating in hunter mode all day, but now the sound of her voice awoke in him something more tender. And tenderness evoked fear.

"Catherine, I don't want you to be scared, but it might be good if you keep a close eye on things around the house. And on our street. Has there been anything unusual that you've noticed?"

"What do you mean? Like what?"

"I don't know. Strange phone calls. Hang-ups, maybe."

"No. Nothing at all. Why?"

"Nothing. Old business that keeps resurfacing. We just need to be careful for the next little while."

"John, there's something else we have to worry about. I'll meet you at the airport."

"Why? What's up?"

"I've just come back from the hospital. Your father's in intensive care."

14

ABOUT THE TIME CARDINAL had taken off for New York, Lise Delorme was finishing the more prosaic task of designing and running off Missing Person flyers bearing Dr. Cates's photograph: Have you seen this person? it said, and gave Delorme's phone number at the bottom. Szelagy was spending his Wednesday canvassing Dr. Cates's neighbors in the Twickenham. Delorme left half the flyers on Szelagy's desk, then went down to the ident section.

Of all the rooms in the police station just then, ident was the one that was suffering the most. Their entire ceiling was gone, and they had set up makeshift plastic tents over their desks and file cabinets. The plastic kept the dust off their equipment, and also did a neat job of keeping out the ventilation. What it didn't keep out was the noise of construction above them.

"How can you work in here?" Delorme said to Arsenault. She had to shout over the screech of a metal drill. "There's no air."

"Air?" Arsenault said. "My hearing's being destroyed and you're worried about air?"

Collingwood looked up at Delorme for a moment, then back to his computer, imperturbable as a monk.

Delorme and Arsenault stepped into the hall.

"What can you give me from Dr. Cates's office?"

"It's a doctor's office—they keep it clean. I hope you weren't expecting a zillion fingerprints or anything."

"One would be fine."

"Well, we got a lot more than that, but mostly they belong to Dr. Cates and her assistant. We're running the rest for records, but nothing so far."

"And the bandage wrapper?"

"Prints from the doctor. Nothing else."

"You're breaking my heart, Paul. What about the paper from the examining table? The assistant swears it was changed Monday night, but yesterday morning it had been used."

"No hair, no fiber, unfortunately. But we did come up with some microscopic blood drops. We typed it AB-negative."

"That's rare, isn't it?"

"Pretty rare. We've sent it down to the Forensic Center for DNA analysis, but you know the drill. It's going to take a while."

DELORME DROVE THROUGH a light rain to the home of Dr. Raymond Choquette. Ray Choquette had been in practice in Algonquin Bay for twenty-five years. He lived in a three-story red-brick house on Baxter, a tiny, sloping side street less than four blocks from St. Francis hospital. Delorme could name at least three doctors off the top of her head who lived on Baxter. Her parents used to bring her to a doctor named Renaud who had lived on this street. He had been a gruff old codger, a throat specialist who always wore a reflective lamp on his forehead. He had always threatened to take Delorme's tonsils out, but died before he got the chance.

There was a Toyota RAV4 parked by the side door of the Choquette home. The temperature was dropping now, and the Toyota was covered with a fine glaze of ice. Delorme parked behind it, jotting down the license number before she got out of the car.

When Choquette opened the door on the front porch, Delorme showed her badge and introduced herself in French.

"You're lucky you caught me," Choquette said in English. "This time tomorrow the wife and I'll be in Puerto Rico." He was a tall man in his mid-fifties, with a ruddy complexion that made him look jolly—which Delorme suspected he was not—and a long straight nose made him look snobbish, which Delorme suspected he was.

Delorme continued in English. "Dr. Choquette, do you know a woman named Winter Cates?"

"Yes, of course I do. She's taking over my practice. Took over, I should say. Is there some kind of trouble? Don't tell me the place has been broken into again . . ."

"I'm afraid Dr. Cates is missing."

"Missing? What does that mean, exactly? She hasn't shown up for work?"

"She hasn't been seen or spoken to since late Monday night when she was home watching TV. Yesterday morning she missed a surgery she was scheduled to assist at, and she hasn't shown up for her office hours, either."

"Perhaps she had an accident. All this rain—and now it's turning to ice."

"Dr. Cates is missing. Her car isn't."

"Oh dear. That sounds bad. Are you sure? I saw her just a few days ago."

"Do you mind if I come in and ask a few questions?"

Dr. Choquette's ruddy face sagged a little, but he made a show of good cheer. "By all means. Come in, come in. Anything I can do to help . . ."

Choquette led Delorme into a small TV room. It was tiny, cozy, full of bookshelves stacked with English titles. Delorme had a sudden sense that Dr. Choquette was one of those Ontario French Canadians, rare these days, who attach themselves entirely to the English culture and forsake their own background. Many of the shelves contained golfing videos and trophies. Apparently Dr. Choquette was a regular at the local tournaments. There were small trophies and large ones, golden men wielding golden clubs, plaques, cups, mugs, and fixtures from various courses he had played at. A photograph on the wall showed Dr. Choquette in plaid pants and yellow cardigan next to some famous golfer, Delorme wasn't sure if it was Jack Nicklaus or the other one. Except for Tiger Woods, all golfers looked the same to her: men in funny pants.

"I hope nothing's happened to her," Choquette kept saying. "I just hope she's all right."

"You said you saw her recently. When was that, exactly?"

"It was at Wal-Mart. Yes, it was at Wal-Mart, and I know that was Thursday."

"Did she seem under any particular stress to you?"

"Not at all. She's a chipper thing. Intrepid, is my impression—you know, nothing gets her down."

"Any enemies that you know about? Anyone she was afraid of? Worried about?"

"Winter? I can't imagine her having an enemy in the world. She's totally gregarious. Been here six months and already she's got more friends at the hospital than I had in my first six years. And I'll tell you her secret: She loves to assist."

"Assist?"

"In the O.R. Surgery. She let it be known right away that she liked to assist, and that's rare."

"Why's that?"

"Why?" Choquette looked at Delorme as if she was a dolt. "Because it doesn't pay, that's why. The Ontario government in its infinite wisdom has structured payments so that a GP is much better off seeing patients in his own practice than assisting at surgery. Spend two hours in the O.R. and you get paid the same as treating two or three patients. Obviously, you can see a lot more than two or three patients in that time. These days, the Hippocratic oath may as well be a vow of poverty. Do you know what I get paid if I set your broken arm? Less than half what a vet gets paid for putting a splint on your dog. Please. Don't get me started on that subject. All you need to know about Winter Cates is that she's really well-liked in the medical community. Totally unruffled sort, and a great sense of humor. Believe me, a sense of humor is highly prized in the O.R."

"It goes a long way in police work, too," Delorme said.

More questions elicited the information that Dr. Winter Cates interned at Sick Kids, did her residency at Toronto General.

"Dr. Cates is an attractive person," Delorme said. "Do you know anything about her romantic life at all?"

"There you have me. I wouldn't know a thing. I had the impression she had someone in Sudbury, but beyond that I can't help you. Dr. Cates loves her work, and all we ever talk about is medicine."

"And you sold her your practice, is that correct?"

"Sold? No, you can't sell a practice, not in this province, anyway. No, no. I met her down at Toronto General when she was doing her residency and like everybody else was totally charmed. She said she'd love to set up in Algonquin Bay, and I mulled that over. I've been planning to retire for a decade at least. Anyway, I offered to take her on as a partner for six months and then I'd make my graceful exit. Which I have done."

"Dr. Choquette, when did you purchase your tickets to Puerto Rico?"

"Months ago. I don't see what my tickets have to do with anything."

"May I see them, please?"

The doctor rose, red in the face, and Delorme could see him working to restrain his temper as he left the room. He returned a moment later with the tickets and handed them over without a word. Two round-trip tickets to Puerto Rico, purchased in November, returning in one week.

"Thank you." Delorme handed back the tickets. "Where are you planning to stay?"

"A lovely resort called Palmas del Mar, on the south coast. Do you know it?"

"No." Having no interest in Caribbean vacations, Delorme was not entirely sure where Puerto Rico was, other than somewhere past Florida.

"Gorgeous place. Perfect location—a little short on beachfront, but they make up for it with one of the finest golf courses you've ever seen."

"And can you tell me where you were Monday night, Doctor? Round about midnight?"

"Playing bridge with friends. We have a regular Monday night game that—God damn it, surely you can't suspect me of having anything to do with this? A young doctor goes missing, what's that got to do with me, for God's sake?"

Delorme took her time to respond, watching a vein that throbbed in Dr. Choquette's temple. "You have financial dealings with Dr. Cates. All right, you didn't sell her your practice, but there's a large office full of equipment. My understanding is you had a disagreement over what was included in the transfer of your practice. And you were angry about it."

"Oh, really." Dr. Choquette crossed his arms and looked Delorme up and down. "I'd love to know who you've been talking to."

"Dr. Cates is refusing to pay you what you think the stuff is worth, is that it?"

"Nothing so dramatic, I'm afraid. I should have used a lawyer—I normally do for all my business dealings—but for some reason I didn't, in this case. Maybe because Winter's so—well, she's very appealing, let's say. We are having a dispute over depreciation. Do you know how much an examining table costs new? I thought we had found a figure comfortably in the middle between what I could get for the stuff if I put it up for sale, and what Winter would have to pay if she had to buy it new. Apparently I was wrong. I mean, ask her, if you think I'm lying."

"Dr. Cates isn't here to ask, unfortunately. How much money was involved?"

"Not a fortune. A couple of thousand. It's the principle of the thing. Look, she's probably got eighty to a hundred grand in education costs to pay off and every penny counts. No doubt she really believes we agreed to the lower figure, but it's just wishful thinking on her part. Anyway, it's not a big deal. Now, if you don't have any more questions . . ."

"No more questions. But I'll need the names of your bridge partners."

NEXT STOP: Glenn Freemont, unpleasant patient.

Freemont answered the door in his bathrobe—a bathrobe that looked as if it had seen several previous owners, at least one of whom had died in it. He was a runt of a man in his mid-thirties, with the oiliest hair Delorme had ever seen.

"Mr. Freemont, I'm investigating the disappearance of Dr. Winter Cates," Delorme said, after she had introduced herself. "May I come in and ask a few questions?" Mr. Freemont's basement apartment had no awning, and Delorme had no umbrella. Icy rain was dripping down her neck.

"Why?" Freemont was leaning with his hand against the doorjamb, as if to block any sudden moves.

"You're a patient of Dr. Cates's. I need to ask you some questions."

"She's got a million patients. Why are you coming to me?"

"Mr. Freemont, would you rather have a thorough scrutiny of your Workmen's Compensation? Maybe I should just give them a call."

"Go ahead. I'm cut off anyway, those jerks. I got a bad back. I never used to have a bad back. And the reason I got one now is because I lug cans of paint up and down two flights of stairs all day. Try it sometime. See how you like it."

"You had a screaming fit at Dr. Cates's office. Was that because she wouldn't back up your claim?"

"It wasn't no screaming fit. We had a discussion, that's all."

"According to witnesses, you slammed the desk with your fist and kicked over a plant."

"She called me a liar. I don't take that kind of shit. Not from anyone."

"Can you tell me where you were Monday night? Monday night around midnight?"

"Monday night? Yeah, I can tell you where I was Monday night. I was in Toronto."

"Why were you down there?"

Freemont hooked an index finger into his right cheek and pulled it back. A glimmer of pink, crisscrossed with black stitches. "Gum surgery. Early Tuesday morning. I drove down the day before, stayed at a hotel. Wait there."

Freemont closed the door. Delorme pulled up the hood on her anorak. Rain pattered on nylon. A film of ice was forming over the puddles at her feet.

Two minutes later Freemont came back with a fistful of papers. He handed them to Delorme one by one. "Receipt from the Colony Hotel. Receipt from the filling station on Spadina. Receipt from my periodontist. He wears black scrubs and he charges me a fucking fortune."

"Do you always keep such careful records?" Delorme said, making a note of the periodontist's name and number.

"Only when I plan to get reimbursed from OHIP."

"That'll be difficult. The province doesn't cover dental work."

Freemont snatched the receipts back. "Shows how much you know."

"Thank you, Mr. Freemont. I appreciate your cooperation."

"Oh, no. Thank *you*, Officer. And you have a wonderful day."

Before Delorme reached her car, she heard Freemont scream from behind the closed door, "Bitch!"

BOTH THE HOTEL and the periodontist backed up everything Glenn Freemont had said; Delorme made the calls first thing when she got back to the station. She wrote up some notes on her interviews and handed off the names of Dr. Choquette's bridge partners to Szelagy for follow-up.

She ate lunch at her desk, contemplating the stack of flyers, Dr. Cates's pretty face staring up at her. The construction crew was hammering and drilling upstairs, making it hard to think. She looked out the window at the parking lot. The rain had stopped an hour before, and now the day had turned bright and sunny; even the most mundane objects—trees, telephone poles, and mailboxes with their patina of ice—shimmered like figments in an ecstatic vision. As Delorme scanned the scene outside, the deep blue of the sky seemed to flash against the rooftops.

Her phone rang.

"Delorme. CID."

It was a man named Ted Pascoe, a camera salesman at Milton's Photo, younger brother of one Frank Pascoe, whom Delorme had put away for credit-card fraud. Ted Pascoe was so frantic she could hardly make out what he was saying—something about a dead body in the woods.

"Slow down, Mr. Pascoe. Slow down. Where are you?"

"Um, pay phone near the NorthWind Tavern. You know the tavern out past Algonquin Mall?"

Delorme knew it well. At one time she had had a boyfriend who liked his English beer. They used to go to the North Wind practically every Friday night for fish and chips. Unfortunately, that was about as exciting as that particular romance ever got.

"I was taking pictures up the hill out toward Four Mile Bay. Took the four-by-four, just looking for a good shot, you know. And I came across this body. A woman. Looks like she froze to death."

"Was there anyone else with you?"

"No. I like to be alone when I photograph. You can't have someone tapping their foot waiting for you. You start rushing things, you forget to bracket, you don't try all the angles. It's really not very—"

"What's the road like? Can we get a van in there?"

"No, no. This is strictly RV country."

"Okay, Mr. Pascoe. Stay where you are. Don't tell anyone else what you found. We'll be there in a few minutes."

Delorme knocked on Daniel Chouinard's door and entered without waiting for an okay. He listened intently as she summarized the phone call. "So, it could be your missing doctor," he said.

"I'd say there's a good chance."

"You'll need help for this. Too bad McLeod's out of town. Take Szelagy. You'll need ident, too."

He dialed an extension. "Arsenault, put down the sports section. You and Collingwood have got some actual work to do. And bring your Land Rover. Sounds like the ident van isn't going to do it."

He hung up and said. "What are you waiting for? Hit the road."

"I haven't called the coroner yet."

"I'll do it. You get moving," Chouinard said, adding wistfully, "Another body in the woods. I wish I was going with you."

"Sorry," Delorme said. "You're strictly a big-picture guy now."

"I know." Chouinard sighed and tossed the stub of a pencil into his wastebasket, where it landed with a clang. "And ain't that a shame."

KEN SZELAGY HAD a tendency to chatter. They got into the car, and it was like pulling the string on a Chatty Cathy: the wife, the kids, the hockey game. Delorme managed to steer him briefly onto the subject of Dr. Cates's neighbors.

"A lot of people are away just now—down in the Bahamas or wherever—so there weren't actually that many people to talk to. Typical apartment building—I mean, nobody really knows anybody else. I think you could die in that building and no one would know. Anyway, the upshot is no one saw or heard anything unusual Monday night or Tuesday morning. Everyone was either watching TV or in bed, and they didn't hear a thing."

"It's so strange," Delorme said. "If someone abducted her, you'd think somebody would hear a commotion of some kind."

"She could have went somewhere willingly. We just don't know yet. She could have gone off with someone she knew, then there's an accident or something else happens and that's why no one's heard from her."

Szelagy veered off the subject again and started talking about his family. Delorme found herself wishing for Cardinal, who tended to be as quiet as she was. Szelagy moved on to his in-laws, his mortgage, his car-insurance premiums; he was a force of nature.

"Szelagy!"

"What?"

"Cool it, for God's sake."

"Just being sociable. More than I can say for you."

The truth was, for sheer amiability there was no one on the force who could touch Szelagy. He was just a natural-born nice guy, and Delorme felt bad for jumping on him. She drove the next few blocks in guilty silence.

"Sorry," she said at the next light. "I'm just thinking about Dr. Cates."

"That's okay," Szelagy said. Then he was off on the merits of the snowmobile he'd just bought for the kids. Really, the new Bombardiers were so fast, they were practically Satanic.

They continued out along Summer and then across the bypass onto Highway 63. Ice glittered on every roof, every wire, every bough. The sky was pure cerulean. Sunlight was refracted off the trees and rooftops, in piercing white rays when you were close but from a distance the silvery glitter of tinsel.

The highway itself was clear of ice, and they made it to the North-Wind in less than twenty minutes. Ted Pascoe was leaning against his Jeep Wrangler, smoking a cigarette. "I don't even smoke anymore," he said by way of greeting. "Quit two years ago, but this thing really rattled me. I never saw a dead person before—well my dad, but that was different. I'm shaking." He held out a quivering hand for verification.

Delorme introduced Szelagy, then asked Pascoe what time he had found the body.

"About forty-five minutes ago. I came straight here and called." He gestured toward the pay phone.

"And you were alone?"

"Just me and the camera. Don't get ice like this too often—I wanted to get out there before it melts. Was on a logging road about half a mile east of here."

Arsenault and Collingwood pulled up in a Land Rover. Delorme gave them the one-minute signal. "Mr. Pascoe, why don't you drive us right back to the spot, and we'll have the scene men follow along behind."

A Lexus pulled off the highway, and Delorme groaned inwardly. The role of coroner was filled by several doctors who worked on rotation. It was bad luck to draw Dr. Barnhouse twice in a row.

"You're going to have to ride along with Arsenault and Collingwood, Doctor. Don't think that beautiful car of yours'll make it, where we're going."

"Marvelous," he said without humor. "Fantastic." But he got out of the car, black bag in hand.

Whatever logging had been done in the Algonquin Bay region had been finished half a century before, but the old access roads remained. They were forgotten for decades, until the craze for recreational vehicles made them once more passable. The recent warm weather had reduced the snowpack to little more than a few inches, and the ice on top was a thin crust. The resulting traction was better than on the streets in town.

Here the trees were all pine. Their boughs were weighted down, but the trees themselves, selected over millennia for this environment, remained erect. Rays of light, bright as lasers, shot out from icy carapaces.

"This is where I got out," Pascoe said. "Didn't want to risk driving around that." He pointed to a felled tree blocking the road ahead.

They got out of the car and waited for Arsenault and Collingwood. Delorme said, "Did you come back to the car the same way you went in?"

"Yup." He pointed to footprints in the snow. "Those are my tracks. I didn't notice any others, but then, I wasn't looking."

Delorme and Szelagy led the way. Pascoe stayed close behind, followed by Arsenault, Collingwood, and Dr. Barnhouse. They had been walking for less than five minutes when Pascoe said from behind, "Up ahead. Just beyond that stump. I nearly tripped over her."

Working in Special Investigations for six years, Delorme had not had to face any dead bodies. Before that, as a constable, she had of course seen the usual victims of car accidents or drownings. The scenes, being death scenes, always had an air of hopelessness about them, even if the victim perished in a cheerfully decorated living room. Sometimes the circumstances were tawdry: men hanging naked, pornography scattered about their pale feet. Sometimes they were frightening: the scene of a raging fire, marks of its ferocity everywhere. Sometimes they were eerie: an abandoned mineshaft in the middle of a winter night. What Delorme had never seen, in all her years in police work, was a death scene so beautiful.

She and Szelagy and the others stood at the edge of a scene from a fairy tale. All around them, the woods shimmered as if the trees were made of jewelry. There was no sound but the click of branches, and from farther off the buzz of a snowmobile. Sunlight bounced off every surface, making the scene more appropriate for a tale of magic, rather than a tragedy, the kind of story in which statues come to life.

But the figure before them would not be coming to life. The dead woman lay on her left side in a position of repose, one knee and one arm drawn up as if for balance. There was no obvious sign of violence, no cuts or bruises. Photographed from a distance, she might have appeared to be asleep. But there is nothing more still than a dead body, and no mistaking it for anything else. This one was naked, covered with a glaze of ice. Even the long black hair that fell in tendrils across her face was encased in ice. It was as if she were under a spell—the victim of a jealous wizard, a wicked witch.

"There's nothing to be gained by standing around gaping," Barnhouse observed.

"It's called assessing the scene," Delorme said. "Maybe you, you prefer to barge in and trample over evidence, but we're going to take some pictures first."

"You will not." Barnhouse did not take contradiction well. Coming from a woman, it had a visible effect on his blood pressure, and made him sputter. "You will not," he repeated. "I am the coroner and I am in charge here."

"Only until such time as foul play has been established."

"Which is what I intend to do, if you'll only let me go about my work."

"The victim is naked in the middle of a frozen forest. Me, as far as I'm concerned, foul play is already established."

Szelagy gave her a take-it-easy look, and Delorme mentally started counting to ten.

"I didn't realize you're a trained pathologist," Barnhouse went on. "Perhaps you don't need a coroner at all."

Delorme said, "Doctor, we need you to take a look at her. Just let us get some pictures first before the bunch of us destroy any evidence."

"We'll set the video cam back here," Arsenault said. "Leave it on wide angle."

Collingwood was already snapping away with still camera and measuring tape at the tracks that led into the clearing. There appeared to be only one set. He turned to Pascoe. "Could you lift your foot for me, sir?"

Pascoe awkwardly obliged, balancing himself against a tree. Collingwood snapped a couple of pictures of his hiking boots.

Arsenault moved in closer and shot a roll of pictures of the body, and then Delorme, Szelagy, and the coroner moved closer. Dr. Barnhouse clutched a microcassette recorder in his fist and muttered into it as he leaned over the body: well-nourished woman, early thirties, discoloration around the throat suggesting strangulation.

"There's her clothes," Delorme said. They were strewn to one side, frozen into a violent still life. The veneer of ice precluded close examination, but there were buttons torn off, the stretched neck of a sweater.

"Looks like she was killed here," Szelagy said.

"Possibly," Barnhouse said. "But look at the lividity." He pointed with a latex-gloved finger at the purpling of the lower leg and arm. "Blood traveled where gravity took it—backs of her shoulders and legs. She didn't die in this position. She could have been killed here and moved by some-one after death. Or she could have been killed somewhere else and brought here."

"But the clothes . . ." Delorme said.

"Yes, well. No doubt there's some explanation, but I doubt that it's medical."

"Can you give us a ballpark idea when she died?"

"She's covered with ice, so obviously she must've been here during the rain—before it froze. On the other hand, there's very little deterioration. So she hasn't been lying out here for much of the warm spell. So I'd say she was dumped here late Monday, maybe Tuesday morning. But you know, with the refrigeration effect out here, it'll be hard to pin down time of death without other indications. Now, give me a hand, here. I want to turn the body."

Delorme put a gloved hand under the extended knee and lifted. The film of ice on the limbs splintered noisily and slid away. The dark hair re-mained stiff across half the facial features.

"Bruising in vaginal area indicates possible rape. There are also notice-able contusions around the throat. Strangulation is a possibility. They'll have to open her up—look for petechial hemorrhaging in the lungs. Let's get a look at you, now." The stiffened hair crackled as Barnhouse moved it aside. "Oh, my," he said. "I know this woman."

"Guess we can hold off on distributing those flyers," Szelagy said.

Delorme contemplated the icy features, the milky sheen on the half-open eyes. She thought of all the patients this young Dr. Cates would have helped—thousands, probably—had she been allowed to live. She wondered what kind of person could have done this to her. Her mind traveled forward into the things that would have to be done, informing Dr. Cates's parents foremost among them.

She looked at Barnhouse. "We know Dr. Cates was home at eleven-thirty P.M. Monday night. A friend spoke to her. But we know from her phone machine she wasn't answering her phone early Tuesday morning."

"That would be consistent with what I see here. No doubt the patholo-gist will give you more."

"How long do you think it'll take the Forensic Center to get back to us?"

"Now, there you're in luck. Have you worked with Dr. Lortie down there?"

"No."

"He's one of their top pathologists. As it happens, he's here in town assessing regional requirements. I don't think I'll have any trouble getting him to handle the case right here. It would save taxpayer resources and so on."

"It would sure save us a lot of time," Delorme said.

"God knows," Dr. Barnhouse said, nodding at the dead woman, "it's the least we can do for her."

They fell silent. From the glittering woods, there was no sound but the ticking of branches.

15

WHILE THE IDENT TEAM went about their
work in the woods, Delorme drove to Sudbury, eighty miles west of Algonquin Bay. The shimmer of ice made the passing telephone poles, the
drooping wires, the angular rock-cuts bright and interesting, but Delorme's thoughts stayed mostly on that scene in the woods.

A crime of passion? Perhaps Craig Simmons had finally exploded in
the rage of a jilted lover. Certainly there were no other suspects for this
type of crime in Dr. Cates's life. A man says he was watching the hockey
game at home and can't prove it, well, in the absence of evidence to the
contrary, what can you do? Dr. Choquette's alibi still had to be checked
out, but he wasn't high on Delorme's list. And two bodies found in the
woods within a few days of each other? If Craig Simmons were ruled out,
the assumption would have to be that Dr. Cates was somehow connected
to the dead American. In that case, why did one get fed to the bears and
not the other?

For now, there were Dr. Cates's parents to face. Delorme had already
informed them by telephone, but it was essential to see them in person,
unfortunately. Talking to the bereaved was easily the worst aspect of
working homicide, and the only aspect that made Delorme long for the
comparative cleanliness of Special Investigations. Emotional cleanliness.
At least in Special, where she had put in six years and made some big
cases, you didn't have to tell anybody their daughter was dead. You didn't
have to stand in a room, all but drowning in their pain.

Which, half an hour later, was exactly what Delorme was doing. On
the mantelpiece across from her sat a graduation picture of Winter
Cates, her smile a promise of joy and success. Her mother was hunched

in a corner armchair, handkerchief clutched in her hand, a plump woman in her mid-sixties, yet still with something of the peaches-and-cream face in her daughter's photograph. Her father, a square man with a white beard and white hair combed forward in a fringe, was a professor of English literature at Laurentian University. He looked like a Roman senator.

"This Craig Simmons," Professor Cates said. "I knew he was a mistake from the start. We both did. Winter was only sixteen when she met him, and he was handsome and athletic and a football player and all those things that sixteen-year-olds think matter. But it was obvious to any adult that there was something wrong with him. He was too intense. Too doting. He hung on to Winter, literally, all the time. They'd be standing in the foyer right there, and he'd be gripping her elbow like a little old man."

"And he'd stare at her all the time," Mrs. Cates said softly. Her eyes were reddened, although she was not crying now. "Stare in a way that was not natural. Stare at her whenever she spoke. He'd be staring at her mouth as if her every word was life and death to him."

"Winter was a kid," Professor Cates said. "She couldn't see what was going on. I suppose she just thought he was super-romantic. But anyone with a little experience knows obsession when they see it. The shame of it is, that's the only kind of love that gets any kind of attention these days. In books and movies, I mean. Songs. No one's allowed to love quietly. No, no, it always has to be Sturm and Drang."

In Delorme's experience, love usually was a matter of Sturm and Drang, but she wasn't about to debate Professor Cates on the point.

"Craig Simmons never loved anybody but himself," he went on. "He's like that obsessive little creep who shot John Lennon. Or like any other maniac who can't stand to be rejected, because they don't really love anyone else. The other person's feelings don't enter into it. Do you think he cared a damn whether Winter was happy or not? He did not. We talked to her last week, and she said she was sick and tired of him. She wasn't talking to him anymore, and she wasn't taking his calls. See, with the

Craig Simmonses of this world, it's all Me, Me, Me. Capital *M*. Nothing else exists. And when something like a resounding No forces them to acknowledge that they do not in fact own the universe, it's like annihilation for them, and they have to strike back. Which is exactly what that bastard did."

The professor's voice was getting louder and louder. His wife reached over and touched his wrist, but he took no notice.

"That idiot murdered my daughter, and I want to see justice, Detective Delorme. I want to see that murdering bastard rot in prison for the rest of his life. I suppose he raped her?" The senatorial eyebrows rose as if he were making a routine inquiry.

Delorme had been dreading that question, and yet found herself unprepared for it. "There are indications, I'm afraid."

Professor Cates spun away from her as if he had been shot. He sank to the sofa and folded over his knees. Mrs. Cates rose from her chair and sat beside him, resting her hand on his back.

"The funny thing about Craig Simmons . . ." Mrs. Cates spoke softly, almost inaudibly. "Everything my husband says is true. Craig did behave in that way. And yet I always had the sense that he had learned it somewhere."

"Well, yes," said the professor. "He learned it from the movies, from his parents, from his childhood, from God knows where, and who cares?"

"That's not what I meant. I meant it was like he learned it the way an actor learns a part. As if he'd read somewhere that that's the way you're supposed to behave and by God that's the way he was going to behave. You sensed he knew it was inappropriate, but he was doing it anyway—and that was really upsetting."

"Did Mr. Simmons ever threaten your daughter in any way?"

Mrs. Cates looked up at the ceiling, trying to keep the tears from spilling over. "Never," she said. "Not once."

Professor Cates sat up so swiftly that in other circumstances it might have been comic. "What do you mean? That boy used to show up here all the time, uninvited. He'd show up to walk her to school—which would have been one thing if they had been going out together. But she had broken up with him. 'Daddy, he's here again,' she'd say, and I'd have to go out and tell him to beat it. Not that it did any good. He'd be back again a week later."

"I don't think that's what the detective meant by a threat, dear."

"How many unwanted phone calls were there? Hundreds? Thousands?"

"It's true, he used to call all the time," Mrs. Cates said. "I felt sorry for him at first. Well, one did. He was so clearly desperate."

"Don't you start forgiving this bastard. Don't you even think of forgiving him."

"I'm not, dear. I'm just telling it the way it was. He never threatened to harm Winter. He just wanted to talk to her. To see her. It was overwhelming for a sixteen-year-old, as you can imagine."

"Sometimes he'd be out there. Just sitting out there in his car." The professor jabbed a finger in the direction of the street. "Even that was enough to make you uneasy."

"But then years went by and he didn't bother her," Delorme said. "Did I understand that right? When she was at college?"

"That's true," Mrs. Cates said. "She never complained about him the whole time she was in Ottawa. Mind you, for most of that time he was out west. He could only visit once or twice. He was at the Mountie training depot in Regina, and then they assigned him somewhere way up north. I find it terrifying that someone like Craig Simmons is walking around as a police officer. Armed, no less."

"And Winter agreed to see him on a friendly basis after that? After she finished her degree?"

"She felt sorry for him," Professor Cates said. "God knows why. I never did. But one thing you must understand. Winter wanted to set up practice in Sudbury. The only reason she didn't was because he was here. Unfortunately, Algonquin Bay wasn't far enough away. Probably nowhere would have been."

Delorme stayed another fifteen minutes without getting a lot more information. Professor Cates followed her out onto their glassed-in porch. The suburban scene shone around them.

"Listen," Professor Cates said, "when do you think you'll be arresting him?"

"We don't have enough evidence to do that."

"But you know he did it, right?"

"We don't have any firm suspects at this point. Mr. Simmons's behavior may have been upsetting, but that doesn't make him guilty."

Professor Cates looked her up and down as if grading her performance. Delorme could see the F coming. "Now you just tell me one thing," he said. "You just tell me what good is the organization you work for, if you can't lock such a man up?"

The Cateses' suffering clung to Delorme all the way home. She tried to imagine the devastation of losing a child, but knew she could not. The young doctor's face hovered before her, and Delorme vowed again to catch the person who had stolen her future from her.

Her thoughts turned once again to the obsessive Corporal Simmons, and she found herself remembering an obsessive former boyfriend of her own, named René. She still heard from him occasionally, usually at two in the morning. He would be drunk and maudlin and half the time threatening to kill himself. Once he had shown up on her doorstep when she had been with another man. There they were kissing on the couch, when the doorbell rings and there's René tottering on the front steps, slamming his palms on her screen door. It had made the new boyfriend extremely nervous, and he never did come back after that. Last she'd heard, René was in Vancouver—and please God let him stay there.

Trouble was, there weren't a lot of ideal men in Algonquin Bay, and Delorme wasn't about to get romantically entwined with anyone in the department. It would have been nice if someone like Cardinal—not Cardinal himself, needless to say—appeared on her doorstep. Cardinal was the least obsessive man she'd ever met. Talk about steadiness, Professor. You couldn't say Cardinal was a happy man—he was a brooder, maybe even kind of depressed—but he never spoke of his wife with anything but happiness and affection. He never mentioned her illness, not once. And yet his life with her must be difficult—according to McLeod, Cardinal had raised his daughter practically on his own. The truth was, Cardinal could be a pain to work with, he could make mistakes—just look at that unfortunate Bouchard business in his past—but you could bet your life on someone like Cardinal, and he'd never let you down.

Delorme had to brake for a truck that pulled onto the highway near Sturgeon Falls. Good grief, she thought, why am I thinking about Cardinal? He sure as hell never thinks about me. She turned on the radio. A newscaster announced that another pipe bomb had gone off outside a Montreal restaurant, courtesy of the French Self-Defense League, protesting the restaurant's English sign. Delorme switched to a French pop station—Celine Dion wailing about lost love—and resolved to banish John Cardinal from her mind.

BACK AT THE STATION, Delorme put in a call to the coroner's office up at the Ontario Hospital. She spoke first to Dr. Barnhouse, who handed the phone over to the visiting pathologist, Dr. Alain Lortie. He sounded young but confident.

"This woman died of strangulation, no question at all. We've got hemorrhaging in the lungs and in the eyes, not to mention a fractured hyoid bone in the throat. My guess is somebody pretty strong did it."

"And what about rape, doctor? We found her clothes right nearby in the woods, torn off."

"Clothes torn off could indicate sexual violence. Vaginal bruising— and we have some here—also is usually an indicator. I'd ignore the clothes, though, because the lividity and the stage of insect activity indicate she was killed somewhere else. You wouldn't get flies outside this time of year, so she was probably killed indoors. So tearing the clothes off seems like an afterthought. No semen on or in the body, no vaginal or anal tearing. My gut feeling is that this woman was not raped."

"Are you sure about that?"

"Can't prove a negative, Detective. It's just my feeling."

"But someone made it appear like rape?"

"Looks that way."

"What about time of death?"

"Stomach contents: two chocolate cookies, not much else."

"Well, we know she was eating those cookies at eleven thirty P.M., Monday night. She was talking to a friend on the phone."

"Well, from where they'd got to in her digestive tract, I'd say she was killed within an hour or so of that phone call. Nothing else of interest, I'm afraid. I'll fax you my full report."

"Thank you so much for doing this, Doctor. I know you weren't in town to perform autopsies."

"Glad to help out."

Delorme tucked the time of death away in her mental file labeled "uncontested facts" and wandered down to the pantry. There was a bulletin board next to the Coke machine, and Delorme stopped to read it, she always did. In addition to the For Sale notices, there was a typed list of license plates: numbers taken down at the Northtown Mini-mall.

The video arcade at the mini-mall had recently become something of a neighborhood nuisance. Teenagers were hanging out until all hours, smoking dope and making a racket. Cops on the beat were instructed to take down the license numbers of any vehicles parked near the store after eleven o'clock at night. It was meant to be a low-cost, laid-back effort at getting rid of whatever dealer was supplying the kids with their grass. The list of license plates was posted in the pantry under the sardonic heading ALGONQUIN BAY'S MOST WANTED!

Keeping track of the plate numbers was a totally informal, off-the-books kind of operation—if you could even call it an operation. It was the sort of thing the chief could plausibly claim as an "ongoing effort" to deal with a minor problem. "We are closely monitoring the situation," R.J. could say, and still look at himself in the mirror. In short, no one took the license list very seriously—it was pinned to the bulletin board beside the Coke machine along with notices of exercise machines for sale and cottages for rent—still, everyone glanced at it.

Delorme put a loony in the Coke machine and hit the Diet Coke button, only to have the machine deliver regular Coke. She stood there sipping from the can, looking at a picture of hockey equipment for sale—a complete kids' goalie outfit for "only" five hundred dollars. She read an ad looking for homes for six tabby kittens, and one looking for a "dirt-cheap" laptop. *See Nancy Newcombe* some wag had written; Nancy Newcombe ran the evidence room.

Just as Delorme was contemplating the number of calories in the Coke, her eyes fell upon the list of license numbers. And there it was, right at the top: PAL 474, easy enough to remember, and Delorme quickly flipped open her notebook to double check. But the thing that made Delorme's blood hammer in her veins wasn't the plate number itself but the date and time on which the beat cop had made a note of it: Monday, 11:00 P.M.

A LAW-ABIDING CITIZEN can drive from Algonquin Bay to Mattawa in about thirty-five minutes. Delorme made it in under twenty. The Simmons cottage loomed at the end of the driveway in mauve Victorian splendor. To the gingerbread siding, the frozen rain had now added a layer of crystalline icing. Craig Simmons's Jeep was still there. In Delorme's mind, the license plate could have been a neon sign, flashing the word "guilty" in letters of blazing scarlet.

Delorme rang the front doorbell, but there was no answer. She found Simmons on the far side of the boathouse, attaching a complicated-looking lock to the door. The Mattawa River, black and deep in this area, swirled and flowed behind him. He gave Delorme the briefest glance and went on with his work.

"Corporal Simmons, I have a few more questions for you."

"She's dead. I heard on the news. I really don't feel like talking to you right now."

"Corporal Simmons, you're a Mountie. You know I have to do this. Don't make it harder than it has to be."

Simmons looked at her with disgust. He dropped his screwdriver into a toolbox with a clatter and headed up toward the house.

Delorme followed him inside. The place smelled of coffee. Simmons poured himself a cup and offered it to Delorme. When she declined, he took it into the living room, where he sat on the edge of a recamier couch and buried his face in his hands. Delorme tensed for another explosion. But when the corporal pulled his hands away, he just stared at them as if they held an open book. "I knew she was dead, right from the start. As soon as she went missing. Winter's just not the type to go missing."

"You seem to be taking it pretty calmly."

"Calm? No, I wouldn't say calm."

Delorme sat on the edge of a wing chair. "Certainly calmer than the other day."

"You think I killed Winter. And you think I'm calm because I killed her."

Delorme shrugged. "If the shoe fits . . ."

"You don't think it's possible to be calm and yet in a great deal of pain?" Simmons sipped coffee from a delicate floral cup, an absurd cup for so muscular a man. "Can't you understand that knowing for sure Winter's dead is less stressful than wondering where she is? Wondering if she's lying somewhere injured or in pain? I'm sitting here devastated, but at the same time, yes, I'm feeling less . . . stress, for lack of a better word."

"I would've thought you'd be feeling a lot more, considering you don't have an alibi—other than the hockey game you say you watched Monday night."

"But I know I'm innocent, don't I. So that'll be bothering you more than it does me. Ever since I met Winter—that was over ten years ago, now, back when we were in high school—I've wanted nothing more than to be with her. But it was never the same for her. Oh, she was fond of me. There were things about me she liked. But I wanted to marry her, and she would never agree. It was excruciating."

Simmons contemplated the steam rising from his coffee. He smoothed back his fringe of pale hair. He would have been attractive, Delorme thought, if he wasn't such a fake, such an actor.

"From the time we met it was like I had this motor going inside me—gotta have her, gotta have her, gotta have her." He ran the words together like a revving engine. "Day after day, year after year, my entire focus was on trying to get Winter to love me. I would do anything. When I was at the training depot out in Regina I would sometimes fly all the way to Ottawa—it cost me a fortune!—just to be with her for one day. One day!

"And letters. I wrote her endless letters, telling her how much I loved her. I even started reading about medicine, just because that's what she was studying. Can you imagine?"

"Look, Corporal Simmons, it's no news to me that you were hung up on Dr. Cates. That was obvious from your phone messages."

"You know what it was like?" Simmons looked at her, and Delorme saw he didn't really want an answer. "It was like running on high revs year after year after year. And you know what? It's over now. So even though I'm devastated that Winter's gone, it's also as if this weight has been lifted. I don't have to try anymore. It's over. There's nothing I can do about it, and I don't have to win her over anymore, and so in some weird way it's kind of a relief."

"Well, that's nice for you," Delorme said. "I'm sure Dr. Cates wouldn't have minded dying if she knew how good it was going to make you feel. She probably would have done it a lot sooner."

"You can't really suspect me, Detective. I'm being more honest than most people would be in this situation."

"Of course you are. Me, I'm very impressed. And besides, you were here watching the hockey game when she was killed, no? That's what you said."

"That's what I said. And it's the truth."

"Then why was your Jeep Wrangler, license number PAL 474, spotted at the Northtown Mini-mall in Algonquin Bay Monday night? Shortly before Dr. Cates was killed."

Simmons lowered his coffee cup to the table, so slowly that it made no sound. All the color drained from his face. Then he leaned forward and put his face once more in his hands.

"A court of law is going to have a hard time appreciating your so-called honesty, Corporal Simmons. You said you were here when Winter was murdered, but you weren't. You were in Algonquin Bay."

"Oh, God," Simmons said into his hands. "Oh, merciful God."

16

EVEN THE ICE couldn't keep the teen-
agers from hanging around the Northtown Mini-mall. The Cosmic Arcade had at least a half-dozen kids standing under the awning, smoking
cigarettes and jostling one another and belching and in general being ob-
noxious in all the ways teenagers have perfected.

You have to wonder how they can stand it, Delorme was thinking. I sure
wouldn't want to be standing out there this time of year with my navel ex-
posed. Then again, I wouldn't be doing that in midsummer, either.

Delorme and Craig Simmons had driven here in their separate vehicles,
and now he was sitting beside her on the front seat of the unmarked.
Their attention was not on the games arcade. The Northtown Mini-mall
also housed an electronics parts store, several empty storefronts, and Fantasy XXX Video.

It was the video store that Delorme and Simmons were watching. The
neon sign flashed blurry rubies on the windshield, where ice had melted.
Delorme flicked on the wipers, and the shop came once again into focus.

"You can't tell anybody about this," Simmons said. "Ever. Obviously
I'd be finished on the force."

"Assuming it turns out to be true."

"I'm very careful. I never do this in Sudbury or Mattawa, places where
I'm known."

"Careful? When you don't even know who you're . . . I wouldn't exactly call that careful."

Simmons drew a face in the mist on the passenger window. "It's a kink,
all right? It's nothing to get sanctimonious about. A lot of people do it."

"A lot of men, you mean."

"All right, a lot of men."

Delorme looked at her watch. "It's going on eleven thirty, now. There's no reason to think this guy's going to show. If he exists."

"He said he comes by three or four nights a week. He said if I wanted to meet up again, he'd probably be here."

"Three or four nights a week. You must not give much of a damn about your health, if you—"

"There he is," Simmons said. "That's him."

He pointed to a middle-aged man in a tan raincoat who was locking the door of a battered Caprice. The man looked briefly around the parking lot and headed toward the video store.

"Wait here," Delorme said. She got out of the car and came up behind the man before he reached the store. "Excuse me, sir. I need to talk to you."

The man turned, frowning.

"Is this your glove?" Delorme held up a brown leather glove, brand new.

The man felt in his pockets, pulled out one glove. "Why, yes, I guess it is."

He reached for the glove, but Delorme pulled out her badge. "I have a few questions for you. It'll only take a minute."

The man stepped back. "What's going on? Why should I answer any questions?"

"Because you happen to be a witness in a murder case."

"Murder? I have no idea what you're talking about." He stepped past Delorme, back toward his car.

"I'm sure you don't. But you saw a young man right here in this parking lot on Saturday night. You were in his car. The Jeep Wrangler, remember?"

"You have no right to ask me anything. You can't harass me like this," he said, and opened his car door. "I have a very good lawyer."

"You also have a wife, I notice from that ring on your hand. You'd probably prefer to answer questions here than at your house, no?"

The man folded his arms. He looked at the ground and shook his head. "I don't believe this."

Delorme came closer. "Listen. I have less than no interest in your sex life. All I need you to do is confirm a few things."

"Great. Like I have nothing better to do."

"Right at this moment, that's probably true." Delorme signaled to Simmons. He got out of the car and walked round to stand on the driver's side. He was about twenty yards away. "Do you recognize him?"

"Yes. All right? It's called consenting adults. Can I go now?"

"What time were you with him on Saturday night?"

"I don't know. Around midnight."

"We're talking about a murder. Be more specific."

"I first noticed him about eleven thirty, when I went into the store. I looked around for a while. When I came out, he was still there. A little while later we, uh, spent some time together in his Jeep."

"From when until when? I need you to be specific."

"From about twelve-thirty, maybe till one o'clock. I went straight home after, and the clock on the mantel said one-thirty."

"So, you left here about one. Did he leave, too?"

"He was still here."

"I'll need to see some ID, in case we need to call you about any of this."

"I don't see why you need my—"

"Just show me the ID, will you?"

The man produced a driver's license, and Delorme took down the information. She handed it back to him.

"I'd like my glove back, please."

"No. We'll have to hang on to that. But thanks for your cooperation."

"As if I had any choice."

The man got into his car and slammed the door and was out of the parking lot in under three seconds flat.

"He corroborated my statement, didn't he," Simmons said. "What did he say?"

"He said, 'Once you've had a Mountie, you never go back.'"

"It's just lucky he lost that glove in my car. He probably wouldn't have admitted a thing, otherwise."

"Corporal Simmons, listen to me. I won't be telling anyone about this incident unless it's absolutely necessary. Right now, I don't see why it would be. But my advice to you is find yourself a line of work where it doesn't matter if you're gay."

"That's brilliant, Detective. I'd love being a hairdresser."

"Think of how confusing it must have been for Dr. Cates. All this time you're clinging to her—she didn't know she was just cover. Although she must've suspected you were gay."

"You don't seem to get it, Detective. Winter wasn't just cover. I really loved her. And I don't think of myself as gay."

Delorme watched him drive away. It was raining again; even the teenagers had decided to pack it in. Delorme let the fat, icy drops fall on her for a few moments as she tried to absorb the day's work. But all she could really think was that no matter how long she stayed on this job, and no matter how long she lived, she would never—and she mentally italicized the word *never*—understand men.

17

CARDINAL HAD MANAGED to catch the last flight leaving Toronto that Wednesday for Algonquin Bay. "Thank God, you're back," Catherine said the moment he stepped off the tarmac. She looked pale, the lines on her face deeper.

"How is he?"

"Stable. I'm not sure exactly what that means, but they say he's stable."

They drove down a glistening Airport Hill toward City Hospital, Cardinal fighting an uprush of panic.

"He was having trouble breathing," Catherine told him. "I'd dropped him at home, and he was putting groceries away, when suddenly he was feeling like he couldn't breathe. Anyway, he called his cardiologist—who called an ambulance, thank God—and now he's in the ICU."

His father seemed in many ways an indestructible man, but Cardinal suddenly feared that he might become incapacitated, that he would have to live with Cardinal and Catherine, and they'd oversee his final months or years, wheeling him about, changing his diaper. Then Cardinal's Catholic conscience rounded on him and threatened centuries of hellfire for that selfish thought.

At the intensive care unit they were informed that Stan Cardinal had been moved to cardiac care on the fourth floor. The nurse told Cardinal his father was resting comfortably. "We've adjusted his medication, and he seems to be responding well. I suspect he'll be discharged tomorrow."

"Can I see him?"

"Keep it to five minutes. We don't want to tire him out."

"Which room is he in?"

"He's in one of the 'Mantis' suites, I'm afraid—one of the curtained-off areas down the hall."

"Wait a minute. My father's having heart failure, and you're telling me you've got him parked in the hall?"

"I'm sorry. Cutbacks courtesy of the government. A bed in the hall is the best we can do right now."

"I saw him already," Catherine said gently. "Why don't I just wait here for you?"

There were three so-called Mantis suites. Cardinal's father was in the last one, his curtain pulled back so he got some light from a window that looked out across railroad tracks and the schoolyard of Algonquin High. The glass was blurry with rain.

The bed was cranked upward at a thirty-degree angle. Stan Cardinal lay sunken against the pillows, his head drooping to one side as if the weight of the clear plastic tube taped to his nostril was too much to bear. His eyes were closed, but as Cardinal approached, they fluttered open.

"Look who's here." His father's voice sounded much stronger than he looked. "The forces of law and order."

"How you feeling?"

"Like an elephant's sitting on my chest. It's better, though. Earlier, it was two elephants and a rhinoceros."

"The nurse says they'll probably send you home tomorrow."

"I wish they'd send me home right now."

"Well, they seem pleased with how you're doing." Cardinal could hear the false note of optimism in his own voice.

"I feel fine. I really do. I only called the cardiologist to see about my prescription—I didn't expect him to haul off and call an ambulance."

"Well, you must have needed it."

His father shrugged, and winced. His skin was gray and papery, his eyes watery.

"Are you all right? Do you need the nurse?"

"I'm fine, for God's sake. I just want to go home. How the hell do they expect you to get better in a hospital? What you really need is to be surrounded by your own things, watch your own television, make tea in your own pot. This place, you're at the mercy of everybody. Stuck in the hall like a sideshow. You ring and ring and they just wander by whenever they please. At home I can fix what I want, when I want. I don't have to rely on these little Dairy Queen dollies to bring it to me."

"I better go. They told me not to stay long."

"Yeah, get outa here. I'll call you soon's they give me my walking papers."

AS THEY WERE DRIVING HOME, Catherine reached over and touched Cardinal's shoulder. "Maybe your dad should come and live with us for a while. You know, if the doctors say he needs to have someone around all the time, he can stay with us. I'm fine with that, if you are. I wouldn't say so if I wasn't."

"I don't think he'd stay with us, anyway," Cardinal said. "You know, when Mom died, I wasn't sure he was going to make it, he was so . . . shipwrecked. But he pulled it together and got himself that little house, and there he was at the age of seventy-one, living on his own for the first time since he was twenty-something. He's never said so, but he's really proud of that. Self-sufficiency. Independence. It's everything to him."

"I know, sweetheart. I'm just saying, if he needs to have people around him, we can have him with us."

Cardinal nodded. He found it hard to look into Catherine's eyes—she, who had suffered so much, offering her helping hand.

She asked him about work.

He gave her a brief rundown of his New York trip.

"Did you get a chance to call Kelly?"

"There wasn't time," Cardinal said. "I had to get back here. The problem with this case is that the luck is all running one way—against us and for whoever it is we're after. I'm just not getting anywhere."

Cardinal went inside the house with Catherine but only long enough to see that everything was all right. Trying not to be too obvious about it, he checked the doors and windows for signs of tampering. There were none.

"It's ten o'clock at night and you've still got your coat on," Catherine said. "You're not going back to work at this hour, I hope."

" 'Fraid so. Shouldn't be long, though."

CARDINAL'S NEXT STOP WAS the Hilltop Motel, a red-brick oblong located, as the name suggests, at the top of Algonquin. He parked in an unobtrusive corner. There were only three cars in the lot, and the asphalt gleamed with black ice. Cardinal had already checked to see if Squier was still registered, but the slot in front of number eleven was empty.

While he was waiting, Cardinal listened to the news. The provincial election was gearing up. Premier Mantis had announced he would indeed run again: It was time to stay the course, not to rock the boat. His Liberal opponent, not to be outdone in clichés, thought it was time for a new dawn.

A few minutes later Calvin Squier pulled in.

Cardinal jumped out of the car and called across the lot, "Hey, Squier!"

Squier turned at the doorway of room eleven, key in hand. "Hiya, John. How've you been?"

"Fine. Been traveling," Cardinal had one hand thrust out to shake. When Squier reached out he slapped the cuffs on him. On the slick pavement, it was beautiful: Cardinal pulled down and sideways and Squier went down like a bagged moose, his cell phone skittering across the ice. Cardinal had the other cuff on him before he had time to catch his breath.

"Hey, come on, John. What's going on, here?"

"Calvin Squier, you are under arrest for interfering with an investigation, for obstructing justice, for public mischief, and for anything else I can think of before I get to the Crown's office."

"Oh, no," Squier said. "This is awful."

"Are you sure you wouldn't like to resist arrest? It would go a long way toward improving my mood."

"Come on, John. Let me up."

Cardinal kept his knee planted on Squier's back while he read him his rights, enunciating every word clearly. "Do you understand these rights?"

"John, you're going to get me in serious trouble. You don't want to do that, do you?"

"You seem to be under the impression that we're friends, Squier. I don't know what gives you that idea. I can't remember when I met anybody I liked less—and I meet a lot of unpleasant people."

Squier had trouble getting to his feet with his hands cuffed. Cardinal steadied him and then led him across the parking lot to the car.

"This is pure pettiness, isn't it," Squier said from the backseat. "You're just getting even for my taking your gun away the night we met."

"Just keep talking, Squier. It always puts me in such a good mood, the sound of your voice."

"I think if you look at this objectively, you'll find you're behaving unfairly."

"Christ, Squier. How'd you ever think you could get away with it?"

"I'm not sure what you're referring to."

"Pretending that our murder victim was one Howard Matlock when clearly you knew he was someone else."

"I never said he was Howard Matlock, as such. You found a wallet in his hotel room and you made that assumption."

"Which you confirmed by your mythical trip to New York. By pretending to assist in this investigation when you are in fact actively blocking it. All that crap about the CADS base and WARR. It was all a crock, wasn't it?"

"John, I realize that candor is the soul of good teamwork. But I work for Security Intelligence. Obviously I'm not at liberty to explain all my actions to you."

"I don't care. Explain them to the judge."

18

THAT WAS WEDNESDAY. On Thursday, Cardinal was sitting at the breakfast table finishing his second cup of coffee when the local news came on the radio. The lead item was the murder of Winter Cates.

"Isn't that your father's new doctor?" Catherine said.

Cardinal leaned across the table and turned the radio up. The newscaster didn't have a lot of information. Dr. Cates, thirty-two, had been raped and strangled sometime Monday night in a wooded area north of the city. Police had no suspects.

"My God," Cardinal said. "I can't believe it. We just saw her on Monday."

"It's horrible," Catherine said.

"I only met her the once, but I liked her right away. And she seemed like a first-class doctor."

Cardinal picked up the phone and dialed Delorme's home number. When the answering machine picked up, he put the phone down again.

ON THE DRIVE INTO TOWN, Cardinal thought about the young physician who had handled his father so well and gotten him treatment so fast. She had seemed so smart, so intent on helping, and there was something especially awful about the murder of a doctor.

It was still early when Cardinal got to the squad room, but Delorme was already there.

"I just heard about Winter Cates on the radio," Cardinal said. "I still can't get over it. She was raped, too?"

"There were signs of sexual assault, but no—the pathologist is pretty sure she wasn't raped. Somebody sure killed her, though," Delorme said. "And I don't have a clue who it is."

"I thought you were focusing on Corporal Simmons. How'd Musgrave take that, by the way?"

"Musgrave was fine. Told me where to find him, in fact. Also told me Simmons was not the guy, which turned out to be correct."

"He has an alibi? What is it?"

Delorme winced. "I'd rather not say—I made a promise—but believe me, it wasn't in the corporal's interest to tell me about it."

Delorme brought Cardinal up to date on the case from seeing the body in the woods to ruling Simmons out. She laid particular emphasis on Dr. Cates's office. "The assistant is certain that paper on the examining table was used after they closed Monday night. Of course we're waiting for DNA results, but the blood we found is AB-negative, which is rare." She finished by voicing Cardinal's own thought. "You know, two bodies in the woods in the space of three days. You have to think they're probably connected."

"It does seem likely. But what's our link? Let me tell you where I'm at with Matlock, and maybe we can come up with something. His name is not Matlock, for starters. And he wasn't any chartered accountant, either."

Cardinal was interrupted by the phone.

"Cardinal, CID."

"Ed Beacom, Beacom Security. Looks like we're going to be working together again."

"Wonderful. What are you talking about, Ed?" Ed Beacom was a former cop who would have never made it up the ranks. It wasn't incompetence; Beacom just had a grudge against the world and it made him annoying to work with.

"The Mantis fund-raiser?"

Cardinal covered the mouthpiece. "Did Chouinard tell you about this fund-raiser we have to work security on?"

"The Conservative thing," Delorme said. "Yeah, he told me. Just what I want to be doing in the middle of a murder case."

"Listen, Ed," Cardinal said into the phone, "we've got everything hitting the fan just now. Can I call you back?"

"Oh, sure. I know how important you guys are. Wouldn't want to hold up the wheels of justice."

"Are you going to give me your number?"

Beacom gave it to him, and he hung up.

"Where were we?"

"You were telling me Matlock's not Matlock."

Cardinal told Delorme about Squier's deception, about Shackley's real background, and about his trip to New York. Delorme's attention was intense; her brown eyes fixed on him the whole time.

"Quebec? Nineteen seventy?" Delorme said when he was done. "That was like a thousand years ago. You really think that's going to lead anywhere?"

"The minute I have any other leads, I'll follow them."

"And this Squier character," Delorme said. "Why did he lie about who Shackley was? Why does CSIS want to keep Shackley's identity a big secret? Why actively mislead you?"

"Clearly CSIS wants this case to stay buried."

"Yes, but why?"

"An excellent question. I suggest we put it to Calvin Squier."

As they passed the front desk, Duty Sergeant Mary Flower yelled to Cardinal, "Come here, Detective. I need to talk to you."

Cardinal waved her off. "Be right back."

He and Delorme headed back toward the cells.

"I think we should start by zeroing in on how CSIS knew to look for Miles Shackley at the airport," Cardinal said. "On why Miles Shackley was Code Red. It could be something totally simple that'll rule out a connection to Algonquin Bay, or it could lead somewhere that brings us to Dr. Cates."

They passed the pink cell where a drunk was drying out, the cell that had recently suffered a flood and stank of mildew, the cells that had held Paul Bressard and Thierry Ferand until they had made bail, and then they were in front of the last cell on the right, where Calvin Squier of the Canadian Security Intelligence Service was housed. It was empty.

"Must be in an interview room with an attorney," Cardinal said. "Let's go back out front."

They went back to the desk.

"What's up with Squier?" Cardinal asked Mary Flower. "He's not in his cell."

"That's what I wanted to tell you," Flower said. "Calvin Squier is gone. Calvin Squier has vamoosed. Calvin Squier is free as a bird. The Crown Attorney sprung him last night about two seconds after you left."

"TELL ME YOU DIDN'T cave into the Crown on this," Cardinal said to Chouinard. "Tell me you didn't hide under your desk the minute CSIS whimpered."

"Don't give me that, Cardinal. They had the chief in on this, the Crown, you name it. This wasn't up to me, not that I objected too strongly. Playing by the rules doesn't make anybody a wimp. And breaking them doesn't make you a hero." They were in the detective sergeant's office. He had hung up a large Montreal Canadiens calendar behind his desk.

"Talk to Calvin Squier about breaking the rules," Cardinal said. "Calvin Squier completely derailed a murder investigation by implying he had interviewed the next of kin and investigated background when he hadn't done any such thing. Calvin Squier invented a completely fictitious story involving the CADS base and American terrorists. And Calvin Squier also failed to share a crucial piece of information with both us and the RCMP, namely the victim's true identity. If that doesn't qualify as obstruction of justice I don't know what does."

"CSIS is an intelligence operation. You know that. It does not operate under the same rules as everybody else."

"Not in Algonquin Bay, obviously."

"You arrested an agent of a federal institution without consulting me or the chief or the Crown. Reginald Rose is absolutely livid, and if I were you I'd avoid the chief, too. You'll be lucky if you don't get hit with some charges yourself. I'm telling you, Rose was furious. And he had every right to be."

"That doesn't give Squier the right to mislead an investigation. If he had his way, we'd still be trying to figure out who killed Howard Matlock, who is not dead, instead of Miles Shackley, who is."

"All right. Squier withheld evidence. That is not a crime for which you pull a civil servant off the street without a warrant. Why didn't you go to the Crown first?"

"Because it was late. Calvin Squier was withholding information relevant to my investigation."

"That makes him a witness, not a criminal. Cardinal, you and I have worked lots of cases together. Frankly, I'm surprised."

"Likewise."

"Oh, really?" Chouinard stood up, and for a moment Cardinal thought he was going to hit him; his predecessor would have. But Chouinard merely gripped the edge of the desk and took several deep breaths.

"So who'd they bring down on you?" Cardinal said. "I'm assuming somebody pretty heavy."

"It's not a matter of who, it's a matter of who's right."

"Who'd they bring down on you?"

"You were out of line arresting a CSIS agent, and the Ottawa office saw fit to point that out to me."

"Ottawa. Well, that should tell you something. Squier works out of Toronto. Which makes you wonder what Ottawa is trying to hide."

"They're preserving their jurisdiction over cases that involve terrorism. It's not just their right. It's their duty. You're forgetting about the CADS base."

"I told you: CADS security has no record of any breaches. Squier made all of that up. And I don't believe he was connected with any American groups. If there's any terrorism involved in this case it happened in

Quebec more than thirty years ago. Surely our duty to catch murderers trumps that one." Cardinal opened the door. "If I rush, I might be able to arrest him again before he gets out of town."

"Don't even think of it, Cardinal. They will come down on you from a very great height if you do! Do the words 'false arrest' mean anything to you?"

Cardinal could hear the detective sergeant's voice all the way to the ground floor.

He actually had no intention of chasing down Squier again. He drove to the nearest Country Style and bought himself a coffee, then sat in his car, sipping it, while he tried to calm down. Last night's rain had added another layer of ice to everything it touched. All the cars in the lot looked laminated, except where scrapers had been applied to scratch out some visibility.

A barrel-chested man with no hair whatsoever got out of a four-by-four and headed for the Country Style entrance. Cardinal thought for a moment it was Kiki B., and all his reflexes went on high alert. But the man turned slightly as he opened the door, and Cardinal saw that it was not Kiki. He tried to forget his fear—and his anger at Chouinard—and to focus instead on the things that needed to be done.

DELORME WAS WRITING UP her report on Craig Simmons. The difficulty was how to word it so that the corporal was thoroughly cleared without mentioning the sexual angle.

"Boo!"

"Very funny, Szelagy. One day, you're going to do that and you're going to get shot."

"You looked so intense, I couldn't resist." Szelagy hung his coat over the back of his chair and sat down heavily. Delorme liked Szelagy, but sometimes she wished his desk was in another room.

"Just wanted to tell you," he said. "I'm striking out big time on Dr. Cates's neighbors. I swear everybody in that building is either on vacation or away on business. Pretty upscale place, I guess. Super tells me it's owned by Paul Laroche."

Delorme swiveled around to face him. "Really? Paul Laroche?"

"Yeah. Why 'really'?"

"Well, Laroche is a pretty big deal—in the francophone community, anyway. Did anybody talk to him yet?"

"You think we should? It's not like he lives there."

Delorme dialed Cardinal's cell-phone number. When he answered, she said, "Are you still feeling sorry for yourself?"

"Yes, as a matter of fact."

"Well, why don't we go talk to Paul Laroche? He owns the building Winter Cates lived in."

"That doesn't mean he knew her."

"We won't know till we ask."

"You forget—I'm not working the Cates case, remember?"

"No, but you're working security for Laroche's fund-raiser. Can't hurt to talk to the guy."

THEY MET OUTSIDE Laroche Real Estate, which was located in a beautifully re-stored Edwardian house on MacIntosh with porthole windows and an ornate L-shaped verandah. A glossy young woman directed them to the Mantis campaign headquarters a few doors down. It was a converted store-front that had been vacant for years, the interior furnished with old metal desks and what looked like a hundred phones. Many of these were manned by middle-aged housewives, but there was also a platoon of eager-looking young men in shirtsleeves. It was one of these, a kid no more than eighteen, who went to fetch Laroche. So young, Cardinal thought, and so conservative.

"Detective Cardinal," Laroche said when he came out. "How nice to see you again." He handed a stack of paper to a pimply assistant and said, "These are fine."

Cardinal introduced Delorme.

"The notorious Detective Delorme," Laroche said with a smile. "I'll have to watch what I say."

He led them back to an ugly little cubicle with cheap pine paneling and metal bookshelves full of videotapes. One wall was dominated by a huge poster of a smiling Premier Mantis standing in front of the Ontario flag. On the windowsill, a combined TV/VCR was playing a tape of Mantis joking with reporters outside Queen's Park; the sound was off. A snapshot on a bookshelf showed Laroche and Mantis dressed in hunting gear, grinning amid brilliant fall foliage.

The only seating consisted of task chairs rolled up against a table with three computers and telephones on it.

"Have a seat," Laroche said. "I don't imagine you're used to such luxury."

"No, I feel right at home," Cardinal said.

"You've met with Ed Beacom, I take it. Have you worked out the security arrangements?"

"We'll be meeting with Ed soon," Cardinal said. "That isn't actually what we came to talk about."

"Oh?"

Cardinal looked at Delorme: It's your case.

"Mr. Laroche," Delorme said. "Did you know Winter Cates?"

"The young woman who was murdered? I assume the reason you're asking is because she lived in one of my buildings."

"Did you know her?"

"I met her once. I happened to be at the Twickenham the day she moved in. Lovely young woman. Good doctor, too, from what I hear. It's a terrible crime."

"When you met her, was there anything about her that gave you cause for concern?"

"I'm not sure what you mean."

"Perhaps there was something unusual on her rental application. Or maybe there was someone with her . . ."

"Just a couple of moving men, I think."

"And you never saw her again."

"I own a lot of buildings. I don't manage them day-to-day."

"I know," Delorme said. "I used to be one of your tenants."

"Really?" Laroche said. "Which building?"

"The Balmoral, over on MacPherson. Not for long, though."

"Well, I'm sorry we didn't keep you."

"Too expensive. The city doesn't pay me enough."

Laroche laughed. He said something in French that Cardinal didn't catch, and Delorme said something back. Cardinal sensed that she found Laroche attractive, even though he must have had twenty-something years on her. Perhaps it was the dark good looks, graying at the edges. Or perhaps it was the self-assurance that wafted around him like expensive aftershave.

"I'm glad you came by," Laroche said. "I was going to call R. J. and run an idea by him. It's the first time one of my tenants has been murdered, and I have to say I don't like it one bit. I was wondering if a reward would be any use. Understand," he said, touching Delorme's sleeve, "I don't want to blunder in where I'm not wanted. I know sometimes rewards can help, and if that's the case with this matter, then I'd be prepared to put up twenty thousand or so."

Delorme looked at Cardinal. Cardinal just shrugged; it was her call.

"It's very generous of you," Delorme said. "But it's early days, yet. What makes you think we wouldn't catch the killer without a reward?"

"I don't doubt your competence, Detective. After Mayor Wells—not to mention the Windigo case—who could? It's just that Dr. Cates was a young woman, full of promise."

"And she was your tenant."

"This would be entirely anonymous, of course. But as I say, I don't want to interfere if you think it won't help."

Delorme glanced at Cardinal and back to Laroche. "My feeling is, it's too early. This isn't a case where we suspect a group of people. If it was a gang thing, or a drug thing, I would say go for it. You get one of them to turn on the others, it's the fastest way to make your case. But we're looking at a one-off crime, here. So I don't think it would do much good—unless you're offering the reward to the killer for turning himself in."

Laroche smiled. "Not what I had in mind, Detective. It must serve you well in your line of work, that sense of humor."

Delorme shrugged. "You asked my opinion," she said. "That's it."

"Well, let me know if you change your mind," Laroche said. "It's an open offer."

"DO YOU THINK it was odd, him offering a reward?" Cardinal said when they were outside.

"Not really. That's the kind of guy he is. He's a real force in the francophone community—very active in the church and charities and so on. What I like about him, he never takes credit for anything."

"You just think he's sexy," Cardinal said.

"You have no idea what I think," Delorme said. But she didn't deny it, Cardinal noticed.

When he got back to the station, Cardinal went straight to the evidence room, where he signed out the box of Matlock-Shackley's personal effects that had been removed from the cabin at Loon Lodge. He took it back to his desk, where he proceeded to remove items in no particular order. He wasn't sure what he was looking for; it was just that, now that the dead man's identity had changed, the things he had left behind might look different, perhaps lead in new directions.

Cardinal pulled out a shaving kit, a compact silver case that unfolded into a mirror. A small metal handle screwed into separate razor or toothbrush heads. It had a pleasing precision about it, like the parts of a gun. He wasn't sure if the kit was expensive or not; he'd never seen one like it. The manufacturer's logo was engraved into the case, above the words MADE IN FRANCE. Of course, that didn't necessarily mean Shackley bought it there.

The question of price made him take a closer look at the clothes. He pulled out a Brooks Brothers blazer, shiny at the elbows, frayed at the cuffs. The two shirts also had good labels and were also exceedingly worn, as if Shackley hadn't bought anything new in twenty years. Cardinal pulled out a sock with a hole in the heel. Apparently the CIA's retirement plan was stingy.

He wished once again that they would find the damn car. There could be something crucial there. In fact, Shackley might have been murdered in the car. Why else would the killer take so much trouble to hide it or destroy it? Red Escort? Avis sticker? Why hadn't it turned up yet? He pulled the dead man's plane ticket from the box, New York return to Toronto, American Airlines, five hundred dollars. Shackley had booked the flight a month before, lots of advance notice; why had he paid so much for a coach fare?

Cardinal looked at the codes. Ah yes, no restrictions. Shackley wanted to be able to change his return date. Which suggested he hadn't been sure how long he was going to be here. Whatever he was working on, the outcome hadn't been certain.

And why had he been calling Montreal? Was there a connection there that had led him to Algonquin Bay?

Cardinal rubbed his forehead. He had the feeling there was some important deduction to be made here, that someone with a faster mind would be able to make right away, but it was beyond him. "I don't know," he muttered.

"Talking to yourself again?" Delorme said. She sat down next to him.

"Yeah. And it's not helping."

"What about the phone bills? You said he made some calls to Montreal?"

"They're all unlisted. The only number I got through to was something called the Beau Soleil Day Care Center."

"A sixty-year-old New Yorker, he's calling a Montreal day-care center?"

"I know. Musgrave's got their Montreal guys tracing the others."

He was telling Delorme about the negative he had found in Shackley's apartment when Paul Arsenault came in. Cardinal called across the squad room. "Hey, Arsenault. Did you develop that negative?"

"What's the matter? You don't check your inbox?" Arsenault grabbed a manila envelope out of Cardinal's interoffice mailbox and tossed it onto his desk. "And before you ask: No, there were no fingerprints on the negative."

Cardinal undid the clasp of the envelope and slid out two eight-by-twelve prints of the same photograph, handing one to Delorme. Black and white. A group shot of four young people: one woman, three men. Two of the men had long sideburns and mustaches; the third had a full beard. Cardinal held it up to the light. They looked happy, confident, grinning broadly for the camera, posed in front of two curtainless windows. Outside the windows, a view of trees and a church spire glinting in the sunlight.

"Pretty long hair," Delorme noted. She was peering nearsightedly at her copy. "And look at the shirts on the guys, those collars."

"Could be from the seventies," Cardinal said.

"They look like a bunch of lumberjacks, except for the girl."

"Hey, everybody." Ken Szelagy stuck his head in the door, yelling over the top of the cubicles. He was holding a cell phone to one ear. "Time to saddle up. Sounds like we've got the car."

THE RED FORD ESCORT was at the bottom of a disused quarry just off Highway 17. It had been found by a hiking enthusiast named Vince Carey. He had a completely shaved head and a small tattoo of an eagle at the top of his neck.

"I was disgusted," he told Cardinal. "I mean, you can't just dump a car in the middle of the forest, even if it is a former quarry."

"What made you come hiking through here in the middle of winter?"

"Well, it's so beautiful with the ice over everything. And this area used to be kinda cool, you know? Last time I was through here—must've been about three years ago—runoff had formed a natural reservoir, almost a tiny lake, up to about there." He pointed to a moss-green line in the side of the granite cliffs.

"Did you see anyone else in the area today?"

"Not a soul. Nice and quiet." Carey ran a hand over his scalp. "When I saw the water was gone, I thought I'd climb along the side of the cliff. Didn't expect to see a damn car at the bottom. Pissed me off. So when I climbed back up to the highway later, I called Natural Resources to tell 'em about it, but they told me if it was a vehicle I should call you guys. Which is what I did."

"Okay, thanks for your help, Mr. Carey," Cardinal said. "We'll call you if we need anything more."

"My pleasure." He looked down the cliff to where Szelagy, Arsenault, and Collingwood were crawling around the overturned car and back to Cardinal. "Sure are a lot of you for one abandoned car, aren't there?"

"We like to be thorough."

Cardinal made his way down the rocks with extreme care, wary of the icy glaze. Thinking, This could be a gold mine. Finally the luck might be turning his way.

The car lay on its back, nose first in about three feet of water. Most of the roof had been crushed level with the rest of the body, and one wheel was missing entirely.

"Looks promising," Arsenault said. "We can see an exit mark where a bullet went through the passenger-side door."

"What about the interior?" Cardinal said. "Has the water destroyed everything?"

"Way it stands now, the water's barely into the cabin. We don't want to get too close, though, in case we shift the weight and tip it over. It may have washed away some hair and fiber, but if there's any blood by that exit mark, it should be still dry. The hard part's going to be getting the car out. Tow truck's not going to work."

Cardinal looked from the wreck up to the top of the cliff, a distance of at least seventy-five feet that consisted almost entirely of jagged granite. "Don Deckard," he said. "He's the only guy."

THEY HEARD THE CRANE before they saw it. First there was a rumble in the earth, and then the grinding of gears, and finally the sound of a massive combustion engine straining to conquer a hill. Then the machine itself appeared, a colossal vehicle consisting almost entirely of huge wheels. On its back, it carried the steel columns of the crane, now folded up like a boy's construction toy. It stopped at the crest of the hill and Don Deckard jumped down from the cab.

Deckard looked like a dinosaur from the 1960s who had been somehow propelled against his will into the next century. He wore black jeans with studs up the outside seams and a beaded buckskin jacket with an elaborate fringe. His graying hair was tied back in a ponytail, and his eyes were bright red as if he'd just smoked a joint.

"Hey, man." He gave Cardinal a high five; they'd worked together a few times over the years. "Long time no see. What have you got for me?"

Cardinal led him down toward the car.

"Where does he live?" Szelagy said to Arsenault. "Woodstock?"

"You don't know Deckard? This guy's a legend. See that little item, there?"

Arsenault pointed to the crane. Even folded up the thing looked the length of a small high-rise. "It's worth about half a million dollars. Sank in Lake Superior ten years ago—I forget what they were doing with it. Anyway, the company that owned it wrote it off as a complete loss. Even the insurance company wrote it off. But Deckard went out there with about six guys and a barge and hauled that thing out of three hundred feet of ice-cold water."

It took Deckard just under an hour to get his crane set up and in position. Then the beam swung out over the quarry and lowered a steel cable with a canvas sling on the end. Giant airbags intended for use in raising sunken vessels were wedged between the car and the rocks and then inflated to stop the car from shifting. The sling was slipped into position, and a few moments later the car was pulled high into the air above the gorge.

In the cab of the crane, Deckard pulled his levers and spun his wheels until the car settled, still upside down, on the back of a flatbed truck.

Deckard stepped out of his cab, and all four cops applauded. He bowed deeply and jumped down from the crane. He gave Cardinal another high five. "Piece of cake, man. Piece of cake."

Arsenault and Collingwood were already on the back of the flatbed. They used a "jaws of life" machine to pry open a space between the crushed roof and the seats.

"Windows were all open when it went over," Arsenault said. "Clearly the guy thought he was going to sink it. Probably came here at night and sent it over the cliff, thinking the water was deeper."

Arsenault and Collingwood found several items of limited interest: a blurry rental agreement in the name of Howard Matlock, a pair of aviator clip-on sunglasses, and an empty Coke can still in the cup holder. These and the entire car would be fumed for prints when they had dried off.

"It's actually the passenger we want to focus on," Cardinal said. "We know a fair bit about the victim and nothing about who killed him."

Collingwood was going over the back of the passenger seat with a pair of tweezers. He turned to Cardinal and emitted a single word. "Blood."

"On the passenger side? You're sure?"

Collingwood didn't reply. He pulled a carpet-cutter from his toolkit and peeled away the seat cover, exposing the padding. There was no mistaking the brownish stain beneath.

"We don't want to wait ten days for DNA results," Cardinal said. "Is there any way in the meantime we can be sure this is from the passenger and not the driver?"

"We can type them right now," Arsenault said. "It's possible they're the same type, but it's worth a shot, no?"

Arsenault retrieved a handheld device from the ident van. For the next fifteen minutes he and Collingwood labored over the stains. Cardinal waited, staring across the lake at the leaden sky. Mountains of cloud were massing on the horizon, threatening even more rain, which would mean even more ice.

Arsenault came up behind him, footsteps crunching on the ice. "Driver's O-negative," he said.

"And the passenger?"

"We've got the passenger, too. AB-negative."

Cardinal whipped out his cell phone and called Delorme. "Didn't you tell me the blood you found in Dr. Cates's office was AB-negative?"

"That's right. We got it off the paper from the examining table."

"This could link the two cases," Cardinal said. "The killer shoots Shackley but he gets shot, too. The bullet's still in him, but he can't go to a hospital because they have to report gunshot wounds. So he grabs Dr. Cates and forces her to treat him."

"Then kills her to keep her quiet. It's looking good. And I've got some other news for you."

"Oh?"

"Musgrave stopped by. You're not gonna believe who Shackley was calling."

CHOUINARD LISTENED TO Cardinal's proposal with no sign of excitement or even interest. When Cardinal had finished laying it out, Chouinard responded in the tranquil tones that made him sound so much more intelligent than he was.

"Clearly, you have to go to Montreal, no question about that. I'm not so sure about Delorme, though."

"Detective Delorme," Cardinal said, "how would you rate my French?"

"What French? I've heard you, and it's not French. It's more like a kind of Frankenstein sort of . . ."

"What are you so worried about, Cardinal? Everybody in Montreal speaks English, you know."

"That's not true," Delorme said. "That's not even close to true."

"Well, maybe it's changed since the last time I was there. Take a dictionary with you. I'm just not persuaded your two cases are the same killer."

"D.S., think about it," Cardinal said. "Cates is the second dead body in the woods in three days. Shouldn't we assume it's part of the Shackley murder until there's some reason to think otherwise?"

"We've got lots of reasons to think otherwise," Chouinard said. "One body's a man, the other's a woman. One's eaten by bears, one not. One's a visitor, one lived here in town . . ."

"Wait a minute," Delorme said. "What are the chances of two killers in a town this size having AB-negative blood?"

"Blood type is not a positive ID."

"Suppose he shoots Shackley and gets wounded himself," Cardinal said. "A small wound. There wasn't much blood on the passenger side."

"I get that. He needs a doctor. But why feed Shackley to the bears and not do the same with the doctor?"

"There's a number of possibilities. Number one: I think we can agree it's unlikely that Dr. Cates was murdered because of any mob involvement. If she was killed by the same person, that means Bressard wasn't hired by Leon Petrucci to dispose of Shackley's body, he was hired by someone else *pretending* to be Petrucci. Petrucci's well-known in this town. A lot of people know he can't talk, that he writes notes. It all came out when Bressard was on trial for assault years ago—it was all over *The Algonquin Lode*. Maybe our killer figures he can't fool Bressard twice. Maybe he doesn't want to *pay* him twice."

"In any case," Delorme said. "He gets wounded Saturday night in the altercation with Shackley. Maybe he thinks he can tough it out. Maybe he thinks he can live with it. By Monday it's hurting like hell or maybe it's still bleeding. Now he knows for sure he needs a doctor."

"Why Dr. Cates?"

"We don't know that yet," Delorme said.

"But you've checked out her patients. You've checked out her colleagues."

"Which is why I should go to Montreal with Cardinal. Two of us will be able to follow up on those phone numbers faster than one. And if we find out who Shackley was after, we'll know who the killer is."

"God, I hate decisions," Chouinard said. "Wait till you have to worry about budgets and you'll know how it feels."

"So I go too, right?"

"Don't you dare spend one minute longer than necessary."

19

RCMP HEADQUARTERS, "C" Division, Mon-treal. The atmosphere calm and businesslike, everyone polite. Cardinal wondered if he had wandered into the wrong building by mistake. He and Delorme had just come from checking in at the Regent Hotel—a tiny concrete box utterly without character, next to the expressway—and the comparatively plush interior of C Division was a welcome change.

"This place is more like an insurance company than a police station," Delorme said.

They'd been given a small interview room for their first meeting with Sergeant Raymond Ducharme. Cardinal figured Ducharme had to be sixty-five if a day, what with all the lines in his ruddy face. He had the body of a swimmer and the head of a philosopher—wide brow, sharp features, and thin, sarcastic mouth. His teeth looked too good to be real.

"So, you're friends of Malcolm Musgrave," Ducharme said. His French Canadian accent was bracing. "I've known him since he was that high." He made a gesture slightly above knee-level.

"Really?" Cardinal said. "I can't imagine Malcolm Musgrave 'that high.'"

"For sure," Ducharme said. "I used to work with his dad, eh? Back in the good old days. His dad was one of the best. Please, have a seat. Can I get you something to drink? Coke? Coffee? You're sure? All right. Now, I've had a chance to take a look at the photograph you sent me, but let me start by asking how much you remember about the October Crisis."

"October 1970," Cardinal said. "A couple of guys were kidnapped by the FLQ, Raoul Duquette, a provincial cabinet minister, was killed. That's about it."

"I was a little kid," Delorme said. "I don't remember anything."

Sergeant Ducharme raised a pedagogical finger. "Time for a refresher, then."

Cardinal took out his pen.

"It's La Belle Province, late 1960s. We've got strikes left and right: The cab drivers, the students, even the cops, they go on strike. Some of the demonstrators, they get out of hand and heads get broken, one or two individuals get killed. Out of this anarchy rises a group known as the Front de libération du Québec, or FLQ for short. The FLQ starts putting bombs in mailboxes in Montreal and Quebec City. What do they want? They want Quebec to separate from Canada and become its own country.

"Other organizations want the same thing. The Parti Quebecois, for example. The difference is that the PQ aim to do it through the democratic process. The FLQ don't give a damn about the democratic process. They want their own country now, and they're going to get it by violence.

"So bombs start going off. Mostly they're small, and mostly no one gets hurt. But cases of dynamite keep getting stolen from construction sites around the city. In fact, a lot of the dynamite came from the construction of Expo '67, which was supposed to celebrate a hundred years of Canadian nationhood. Some people, they thought this showed the FLQ had a sense of humor. What it really showed was that some of the FLQ worked in construction.

"Anyway, they start putting bombs in mailboxes. Some in Quebec City, some in Ottawa, but mostly they put them in mailboxes on the charming streets of Westmount, home of the wealthier Anglos in Montreal. Also the home of yours truly: RCMP C Division." He waved a hand at the window, where sparse flakes of snow drifted over the green slope of Mount Royal.

"But then people start getting killed or maimed. One of the men on our bomb squad had both his hands blown off trying to defuse a bomb. And a security guard died at a building the FLQ thought was empty. Champions of the working class, they call themselves, but I don't think the security guard's widow would agree. Anyway, by now we're going all-out to catch these bastards.

"October 5, 1970. The home of British Trade Consul Stuart Hawthorne. Doorbell rings, the maid answers. There's a man at the door with a long package. 'Birthday present for Mr. Hawthorne,' he says. The maid moves to open the door and suddenly four men are in the hallway, the box is open, and a machine gun is pointing in her face. They drag Mr. Hawthorne out of the bathroom where he's shaving, and less than five minutes later he's blindfolded in the backseat of a car.

"Communiqués are sent, demands are made. The so-called Liberation cell of the FLQ has a lot of demands, but the biggest ones are freedom for twenty-three so-called political prisoners, five hundred thousand dollars in what they refer to as a voluntary tax, and safe conduct to Cuba for the kidnappers and the freed prisoners. Anything less will result in the execution of Mr. Hawthorne."

"Why did they kidnap someone from another country?" Cardinal asked. "Why not go for someone closer to home?"

"That's exactly what other members in the FLQ asked themselves. The federal government is still putting together its kidnap task force when another cell strikes, the Chénier cell. This time they kidnap Raoul Duquette, provincial Minister of Education.

"The government stalls for time. I was with the Security Service back then, and we set up a Combined Anti-Terrorist Squad—the CAT Squad—made up of Mounties, Provincial Police, and the Montreal Police. Within forty-eight hours we knew who the kidnappers were. What we didn't know was where they were. I was convinced then and I'm convinced today that if we'd had another couple of days, we could've found them. But people were panicking.

"The federal government—Pierre Trudeau—is ready to call in the army. Literally. All he needs is a letter from the mayor of Montreal and the premier of Quebec asking for help dealing with an 'apprehended insurrection.' Those are the actual words required by the War Measures Act. Well, he has a minister dictate the letters, and sure enough they have the signatures two hours later. That night, October 16, 1970, at midnight, he declares war measures in force.

"Suddenly we don't need warrants anymore. We don't have to lay charges for thirty days. We round up everybody, and I mean everybody, from cab drivers to nightclub singers—anybody who ever said anything nice about separation. We lock 'em up and we ask 'em who they know.

"The embarrassing truth is, they don't know anybody. Of the five hundred and forty people we rounded up, only thirty were charged with anything, and only a dozen were convicted, mostly for stupid weapons offenses. We did not find any huge cache of arms, we did not find any gigantic network of terrorists."

"Suspending civil rights?" Delorme said. "The Americans didn't even do that after September eleventh. For immigrants, maybe, but not for citizens."

"You're right," Ducharme said. "The Trudeau government wanted to send a message to the terrorists that violent acts would cost them far more than they could possibly be worth. The Chénier cell understood it differently. They understood it to mean that all the negotiations of the past few days had been completely phony. They gave their answer the next day: They murdered Raoul Duquette."

"But you got the diplomat out," Cardinal said. "Stuart Hawthorne?"

"We got Hawthorne out. It took two months, but we got him out alive. His kidnappers went to Cuba, then to Paris, and eventually most of them came back here and served some time—not much—and then settled down.

"The people who killed Duquette were caught and sent to prison. Unfortunately, we couldn't prove which one of them did the actual killing, so they only did twelve years.

"Which brings us to your photograph."

Ducharme held up the group photograph Cardinal had found in Shackley's files.

"The one on the left with the curly hair is Daniel Lemoyne, leader of the Chénier cell. The young man on the right is Bernard Theroux. In his initial confession he said that he held Duquette down while Lemoyne strangled him. He later recanted this confession, and his lawyer got it thrown out of court."

"What about the young woman?" Cardinal said. "She looks like a teenager."

"She must have been a fringe member, if she was a member at all. I don't have anything on her yet. Same with the other young man, the bearded one in the striped shirt. I know the faces of the major players by heart, but these two . . ."

"They're not members of the Chénier cell?"

"I don't think so. Not that I recall. I'm sorry. Normally, we'd be able to come up with that information right away, but this was long before the age of computerization here, and the files are in transit back from Ottawa. CSIS grabbed them a while back. It's like the Kennedy assassination, you know—every five years some wiseacre decides it's time to revisit the October Crisis. We should have everything back in a day or two, and then you'll get your IDs."

"It's hard to believe this stuff," Delorme said. "It seems so crazy now."

"Really?" Sergeant Ducharme said. "Just in the past year we've had the French Self-Defense League putting bombs in front of coffee shops and restaurants because they have signs in English. Passions run high, even today."

"And the other photograph?" Cardinal pointed to a picture of Miles Shackley circa 1970. Musgrave had sent it to him and to Ducharme. When Cardinal had asked how he had got hold of it, Musgrave had said, "I'm a Mountie, Cardinal. I have superhuman powers."

"Miles Shackley was an American who worked here around the time of the crisis. We had a few CIA people working with us on the CAT Squad. Well, don't look like that, it was perfectly natural. They had the Black Panthers and the Weathermen to deal with, and terrorism was becoming an international problem. It would have been stupid not to have them involved.

"Personally I didn't care for Shackley. Not that it mattered—I was very low on the totem pole. He was working with Lieutenant Fougère and Corporal Sauvé—Fougère died a few years ago, unfortunately, but no doubt you'll be talking to Sauvé. They were the top guys, the three of them, and they got along fine. I don't remember anything else about Shackley, and the file is of course with the others, but I hope to have it back in a few days."

"What was Shackley's function in the CAT Squad?" Cardinal said.

"Liaison, probably. Maybe more, but I don't know. He would have given us help tracing financing, tracing connections between various groups. Oh, and I believe he was following a particular Black Panther who was hiding out up here. The FLQ were getting guns from the Panthers in return for sheltering them when they came up here on the run."

"And Musgrave told us about the phone numbers," Cardinal said.

"Yes, the phone numbers. Now, there it gets interesting."

COMPARED TO WHAT WAS happening in Algonquin Bay, Montreal and environs were enjoying a normal winter. The snow looked about three feet deep, and at corners and intersections it was heaped so high Cardinal had to nose the car out into the intersection to see what was coming down the street.

But it was getting warmer here, too. The branches hung heavy and the icicles dripped, and as Cardinal drove along Highway 20 toward the Eastern Townships, the light snow had turned to drizzle. The damp painted the trunks of the trees deep black, so that the landscape, once he was beyond the city limits, was at once both wintry and misty, the blacks and whites stark. The sky was so dark it gave the day a feel of twilight, even though Cardinal had just finished lunch.

He and Delorme had divided the work between them: Delorme had headed into town to talk to a former FLQ member, and Cardinal was on his way to interview Robert Sauvé, former second-in-command of the CAT Squad. Sauvé's was the first number Shackley had called from New York, and he had called it several times.

"Here's what you have to know about Sauvé," Sergeant Ducharme had said. "A few years after the October Crisis, on June 13, 1973, to be exact, about three thirty in the morning, the citizens of Westmount were woken up by a loud blast. A bomb had gone off outside the home of one Joseph P. Felstein, founder of Felstein supermarkets. Blew out windows along the entire street.

"Police arrive and find a hole in the ground, still smoking, and a trail of blood leading them to a car parked half a block away. Slumped in the front seat they find a guy with his hands torn up, half his face blown away, and his guts hanging out.

"They take him to the hospital, and the guy goes into surgery. For a while it looks like he isn't going to make it, but call it a miracle of Montreal medicine. The guy lives. Of course his jaw is wired up, fingers are missing, his left eye is gone, but he's alive. Unfortunately, he isn't talking. Won't even tell anyone his name.

"It doesn't take the Montreal police long to find out. The car was a rental, but they trace it to Corporal Robert Sauvé of the Combined Anti-Terrorist Squad. You remember when the Mounties got hauled on the carpet by the Keable Commission? We burned a barn the FLQ was using for meetings, we raided René Levesque's offices for mailing lists, planted illegal wiretaps. Very bad boys, the Keable Commission said."

"I remember," Cardinal said. "It was on the news every night for months."

"Corporal Robert Sauvé was the reason it happened. If it hadn't been for him, the Mounties would still be running the Security Service in this country. CSIS would never have been invented. For weeks, Sauvé doesn't say anything. The Montreal cops charge him with everything they can think of and still he doesn't cooperate.

"The judge didn't like his attitude. He was found guilty on all counts and the judge hands him twelve years. Twelve years for blowing himself up and breaking a few windows. Suddenly Sauvé finds his voice.

"'Twelve years,' he says. 'Twelve years, and nobody got hurt except me. I did far worse things when I was in the antiterrorist squad. Far worse.' And that's what started the ball rolling. The end result of all the investigations and commissions was the creation of CSIS. A lot of good men lost their jobs. Alan Musgrave, for one."

"Musgrave's father?" Delorme said.

"Alan got the boot. It didn't help his drinking problem, and six months later he killed himself. Broke my heart, that did."

"Jesus," Cardinal said. "No wonder Musgrave can't stand CSIS."

"There's lots of reasons to be upset with CSIS, but that's a pretty good one."

"I still don't understand," Cardinal said. "Why did Sauvé blow up the department-store guy?"

"They can't be sure, because the son of a bitch, he never cooperated. They think it was a freelance job he did for the mob. The Cotroni family controlled a rival chain of grocery stores and they wanted to send a message. Sauvé was the messenger."

"A pretty drastic career change," Delorme said. "How do you go from working for the RCMP to working for the mafia?"

"You'll have to ask Mr. Sauvé."

SAUVÉ'S CONNECTION to the mafia made Cardinal wonder if there wouldn't turn out to be a link to Leon Petrucci. Somehow, he just couldn't see a small-time mobster known mostly for his grip on Algonquin Bay's coin-operated soda machines suddenly ordering the murder of an American and a doctor. Nevertheless, he decided to keep an open mind on the matter.

He turned off the highway and followed a side road past increasingly desperate-looking farms for several miles. Then a crooked sign pointed the way to Séguinville, which turned out to be not a ville at all, but a cross-roads. A light drizzle fell across deserted fields. Sauvé's place was another two miles down the jagged—and barely plowed—road that zigzagged off to the north.

The house itself was all but hidden behind a stand of birches inter-woven with tangled brush. It appeared to be a two-story structure from the road, but on pulling into the appalling driveway, Cardinal saw that half of the upper story had fallen away. In summer, it would look even worse; winter had softened the broken edges of the walls with hillocks of snow.

A pickup truck, much dented, was parked in front of a skeletal barn, the last standing wall of which consisted of a rusted sign advertising Laurentide ale. Beyond this, a boat was balanced on a hoist, its prow and bridge rounded with snow. It was not the type of boat one commonly saw in a driveway or backyard, not a pleasure craft. It was a tugboat, seventy years old at least, and yet it was tilted skyward as if breasting the waves of an invisible river. Cardinal wouldn't have trusted the seams on land, nevermind the St. Lawrence.

Robert Sauvé himself was out of the house and in the driveway before Cardinal had even stepped out of the car. The former corporal held a twelve-gauge shotgun at gut level. Even from this distance, the left half of his face had a caved-in look, just like his house. One eye squinted at Cardinal, the other—the glass one—maintained an unsettling calm. He didn't have a beard, but it had been many days since his face had seen a razor. He said one word, and it was a challenge, not a greeting. *"Bonjour."*

"Sorry," Cardinal said in French. "My French is not great. Do you speak English?"

The former corporal didn't answer. Cardinal was wishing Delorme was there. He tried English.

"Would you mind pointing that thing away for a minute?"

The shotgun stayed where it was.

Cardinal tried French again. "Listen. I'm not here to make trouble. I'm an Ontario policeman working on an Ontario—" He couldn't remember the word for "case" and settled for "business." *I'm working on an Ontario business.* Sure, that'll work wonders.

"You RCMP?" The words were heavily accented, but at least they were English.

"Algonquin Bay. Local," Cardinal said, keeping his hands well away from his body. "You want to see the badge? I'll have to reach into my back pocket."

"Very slow."

Cardinal reached back and extracted the ID folder from his pocket. He held it out in front of him, and Sauvé took two steps forward, squinting at it with his one good eye.

"What's an Ontario cop want with me?" The left side of Sauvé's mouth stayed frozen. His voice sounded unused, but perhaps it was just the English that was rusty.

"I've got a dead American on my hands, an ex-CIA employee named Miles Shackley, who was in Quebec about thirty years ago. Nineteen-seventy, to be exact. He was active during the October Crisis and we think his murder may have something to do with that. We also know he was recently in contact with you."

"So? An ex-CIA employee phones an ex-RCMP employee, it's not illegal."

"I need to know what he wanted. Can we go in out of the cold for a few minutes, Mr. Sauvé?" Cardinal rubbed his hands together briskly. "I'm not used to these Quebec winters, and it's a little damp out here."

"It's not cold," Sauvé said, not moving.

"You worked on the CAT Squad. And you worked with Shackley."

"I worked with a lot of CIA people. The day Hawthorne got kidnapped they were coming out of the walls. Thirty or forty of them at headquarters alone."

"What was Miles Shackley's function on the CAT Squad?"

"I don't remember."

"Take your time."

"I don't need time." Sauvé turned his back and limped toward his ruin of a house.

"Mr. Sauvé, wait. I need your help."

Sauvé didn't even turn around.

"Don't you remember what it's like? Being neck-deep in a case that isn't going anywhere? I'm looking for one little break that could make all the difference."

Now, Sauvé turned with great difficulty and faced him again. "I talked to every commission in the country. I told them everything I knew. And still I spent twelve years of my life in prison. A former Mountie. What kind of treatment do you think I got there? You think I have any affection for law enforcement?"

"I have nothing to do with the people who put you away. I'm just trying to break a case in a small Ontario city."

Sauvé hauled himself up the sagging steps of the porch. As he bent to open the door, his teeth gleamed in the light. It might have been because of his disfigurement, the skin pulled tight across the reconstructed jaw, but Cardinal suspected that former Corporal Robert Sauvé was laughing.

20

"BERNARD THEROUX," Sergeant Ducharme had said. "The second phone number belongs to Bernard Theroux. In nineteen seventy, nineteen years old. Member of the Chénier cell and, along with Daniel Lemoyne, served twelve years in the penitentiary for the kidnapping of Raoul Duquette. Married to one Françoise Coutrelle, a fringe member of the FLQ, a supporter rather than an actual terrorist. She was never charged with anything. They were occasional associates of one Simone Rouault, but we'll talk about Simone Rouault later.

"As far as we know, Bernard and Françoise Theroux no longer have any connection to terrorist activities, or criminal activities of any kind. Still, this is definitely their phone number, and you have to wonder why your American is calling them three weeks before he turns up dead."

YOU CERTAINLY DO, Delorme was thinking half an hour later. She was trying to steer her way through the middle of Montreal without getting in a multi-car pileup. The rain was not heavy, but apparently it was enough to sow confusion among the local motorists.

At the next stoplight, she dialed Szelagy on her cell phone.

"What did you come up with on Dr. Choquette? Was he where he says he was on Monday night?"

"This guy, I'm telling you. He oughta teach a course at alibi school," Szelagy said. "Not only does he have three witnesses who were playing bridge with him. All three of them are like gold-plated. One's the head of the Ontario Hospital, one's a trustee on the school board, and the other one's local director of the Children's Aid Society. Put them in a room, you've got an instant board of directors."

"You talked to all three of them independently?"

"All three. They were all so polite, too. I wish my friends had manners like that."

"Fat chance. Your friends are all cops."

Delorme's cell phone rang before she had even put it away, Malcolm Musgrave.

"So, are you finished harassing my detachment now, Sergeant Delorme? Or will you be coming to interview all of us?"

"Don't give me a hard time about Simmons. You know I had to check him out."

"And—don't tell me, let me guess—he turned out to be neither a kidnapper nor a murderer, correct? I mean, I do try to keep kidnappers and murderers off my team if I can help it."

"Craig Simmons is no longer a suspect in this case," Delorme said. "Let's leave it at that."

"And we're all going to be very circumspect about how we handle an RCMP officer's private life, aren't we?"

"I'm not sure what you mean."

A man in a black Saab swooped in front of her, making an illegal left turn—and had the gall to curse at her. She had an impulse to pull him over, not that she had any jurisdiction in Montreal.

"I think you know exactly what I mean," Musgrave said. "There's not a police officer alive who wants their private life made public—not me, not your partner, and not Craig Simmons—or perhaps you're some kind of saintly exception."

"You're telling me you know? I mean, you know about the corporal's—"

"Stop right there, Delorme. I know everything I need to know about my men—and women, for that matter. I'm just underlining a mutual understanding that I hope we have. Do I need to say anything more?"

"No," Delorme said. "You've made yourself perfectly clear, as always."

"Enjoy Montreal," Musgrave said. "Nice town."

The Theroux address was on St. Hubert Street in Villeray, almost the exact center of Montreal. Although the area was predominantly French, Delorme also noted signs in Italian, Portuguese, and Arabic. The pedestrians looked to be a mix of students and working class. Dusty old fabric stores alternated with new boutiques and tiny cafés.

Delorme parked the unmarked RCMP car in front of a ribbon shop. Number 7540, the address she was looking for, was half a block south, among a brood of small, square houses lined up as if for protection behind a Greek Orthodox church. She rang the doorbell, noting the two brass signs next to it. One said THEROUX, the other said BEAU SOLEIL. While she was waiting, it started to rain.

The door was answered by a plump, middle-aged woman with dark rings of curly hair framing her face. "Oui?"

"Madame Theroux?"

"Oui?"

Delorme told her in French that she was a police officer from northern Ontario in need of help on a case and that she believed Mr. Theroux could be of assistance. Shouts and chatter of little children rang out in the background. A small crash was followed by the howl of an outraged toddler.

"I'm sorry," the woman said. "My husband doesn't speak to police."

A small, lithe man with dark eyes and dark hair streaked with gray appeared behind her, putting on his coat. "Get lost," he snapped at Delorme. "You heard what my wife said."

"Nobody's after you," Delorme said. "I just need some information."

"Just some information? Is that all?" The man pushed by her and started down the stairs. "Information gets people killed."

He hopped into his truck and drove away.

"Sorry," the woman said. "But I did tell you . . ."

"Yes, you did," Delorme said. "May I perhaps use your phone to call a cab? My partner took the car."

The woman opened the door wider. Delorme entered a front hall that contained a piano and a dozen tiny plastic chairs. To the right, beyond a pair of French doors, a young woman in very tight jeans was leading a group of preschoolers in a round of "Bonhomme, Bonhomme."

"The phone's in the kitchen. This way."

Delorme disconnected the moment she dialed. Then, speaking directly into the dial tone, she ordered a cab. "How long? That's the best you can do? Yes I realize it's raining. All right. Thank you."

Mrs. Theroux was setting out a tray of apple juice and arrowroot biscuits, which she carried into an adjoining dining room. Everywhere the walls were decorated with children's drawings. Several carried declarations of preschool devotion: *"Je t'aime, Françoise!" "Ma deuxième mère,"* and the like with appropriate misspellings. The entire house smelled of soup and something baking. It was hard to imagine a terrorist living here, even a former terrorist.

"The cab is going to be half an hour, I'm afraid," Delorme said.

"It's always that way in the rain. Would you like some coffee?"

"Oh, no, that's all right. Please. Just ignore me."

"I can't ignore you, you're in my house. Have a coffee."

"Thank you. You're very kind."

Pouring the coffee, adding the milk, Françoise Theroux was the picture of domesticity—plump, almost matronly, the sort of woman that reporters interview when they want a mother's opinion on the local school board. The coffee was a dark aromatic roast without a trace of bitterness. Delorme could feel the caffeine illuminating strings of lights along her nerves.

"What time would be a good time to come back?" she said. "I'm afraid it's very important that I speak to your husband."

"Please don't come back." A shadow crossed the woman's face. "Bernard hasn't been involved with anything criminal for thirty years."

"I know. It's thirty years ago we need to talk about. The FLQ, the October Crisis."

"You mustn't come back. Bernard goes crazy whenever the police are around. It brings back that time and he just wants to forget. Maybe I can help you. You probably know I was part of the FLQ, too."

"But you were never charged with anything."

"No. Bernard kept me at arm's length from the more dangerous activities."

"I wonder if you can identify the people in these pictures for me." Delorme showed her the picture of Miles Shackley from his fake driver's license, and the file picture Musgrave had provided. "Can you tell me who this man is?"

"No. He doesn't look familiar. Who is he?"

"I'll come back to him. What about these people?"

Mrs. Theroux took the group picture from Delorme. "Oh, they look so young! They *were* young! That's Bernard in front—he would have been nineteen years old back then. My goodness, he's so skinny. That's Daniel Lemoyne on the left. The girl I don't know. The one on the end, my God, that's Yves Grenelle."

"Yves Grenelle?"

Mrs. Theroux's hand had risen to her mouth.

"Who is Yves Grenelle?"

"It's not him. I must have been mistaken."

"But you were certain it was Yves Grenelle. Why can't you tell me about him?"

"I just can't. Please. I can't help you any more."

"No, I have to ask you about this man." Delorme held up the 1970 picture of Shackley. "Does the name Miles Shackley mean anything to you?"

"No. And I don't recognize that person."

"There are two things you should know before you answer, Mrs. Theroux. The first is that this man called your house less than one month ago. The second is that he has been murdered."

Mrs. Theroux looked up at the ceiling for a few moments, breathing deeply. She got up and went into the other room, collecting cups and cookie plates. Childish voices called her name, begging her to come and draw with them. She came back into the kitchen and set the tray down on the counter, hard.

"Bernard never killed anyone," she said. "He had nothing to do with any murder."

"Excuse me, but your husband was convicted in the death of Raoul Duquette. He confessed to it."

"He was convicted for kidnapping, not for murder. And his confession was thrown out."

"Mrs. Theroux. A man who was known to be involved in the October Crisis called your house last month. That man is now dead. Your husband has been involved in a killing before; it's possible he is involved again."

"Listen to me: My husband never killed anyone. I repeat it for you. Please, take it down. Write it in your notebook, type it in your computer, carve it someplace—anyplace—where you will remember it, because this is God's truth: My husband never killed anyone."

"You're referring now to Raoul Duquette?"

Mrs. Theroux let out a long sigh and lowered herself to a chair. "Yes. I am referring to Raoul Duquette."

"The forensic evidence showed that he was strangled. Your husband said he held Duquette down while Daniel Lemoyne strangled him."

"You have a picture of Bernard. He was nineteen. He weighed one hundred and twenty pounds. Do you know how big Duquette was? He was six foot two, one hundred ninety pounds, a former football player. My husband did not hold him down."

"Mrs. Theroux, the minister's hands were tied. He'd been held prisoner for a week."

A small boy wandered into the kitchen, holding a piece of sketch paper before him like an offering. "Françoise, I made a picture for you."

"Oh, that's lovely, Michel." Mrs. Theroux said, bending low to examine the blue blur of watercolor. "Who is that in the picture?"

"It's my father. He's a policeman."

"In that case, you should show it to Officer Delorme, here—she's with the police, too."

The boy looked up at Delorme, eyes two pools of wonder. "You are a police?"

"Yes. I'm a police too."

"He probably hasn't seen a policewoman before. Robert, are you going to show the detective your lovely picture?"

The boy swiveled toward Delorme, holding the picture uncertainly. It was two swirls of blue and a slash of black.

"It's very good," Delorme said. "He looks like an excellent officer."

The boy turned back to Mrs. Theroux, picture forgotten.

"Françoise, will you read to us now?"

"In a little while, Michel." Mrs. Theroux closed the door after him. She offered Delorme more coffee, which was declined, poured herself another cup, and sat once more at the table, stirring it slowly. "I don't want you to come back here," she said finally. "Our peace here is too fragile, too hard-won. Certain memories can be like earthquakes. So, I will tell you everything I know, because I don't want you harassing my husband. And then I don't want you to come back."

"I don't know what you're going to tell me. I can't make any promises."

"I wouldn't believe them if you did. But I will tell you what really happened all those years ago, and then you won't ever have to come back. If you do, I will say nothing more. Nobody knows the real story. It was as if they'd already decided what the story was before they arrested anybody. But listen to me, and I will tell you the truth.

"The first thing you have to understand is the absolute loyalty we all had for one another. Everyone in the FLQ felt it—absolute and unshakeable—but Bernard and Daniel Lemoyne in particular. They met at a demonstration. We were always going to demonstrations in those days. At one of these—perhaps it was the one in support of the Seven-Up workers, I don't know, or perhaps the taxi drivers. In any case, Bernard was injured, bleeding from the head where some bastard cop had hit him with a billy club. Sorry, but . . ."

"It's all right. I don't have any love for violent cops."

"Anyway, there he is, bleeding in the back of the paddy wagon. Daniel Lemoyne tore up his own shirt to make a bandage."

"Comrades in arms," Delorme said.

"Comrades in arms. Exactly. They became like that." She held up two fingers, crossed. "Inseparable. But there isn't a day that goes by I wish they hadn't met. I don't know about Lemoyne—I think he would have been the same no matter who he was with, but I'm sure that Bernard would never have kidnapped anyone if he hadn't met Lemoyne. Bernard was always for group action, mobilizing the people. He wasn't one for individual plots. But somehow it became a shared madness, this kidnapping."

"A madness they shared with Yves Grenelle, no? Why has his name never come up before?"

"Yves Grenelle was never caught, never charged with anything." The woman's manner suddenly changed. She looked down at her hands as if she held between them a fragile screen on which the events of her youth played out. "That was part of the agreement, you understand."

"Agreement?"

"Among the members of the cell. It was like blood brothers. The agreement was that if the cops found them, anyone who got away was never to be mentioned—not to the cops, not to the press, not to anyone. It was to be as if he or she never existed.

"That's what happened with Yves Grenelle. He was not captured with the others. He disappeared off the face of the earth the day Raoul Duquette was killed. Nobody has heard from him since that day. Probably he went to France—a lot of people did when things got hot. Mostly they came back. But Grenelle was never seen again."

"How was he recruited, this Grenelle? Was he a friend of your husband? A friend of Lemoyne?"

"He must have been a friend of Lemoyne's. Bernard didn't know him. I think he was introduced to Lemoyne a year or two previously by Simone Rouault. That's who you should talk to if you want to know about recruitment. She was so beautiful, they could have made posters of her and the membership would have tripled overnight. She brought a lot of the young men in. She gave the revolution a pretty face, a beautiful mouth. And of course she fucked everybody in sight."

"I've heard the name. Were you close?"

"We were friendly. We didn't see much of her, because of the need to stay separate, but she was something. A real character." Mrs. Theroux shook her head, remembering. "She drank nothing but champagne. French champagne—Veuve Clicquot, that was it. And she was always smoking Gitanes. I hated those things. They smelled like cigars. I'm telling you, if you talk to Simone, take her a bottle of Veuve Clicquot and she'll tell you her life story."

"But Simone Rouault was with the Liberation cell, the cell that kidnapped Hawthorne, no? So she and Grenelle couldn't have met."

"Oh, but they could, you see. Grenelle was the contact between the cells. He moved back and forth. A big talker, Grenelle, always full of ideas, always wanting action, always wanting to move ahead. Bernard and even Lemoyne were, I don't know, more thoughtful."

"So, how did Grenelle avoid being caught?"

"Partly because of my husband. Bernard is a carpenter, like his father. Before they kidnapped Duquette, they had arranged another safe house as a fallback. A place on the South Shore. Bernard built a false wall inside a closet. That was the extent of their escape plan. It seems pitiful, in retrospect, but you see, they never intended to kill anyone, so they never planned an elaborate escape."

"That's not what the communiqués said. They threatened to execute Duquette from the first day."

"They were negotiating. Using their hostage for leverage. You don't believe me, but it's true—thirty years later I have no reason to lie. They were astounded by how the government reacted. Suspending civil rights. Calling out the army. Nobody saw that coming. Bernard and Daniel thought they had a pretty good chance of getting a couple of the political prisoners released. Nobody thought the government would let the hostages die. At worst, they figured they themselves would get transport to Cuba or Algeria or somewhere."

"You would have gone to Cuba with your husband?"

"Yes, of course. Algeria. Anywhere." Mrs. Theroux shrugged. "I was young."

"And you never believed they would kill anyone. Even when they kidnapped a provincial cabinet minister like Duquette?"

"No. It never occurred to me. Not for one second." She stood up and went to look out the window. Delorme thought it was only so she could turn away. "This taxi of yours is taking a long time."

"Yes. If they don't come in a few minutes I'll call again."

The door opened and a little girl came in, her face the image of tragedy. "Sasha spilled paint all over my picture."

"Well, that's a shame, Monique." Mrs. Theroux leaned forward and placed a hand on the girl's shoulder. "I'm sure he didn't mean to."

"He did! Sasha's mean!"

"Well, you go back and talk to Gabrielle about it. You can always draw another one, you know."

"I don't want to!"

"Well, you talk to Gabrielle about it."

Mrs. Theroux held the door open for her, and a gust of children's racket blew in from the other room. She sat across from Delorme again and stirred her coffee till Delorme thought it would evaporate.

"It never occurred to me that Bernard would be involved with a murder. I know my husband. I know him now, I knew him then. Blowing up statues, yes. Attacking corporations, yes—in the middle of the night, with no one around and a warning given. But to kill someone in cold blood. Never. It's just not in him."

She frowned and rubbed her forehead as if she could wipe away the memories.

"After four or five days, the pressure was really on. Army and police everywhere. The three men are trying to decide what to do. Grenelle, the big talker, is all for killing Duquette, but Lemoyne and Bernard need time to think. They go to a friend's place, someone in the support network to discuss what to do, just the two of them, leaving Grenelle to keep watch on the minister. After a long hard debate, they decide there's nothing to be gained by killing their hostage. The army was everywhere, the government was refusing to negotiate, it looked like the entire thing was lost, you understand? They decided not to kill Raoul Duquette.

"They go back to the house to tell Grenelle of their decision. They come in, they find him in the kitchen, staring out the window, not saying a word—which was unusual for him, such a big mouth he was. Now he was sitting there staring out the window, Bernard told me, like he'd been hit on the head with a hammer.

"They tell him they've decided not to kill Duquette. They tell him the reasons. They go over the pros and cons. They tell him it was a hard decision but they believe it's the right one. All this time, Grenelle is saying nothing. Not one word. He just keeps staring out that window.

"Finally, he turns to them. Looks them both up and down and shakes his head, disappointed.

" 'What?' they say. 'What's the matter? If you don't agree, say so. Just don't keep staring at nothing like a dumb ox. Say what's on your mind.'

" 'You're too late,' he tells them.

" 'Too late,' they say. 'What do you mean "too late"?'

" 'I killed him,' Grenelle says, and then he bursts into tears. This big strong guy, Mr. Action, crying like a little baby. Bernard and Lemoyne run into the next room and find it's true. Duquette is lying in a heap near the window—no breath, no pulse, and around his neck this terrible bruise. The window is broken and there's a mess like there was a struggle.

"They go back into the kitchen where Grenelle is still crying. Eventually they get him to calm down.

" 'Tell us what happened,' Bernard says. 'He tried to escape?'

"Grenelle tells them Duquette somehow got his ropes off. Grenelle's in the kitchen, listening to the news. Suddenly he hears a crash. He runs into the bedroom, and there's Duquette halfway out the window. Grenelle hauls him back in, but he fights like a wild man, hysterical. Grenelle shows them his eye where it's starting to turn black. Anyway, he and Duquette fight, and eventually Grenelle gets him down on his stomach and pulls like hell on his sweater. All he wants to do is calm him down, knock him out. He lets go, and Duquette starts fighting again. So again he pulls back on the sweater. This time he's determined to knock the guy out, so he leans back with all his weight, pulling the collar tight against his throat. That was it. Duquette goes unconscious, Grenelle grabs the rope and ties his wrists together. Only problem is, Duquette's not unconscious—he's dead.

"Grenelle tells them all this and starts crying again. The tough-guy revolutionary, suddenly he's a mama's boy. The other two are extremely upset, but also they understand how it could happen. They have a whole new set of decisions to make."

"That's for sure," Delorme said. "Do they claim Duquette's death as an accident, in which case they look clumsy and amateurish? Or do they claim it as an execution, in which case they look ruthless—cruel, but revolutionaries?"

"Exactly. They decided to look like revolutionaries. They would stick to the original plan. The whole cell will claim collective responsibility, no matter who gets caught or who gets away. They will say it was a group action.

"So they put the body in the trunk of the car and drive to the St. Hubert Airport. They tell the media where to find it. Then they go to their safe house on the South Shore. Three weeks later the police find the house, and all three manage to squeeze into the false back of the closet. They were in there the whole time the police were searching the place, listening to everything they said. When finally the police left, they waited another twelve hours and then took off in the middle of the night. The police had no one guarding the place, and they just slipped out the back.

"Bernard and Lemoyne were caught within a week, hiding in a barn like a couple of hoboes. Grenelle got away." Mrs. Theroux sighed heavily and bit her lip. "The only one who got away."

Delorme spoke softly. "Why have you never told anyone before?"

"In the first place, there was the oath of loyalty. And Bernard didn't want to tell anyone. He wanted to leave history the way it was." Sounds of toddler outrage issued from the next room. "Not so noisy in there, Sasha! Others are trying to talk!"

"Did it ever occur to anyone that Grenelle was lying? That maybe he sensed his brothers in arms were vacillating—weakening, in his view—

and to save the revolution he went ahead and killed Duquette on his own initiative?"

"Oh, yes. It occurred to everyone, despite all his tears. Grenelle was always the hottest head. The one who wanted more action. Bigger explosions. More press. I even raised it with Bernard during the trial. At first he didn't want to consider it, and later, in prison, he felt it made no difference. Remember, my husband was only convicted of kidnapping, not murder."

"Something else bothers me," Delorme said. "If Grenelle was such a hothead, such a revolutionary, why didn't he take credit for the killing? Why call it an accident? After all, in his view, it's an act of war, no? Isn't he a hero?"

"Oh, yes. He was always bragging about his exploits with the bombs and so on. He was always quick to take credit for any violent action the cell took. I mean, he usually instigated it, so why not?"

"But instead of bragging about killing Duquette, he bursts into tears. From what you tell me, it's out of character."

Mrs. Theroux shrugged. "Perhaps that's how one reacts. I wouldn't know, I've never killed anyone."

Delorme had. A serial murderer named Edie Soames. And it had left her depressed and tearful for weeks.

"This taxi of yours. I'm beginning to think you didn't really call one."

"It's okay, I think the rain is letting up. Thank you for the coffee." Delorme put on her coat. "You say your husband didn't want to consider that Grenelle had killed Duquette on purpose. Why do you suppose that is? I would have thought it would help preserve his self-image as a revolutionary."

Mrs. Theroux had stood up with Delorme. Now she turned away slightly and gathered her apron into her hands. She looked out the window with its fringe of dripping icicles.

"Did he never speak of any other possibilities to you?"

Mrs. Theroux shook her head tightly.

"Did he never, for example—I don't know—did he never mention anything about the scene? The bedroom, when he and Lemoyne returned and found Duquette dead? Did he never mention anything about how it looked? About whether it fit with what Grenelle was telling them about an escape attempt, the broken window, the struggle?"

"My husband was nineteen years old. A carpenter, not a forensics expert."

"Yes, but given the gravity of the situation, the effect on their personal lives—not to mention history—they would want to be sure of what was true and what wasn't. After all, Lemoyne and your husband went to prison for twelve years. If it hadn't been for Grenelle, they might well have gotten off with a trip to Cuba and a couple of years in jail on their return. So what I'm asking is, do you know whether there was anything at the scene that might have made your husband wonder whether Grenelle was something other than what he appeared to be?"

"I don't know what you mean."

"I think you do. I think it's been on your mind for thirty years."

"You'd better go. Bernard was right, we've nothing to gain by talking to cops, and everything to lose."

"Why did Miles Shackley call here, Mrs. Theroux? Less than a month before he was murdered."

"I told you: I don't know any Miles Shackley. But someone did call here a month ago. A stranger. He identified himself as Yves Grenelle's cousin from Trois-Rivières. Bernard says it's true Grenelle was from Trois-Rivières, though whether he had any cousins or not, who knows? Anyway, this 'cousin' says his father has died and part of the estate is supposed to go to Yves, do we know where to find him. We were even suspicious, but who would be looking for him at this point? The RCMP? They never even knew he existed."

"What did you tell him, this stranger who was looking for Grenelle?"

"It was Bernard who got the call. He told him he'd never heard of any Yves Grenelle."

Delorme looked around at the kitchen, the children's drawings, taking in the air of harmless domesticity. "Thank you," she said. "Thank you very much."

"My husband will never speak to you, and now I've told you everything I know. You won't come back, I hope."

"No. That shouldn't be necessary."

Mrs. Theroux, summoned by a delegation of three toddlers to fulfill her duties as reader-in-chief at Beau Soleil Day Care Center, disappeared into the other room. Delorme let herself out the front door.

Outside, the rain had abated, and the streets of Montreal looked clean and new.

21

ON HIS WAY BACK to town after his use-
less visit to the former Corporal Sauvé, Cardinal called Catherine, who informed him that his father had been discharged from the hospital and was
now back at home.

"I asked him to come and stay with us, but he wouldn't hear of it. I
didn't push it. You know what he's like."

"How's he seem to you?"

"Not bad, considering. A little wobbly, but he's a tough old bird."

Cardinal told her he thought he'd be home by the next day.

"You'd better not leave it too late. It's raining and it looks like we're
going to get another layer of ice. Could get pretty messy for traveling."

Cardinal had arranged to meet Delorme in a café on St. Denis, but he
was early and it was drizzling again so he ducked into one of the underground malls beneath St. Catherine. Most modern cities have such malls,
of course, and they are particularly popular in cities prone to long winters.
But Montreal hides an entire civilization beneath its streets. Stores of
every variety—pharmacies, department stores, tobacconists, furriers—go
on for mile after mile. Cardinal could see the point, on a rainy day like
today—even more so when the temperature might hit thirty below—but
it wasn't his idea of a good time. Being underground felt oppressive, despite the exuberant trappings, and the lighting made everyone look
washed-out and dissatisfied.

He reached an intersection the size of an airport and took careful note
of the street signs; being underground was disorienting. A cosmetics store
caught his eye, and he stood for a few moments looking in the window,

wondering if there might be something he could take home to Catherine. He noticed a cologne called Torso, with a bottle to match, but it reminded him of autopsies.

At one o'clock he went back to street level and met Delorme, as they had arranged, at the Tasse Toi coffee shop. It was a tiny, touristy crêperie with souvenir matchbooks from around the world attached to the ceiling. The clientele seemed to consist entirely of enormous women from Texas.

"God, am I glad to see you," he said to Delorme.

"I know you can't live without me, Cardinal. It's the only reason I came along."

They each ordered the crêpe special of the day and a coffee, decaf for Cardinal.

"How'd it go with Bernard Theroux?"

"Actually, I saw Françoise Theroux. I think it may have worked out even better."

Cardinal listened quietly, making a few notes. He propped the picture of the young FLQ members against his coffee cup. "So his name's Yves Grenelle, and Miles Shackley was looking for him shortly before he died. That's if Madame Theroux can be believed."

"She's a middle-aged woman with a day-care center and all she wants to do is put this stuff behind her. I think we can believe her. What did you get from Sauvé?"

"Nothing."

"Nothing at all? After going all the way out there?"

"I don't think he liked my French."

"I can agree with him on that one."

"Plus we don't have any leverage on the guy. He's done his time, he keeps to himself, what does he care what a couple of Ontario cops want? I'd probably do the same in his position."

When the check arrived, Cardinal said, "Pretty pricey for a couple of coffees. How do they get away with that?"

"They charge double if you're from Ontario."

They dropped one of the cars at RCMP headquarters and then headed across town toward the Hochelaga district. Delorme consulted a street map spread open across her knees and directed Cardinal through a complicated series of one-way streets.

"Couldn't we just have gone straight along St. Catherine?"

"Not if you want to get there today. This is it."

Cardinal turned onto a depressing little one-way street.

"Wow," Delorme said. "This is a couple of steps down from where Theroux lives."

She remembered what Sergeant Ducharme had told them that morning about Simone Rouault. Simone Rouault, in the sergeant's words, was a real piece of work. She was an informer, among other things. A lot of other things. Simone Rouault was, shall we say, complicated. One minute she was all for the good guys, all law and order and let's toss these bastards in a dungeon and throw away the key. Next minute she was setting off dynamite on Mount Royal. Fond of blowing things up, that woman. A committed separatist who informed for the CAT Squad, and when you figure that one out you let me know. Moody as hell. Fougère used to come back from their meetings looking like he'd gone five rounds with a bobcat. On the bright side, the sergeant had informed them, give Simone Rouault a drink and she'll sell you her mother.

The address was a tiny duplex with a rusted red balcony that sagged from the upper story like a split lip. After an eternity, the door was answered by an ancient woman leaning on a walker. A cigarette dangled from the corner of her mouth, an inch and a half of ash quivering on its tip.

"We're sorry to disturb you," Delorme said in French. "We're looking for Simone Rouault."

"I'm Simone Rouault. What do you want?"

Delorme's rapid-fire French was too much for Cardinal. About the only word he recognized was "Ontario." And Ms. Rouault's response was even more inscrutable. Cardinal hung back behind Delorme, trying to look serious but not threatening.

Finally the woman stood aside. Cardinal and Delorme stepped into a room slightly larger than Cardinal's bedroom at home. "What's the matter with you?" the woman demanded of Cardinal. "Are you deaf-mute?"

"My French isn't very good, I'm afraid."

"That's Ontario for you. Fine. We'll speak English—clumsy language, but it will have to do."

She moved with painful slowness, listing badly to one side. Each step evoked a gasp. She lowered herself slowly to an armchair. There was nothing else to sit on but the bed, a fold-out couch she hadn't bothered to fold back up; Cardinal doubted she had the strength.

"That's okay," Cardinal said. "I'll stand."

"Sit, for God's sake. It's just a bed. It won't bite. I'm damned if I'm going to fold the thing up for you. Bloody monstrosity."

When Cardinal and Delorme sat, the bed sank several inches toward the floor. "Ms. Rouault," Cardinal said, "the case we're working on involves at least one person who was active in the FLQ back in nineteen seventy, and we need to talk to you about that time. You don't have anything to worry about. We're here strictly for information."

"Worried? Honey, I'm not worried. I planted a dozen bombs, wrote twenty-five communiqués, harbored fugitives, aided and abetted enemies of the state, and organized seven bank robberies. Go ahead and arrest me." She held out her bent, tormented wrists for handcuffs.

"We're not here to arrest you."

"Damn right, you're not. You'd have to arrest the entire RCMP if you were going to do that. My associates went to jail. My lovers went to jail. Even my best friend went to jail. But I stayed free. There are reasons for that."

"So we understand," Cardinal said. "In fact, I'm wondering how it is you still live in Montreal, and under the same name."

"Look at me. What can they do to me now? Break in and shoot a little old lady? Let them come, I don't care."

"Well, we're hoping you can—"

She interrupted him: "You know I'm not supposed to talk to you?"

"The events we're interested in were over thirty years ago. I don't think you'll be breaching security at this point."

"CSIS disagrees with you. They called me this morning and told me not to tell you anything."

"Was it Calvin Squier who called?"

"He wouldn't give his name. An older man. French-Canadian. He told me I would be jeopardizing national security if I gave you any information. He even threatened to get my social security taken away. I don't feel the slightest loyalty to them. You see how I live. I doubt that Detective-Lieutenant Jean-Paul Fougère lived like this—in New Brunswick or wherever the hell he retired to before he died. CSIS is the same gang with a new name. If they hadn't called and threatened me, I might not have talked to you, but now they can go fuck themselves as far as I'm concerned."

Delorme reached into her bag and pulled out the oblong box. "Françoise Theroux told me you were fond of this stuff."

The woman took the box and examined it as if it were an object of the utmost rarity. Museum quality. With difficulty, she extracted the bottle and cradled it in her arms like a newborn.

"Are they doing well for themselves, the Therouxs?"

"They seem to make a good living."

"God has a sense of humor, no? The murderer, he makes a good living; I live like a welfare case."

"We need to know about this person," Cardinal said. He handed her the photograph of Shackley as a young man.

She examined it without expression for a few moments before handing it back. A small smile hovered about her dry, cracked lips, and she shook her head gently from side to side. "Such a story I could tell." She nodded at the bottle of champagne. "Open that for me, will you?"

Cardinal picked up the bottle and started removing the foil.

"Always such a pleasure, isn't it?" she said to Delorme. "To watch a strong man work with his hands."

Delorme let that one go.

"Glasses are over there, dear." She gestured toward a row of metal cupboards above a half-size fridge. "Won't you join me?"

"I'd love to," Cardinal said. "But unfortunately . . ."

"Yes, yes. So sad. Can't have intoxicated Mounties running all over the place, can we?"

"We're not Mounties," Delorme said.

"I was speaking metaphorically, my dear. You mustn't be so literal-minded."

Cardinal brought the bottle and a murky champagne flute. He poured her a glass and set the bottle down.

The woman held the glass under her nose a moment and inhaled. "Veuve Clicquot," she said. "Everybody's favorite widow."

"*Veuve* means widow," Delorme said to Cardinal.

"Thank you. I figured."

"There was a time when I drank nothing else." Ms. Rouault took a delicate sip, held the glass before her and examined the color, then took another sip. "It hasn't changed at all—unlike me."

Cardinal and Delorme waited.

"I was beautiful," she said. "That's the first thing you must understand. I was very beautiful."

"That's easy to believe," Cardinal said. Though veined with tiny violet capillaries, the fine high cheekbones were still apparent. The graceful arch of eyebrow. The gray eyes, almost hidden now in folds of skin, were so wide set that in her younger days she would have had a look of wisdom beyond her years.

"It was an intensity I had," she said in a factual tone. "An air of passion, coupled with a necessary aloofness that people found compelling." She reached painfully toward a bookshelf and brought down a photograph of a young woman laughing at the camera. She had magnificent teeth, an invitingly plump upper lip, and the wide gray eyes were absolutely clear.

"At the beach. Summer of nineteen seventy. I was thirty-one." Which put her in her sixties now. She looked closer to eighty.

"Osteoporosis, arthritis, you name it," she said, catching Cardinal's thoughts. "I never did like milk. And I always loved these." She pulled out a pack of Gitanes and lit one. Then she took the photo back in a desiccated claw and drew her index finger not at her younger face but at the clouds in the background of the photo, the hill to the left, foliage on the right. "You see that? You know what that is? Or rather, what that was?"

Cardinal shrugged. "You said you were at the beach."

"Again so literal-minded. The two of you should get married. I was pointing at my future. That's what that was. I still had one then. Would you mind?" She held out her glass to Cardinal and he filled it for her. She took a trembling sip and held the glass in her lap. "My future," she said again. "How strange to think that this body— this face, this room—how strange to think that these were my future. If I'd known that then, of course, I would have hanged myself. You have some time, I take it?"

Cardinal and Delorme nodded.

"That is a great luxury, having time. *Bon*. I have your attention, I have my cigarette, I have a full glass. Let an old lady tell you where her future went.

"I was twenty-nine years old. Not so old, really. But in those days, youth was everything. To be young was regarded as an honor, just as in earlier times to be old was valued as an achievement. A load of crap, either way. Your age is your age and it's not in your control. But back then—I'm talking nineteen sixty-eight, nineteen sixty-nine, now—if you were over thirty you were over the hill. The Beatles were at the height of their fame. It was Trudeaumania—why? Because he was young and handsome—like Kennedy. Good television. There was even a government organization called the Company of Young Canadians. Of course, it was a make-work program designed to hide the high unemployment figures, but it sounded so romantic.

"Fifty percent of the population was under thirty, and that meant we had power. With numbers like that, politicians had to listen. At the universities, students went on strike to change their curriculum, even to have a say in hiring and firing, in tenure. And of course the endless marches against the Vietnam War. They were radical times.

"You'd go to a march, a sit-in, and there'd be not a soul over thirty—or very few. So exhilarating to be surrounded by thousands of people who look just like you. All saying the same things, singing the same things, believing the same things. Of course there's a frightening side to it: So many people all wearing the same things—flak jackets and blue jeans, tie-dyed T-shirts and blue jeans, Indian silk and blue jeans— all saying the same things. George Orwell knew a thing or two."

She took a sip of champagne and a deep drag on her cigarette. She ex-

haled slowly, contemplating the stream of smoke. "I was terrified of growing old. It was the times I lived in, not just my own neurosis. That is point
number one. Point number two: I had married young and badly. My husband considered himself a great artist, but the rest of the world disagreed
and he took it out on me. Anyway, it ended, and I felt all washed up the
moment I turned thirty.

"I was already too old to be involved in the student activities. I had
gone to the University of Montreal for two years, but dropped out when I
got married. After the breakup, I put myself back together very slowly.
Got myself a job with an oil company, about as boring a job as you can
imagine, and took up a serious interest in politics—as much for the social
life as anything.

"I was a separatist back then. René Levesque had formed the Parti
Quebecois, and I believed in it with an absolute passion. Quebec would
become its own sovereign power, but it would remain tied to the rest of
the country with an economic association, like the countries in the European Union have now. And the PQ would achieve this through democratic means: first, get itself elected as the provincial government. Second,
get the people to vote in a referendum for or against separation. Third,
found the new nation.

"I was lonely, desperate to fill my empty hours. I was happy to do all
the legwork, seal the envelopes, lick the stamps, take the leaflets door-to-
door. There were lots of other young Quebecois helping out, so I made a
lot of friends. I'd get up at six in the morning to stand outside the Metro
with our candidate, then do the same thing in the evening after work, and
then the endless planning meetings at night.

"But being young, of course, we thought it would happen right away.
When our candidate lost, and René Levesque lost, I was completely aston-
ished and depressed. And I'll tell you one of the reasons we lost: the FLQ.
The Liberals were quick to associate the PQ with the bombs going off in
Westmount, and it frightened people away. It didn't matter how many
times Levesque said he did not condone violence, that the PQ stood for
democracy; the FLQ scared people, so we lost and we lost badly.

"It affected party workers different ways. One of the young men I worked with, Louis Labrecque, said it made him want to join the FLQ. He even asked me if I'd join, and I was so depressed that I said I might. I didn't think anything would come of it. To tell you the truth, I forgot about it.

"*Bon.* About six months later, he shows up at my door and asks if I would be willing to help the revolution, meaning the FLQ. I said I didn't want anything to do with violence. He said, no, no—no violence. What they needed was money. He asked if I was still working at the oil company. For some reason I had told him about one of my duties there: Once a month the company delivered large sums of money to the various offices to make the payroll. This was in the days before electronic transfers, obviously. But they didn't use a Brinks truck or anything. I just drove along with my boss and delivered these large manila envelopes to the various offices. He sat in the car while I went in with them.

"I told him I was not going to steal from the company where I worked. And he said no, of course not, I would be the victim. They would rob me and my boss as we did our rounds. There was another payday in two weeks, they would do it then. I said I needed time to think about it.

"Well, he looked at me differently then. He didn't like that at all. And I could see in his eyes exactly what he was thinking: If she doesn't go along with it, that means I have opened myself up to the bitch in a completely insecure manner. He would be in trouble with other FLQ members. I can tell you, that look scared me. He gave me three days.

"I couldn't sleep, I was so terrified. If I didn't go along, I felt that I might be killed, and if I did, I was afraid I would go to prison. So, two nights later I put on a blond wig and in the middle of the night I went to the police station and told them I had information about the FLQ. And that's how I met Detective-Lieutenant Jean-Paul Fougère—may he rest in peace."

She took a long pull on her cigarette and contemplated the glowing end. "Jean-Paul Fougère . . . Jean-Paul Fougère was thirty-five, slender, not big at all, and graceful—if graceful is a word you can use about a man—he just moved in a way that was fascinating to me. Just watching him light a cigarette was a pleasure—the way he would hold it while he was talking, or tap it against the ashtray, it was like a performance or something.

"Over the next few months he told me a lot about himself, but you don't need to know that now. All you need to know is that he was high up in the CAT Squad and desperately wanted to infiltrate the FLQ. The cops never had any idea when they would strike next, they had no idea of the size of the threat. They knew who many of the members were—people from the extreme left wing, people in the Communist party, labor activists. But they couldn't prove anything. They needed someone inside.

"Their attempts to recruit informers were pathetic. It made Jean-Paul crazy. You know how they would attempt to recruit someone? They'd simply pick him up on the street, take him to some horrible little hotel, and terrorize him for hours. Pull out their guns and so on. As if this was going to make the poor bastard loyal to the forces of law and order. Or they would threaten some kid with exposure as a homosexual—which might have worked if they had actually picked one who was also close to the FLQ, but they always got it wrong. Bombs are going off all over Montreal and Quebec City and the CAT Squad is just getting nowhere. Jean-Paul's boss is screaming for blood, the Prime Minister is screaming for blood, and they were just at a complete loss. Which is when I came along with my dilemma about the holdup."

"You must have been a godsend," Cardinal said.

"Oh, Jean-Paul couldn't believe his luck. 'What am I going to do about this robbery?' I wailed. 'They'll kill me if I don't go through with it.' 'Oh,' he said. 'You must go through with it, no question.' Just like that. I thought he was crazy. There was no way I wanted to get robbed. What if they shot me or my boss in the process?"

She paused for a moment to pour herself more champagne, filling her glass to the top, careful as a surgeon, making sure nothing foamed over the rim. She lit another cigarette, even though the last one was still smoking in the ashtray and Cardinal's eyes were already stinging. She sipped thoughtfully for a few moments. Then, holding her glass in her lap and staring down into the pale gold liquid as if it were a crystal ball, she said softly, "That was the beginning of my life as an informer."

Delorme leaned forward. Cardinal had almost forgotten she was there, she had that ability, to settle into a quiet so intense that you forgot she was right beside you.

"They didn't warn your company about the hold-up?" she asked.

Rouault shook her head, scattering ashes over her chest and lap. "The company knew nothing. Fougère arranged with the bank to give them all marked bills, but other than that everything proceeded as normal. Payday comes, the boss and I go to make our rounds, same as usual."

"And who actually did the robbery?"

"There were three of them. Labrecque, a more senior guy named Claude Hibert, and a true believer named Grenelle. Yves Grenelle. He was the only amateurish part of the whole thing.

"Three o'clock on the dot, the boss and I are about to deliver the cash to the first office. We stop out front, same place as usual, and before I can get out with the envelope there are two men, one on either side of the car. There's a third, Hibert, I later learned, ready with a car across the street. They demand all our money—wallets and purse to start with so it doesn't look like a setup. And then—as if it's on an impulse—Labrecque grabs the envelope I'm holding.

"It had all gone perfectly smoothly up to that point. Then, completely for no reason, Grenelle bashes my boss in the head. I think it was a black-jack he used. My boss had done nothing. He hadn't resisted in any way. But Grenelle hits him with this thing and knocks him cold. It was stupid, you know, because it raised the crime from armed robbery to robbery with violence, for no reason. And my boss, well I didn't like him—he was al-ways pinching me and making eyes at me—but I didn't dislike him, ei-ther. I certainly didn't want to see him in the hospital for three days, which is what happened. It's not like in the movies where you get bashed in the head and you're perfectly fine two minutes later."

"How did the FLQ respond to your involvement?" Cardinal asked.

"Oh, I was in with flying colors. Labrecque said he'd never seen them so excited. He got a lot of mileage out of it, of course, for having re-cruited me. They got away with five thousand dollars, not realizing it was all marked bills, of course. So they loved me."

"And did you see more of Grenelle?"

"The first thing I said when Labrecque told me I was accepted was I never want to work with Yves Grenelle again. Stupid violence."

Ms. Rouault poured herself more champagne, holding her glass up to the light and turning it slowly. "Over the next few months they mostly used me to recruit new people. They didn't ask me to do anything extreme. Mostly I sat in the Chat Noir café—that's where all the activists hung out—and waited for some young separatist to come on to me. We would talk about the revolution, and pretty soon he'd be committed to the FLQ. It's amazing the trouble an infatuation can get you into.

"The truly fantastic piece of irony, however, was that I had no clue what was being done to me. You see, right from the first night, Detective Fougère treated me like the love of his life. He was so good to me, so considerate, so concerned for my safety. I was in danger all the time of course, leading this double life. I'd be at FLQ meetings in the evening and two hours later I'd be relaying every word to the CAT Squad. I was frightened all the time. My nerves were a ruin. I hardly slept. Couldn't eat. People like Hibert, like Grenelle, they were dead serious. There's not the slightest doubt they would have killed me if they had known what I was up to.

"Well, the result was that I fell totally in love with Fougère." She hung her head for a few moments. Cardinal was about to prompt her with a question when the gray head jerked upright again, and the gray eyes shone. "I just lived for our meetings together. It was the only time I could be real, you see, the only time I could tell the exact truth without fear. After a few months, I can't tell you what a relief that was."

"I can imagine," Delorme said. "It must've been quite addictive."

"Exactly, my dear." Ms. Rouault nodded, spilling ash all over. "Both parts were addictive. The double life—what a sense of power I had. What importance! After being the rejected little housewife, here I was risking my life and saving my country at the same time. Fougère knew I was a separatist of course, but he didn't care. Both of us wanted the FLQ stopped, though for different reasons."

"And he was so kind to me. So tender." She stopped again, her cigarette in midair. The gray eyes looked into an indeterminate distance, as if

Fougère's face hovered amid the smoke. "Just holding his hand meant so much to me. I felt so safe, so secure. Oh, he played me like a violin.

"*Bon.* All these months, Jean-Paul wasn't interested in Labrecque. Too low-level to bother with. Didn't care about Grenelle, either—a blowhard, he called him. Not important. It was Claude Hibert he wanted me to get close to. Hibert wasn't suspected of committing any violent acts, but he had become head of the information cell—the FLQ's public relations office, if you like—he was bound to have contacts with the other cells. So I had two assignments: to win the confidence of Claude Hibert and to become head of my own cell.

"To be convincing as the head of a cell, of course, I would have to be able to blow things up, and put out communiqués. I asked Hibert to get me some dynamite. He refused. 'You're not ready,' he told me. I asked him for FLQ letterhead: We never did find out where they had it made. It had a watermark that went from the top of the page to the bottom—a picture of a *patriote* with a pipe in his teeth and a rifle in his hands. The CAT squad was dying for me to get my hands on the genuine article; I didn't understand why, at the time.

"But I kept bugging Hibert for explosives and letterhead. And he just kept saying, I'll try, I'll try. Fougère was getting more and more fed up. Then one night—it came out of the blue—he took me out to a very special restaurant, Ma Bourgogne. The finest restaurant in the city. Normally, we couldn't do things like that because we couldn't risk being seen together. But Jean-Paul went to infinite trouble—had I don't know how many men watching our backs and securing the area around the restaurant. He was bolstering my ego, showing how highly I was valued by the Squad, and also he was making good use of the romantic setting.

"He knew by now I was crazy about him—I was doing all this as much for him as for Quebec. I loved him totally. And he began the evening by saying—already at the aperitif stage—saying how much he adored me. He was holding my hand and looking into my eyes. All I could see was adoration there. In fact, do you know, I actually thought he was going to propose to me. Hah!"

The exclamation turned into a cough that shook the frail frame. Then the cough became a wheeze. Kleenex was searched for. Drink replenished. Cigarette lit.

"We had our dinner. A magnificent dinner: lobster bisque followed by beef chateaubriand. Champagne, of course. And afterward, Armagnac. To this day, I believe it is the best meal I've ever had. And afterward, over the brandy, Jean-Paul takes my hand. His face is very serious, and I know he's going to say something that will change my life. 'This is hard for me to say, Simone,' he says. 'You've done so much already. Why, really, you're risking your life every day. But, Simone, we need to know just how far you would go to protect your ideals.'

" 'But you've seen how far,' I said. 'You're seeing how far. What do you want me to do? Kill someone?'

"He shakes his head. 'No,' he says, and there's a tremor in his voice.

"By now, I was frightened. I didn't know what he was going to say—but my stomach did, because it was starting to turn over. Suddenly the lobster bisque didn't seem like such a good idea. My heart stopped beating. I broke out into a sweat. I put my glass on the table. I couldn't look him in the eye. 'You want me to fuck someone,' I said.

" 'We don't want you to do anything you feel would be too much,' he said very quickly. 'Use your own judgment, of course. But we feel Hibert has gone as far as he is going to go, and we need something to break the, uh, stalemate.'

"I couldn't look at him. I just leaned forward, kind of rocking back and forth, hugging myself.

" 'Are you all right?' he asks me. Can you imagine? Was I all right? He repeated it I don't know how many times. Was I all right? Was I all right? My God. He could ask me that. Was I all right?

"I told him I was fine.

" 'You'll do it?'

" 'If you want me to.' I looked him in the eye when I said it. I wanted to see how he looked when I said it.

" 'It's not what I want,' he said. 'It couldn't be farther from what I want, Simone. You know that. But in this line of work we don't get to pick and choose.'

" 'I will do it,' I said again—very firmly, as if I was speaking to a deaf person. 'I will do it. If that is what you want. Do you want me to do it?'

"He nodded his head. Now it was he who could not look me in the eye. You see, if he could ask me to do such a thing, then there was no reason not to do it. Clearly I meant nothing to him. From that moment on, I didn't care what I did, who I slept with. I had nothing to lose."

"But you could have walked away," Delorme said. "They couldn't have forced you to do it."

"After what Jean-Paul said to me, I wanted to die. Really, death held no terror for me anymore. And staying undercover in the FLQ seemed like an efficient way to commit suicide. So next time Hibert and I were alone, we slept together and then I no longer felt like dying, I felt dead. I was completely numb.

"I tried to hurt Jean-Paul when I reported back to him. Told him what an extraordinary lover Hibert was, how well endowed, how considerate. None of it true, by the way.

"Jean-Paul didn't even blink. 'Just stick with the relevant facts, Simone,' he said.

"As a tactic, sleeping with Hibert turned out to be a good move. Hibert was now in the position of either worrying that he was sleeping with an informer or trusting me completely. He decided to trust me, and a week later I had a stack of letterhead and three cases of dynamite.

"With the letterhead, I put out communiqués, inventing cell names as I went along. I would announce 'a major blow' to come, for example, and then we would set the dynamite. The high point of my career came when I had eight recruits at one time in my apartment. We're typing up communiqués in one room, and two of them are making a bomb in my bathtub."

Cardinal stirred. "You're telling me the Mounties and the Montreal police let you manufacture bombs in your apartment? I don't believe that."

"They doctored the explosives so they would be inert. Sometimes they would substitute their own dynamite after we'd planted it—that's if they wanted the explosion to actually happen. Other times, they would just let us set a dud. For example, they let us blow up a section of track on the CPR, but they replaced our dud with a small charge that did very little damage. That way, I could keep my credibility. They arrested four guys after that one."

"All people you recruited?"

"All my recruits, yes. They got four years."

Cardinal looked at Delorme, but Delorme was just staring at Simone Rouault, eyebrows in the air.

"Don't look at me like that. You think they were so innocent? These were people who, if they had joined a real cell, would have killed people. We took them out of action before they could do any damage. Listen, I put twenty-seven people in prison, and probably not more than three were FLQ before I met them. And I probably did all of them a favor."

Oh, yes, Cardinal thought, we all have to tell ourselves lies sometimes. God knows he had told himself more than a few in his time. He pulled out the photograph of Shackley again. "Do you recognize this man?"

"Shackley," she said without hesitation. "His name was Miles Shackley. He worked with Jean-Paul. I met him quite a few times. He was American, so I assumed he was CIA, though I was too polite to ask. They were supposed to be partners, but Shackley always behaved as if he was Jean-Paul's instructor. He did have more experience, and I had the impression that he had his own informer very well situated in one of the FLQ cells. An extremely cold man, like a machine, he practically clicked when he walked. I didn't like him at all. When he dropped out of the picture, I didn't miss him one bit."

"Dropped out?" Cardinal said.

"One night he was supposed to be having dinner with Jean-Paul and me. When Jean-Paul showed up alone, I asked where Shackley was, and he said, 'I don't think we'll be seeing Miles Shackley anymore.' He'd had some kind of political blowup with the higher-ups."

"When was this, exactly?"

"August 17, 1970. I remember because that day the FLQ set off four bombs around the city. A man was killed—a security guard—and police were everywhere. For the first time, there was the feeling of crisis in the air."

"And did you ever see Shackley again?"

"Never. I know the CAT Squad was looking for him after Hawthorne was kidnapped—well, looking for him is not the word. They were ransacking the entire city for him. I was under strict instructions to have nothing to do with him. If he contacted me in any way I was to call headquarters immediately. I don't know what he did, but they wanted him as badly as they wanted the FLQ."

"And what about these people? Can you identify them?"

Rouault put her glass down and took the photograph in trembling fingers. "Oh, my," she said. "That's Madeleine. Madeleine Ferrier. Oh, I was so fond of her. She was the only *felquiste* I did like. She was so young. Eighteen, I think, not more than nineteen. I never reported her name to anyone. Surveillants would notice her, of course, and Jean-Paul would ask, but always I would tell him, 'She's no one. She's someone's cousin. She makes them lunch.' And really her involvement was not much more than that. She was crazy about Yves Grenelle and was clearly in the terror game only to be near him. She hung on his every word. But she was just a kid. She never carried explosives, guns, or anything like that. Poor Madeleine. To think she would've been fifty by now."

"Would've been? She died?"

"She didn't die. She was murdered. After the Hawthorne kidnappers were caught, she received a minor sentence for aiding and abetting—not because of anything *I* said—and did six months in jail. Then she totally reformed. Went to university, became a teacher, and did well for herself. She moved to Ontario twelve years ago. We weren't close, but we stayed in touch over the years. I liked her so much, she was the only one I would ever have considered telling the truth about myself, but I didn't have the heart. Anyway, she called to say she was moving to Ontario, I forget where, and the next thing I knew she was dead. The killer was never caught as far as I know."

"Do you remember where she was killed?"

"I don't know, someplace up north. Ontario, you have to love it."

"And you said she had a thing for Yves Grenelle?"

"Yes. That's Grenelle, there." A crooked finger hovered over the youth laughing at the edge of the frame. The thick curly hair and a beard gave him the look of a B-movie desperado.

"How much did you see of Grenelle after your first escapade?"

"Not much. He kept close with Lemoyne and Theroux, people who were in it from the beginning. I'm telling you, he wanted to run the country of Quebec, once it was liberated from the clutches of Pierre Trudeau. He moved up in the ranks very quickly."

"Did you ever hear that he killed the minister? Raoul Duquette?"

"He was certainly capable of it: violent, angry, hungry for action and power. Absolutely, he could have done it. But Daniel Lemoyne and Bernard Theroux confessed to that crime. That's Lemoyne, there."

The bony finger hovered over the heavier young man on the other side of the photograph. "He and Grenelle were great friends, I believe. I was always amazed that Grenelle was not captured with him and Theroux. I heard he fled to Paris."

She bent her head, and there was a silence. Cardinal and Delorme looked at each other, waiting. Cardinal thought Ms. Rouault was trying to remember something, or perhaps grieving for her long-lost love. But then there came a soft fluttering noise, and he realized she was snoring.

Delorme said quietly, "I think we're done here, no?"

Cardinal reached over and stubbed out the cigarette and removed the champagne glass from the old fingers. The bottle on the floor was empty.

22

CARDINAL AND DELORME DROVE to the Regent Hotel and went to their separate rooms, Delorme on the ground floor, Cardinal on the third. When the rattletrap of an elevator took too long to come, he ducked into a damp stairwell.

All Cardinal wanted to do now was have a shower and a nap before dinner, but he had no sooner taken off his shoes than there was a knock at the door. He opened it, and Calvin Squier grinned at him like a long-lost fraternity brother.

"John, listen. Before you say anything, let me apologize. I know I caused you major problems up north, and I just want you to know that—"

Cardinal shut the door.

"John, I'm here to help you."

Cardinal spoke to the door. "Why is it every time you help me I end up in the shit?"

"No, really, this time I'm on your side a hundred percent. And I can't believe, after your interviews today, that you aren't going to need the information I have. Besides which, something's changed that I need to tell you about."

Cardinal swung open the door. "How do you know I had interviews?"

"I can't talk out here in the hall."

Cardinal stood aside, and Squier breezed by, unbuttoning his overcoat.

"Leave it on," Cardinal said. "You're not staying. And anyway, how'd you follow me here? I suppose you have me bugged, too."

Squier looked hurt. "Of course not. See, what you refuse to accept is that I trust you, even though you don't trust me." He held up his hands to ward off accusations. "I know, I know, I caused you problems. That's why I'm here. To make up for it any way I can."

"You can start by telling me who called Simone Rouault and tried to shut her up."

"Well, it wasn't me, I guarantee you that."

"French Canadian. An older man. He claimed to be calling from CSIS. You can see that, from where I stand, that's very easy to believe."

"It could have been one of the Ottawa brass, I've no way of knowing for sure. See, that's the big change I have to tell you about: I quit."

"You quit?"

"You heard me. Calvin Squier and CSIS are now separate and apart."

"I'm sure you'll both be happier."

Squier sat down on the nearest bed. He gave a deep sigh, as if a wave of despair washed over him. "John, there comes a time in every man's life where he's just got to suck it up and do the right thing. The truth is, I have not been happy about the way CSIS has been handling this matter from the beginning. I try to be a good soldier, to do my job and not ask too many questions, but when it comes to out-and-out hampering an ongoing murder investigation, well, that's where I draw the line."

"Uh-huh. And what brought on this change of heart?"

"Well, it was when you arrested me, I guess. That's when the scales dropped from my eyes. I work—worked—for an important organization, and I wanted to believe my superiors were behaving ethically. But it's amazing how being handcuffed face-down on the pavement can make you rethink your position. It just suddenly struck home that I was working for people who don't give a damn about little things like truth and justice."

"—and the American way?"

"Well, now you're making fun of me, and probably I deserve it. But you know what I'm saying. I joined CSIS because I believe in certain things. And I've come to realize my superiors don't share those beliefs. See, you're not the only one they've been keeping in the dark. They wouldn't even let me see the records on Shackley. Why was he code Red in the first place, I wanted to know. No one would clue me in, and they wouldn't release the file—assuming it still exists. And that's why we've parted ways."

"And you've come here to apologize."

"And to help out, if I can."

"Apology accepted, Squier. Goodbye." Cardinal opened the door again.

"Wait, John. Let me finish what I came here to do, and then I'll get out of your hair. You saw Sauvé today. I'm sure the former corporal wasn't much help to you."

"You didn't follow me there," Cardinal said, shutting the door again. "Nobody did."

"No, but you have a logical mind, and Sauvé is the logical place to start. He didn't say diddley, right? Like interviewing a monument, I bet."

"More or less."

Squier made a note on his palmtop. "Fine. We'll get back to Sauvé. Bet you didn't get anywhere with Theroux, either."

"We talked to the wife," Cardinal said. "She turned out to be very helpful."

"Really? Did she tell you her husband didn't kill Raoul Duquette?"

"How did you know that?"

"Look at the file, John. She's been saying that ever since Theroux was sentenced."

"What she says now is that Yves Grenelle murdered him."

"Well, she wouldn't get far with that. Publicly, nobody's heard of Grenelle. And anybody on the CAT Squad can tell you it was unlikely in the extreme. Yves Grenelle was all hat and no cattle. He was not a member of the Chénier cell; he wasn't a member of the Liberation cell. At best, he was liaison between the two. Don't take my word for it; look him up in the file."

"Simone Rouault didn't have any trouble believing Yves Grenelle could have killed Duquette. As far as she knew, he was a violent thug who wanted to rule the world—Quebec at least."

"You talked to Simone Rouault, too. Man, you should see the stuff CSIS has on her. That woman deserves a medal. Do you know how many people she put in jail?"

"She claims twenty-seven."

"That's all she knows about. She was kept in the dark about a lot of things."

"She certainly was," Cardinal said, remembering the look on her face as she recalled Detective Fougère.

"Great woman, no doubt, but not in a position to say who did or did not kill Raoul Duquette."

"She did know Miles Shackley, though."

"Of course she did. He and Fougère were very tight, and Fougère was running her. But Rouault was a low-level informant, John—effective, but low-level."

"They had higher-level informants? Are you going to tell me Daniel Lemoyne was working for the CIA?"

Squier grinned. "That old chestnut."

"As far as I can tell, Simone Rouault was the best informer the Mounties ever had."

"My point is, she can only help you so far. Lieutenant Fougère is dead, and Lemoyne and Theroux won't talk."

"The person I really need to talk to is Yves Grenelle."

"Yves Grenelle dropped off the planet in nineteen seventy and has never been heard from since. Work with what you have. Sauvé's the guy. He was on the CAT Squad. Heck, he was almost running the CAT Squad. And despite his criminal tendencies, he knows everything there is to know about the FLQ."

"Unfortunately, he is also a sphinx."

"Show him this." Squier reached into his satchel and pulled out a manila envelope, folded in half.

Cardinal took it and opened it. "A videotape?"

"I took it as a little parting gift from CSIS. Unlike them, I don't happen to believe that when an American citizen gets killed on our soil nothing should be done about it. Maybe this will make up for some of the trouble we caused you. Anyway, once he gets a look at that, I think you'll find our former Mountie and jailbird a lot more cooperative."

Squier stood up. "I'm glad I got to work with you, John. You know, I'm going to be taking some time off now, to consider my options. And I'm going to be giving some serious thought to joining the police. And that's entirely because of your influence."

"I'll never forgive myself."

"Next job I get, I want to be sure I'm actually helping people. No more of this keep-everybody-in-the-dark business for me. If that's what Ottawa wants, they're not going to have me to help them do it anymore."

Cardinal thought Squier was actually going to salute, but he only adjusted the buttons on his overcoat and shook hands one last time.

"Keep fighting the good fight," he said. And then he was gone.

Cardinal waited a few moments, then went down to Delorme's room and knocked on the door. Delorme answered it, dressed in jeans and T-shirt, her hair still wet from the shower.

"What's going on?" she said. "I thought we were going to meet later for dinner."

"Calvin Squier, formerly of Canadian Security Intelligence, wants to kiss and make up." Cardinal held up the videotape. "He came bearing gifts."

"Great. What are we going to watch it on?"

THEY DROVE BACK to RCMP headquarters. Sergeant Ducharme had left for the day, and that turned out to be problematic. The young Mountie at the front desk wasn't in a hurry to grant admittance to police officers from other provinces, not to mention other agencies. After consulting not one but two superior officers, he called Sergeant Ducharme at home and got the green light.

There was a lengthy search of empty offices. Cardinal and Delorme were finally set up in an interview room with a TV and VCR. The videotape was just under half an hour, and when it was done, Delorme turned to Cardinal and said, "Looks like your CSIS man came through for once."

"I take back everything I said. Let's go eat, and I'll be happy to raise a glass to Calvin Squier."

Twenty minutes later they were sitting in a booth in the Embassy Restaurant on Peel Street. Just as "hotel" was too grand a word for the Regent, so "restaurant" turned out to be too grand a word for the Embassy. Yes, it had tablecloths and banquettes. It had a hostess, and dim lights, and waitresses wearing slinky outfits, and a sign saying PLEASE WAIT TO BE SEATED. But everything else about the place—from the menu to the vinyl upholstery to the coffin-sized aquariums devoid of fish—screamed greasy spoon.

"What do you suppose happened to the goldfish?" Delorme said as they examined menus.

"Probably went to a better restaurant," Cardinal said. "Are you okay with this or do you want to go somewhere else?"

"I'm tired and starving. Let's stay here."

"Do you know what you want? I'm going to have a steak."

"I'm going to have the seafood special."

"I'd be careful. It might be a lot of little goldfish."

"I don't care. I'm going to have plenty of beer with it."

They ordered from a hostile young woman whose goals in life did not include waitressing. Cardinal was just glad she addressed them in English.

When the beers arrived, Cardinal took a sip of his Labatt's and frowned at the bottle. "Tastes funny."

"They make it different for the Quebec market."

"Why would they do that?"

"Because French Canadians have more subtle, sophisticated tastes."

"Oh, sure. Famous for it."

Delorme made a face at him. She had left her hair untied so that it fell in thick, curly waves to her shoulders, and she was wearing a red T-shirt that looked a lot better than any T-shirt had a right to look. There was a tiny black cat embroidered over her sternum.

When their food came, it turned out to be surprisingly good. Cardinal's steak was tender, and cooked exactly medium-rare, the way he liked it. And the expression on Delorme's face was a transparent register of delight.

"Seafood's okay?"

"Okay? It's wonderful."

The good food cheered them up. As they ate, they talked about the ground they had covered that day and what they hoped to cover the next. They still had no clear motive for Shackley's murder, but if luck turned out to be on their side the next day, one might emerge. After a while, they moved on to more personal topics. Cardinal asked after a boyfriend Delorme had mentioned once or twice.

"Steven—wasn't that his name? Sounded like a nice guy from what you told me."

"Oh, yes, he was a very nice guy—except he thought he could screw everything in sight. Sometimes I can see why women become lesbians."

There was a pause. Delorme looked away a moment, then leaned forward a little. "John, we've never talked about it since you nearly resigned last year, but I'm just asking as a friend: Are you still getting pressure from Rick Bouchard and company?"

"A little."

"I knew it. What's going on?"

"He sent a card. He has my home address."

"Your home? What are you going to do?"

"Bouchard still has some time to run on his sentence. I can always hope he screws up and gets a few years tacked on."

"You can't count on that, though."

"Then there's the blowhard factor. He's been in prison twelve years. Is he really going to risk going back there by coming after me? Chances are it's just jailhouse bravado."

"I hope so. Let me know if I can do anything."

"Thanks, Lise. Can we change the subject now?"

"What shall we talk about?"

"Tell me about your worst date ever."

"Oh, that's hard. There's been so many."

Delorme launched into a story about a blind date with a hot-rodder that started out with a speeding ticket and ended with a flat tire in the pouring rain. Throughout dinner, Cardinal couldn't help noticing how different Delorme was, off the job. She had a wonderfully expressive face. Around the station, she conducted herself with a brusque efficiency that kept people at arm's length and was also tough to read. But now, after-hours and in another city, she let down her guard. Her gestures became more emphatic—eyes bulging as she described the ride with her hot-rodder, voice dipping down to a doofus drawl as she recounted things he'd said. Cardinal was touched that she was revealing to him a side that was more emotional, more feminine, and maybe, he thought, more French.

After the plates had been cleared away, the two of them sat quietly.

"You want another beer?" Cardinal said.

Delorme shrugged, breasts momentarily emphasized. She flagged the waitress across the room. "I'll have another beer. And another Labatt's for my father?"

WHEN THEY GOT BACK to the hotel, one of the girls behind the front desk called them over. She spoke French.

"Ms. Delorme, I'm so sorry, but there has been a problem. A pipe has burst on the ground floor and flooded all the rooms. I'm afraid it won't be possible for you to stay in that room."

"That's fine. Put me somewhere else."

"That's the problem. We are completely full. There are no other rooms."

"Did you get that?" Delorme said to Cardinal.

"More or less."

"I swear, next time I'm staying at the Queen Elizabeth."

She turned back to the desk clerk, speaking once more in French. Cardinal didn't catch all of it, but he noted with admiration that Delorme did not lose her temper or raise her voice, even when the bad news got worse.

She turned to Cardinal once more. "There's a Holiday Inn about two kilometers from here. They'll pay for me to stay there."

"Are you sure you don't have anything else?" Cardinal said to the receptionist. "Surely in the entire hotel . . ."

The girl's reply was heavily accented. "Normally, yes, it would not be a problem. But tonight we have a high-school hockey team taking up an entire floor. I'm sorry."

Cardinal's heart went out to Delorme. Suddenly she was looking very small and tired.

"Why don't you stay in my room?" he said. "I'll go to the Holiday Inn."

"No way. I'm not going to put you out."

"Well, the other option is, we both stay in my room. It's got two double beds in it."

Delorme shook her head.

"We can be grownups about it," he said quietly. "I'm not going to jump you."

"And have the whole department making jokes? No, thank you."

"Who's going to know? I'm not going to tell anyone."

"I should go somewhere else."

"It's been a long day. You're tired. And we want to make an early start in the morning. Stay in my room."

"So help me, John, if you tell anyone—and I mean *anyone*—I will never speak to you again."

CARDINAL GOT INTO BED while Delorme was in the bathroom brushing her teeth. He wanted to call Catherine but felt too weird with Delorme around. He pulled out a paperback and forced himself to read a few pages.

When the bathroom door opened, he kept his gaze firmly on the book, but he could see from the corner of his eye that Delorme was still dressed. He rolled onto his side, facing away, and then there was the sound of her undressing, the zipper of her jeans.

A deep sigh as she got into bed. The room was overheated; what would she be wearing under those covers?

Cardinal turned once more onto his back and wondered what to say. He certainly didn't want to say anything too personal, anything that might be construed as provocative, but he didn't feel like going back to the case, either. Was Delorme experiencing anything remotely similar? Was she wondering what to say? Imagining things?

As if by way of answer, Delorme turned her back to him and switched off her light.

Of course, that could be open to interpretation. Was she hoping he would make a move? Lovely, the way her hair spilled in curls on the pillow behind her, the rise of her hip beneath the covers.

She'd called him her father at dinner. Put me in my place, Cardinal thought, reminding him of the twelve-odd years between them. He switched off his own light and resolved not to think about her anymore.

It didn't work, and he lay awake for a long time.

DELORME WAS UP and fully dressed before the wake-up call roused Cardinal. "I'll be in the coffee shop," she said, and then she was gone.

They drove out to the Eastern Townships and down the corduroy road that led to Sauvé's place. The sun had come out, and a stiff wind blew off the surrounding farmland. The fields resembled a swamp, glinting like metal in the sunlight. Cardinal made a couple of calls on his cell phone to the British Consulate. An intensely polite young woman said she would make the necessary inquiries and someone would call him back shortly.

"You okay?" Delorme asked at one point. "You seem a little grumpy."

"Tired," Cardinal said. "I didn't sleep well."

"Really? I slept fine."

Cardinal wondered if she were trying to rub it in, her complete physical indifference to him. But more likely she was just stating a fact: Physical attraction had not entered her head.

They pulled into Sauvé's drive, blocking Sauvé himself, who was just backing out. He leaned on his horn, sending crows and blue jays flapping from the trees. When Cardinal didn't move, Sauvé threw open his truck door and came lurching toward them. "I told you I've got nothing to say to the Mounties, the Sûreté, or any other police. Now get the hell out of my driveway."

"Mr. Sauvé, do you have a VCR? We brought one along in case you don't."

THE INTERIOR OF SAUVÉ'S house was in worse shape than even its owner. Plastic sheeting flapped at the windows in a vain attempt to keep the Quebec winter outside. One wall of the living room was nothing more than struts. Bits of drywall were strewn across the hallway. In the living room there was a lumpy sofa covered with a woolen blanket, where Cardinal and Delorme sat. Sauvé occupied an armchair that spewed stuffing from one arm. A black cat with bald patches prowled around his feet.

Sauvé had a Molson in his hand, and sat crookedly in the chair so that he could focus on the television with his good eye. The tape had been shot at night, from several different angles in a parking lot. It showed Sauvé getting out of his truck and unloading boxes labeled DEPARTMENT OF TRANSPORT. Two men got out of a van and examined the boxes before handing him an envelope. Sauvé drove off while they were loading the boxes into their van. When the tape was over, Sauvé hurled his beer across the room, shattering it against a wall. The smell of hops filled the air, mixing with the smell of mildew.

"Certain parties are willing to forget this episode," Cardinal said, "provided you cooperate with our investigation. And of course provided you cease and desist selling explosives to the French Self-Defense League."

Sauvé rubbed the bristles on his cheeks. Three fingers were missing from his hand. His eye was a drill hole of pure anger. "Tell me something, Detective. Do you really imagine there's a lot of difference between the Mounties and the people you put behind bars?"

"So far, I don't know any Mounties who have fed their murder victims to the bears. But I lead a sheltered life."

"Miles Shackley came up to Algonquin Bay a few days ago," Delorme said. "We think you might know why."

"Well, guess what, sister? I don't. I haven't seen Miles Shackley in over thirty years."

"And yet he called you three weeks ago. Why would that be?"

"He was an old spook and he didn't take well to retirement, okay? He was feeling nostalgic, calling old friends. Going over old ground. Trading war stories. Why shouldn't he call me?"

"You worked together at the CAT Squad, correct?"

"Yes. And our assignment was to cultivate informers in the FLQ. So we did."

"And the two of you worked with Detective Fougère?"

"Not at first. I worked with Fougère after he fucked up. Oh, excuse me, was I speaking ill of the dead? I'm so sorry. Lieutenant Fougère came up with the brilliant idea of Operation Coquette. Mostly because he was screwing the coquette."

"You're referring to Simone Rouault, now?"

"Yeah. Complete slut. Fougère recruits his girlfriend to infiltrate the FLQ and spends the first three months getting her to cozy up to a guy named Claude Hibert. Only one problem, Claude Hibert happened to be my informer."

"He was already working for the CAT Squad?"

"He was my informer—from before I joined the CAT Squad. He'd been mine for eighteen months. Fougère and his *putain* wasted months. So me and Shackley had to take him in hand. Shackley was CIA and a really stand-up guy. One of the few people in the world you could actually count on. When we formed the combined antiterrorist force, he volunteered to join. Didn't have to. He had a cushy assignment in New York before that.

"And resourceful, this guy. Not like Fougère. Shackley came to us, he already had an agent in place. CIA rules were, he wasn't supposed to share with us exactly who it was or where it was. He could share the goods, and rate them for likely accuracy, but the rest was strictly need-to-know."

"But you needed to know, obviously. Otherwise you risked making the same mistake as Fougère."

"Tell it to Langley. In the end it didn't matter, because Shackley and Langley didn't see eye to eye on a lot of things. He told me who his man on the spot was: an individual named Yves Grenelle."

"Did Yves Grenelle kill Raoul Duquette?"

"Read your files. Daniel Lemoyne and Bernard Theroux killed Raoul Duquette. They confessed to it."

Cardinal stood up. "All right. You're clearly in a hurry to go back to prison. Selling explosives to a terrorist group, that should be good for at least another eight years. And of course, as an ex-cop you'll be popular in the cell block."

"I'm telling you the truth. Lemoyne and Theroux—"

"Everyone knows they confessed to killing Duquette. We also know there was such a thing as cell solidarity. That whoever got caught would take the fall, and whoever got away got away. Yves Grenelle got away, right?"

"Yeah, he got away. So what?"

"And he was Shackley's agent, wasn't he."

"Yeah, he was Shackley's. So what?"

"And he killed Duquette. Didn't he."

"If he did, I had nothing to do with it."

"But maybe Shackley did. Suddenly in the middle of the October Crisis, the entire CAT Squad was hot to find Shackley. Why?"

"Maybe because he played a rough game. He didn't pussyfoot around."

"Meaning what? That Grenelle was more than an informer? He was a provocateur, wasn't he? Just like Simone Rouault. Committing more crimes than he was stopping?"

"What if he was?"

"Well, if Detective Fougère had his girlfriend robbing oil companies and planting bombs, I imagine Miles Shackley's man was capable of a lot more. Like killing Raoul Duquette."

Sauvé shrugged. "It's possible."

"That couldn't have been CIA policy. How's it in their interest to foment insurrection in a friendly neighbor?"

"You're right. The CIA would never do a thing like that. Any Chilean
will tell you that. Or you could ask the grateful Guatemalans."

"You're saying that was their policy?"

"Jesus. They don't grow them subtle in Ontario, do they? For the
record, no, I do not think it was CIA policy to foment insurrection in
Canada. Not official policy."

"But?"

"No but. End of story."

"How do you think that tape's going to play on the six o'clock news?
Shall we find out?"

"All right, for Christ's sake! You're asking me things I can't possibly
know! Unofficial CIA policy? Super-secret covert operations? How am I
supposed to know? I was a Mountie, for Christ's sake. If you want to
know what I think, I'll tell you that for free. But it's only hearsay and
guesswork and the only reason I'm in a position to do that is because
Shackley and I were tight. We got close because we were both black sheep
and we both liked to get the job done."

"Fine. We're listening."

Sauvé let out a deep sigh. He began to speak in a monotone, as if he
had lectured on the subject many times. "The U.S. under Nixon was extremely irritated with Canada. First, we suggest they lift the embargo on
Cuba. The Yanks are nuts on the subject of Cuba. Second, we take in
Vietnam draft dodgers by the planeload—not guaranteed to win us love
and understanding in Washington. Third, it's the height of the cold war,
and Trudeau declares us a nuclear-free zone. Nuclear-free. It's not as if we
were maintaining a real army. The States spend billions on defense and
they see us taking a free ride. And fourth, Trudeau's hair is too long. You
think I'm joking, but it's Richard Milhous Nixon we're talking about, Nature's own Master of Paranoia.

"The Nixon bunch wanted a different attitude in their northern neighbor, and they wanted it now. They wanted a conservative in power, some-

one who would see eye-to-eye on little matters like Vietnam and the cold war and nuclear weapons. And the best way to do that, according to the Nixon Department of the Real World, was to scare the living shit out of the Canadian population and get them to vote somebody else in. They had one big problem."

"Pierre Trudeau."

"Pierre Trudeau. These were the days of Trudeaumania. How are they gonna get Canadians to see the light? So they cook up this idea. Quebec is heating up. Why not heat it to the boiling point? Get the rest of Canada really scared. And when the people see just what a pussy Pierre Trudeau is, they'll throw him out and we'll get a red-blooded conservative in there. This wouldn't be a policy, you understand. It would be a what-if. A scenario.

"Shackley's job would have been to assess feasibility. You do that all the time in a security service, run a war game, test out a theory. So Shackley puts a man in place in the FLQ. He gets the guy ultra well-placed. And then when he's ready to rock and roll, the folks at Langley back off. Tell him thanks but no thanks. But Shackley's playing for keeps, see, so he continues to run Grenelle on his own. That's why he disappeared, and that's why, when Hawthorne and Duquette were kidnapped, every cop in Montreal that was looking for Daniel Lemoyne and Bernard Theroux was also looking for Miles Shackley."

"You think he ordered Grenelle to kill Duquette?"

"What's it matter?" Sauvé spat at his propane stove, causing a sudden sizzle like radio static. "Raoul Duquette has been dead for thirty years."

23

CARDINAL AND DELORME STOPPED for lunch at a tiny roadside diner called Chez Marguerite. Cardinal had been mentally rehearsing his order in French, but when Marguerite—an enormous woman with glasses thick as ashtrays—took their orders, she actually laughed.

"Why did she laugh? I thought I got it right."

Delorme shook her head. "It's your accent. You think French Canadian accents are funny, but believe me, it doesn't compare with an Anglo trying to speak French."

"That's it. I'm never speaking French again."

"Don't be silly. You did very well."

"Bloody French. Then they wonder why the rest of the country gets fed up with them."

"Stop it. You sound like McLeod."

"I was kidding."

Delorme looked out the window at the fields across the highway. The sun was still low in the sky, and the light caught coppery highlights in her hair. "You think Sauvé was telling the truth?"

"He certainly had more to gain by telling the truth. And everything he said matched with what we've heard from others. I think that's as much as we're going to get out of Shackley's phone contacts."

The owner brought their food: burger for Cardinal and for Delorme a plate of poutine—a French Canadian concoction of fries, gravy, and melted cheese curds.

"God, Delorme. How can you eat that?"

"Leave me alone. I only eat it when I'm in Quebec."

"Ah, yes. Those subtle, sophisticated French Canadian tastes."

Delorme leveled her earnest brown eyes at him. "You should say *com-mander*," she said. "When you're ordering food? *Je veux commander.*"

They were on Highway 20, just about back in town, when Cardinal's cell phone rang. The voice on the other end was very cultured, very British. "Good afternoon. May I speak with Detective John Cardinal, please?"

"You're speaking to him."

"Ah. I believe you were trying to get hold of me. My name is Hawthorne. Stuart Hawthorne."

STUART HAWTHORNE LOOKED to be in his late sixties, but trim and energetic. His hair, thick and silvery on top, retained traces of its former sandy color at the back near the neck. It was combed away from his brow, forming two swept-back wings above the ears. Cardinal had been expecting a pinstripe suit, but of course Hawthorne was retired now, with no reason to dress up. He wore a soft white shirt with button-down collar, khakis without cuffs, and a pair of Kodiak boots. He looked like a man who would be comfortable on safari, in a TV studio, or doing a bit of gardening in the backyard.

"You know, Detective, CSIS called me," he said, when Cardinal and Delorme picked him up at his Westmount home. "They're very anxious that I not talk to you."

"CSIS doesn't want anyone to talk to us," Cardinal said. "There are aspects of this investigation that don't reflect too well on their old guard."

"Well, that's fine with me. As far as I'm concerned, they made a complete dog's breakfast of the October Crisis back when they were known as the RCMP Security Service. If they'd handled it differently Raoul Duquette might well be alive."

"Did the person who called give a name?"

"He did not. Which immediately made me suspect his motives. He was an older man—well, he would be if he's the old guard—possibly French Canadian. In any case, I'm not about to hinder a murder investigation on the basis of an anonymous call."

They drove a short distance in silence. Then Hawthorne said, "You know, I used to get a lot of requests to do this sort of thing, but I stopped talking to the media more than a decade ago. Last time they contacted me was October, two thousand—thirtieth anniversary of the old business—I told them, No, no, no. Count me out. I just want to forget nineteen seventy—my part in it, anyway. On the other hand, there's not a day goes by I don't think of Raoul Duquette buried up there on Mount Royal."

Delorme drove, and Cardinal sat in back, an arrangement they had worked out ahead of time on the basis that Delorme might present a more sympathetic, not to say more attractive, ear. And it worked. Once they were under way, Hawthorne went on without much prodding. "Bloody media," he said. "I think the CBC people were hoping I'd say something terribly Christian and forgiving toward my kidnappers, but I'm sorry, I don't forgive them. Aside from what it did to me, people forget what they put my family through. You know at one point the media reported me dead—the same day Duquette was killed? Can you imagine what that did to my wife? I had a four-year-old boy, for God's sake. Forgive them? Not bloody likely. Wife was never the same afterward," Hawthorne said. "Harder on her than it was on me. That's what I can't forgive."

Delorme turned north onto a main thoroughfare, having worked out the most efficient route earlier.

Hawthorne watched the passing street life, which seemed to consist mostly of kids on skateboards and Arab women pushing prams. On the phone, Hawthorne had not been at all receptive to their meeting. "Look," he had said. "It was thirty years ago. One wants to get on with life."

And yet, curiously, Hawthorne had not left Canada after the kidnap crisis. Had not even left Quebec. When he had retired in 1988, he had chosen to retire in Montreal, the location of his ordeal. Cardinal asked him about that now.

"Well, I did actually try to go back to England, you know. Lived there for two years. But one gets used to different ways of thinking, different ways of living. To tell you the truth, I find Britain unbearably stodgy these days—despite the superficial modernism of Tony Blair—place still has an air of time-delay about it—twenty years behind the rest of the world."

He turned round to look at Cardinal. "Besides. Despite what happened to me, I've always liked Canadians. The people who kidnapped me were extremists. I had, and to this day still have, many French Canadian friends. But Canadians in general are a happy medium between your hidebound Englishman and your brash American. That's my experience, anyway. Perhaps you disagree."

"I don't know," Delorme said. "Some of my relatives are disgustingly conservative. They scare me sometimes. They vote for guys like Geoff Mantis."

"You notice I'm silent on the point. Diplomatic habits die hard."

Cardinal found himself intrigued by Hawthorne's accent. Oxford or Cambridge, Cardinal knew, but didn't know how he knew. The most ordinary words sounded beautiful. It made Cardinal slightly envious, and he wondered if Delorme felt the same around people from France, assuming she ever met people from France. Hawthorne was smooth, polished, finished, these were the words that came to mind—in a way that Canadians never were. He calls us a happy medium between the Americans and the English, Cardinal thought, but the truth is we're intimidated by both.

"I've never been back," Hawthorne said. "You know, to the house. The CBC asks me to visit. Every five years, like clockwork, some enterprising young producer—they're always named Mindy if they're anglo and Lise if they're French. . . ."

"That's my name," Delorme put in.

"In that case," Hawthorne said, "you should be working for the CBC." Delorme laughed.

"Anyway, as I say, the phone rings every five years and it's Mindy or Lise wanting to know would I mind very much taking a trip down memory lane. Reminisce about my time among the terrorists, and perhaps a trip to the actual house. On camera, of course.

" 'Actually,' I tell them, Bartleby-like, 'I should prefer not to.' This they take as great encouragement. They become smitten waifs whose ardor is only increased by rejection. For the next four weeks they call and call, ask me to lunch, ask me to dinner, suggest coming round to the house—

as if that is a great inducement—and all but offer me their firstborn child to give them an interview and go back to that blasted house. And I never do," he added, lapsing into a silence as they turned onto Delavigne, a narrow street of bungalows. "I never do."

"I'm sorry if it's not comfortable for you," Cardinal said. "But as I mentioned on the phone, we're desperate for information. It's not for entertainment, it's to catch a murderer."

"Yes, yes. Wouldn't be here, otherwise. Hang on, this is the actual street, isn't it—Delavigne? Yes, the actual street. Of course, I never saw it at the time. Not the street."

"You were blindfolded?" Delorme asked.

"In the car, yes. You know what they blindfolded me with? An old gas mask. Had the eyepieces blacked out. Couldn't see a bloody thing. But I can tell you it terrified me. Didn't know it was a blindfold, did I? Thought they were going to gas me or something. I mean, they were shoving me down in the backseat, threatening me, and then they've got this stinking rubbery thing over my face. Doesn't do much for one's innate sense of optimism."

"Here we are," Delorme said. She pulled into the driveway of a small white bungalow behind a maroon minivan.

"Gosh," Hawthorne said.

Cardinal started to get out of the car.

"Hang on a sec," Hawthorne said. "Would you mind awfully if we just sat here for a minute? It's all a bit of a . . ."

Cardinal closed the door.

"Gosh," Hawthorne said again. "D'you know, if I'd walked by this place, I'd never have known it was the one. Never in a million years. Well, of course, I never saw it properly, being blindfolded. That is, I did and I didn't. I caught glimpses of it through the edge of the mask that first day. And then on the last day, when they finally drove me out of here. I came out and got into the back of this old wreck of a car they had, and I saw it as we drove away. But it looked quite different somehow."

"It's the house, sir. The number's the same. And I've looked at the old news photos. Only difference is they've added a carport."

"Oh, I'm sure you're right. I'm sure it's the house. It's just that, in my mind, in my memory, it's become such a nightmarish thing. Not so much anymore, of course, more in the first five years or so, when I'd dream about it. Think about it. But the point is, that's the real shape it took on for me, the shape in my mind. Not this place we're looking at now."

"I'm sorry to put you through this, sir." Cardinal wasn't sure why he kept calling him sir. There was hardly anyone he ever called sir. That damn accent.

"No, no. Not at all. It's probably good for me in fact. Slaying-the-dragon sort of thing. It's just a little house on a quiet street. Not a torture chamber. No, no, I'm sure that's good." Hawthorne slapped his knees. "Righty-ho. Lead on."

They were met at the door by Al Lamotte, the present owner of the house. Delorme had talked to him on the phone, making the arrangements. Like her, he was in his mid-thirties, and had no strong memories of the political events of 1970. The house had changed hands a dozen times since then; Lamotte had been living there with his wife and son for two years. The wife and son were out just now.

"Look," he said, after introductions were made, "I'll just stay out of your way, all right? You just wander where you have to wander, and I'll be in the kitchen."

"Thanks, Mr. Lamotte," Cardinal said. "It's very kind of you."

Lamotte made a deprecating gesture and went into the kitchen.

Hawthorne had been standing, hands jauntily on hips, surveying the place. Outside the living-room window, trees and a distant steeple glittered in the sunlight.

Cardinal looked at him expectantly.

"I never saw the living room till the end. It was almost totally bare. A few sleeping bags, a couple of hard chairs. They clearly hadn't expected the thing to take more than a couple of days. I was kept in the bedroom the whole time. Always an armed guard by the door. Don't remember much else about this room. Place was surrounded by police and about six thousand army troops. I just wanted to be out of here before the bullets started flying." Hawthorne's voice quavered a little. A crack in the smooth finish.

"They kept me in the bedroom at all times, except when I needed the bathroom. They even went in there with me, for God's sake. That was depressing." Hawthorne turned to face them. "Look, I really don't think I'm going to have any great revelations. It's all too long ago. And of course I haven't wanted to remember, I've wanted to forget."

"Can we take a look at the bedroom?" It was Delorme who spoke, and Cardinal was glad. It was hard to see a cool man like Hawthorne tremble.

The Englishman tucked his chin into his chest. It was as close as he came to a nod. Then Delorme turned, and he followed her down the dim corridor like a boy.

Cardinal stayed in the hallway where the light from the bedroom fell in a bright slant. Hawthorne hunched at the far side of the room, hands in pockets, chin tucked in as if he were standing in a high wind.

It was a child's room now, the domain—to judge by the sports gear—of a ten- or eleven-year-old boy. An enormous teddy bear sat hunched in one corner. On the wall a colorful kite hung waiting for summer, a Montreal Canadiens poster beside it. A yellow dresser with several drawers hanging open was strewn with video games, comic books, and collectible cards with pictures of witches and wizards on them. There was a small desk with a computer. The screensaver showed a Tyrannosaurus rex in full roar. There was a faint smell of new sneakers.

"Oh my," Hawthorne said quietly.

Cardinal and Delorme waited. Hawthorne shifted his weight, looking around.

"I'm glad it's a child's room," he said, without explanation. Cardinal didn't think he was talking to them, anyway. "It's like revisiting a battlefield. Gettysburg or Poitiers. Ever been? A few quiet hills, flowers and grass waving in the wind. You'd never know what took place here.

"Of course, it seems so small, now. Two kidnappings, one murder. A blip on the screen, compared to September eleventh. But it's a terrifying thing to be kidnapped." He turned to Delorme. "Two months I spent in here. Two months."

"It's a long time."

"Wasn't so bad at first. After the initial shock, I mean. They were polite, made sure I was comfortable—or as comfortable as you can be with your ankles tied and a hood on your head. It was a pillowcase torn open along one seam. I could see straight ahead, but no peripheral vision. Had a marvelous view of that wall for two months. They kept reassuring me that they weren't going to hurt me, that I was just a pawn, etcetera, something to trade. I suppose they were quite deferential, in their way."

He turned to face the window. "That was boarded up. I fantasized about slowly loosening the board and one day jumping out, but there was always an armed guard watching me. They used to bring me books to read—political stuff at first, and later paperback thrillers." He sighed, and there was a shudder in his breath.

"How many were here?" Cardinal asked, but Hawthorne seemed not to hear. He continued with his muttered tour of the past, now pointing at a corner, now nodding toward a wall.

"The bed was a single cot. Comfortable enough, I suppose, but very narrow. Made it easier for them to tie me."

A turn, a nod.

"Canvas chair by the door. Always someone in it, too. They were always armed but never flashed the weapon or anything. Having it was enough."

A turn, a nod.

"Fold-out card table here. Two little fold-up chairs. Where I ate. Lot of takeout food, of course. But there was a woman who cooked occasionally. Madeleine, her name was. She made a good tourtiere, other dishes. Even baked things sometimes. She seemed to feel guilty about the whole enterprise. 'Don't worry,' she would whisper to me once in a while. 'Don't worry. You'll be all right.'"

The memory seemed to pluck some string of emotion in him that had been hitherto silent. He squeezed the bridge of his nose between thumb and forefinger.

"And you know—I was all right. I really was all right. They had the television or radio on all the time, so I was up to date with the news. And it sounded as if the provincial government was doing everything it could to negotiate an end to the thing. But then Ottawa called out the army. The minute they declared the War Measures Act, the air was sucked right out of this place. The kidnappers weren't expecting that, you see. They thought there were real negotiations going on. But once Ottawa took over . . ."

With the tip of his Kodiak boot, Hawthorne traced the outline of a tiger in the rug at his feet. "Once they thought the negotiations were hopeless, they became frightened. Well, you saw what happened with the other cell. The day after War Measures were declared, they killed Raoul Duquette. . . ."

The tip of his boot traced the tiger's muzzle, around to the ears, back down to the chin.

"That poor man has been in his grave for thirty years. And it's entirely a matter of luck. He got with the more violent group. People have suggested he argued with his kidnappers, but I'm sure he was not so foolish as to antagonize them. No, he just had the bad luck to be taken by people who were willing to kill. My kidnappers were not, and I don't for one minute put it down to my diplomatic skills. Although I did joke with them and so on, as much as possible.

"The important thing was to humanize myself in their eyes, without in any way kowtowing. Just to keep them thinking of me as a person, not an object. Disposable. I remember once, one of them let an enormous fart, and I said, 'Ah. *Votre arme secrète*. Your secret weapon. They got a laugh out of that."

"How many people held you?" Delorme said.

"Four. Jacques Savard, Robert Villeneuve, the girl, Madeleine, and a man who came and went named Yves. He was the only one who threatened me. 'Don't think we won't do it,' he'd say. 'I could snap your neck like this!' and he'd snap his fingers. Bloody brute. World's full of people like him, unfortunately."

"You never heard his last name?"

"Never. He insisted everyone just call him comrade or soldier, but the girl slipped once or twice, calling him Yves. He never stayed more than half an hour, thank God. I think he was mostly relaying messages." Hawthorne suddenly swung round and strode toward the bedroom door. "I really can't be in here anymore, it's just too much."

In the living room he leaned against the back of an armchair, breathing heavily.

"Everything all right?" the owner called from the kitchen.

"Fine," Cardinal said. "We'll be gone in a minute."

"Why don't you sit down," Delorme said. "Take a breather."

"No, it's all right. I'm fine. Sorry about the little display." Hawthorne managed a smile, but sweat had beaded on his forehead.

Cardinal pulled out the photograph of Miles Shackley. "Do you recognize this man?"

"No. Should I?"

"Not necessarily. And these people?" Cardinal showed him the photo. Four smiling terrorists with the window behind them.

"Well, Lemoyne and Theroux I recognize from the newspaper accounts. They were never here, as far as I know. They were busy killing Mr. Duquette. That's Madeleine, the one who would occasionally cook."

"And the man on the end?" Cardinal pointed to the man with the black curls, the striped T-shirt.

"I'm not likely to forget that man. He's the one they called Yves. The bully of the group."

"We believe his name is Yves Grenelle," Cardinal said.

"May have been. Understand, I didn't want to know anything. I wanted to be as little threat to them as possible. Didn't want to give them any reason to kill me—other than the political one. You tell me that's Yves Grenelle, I'll believe you. I never heard the full name. I just knew him as a right bastard, if you'll forgive the technical term."

"How did you see his face?" Delorme said. "You were blindfolded, no?"

"That man didn't care whether I saw his face. And that terrified me. One time he pulled my hood off, when Madeleine was in the room."

"Did he come round throughout your time here? Were his visits regular?"

"Not at all. He came three or four times toward the beginning. After that I never saw him again. Which doesn't mean he didn't come. I was locked away in the bedroom."

"But you never saw him after the second week?"

"I don't believe so. The news was on all the time, and I know he didn't come around after they killed Duquette. I'd have remembered that, because he scared me bad before that. After Duquette was dead, they all scared me. I was terrified he would come round again and stir them up, but if he did come, I didn't see him." Hawthorne suddenly got to his feet. "Look, I think I've been all the help I can, Detective. Now, if you'll excuse me, I'd very much like to go home."

Cardinal went to the kitchen to thank the owner of the house.

"You're welcome," Lamotte said. "Hell of a thing that happened here. Hell of a thing. I'm glad it's not, you know, the other house. The one where they . . ."

"Right," said Cardinal. "Thanks again."

"Was that the fellow they kidnapped? The diplomat?"

"I can't tell you anything, I'm afraid. It's an investigation in progress."

"After thirty years? Doesn't sound like much progress."

"Well, you know," Cardinal said. "Slow but steady wins the race."

"Yeah, right. And if you believe that . . . What's wrong?"

"That window," Cardinal said, speaking to himself, really. "That steeple in the distance."

"Ste Agathe. Still the tallest thing in the neighborhood."

The neogothic lines of the steeple looked stagey against the heavy cloud. Cardinal pulled the photograph out of his pocket, the four grinning young terrorists. The view outside the window looked different. It had been summer then; the trees outside were green and full. But the view across the street was otherwise the same. A brown wooden ranch house with a fat cedar outside, and off to the right, above distant rooftops, the steeple of Ste. Agathe. "It was taken here," Cardinal said. "The picture was taken in this room."

"For sure," said Mr. Lamotte, who was peering over his shoulder. "That's the house across the street. And there's the church."

Cardinal couldn't wait to tell Delorme, but when he got into the car he found Hawthorne sobbing in the front seat like a child, and Delorme looking for once at a loss.

They waited a couple of minutes. Hawthorne pulled out a handkerchief and wiped his eyes, blew his nose thoroughly, and then sat back, exhausted. "God," he said, and shook his head slowly back and forth. "You want to know the truly stupid thing?"

"Sure," Cardinal said.

"I told them this on the first day. They'd sat me down and got the hood on me and had my wrist manacled to the bed frame. They'd finished cheering each other for their wonderful victory, etcetera. And when it was quiet and there were just two of them in the room, I said to them, 'Mes pauvres amis,' I said. 'I have some bad news for you, I'm afraid. The truth is, I'm not even English, you see. So, if you think Her Majesty's Government is going to lift a finger to save me, you're sadly mistaken.'"

Delorme looked at him. "You're not English?"

"No, madam. That's the ridiculous thing." Hawthorne shook his head in amazement at the scope of human folly, and his next statement came out in a tone of wonder. "I'm Irish."

24

THE REST OF THE DAY was given over to
the dreariness that is contemporary travel. First there was the rainy drive
out to Dorval Airport. Then there was a long wait made worse by Air
Canada's refusal to impart any information beyond "icy conditions in Ontario." They both pulled out their cell phones; Cardinal called Musgrave.

"Here's something for you to file under certifiable facts," Musgrave
said. "Leon Petrucci did not order your man to be killed, and Leon
Petrucci didn't order Paul Bressard to feed him to the bears, and Leon
Petrucci didn't write that note."

"Why not?"

"Because Leon Petrucci is dead."

"Dead?"

"Yes. Leon Petrucci is thoroughly, completely, totally dead. He had another operation down at Toronto Mount Sinai two months ago and he fell
into a coma and never woke up. He died a week ago last Tuesday. Long
before your victim showed up in Algonquin Bay."

"How come it wasn't in the papers?"

"It will be. He wasn't registered under his real name."

"You're sure about all this."

"Cardinal, I work for the RCMP. Organized crime is what we do.
Whoever killed Miles Shackley, believe me, it wasn't Leon Petrucci. And
while we're on the subject of interagency cooperation, I'd like to thank
you for letting me know Squier quit," Musgrave said. "Nothing like keeping me up to the minute."

"Sorry. Really, there hasn't been a chance. You know, Squier actually
turned out to be helpful in the end."

"By accident, no doubt. I have to tell you, though, my man at CSIS tells me the pressure came from very high up. Yesterday morning they get a visit—not a call, a personal visit—from Jim Coulter. Do you know who Jim Coulter is?"

"Name's familiar."

"Deputy chief of CSIS operations in Ottawa, and a real bastard—former Mountie, too, so I know whereof I speak. Anyway, Jim Coulter has a confab with CSIS Toronto, and two hours later Calvin Squier is out the door. You do the math. Squier may say he quit, but I think he *got* quit."

"Well, we've figured out why CSIS trailed Shackley. They don't want it coming to light that Raoul Duquette was murdered by a CIA informer—an informer run by an agent working on our CAT Squad."

"Ouch. Yeah, that wouldn't exactly enhance their image."

"Listen, do you guys have someone who can age a photograph?"

"Yeah, sure. Tony Catrell'll do it for you."

"You got a number for him?"

There was a pause.

"You still there?" Cardinal said.

"Still here. Just rethinking this age progression business. You know what? Don't use Tony. Tony's a nuts-and-bolts guy. Knows everything there is to know about the software, but, I don't know. He's a bit of a cold fish. No, I think you wanna take this to Miriam Stead at Toronto Police."

"I figured it'd be faster using one of your guys."

"Miriam Stead is like the guru of age progression. Been doing this stuff for thirty years. There's nobody better. Nobody faster, either. The difference is, Tony'll give you a likeness. But Miriam—Miriam's an artist. I don't know how she does it, but you give Miriam Stead a photograph, she'll give you back a human being. She's also a workaholic, who likes to spend her weekends in the office. By the way, do you have any idea what the weather's doing up here?"

"What, is it snowing?"

Musgrave just chuckled and hung up.

. . .

THEIR PLANE TOOK OFF at four o'clock. Cardinal slept most of the way to Toronto.

"Boy, you sure conked out," Delorme said when he woke up, rubbing his eyes. "Are you all right?"

"Little out of it. Had trouble sleeping last night."

"Yeah, that room was overheated."

"Frankly, it was because you were in the room. It was distracting."

"Come on, Cardinal. That's ridiculous."

"Don't give me that, like it's some big shock. You think because I'm married I'm not attracted to women? Do I look like a choirboy to you?"

"No."

"So what's the big mystery?"

"Nothing. I'm just surprised, okay? That's legal, right, for me to be surprised?"

"Jesus. Forget I said anything, all right?"

"Fine. It's forgotten."

They landed in Toronto only to find their connecting flight to Algonquin Bay had been canceled. Once more, the laconic explanation: Icy conditions.

"Oh, man," Delorme said. "I don't want to spend another night in a big city."

"I'll call Jerry Commanda. Maybe we can catch a ride on an OPP chopper. Anyway, there's one good thing about this."

"Really?" Delorme said. "I wish you'd tell me what it is."

"Toronto's ident headquarters is at Jane and Wilson. That's actually not too far from here. We can take a cab."

"Fabulous," Delorme said. "Just fabulous."

They were met at the front desk of ident headquarters by Miriam Stead. Whatever Cardinal had been expecting, Miriam Stead was not it. She had white hair, short and spiky, and silver hoop earrings. She wore a gray turtleneck over black jeans and a pair of scarlet Keds. There wasn't a trace of fat on her, and if it weren't for the gray hair, she could've been mid-forties. A marathoner, Cardinal thought. Got to be.

She brought them back to her workstation, which was a cubicle furnished mostly with machines Cardinal didn't recognize and two Mac computers with gigantic screens, one of which showed the image of a desiccated skull.

"He's cute," Delorme said.

"Sorry," Ms. Stead said, and clicked the image into oblivion. "Reconstruction project, obviously. That's mostly what I do—reconstruction and missing kids. But I understand you have something a little different for me."

Cardinal handed her the group photograph and told her what they needed. While he was talking, Ms. Stead slipped the picture into a flatbed scanner, and it appeared bit by bit on the Mac screen behind her. Still listening, she swiveled around and went to work with her mouse—now cropping, now enlarging—until the head and shoulders of Yves Grenelle all but filled the screen.

"If you don't know his real name, then I don't imagine you'll be giving me any photos of Ma and Pa and Gramps, right?"

"Sorry."

"That's mostly what we use, of course. With a missing kid, if you want to know what they look like seven years later, you age them toward Mom and Dad. Without that kind of input, we don't know whether your man is likely to be skinny or fat, hairy or bald."

"Maybe this isn't such a great idea, then," Delorme said.

"Oh, no, I can help you. What we're talking about is the human being's battle with gravity. Basically everything sinks—flesh heads earthward, cartilage lengthens, the nose starts to sag. It's a terrible flaw in the design. But what we do in a situation like this where there's no genetic input is we'll give you several possibilities—using the variables I just mentioned and also updating hairstyles and so on. What can you tell me about your fella's lifestyle? Is he a drinker? A smoker? Weightlifter? Health nut? All of that affects how people age."

"Well, now you're making me feel dumb," Cardinal said. "I didn't even ask anyone about those things. Coming here was pretty spur-of-the-moment."

"That's all right. I may be a civilian, but I do realize you people aren't trying to make my job more difficult, even if that is invariably what you do."

"What are the chances of any of your variations being close to reality?" Delorme asked.

"If he's got fat and bald, then the version that's fat and bald will look a lot like him. Not just a little. A lot. Obviously you can't use it for court-room ID without fingerprints or DNA or something, but the truth is, the proportions of your face don't change. That's why—say you haven't seen someone for thirty, forty years. The moment you get up close and they start to speak, you're looking in their eyes, you know it's them."

"To give us all these variations," Cardinal said. "That's going to take a few days, I suppose."

"You should have them by tomorrow."

"Really? Musgrave said you were good."

"Sergeant Musgrave of the Mounties! I love that man! I swear, he must've been born wearing a tunic and a Smoky hat."

"She's right about people aging differently," Delorme said when they had gone back to the front desk. "I hope I look that good when I'm her age."

"Keep eating that poutine," Cardinal said.

"Did you see that plaque in her cubicle?"

"I did. Miriam Stead finished among the first twenty seniors in the New York marathon last year."

After what seemed like a thousand phone calls back and forth to Jerry Commanda at OPP ("Jesus, stay in Toronto, Cardinal. This town is frozen solid, I kid you not"), Cardinal managed to arrange a helicopter ride courtesy of the Ontario Provincial Police.

IT WAS ONE THING to hear about icy conditions and quite another to see them firsthand. The pilot told them things were supposed to be "pretty hairy" up in Algonquin Bay, but people were always saying that about the weather up there. "We got a two- or three-hour break in the rain for now, so we'll be fine. Runway's useless for planes, though," he told them. Rotor noise made conversation difficult after that, and it was too dark to see much from the air.

As they were passing over Bracebridge, Delorme jabbed a gloved finger toward the ground. She shouted to Cardinal: "No cars!"

It was true. The highway unfurled like a pale gray ribbon among the hills, completely empty. A ghost highway.

Even so, the helicopter ride went so smoothly that it was hard to understand why the regular flight had been canceled—until they landed. The pilot stepped down first, and fell flat on his face; the tarmac was a sheet of solid ice. Except for two security guards and a lonely-looking maintenance man, the airport itself was deserted.

"This is weird," Delorme said. "It's like a dream I used to have all the time."

The pilot's wife was waiting for him in the parking lot, motor running. Cardinal and Delorme turned down the offer of a ride—foolishly, as it turned out. The car Delorme had left at the airport was now an ice sculpture. It took them half an hour to open the doors, using a pair of hammers they managed to borrow from the maintenance man.

It was frustrating work—Cardinal fell to his knees more than once—and his desire to be home and warm became more intense by the minute. Delorme, somehow immune to gravity, managed to work efficiently without falling once, though she did let fly with several curses, the first French Cardinal had learned—in the playground, not in class.

The highway into town was treacherous, even though it had been heavily salted. Abandoned cars were strewn at crazy angles on the shoulders and in the culverts. There were no pedestrians anywhere. There was exactly one other car on the road, a red minivan just ahead of them that several times threatened to go off the road.

It was nine thirty by the time Delorme turned onto Madonna Road. Less than a hundred yards after the turnoff she had to stop for a gigantic branch that had snapped from a frozen poplar. Cardinal knew the tree well. In summer, after a heavy rain, it was the branch that hung lowest, and by August it would sometimes brush the roof of the car as he drove by. It was no wonder the thing had broken; it was encased in a good half inch of ice. As Cardinal dragged it to the side of the road, it sounded like the snapping of a thousand small bones.

"Listen," he said, back in the car. "About what I said—about last night."

Delorme frowned at the road ahead, her face pale in a stripe of passing moonlight. "Don't worry about it."

"I'm sorry I said it. I'd just woke up from a serious nap and I wasn't thinking clearly. It was unprofessional, and I don't want it to get in the way."

"It won't. Not on my side, anyway." Delorme slowed very gradually to a stop. "I don't think I'll try your driveway with this ice."

"So, we're okay on that?"

"We're fine," Delorme said.

Cardinal waited for her to say something more, but she just stared straight ahead, waiting for him to get out.

"I'll see you tomorrow, then," he said.

"Yeah. See you tomorrow."

Catherine had put salt down on the driveway, but even so, it was hard to walk up the slope without falling. He had to cling to the handrail of the back stairs.

"Catherine?" he called as he stepped into the kitchen.

Catherine came in and gave him a hug. "I'm afraid you've come home to a bit of a crowd scene. Tess and Abby are here. The lights are out over in Ferris, so I invited Sally to stay here."

"They're sleeping over?"

"They have no heat at their place. Thank God we have the woodstove. Half the city has no heat."

"Hi, John." Sally Westlake, a square-built blonde in a reindeer sweat-shirt, waved to him from the living room. "Sorry to land on you like this."

"No, no. You're welcome, Sally. Stay as long as you want. How long's your power been out?"

"Since last night. Every time they get it going, it fails again in half an hour or so."

"Is it just in Ferris? The lights were still on up on Airport Road."

There was a terrific explosion outside.

"What the hell was that!"

"A branch," Catherine said. "They fall from the trees and just shatter and it makes that incredible sound. It makes going to sleep a real challenge."

"Makes me jump out of my skin every time," Sally said.

Cardinal drew Catherine aside. "Have you talked to Dad?"

"A couple of hours ago. He seemed fine. Wouldn't come down here, of course."

"I better go check on him. I'm not going to be able to sleep otherwise. Speaking of which, we're not exactly the Sheraton, here. I guess Sally and the girls can stay in Kelly's room, and if I can persuade Dad to stay with us he can have the pullout couch."

"He hates the pullout couch. If he comes we'll just have to think of something else."

CARDINAL WAS AT THE TOP of Airport Hill again when the power went out. Without a sound the highway turned to utter blackness, as if someone had thrown a tarp over the car. He pulled to the side of the road and waited for his vision to adjust before pulling out again.

The Camry crept along the crest of Airport Hill, headlights carving cones of visibility into the darkness, and then onto Cunningham. The dirt road was even worse going. The surface had not been salted, and it was like trying to drive on a hockey rink. Cardinal stayed in low gear. The blackness outside the car was so complete, he was not at all sure he'd be able to see his father's place, but as he crawled around the last curve on Cunningham, the moon emerged from behind a cloud, and the white trim of his father's house took shape against the trees. The verdigris squirrel was a black silhouette against a moonlit cloud, icicles hanging from its nose and tail.

The house was dark.

Cardinal stepped round to the back porch. There was a phosphorescent glow from inside. His father heard the noise and came to the back door, wearing his coat.

"What the hell are you doing here?"

"Nice to see you too, Dad. I came to see how you're making out up here."

"I'm just fine, thank you." His father stared at him from the shadows of the kitchen. Behind him, a Coleman lamp hissed on the table.

"But you've got no power."

"Believe it or not, John, I knew that before you got here."

"Dad, you've got no heat. Why don't you come down to our place for the night?"

"Because I'm fine right here. It's not that cold out, I've got my Coleman lamp going strong, and I've got a good book. I've got a transistor radio and a Coleman stove, too—case I have to heat water."

"You can't use a Coleman stove, Dad. The carbon monoxide will kill you."

His father blinked at him. "I know that. I'll use it on the porch."

"Dad, come to our place. The power could be out for hours."

"I'm fine right here. Now, unless there was something else you needed?"

"Dad—"

"Goodnight, John. Oh—how was Montreal?"

"It was fine. Look, just because you spend a night with us doesn't mean you're totally dependent, you know. It's an ice storm, for God's sake. Don't you think you're being a little unreasonable?"

"Never liked Montreal—probably because I don't speak French. Never saw the need. Well, thanks for dropping by, John. I suppose I'll see you for lunch on Tuesday."

"Dad, for God's sake, what are you going to do—sleep under forty pounds of blankets?"

"That's exactly what I plan to do. Not forty pounds, but I've got my down coat and a down sleeping bag, and I'll sleep in front of the fireplace."

"On what?"

"On my damn mattress, that's what. It's all set up and there's nothing to worry about."

"You dragged the mattress by yourself? Your heart's not up to that kind of strain anymore."

"Nice of you to remind me. But if I'd have asked you to help with the mattress you'd have given me a lecture about staying with you. Can't you see I'm fine up here? Is that so hard to believe? You know I looked after myself for thirty-four years before you were born, and I'm perfectly capable of looking after myself now. The power will be on in a couple of hours, and there'll be no need to have this discussion. Not that there's any need now. Goodnight."

"I'll put some more firewood up on the porch," Cardinal said, but his father was already closing the door.

As Cardinal turned off Airport Hill onto Algonquin, the city, which normally glittered like a box of rhinestones, lay below him in a pool of darkness. The smell of wood smoke was strong. When the moon appeared, he could see streams of smoke bending like saplings toward the east, as if the whole town was sailing west. Even the traffic lights were out. Cardinal counted six separate hydro crews on his way back to Madonna Road.

When he got home again he stood for a while by the side of the house, listening—he wasn't sure for what. If Bouchard came after him, it wouldn't likely happen on a night like this. But he listened all the same. The only sounds were the click and chatter of icy branches.

"He wouldn't come?" Catherine asked as soon as Cardinal was in the door.

"Nope. He'd rather freeze his ass off up there than spend the night in his son's home. He's got no heat except the fireplace. And he was planning to cook on the Coleman—a very efficient way to kill yourself. Anyway, I put some firewood by the back door. He should be all right for the night."

"I'll talk to him tomorrow, John. Why don't you sit down and I'll heat up some chili for you?"

"Sally asleep?"

"Uh-huh. I hope you don't mind that I invited them here."

"Of course not. You always do the right thing."

Catherine placed the bowl of chili in front of him and he told her about Montreal. He told her about interviewing the players in the crisis of thirty years before, about his feeling that he had been walking through a time warp, about how he had missed her.

"Oh, I nearly forgot to mention," he added. "I slept with another woman in Montreal."

"You did?"

"Well, in the same room anyway. Delorme got flooded out of hers, and the hotel didn't have any others. There was an extra bed in mine."

"Lise is very good looking."

"Yes, she is."

"It must have been quite a temptation."

"It wasn't like sharing with McLeod. That's for sure."

25

THE RAIN BEGAN to fall once more in the early hours of the morning. It fell in large drops that tumbled through a layer of cold air hovering just above the ground. Each drop, upon impact with the previous layer of ice, was transformed instantly to more ice. The rain froze on the rooftops, it froze on the cars. It froze on the streetlamps and highways. It froze on the trunks of trees and on the tiniest branches. It froze on the hydro wires, on the mailboxes, and on the traffic lights. It froze on the roof of the cathedral, glazing its spire and cross. It froze on the wooden apex of the modernist synagogue, and it froze on the stone arch in Ferris Park that says GATEWAY TO THE NORTH.

Cardinal had seen many ice storms, but never one like this. On Monday he drove into town with absurd slowness; the city around him had been transformed into a gigantic chandelier.

He got to work—late, of course—and found that the storm had sealed the Algonquin Bay police station not just in a carapace of ice, but into a kind of muffled peace. Several people failed to show up for duty, as did the entire construction crew, and a pleasant quiet hung over the place.

Somewhere someone was whistling—probably Chouinard—and Nancy Newcombe, in charge of the evidence room, was admonishing someone to fill in the date (legibly, thank you very much) beside his or her signature. At the desk next to Cardinal, Delorme was murmuring into the phone. It was amazing to Cardinal how quietly Delorme could conduct business. It always sounded as if she were imparting secrets to a lover, but she was invariably just doing the footwork like everyone else.

Power had been restored to Airport Hill and Cunningham Road—

Cardinal had made sure, first thing. But he had resisted the impulse to drive up there and check on his father. Catherine would call Stan from home; he wouldn't resent hearing from her. Coming home had brought Cardinal a curious kind of tranquility—transient, he knew—but he savored it as he sat in the early morning silence. That silence was blown into tiny pieces by a voice suddenly booming out from the front counter.

"Disgusting! Who ordered up this ridiculous weather? I go away for two weeks and the entire city falls apart." This delivered at ten on the volume knob, in the window-rattling voice of Detective Ian McLeod, Cardinal's sometime partner, elder colleague, and paranoid pain in the ass.

McLeod was in his late fifties, a solid, foul-mouthed, barrel-shaped knot of muscle topped with a short frizz of graying red hair. Lately, and for reasons known only to himself, McLeod had taken to calling his colleagues "Doctor." Cardinal found it faintly irritating, but most things about McLeod were irritating.

"Dr. Cardinal is doing rounds, I see. Or are you performing surgery today—extracting confessions from some hopelessly comatose criminal?"

"I wish. How was Florida?"

"Florida was wonderful. Lots of sunshine. The sun down there actually gives off some heat! Great food! But the place is crawling with Cubans and geezers. I'm telling you, coming back here, it feels fabulous to look around and see people walking unassisted—trying to, anyway. Half the Sunshine State is over eighty and the other half doesn't speak English."

Delorme covered the mouthpiece of the phone. "For God's sake, McLeod, I'm trying to work, here."

"Then you got the French Canadians." McLeod jerked his chin in Delorme's direction. "Getting so there's no point going away. Goddamn frogs. It's like being at work."

McLeod settled his big frame on the chair next to Cardinal's and demanded to know everything about their cases. Delorme was off the phone now, and they told him the story, finishing up with their trip to Montreal.

"Goddamn," McLeod said in a tone of wonder several times. And when they were finished: "I can't get over the bears. I mean, I've heard of getting rid of evidence, but this is going too far." Eventually he wandered over to his own desk, where he proceeded to bellow into the phone.

Cardinal's phone rang; it was Musgrave on the other end.

"I have finally managed to pry some information out of the FBI," he said. "I don't know what those guys do for a living, but sharing information isn't one of them."

"They give you anything on Shackley?"

"Turns out Mr. Shackley has a record, after all. Seems our former CIA hard case was nabbed for a little extortion back in 'ninety-two. Tried to put the arm on a former operative of theirs, one Diego Aguilar, who used to do cocaine runs up the Gulf coast and who was also—only coincidentally, of course—working for the CIA. Shackley was part of the team that ran him. When Shackley hit hard times, he went to Aguilar for help. When Aguilar failed to be generous and supportive, Shackley threatened to expose his drug background. Even had copies of surveillance videotapes as backup."

"And his victim just toughed it out? Went to the cops?"

"Better. Shackley made a slight miscalculation with this Aguilar guy— he failed to notice that the guy never stopped working for the CIA, although now it's as a communications network consultant to Latin American countries. So he just put in a complaint to Langley, and they had the local police pick Shackley up. Did six years for that little stunt."

Cardinal went over to Delorme's desk and propped the FLQ snapshot on her keyboard.

"Musgrave tells me Shackley did time for trying to extort money out of a tough guy used to do work for the CIA. That gives us motive. I think he was up to his old tricks again—using this photograph—and I think this time his target was Yves Grenelle."

"Yves Grenelle under another name, you mean."

"Under another name and thirty years later. Presumably a French Canadian name. In fact, maybe that's who tried to stop Rouault and Hawthorne from talking to us. Maybe it wasn't CSIS."

"They both said it was an older man," Delorme said. "But Hawthorne wasn't certain he was French Canadian."

"Rouault was. So who does that give us?"

"Paul Bressard? But you've cleared him, right?"

"Bressard's not old enough. He would have been nine or ten in nineteen seventy. Of course there's always Dr. Choquette. He's certainly the right age, and he was angry at Winter Cates."

"It's not Dr. Choquette. He's got several witnesses who were playing cards with him when Dr. Cates was kidnapped. Strong witnesses, too."

"Well, Miles Shackley comes up here to blackmail Yves Grenelle, whoever he is, who's been living under a new identity for God knows how long. He arranges a meeting, shows him what he's got, and there's a fight. Shackley is killed, but Grenelle is injured too."

"If I was threatening someone with blackmail, I think I'd keep a gun on them."

"So would I. Maybe Grenelle makes a grab for it and gets shot, but he manages to kill Shackley. He dumps the body in the woods and sinks the car. He tries to go on with his life. But he's got a bullet in him, or he's at least got a bad enough hole in him he can't fix it himself."

"He has to find a doctor, we know that. It keeps bringing us back to the same question: Why pick Winter Cates?"

"That's the tough one. She's new in town, which narrows it down to neighbors and patients—both of which have come up clean. But this time at least we know what the killer looked like thirty years ago. Plus we'll have whatever Miriam Stead comes up with."

"I know how different I looked thirty years ago: I was wearing snowsuits and Mickey Mouse ears. What about you?"

"I had hair down to my shoulders."

"I don't believe it."

"It's true. I had John Lennon hair."

McLeod came wandering around the divider looking uncharacteristically contemplative.

"What's up?" Cardinal said. "You look like you've found religion."

"The Cates thing. You said it was made to look like rape but no rape had occurred?"

"She was naked and her clothes had been torn off, but there was no sign of penetration. That's not conclusive, of course. Why? What's on your mind?"

"Old case of mine. Ten years ago, maybe. Situation where a woman was murdered, found outdoors, naked, clothes all ripped, but no sign of penetration."

"Couldn't have been ten years ago—I'd've remembered."

"Twelve, then. It was before you moved here from Toronto. Man, we busted our asses on that case and we just never got lucky. Came up with nothing. Absolutely nothing. I worked it with Turgeon." Dick Turgeon was an old-timer who had worked with McLeod for years. He'd died of a heart attack exactly two weeks after his retirement party—a fact that could still elicit reams of morbid philosophy from McLeod.

"I don't suppose you remember the name of the victim? Anything useful like that?"

"It'll come to me. She was mid-thirties, good-looking. Hadn't been in town more than a couple of months." McLeod snapped his fingers. "Ferrier. That was her name."

"Madeleine Ferrier?"

"Madeleine Ferrier. How'd you know?"

"A little coquette told us," Delorme said. She filled McLeod in quickly on the CAT Squad's prize informer. "According to Simone Rouault, Madeleine Ferrier was with the FLQ in nineteen seventy. She played a very minor role, did some time on a minor charge, then apparently re-formed. Moved to Ontario."

"That's right," McLeod said. "I remember she had some history. We tried like hell to find a connection between her murder and the FLQ, but there was nothing. Nada."

"Well, get this," Cardinal said. "Madeleine Ferrier was at one time crazy about Yves Grenelle."

"I'm missing something," McLeod said. "Why's that important?"

"Because she wouldn't be likely to forget his face, even after almost twenty years, which is how much time there was between her FLQ activities and her arrival in Algonquin Bay."

Cardinal and Delorme managed to extract the Ferrier file from the archives. It was nearly three inches thick. As an unsolved homicide, it wouldn't have been thinned out for archiving, even after twelve years. They sat at their desks, each with half of the file.

Half an hour passed in silence.

Other than the victim and the way she was killed, nothing about the case seemed to connect it to their present one. Madeleine Ferrier, aged thirty-seven, had moved to Algonquin Bay twelve years previously. A high-school teacher of French and geography, she had been in town two months when she was murdered. She was found in a wooded area between the Algonquin Mall and Trout Lake Road, naked, as McLeod had said, and strangled. Except for the torn clothes, Forensics had found no evidence of rape.

Suspects? None. She hadn't been in town long enough to make any enemies—or any friends for that matter. The wood she was found in was a well-traveled shortcut from the mall to her neighborhood. Anyone could have seen her there.

Since there were no suspects, the stack of supplementary reports was huge. There had been nothing to narrow down the search. Everyone who had been in the mall that evening was interviewed. As were the proprietors of all the stores. As was every tenant in the building where she had rented an apartment. Those alone formed practically a separate file.

"You know, there ought to be an index to a file this size. It would certainly make life a lot easier."

"Right," Cardinal said. "Unless you were the one who had to do the indexing."

"Here's something." Delorme held out a sup headed Interview With Paul Laroche. "Paul Laroche owned the building Dr. Cates lived in, right?"

"Paul Laroche owns a lot of buildings." Cardinal rolled his chair next to Delorme's.

"Well, he didn't own this one. The Willowbank Apartments on Rayne Street. It gives his occupation as real estate agent, but it's for Mason and Barnes Real Estate. He was a small fry back then."

"He may have been a small fry. Mason and Barnes isn't. And this is the first name that comes up in both cases."

They read in silence.

Paul Laroche, then aged forty-five had told Detective Dick Turgeon he had no information about the dead woman. He had seen her in the lobby once or twice, that was it. The night she had been killed, he had been at home, setting up a new stereo he had just bought. Turgeon had had no reason to question Laroche further.

Delorme's phone rang. She listened for a moment, then clamped the phone between ear and shoulder as she typed. "Yes, I've got it. Yes, the attachments are there, too. Thank you so much for your help. We really appreciate it."

Cardinal rolled his chair up beside her.

"Miriam Stead," Delorme said. "She sent everything by e-mail. It'll be sharper than a fax."

Delorme had clicked on an attachment, and it was unfolding now on the screen.

"Wow. I hope he has better fashion sense that that," Cardinal said.

The image showed a man in his mid-fifties, with a Bozo-the-clown-type corona of salt-and-pepper hair. The clown effect was not diminished by the baggy suit and fat tie.

Delorme clicked another attachment. It took a few moments to open. "Oh, boy. Now we've got the Kojak look."

The same features, unsoftened by hair, now had the ruthless aspect of a shipping tycoon, or perhaps an over-the-hill hit man.

"That's why God invented hair," Cardinal said. "Let's see the next one."

Delorme clicked again. This time they didn't even have to wait for the picture file to open all the way. They didn't wait to see the thickening of the neck, the broadening of the shoulders. There was the close-cut, clinging hairstyle, with its flecks of gray like iron filings—that was enough to put it in the ballpark. But the to-the-life resemblance was truly to be seen in the set of the mouth, in the slightly upthrust chin, and most of all in the unstoppable self-confidence of the eyes. Even before it showed the suit and tie of a man of substance, they both said, "Paul Laroche."

"Amazing," Delorme said. "It could have been taken last week."

26

IT WAS NO LATER than six thirty when Cardinal left the station that night, but it was dark as midnight. Out in the parking lot he could hear the traffic honking on the bypass. Normally Algonquin Bay drivers are silent drivers, but the ice was causing delays everywhere, and that northern patience was apparently beginning to wear thin. He got into his car, but before he could put his key in the ignition, a voice from behind him said, "Looks like more rain, doesn't it."

"Kiki. How nice to see you." Cardinal was amazed at how quickly his heart could double its speed. This would be it, then. No more warnings.

"Yeah. Thought I'd stop by."

"You know, just because it's a car doesn't mean I can't have you up for breaking and entering."

"It was open. I just climbed in and fell asleep."

"It was locked. And anyway, it's the same as a house. Just because a house is unlocked doesn't mean you can stop in and have a nap."

Kiki yawned. His leather jacket creaked as he stretched. "Let's go for a drive. I'm tired of sitting in a parking lot."

"Kiki, have you noticed the weather? The entire planet is covered with ice. It's not a good day for a drive. If you're going to shoot me, you'll have to shoot me here in the police station parking lot."

"Not a problem. I have a silencer."

"You must be very proud." Cardinal was easing his right hand under his coat. It wasn't going to be easy getting at the Beretta. It was strapped in his underarm holster on his left side.

"No. It's just a fact. Doesn't call for being proud or unproud. I'm just pointing out that it could be done. Pretty embarrassing for you to be killed outside the cop shop."

"Well it wouldn't bother me, of course. I'd be dead."

"True."

The holster seemed farther away than ever. Cardinal debated whether he should just make a grab for his Beretta and be done with it. The other options were simply getting out of the car, although catching a bullet in the spine before he got the door open didn't appeal to him one bit. Or he could flip around and grab for whatever weapon Kiki was pointing at him through the seat. At least that way he'd be a moving target.

"Do you know a person named Robert Henry Hewitt?"

Wudky. Cardinal would not have put Wudky together with Kiki B. and Rick Bouchard's gang in a thousand years. "Yes, I know Robert," he said. "I didn't realize you two were friends."

"We're not. He's in the same wing as Ricky. Was."

"What do you mean 'was'? Has something happened to Robert?"

"See, that's why you're not a very good cop, Cardinal. You're a terrible judge of character."

"I've been surprised before, it's true."

"Can't keep nothing secret in stir, that's the problem. Somehow your little twerp pal hears that Bouchard is putting a contract out on you. And this upsets him deeply. He goes to Bouchard and tries to talk him out of it. I wish I'd seen that."

Cardinal wished he'd seen it too.

"First he tells him he's wrong about you. John Cardinal would never steal nothing: This is the gospel according to Hewitt. Another bad judge of character, obviously."

"Yeah, Wudky's not the sharpest knife in the drawer."

"What'd you call him?"

"Long story."

"Naturally, Rick begged to differ on the honest-cop part. To the tune of two hundred thousand dollars, as we know. Second point your friend made: John Cardinal is not your typical cop. He busts me, Hewitt says, and then tries to talk the Crown out of sending me away. Is that true, by the way?"

"It is, actually. I know it sounds funny."

"You never did anything like that for me."

"Yes, but you're not a nice person, Kiki."

"This Hewitt is your idea of a nice person?"

"He didn't have your advantages. Anyway, I can imagine how all this moved Bouchard. He's such a soft touch."

"Right. He tells your friend to go away before he decides to skin him alive. Your friend says he has just one more argument to make on your behalf. 'Oh?' says Rick. 'I can't wait to hear it.' And the kid says his third argument is that if Bouchard doesn't call off this contract by tomorrow he's going to kill him."

"Mm. I can see how that would have Bouchard trembling."

"He beat the shit out of Hewitt. Put him in the infirmary for a week. Do you have any idea how sick you have to be to get into the infirmary in Kingston? You have to be like a quarter to dead. But when he gets out, all beat to hell, he goes back to work in the kitchen and—Bam! Goes after Bouchard with a meat cleaver. I hear it was pretty spectacular. I can't help feeling bad for Rick, though, dying that way."

"You're telling me that Robert Henry Hewitt killed Rick Bouchard? That's got to be a joke. Robert is completely harmless."

"Call Kingston. They'll tell you how harmless he is."

"Wudky kills Bouchard and you're here to make it right, is that it?"

"What do you mean? Like revenge?"

"Well, *duh*, Kiki."

"Hell, no. I don't give a shit. I didn't even like Bouchard. Couldn't stand him, if you want to know the truth."

"So why'd you stay with him all those years?"

"He was a good employer. Are you in love with your boss?"

"Good point."

"Oh, I get it!" Kiki slammed the back of the front seat. It was like being rear-ended. "You thought I was back here to kill you!"

Cardinal turned around in the front seat. Kiki was looking at him with genuine wonder and delight, a kid at the circus. He had fewer teeth than a goalie.

"You thought I was coming back to make good on what you owed Rick! That's great! No, I'm not here for any of that. I just come to tell you what happened. To let you know it's all over. There's no one to put a contract out on you now, Cardinal. And no one to pay me even if I did manage to get Bouchard's money out of you."

"Well, of course, you could keep it yourself. Assuming you got any out of me. Which you wouldn't."

"No, no. It wasn't my money in the first place. This was all Rick's grief. Rick's gone, grief's gone. You're a free man, Cardinal. That's all I came to tell you."

"You came all the way up here from Toronto to tell me this?"

Kiki took his woolen cap off and scratched at the pale fuzz on his head. Then he put the cap back on, reaching past Cardinal to adjust the rearview, checking himself out in it.

"To tell you the truth I've been thinking about moving up here."

"Please don't," Cardinal said. "We'd see too much of each other."

"Well, I'm tired of the rat race, you know?"

Cardinal hadn't thought of criminals being in the rat race, but he could see where they might find Toronto as stressful as anyone. More so.

"What are you going to do—take up canoeing? Fishing?"

"Naw. Anything with a boat? No good. But I like it up here. It's clean. It smells nice. That means a lot. Of course, this ice-storm shit is giving me second thoughts. But I wanted to ask you. Would you know of any jobs up here?"

There wasn't a trace of irony in Kiki's broad, flat face.

"Were you thinking of loan-sharking or extortion?"

"Come on, Cardinal. I'm serious. I'm talking legitimate employment, you know? I've got a heavy-equipment operator's license."

"Let me put my mind to it, Kiki. I'll ask around."

"Really? That'd be great. Maybe your friend wasn't all wrong about you."

"You never told me what happened to Robert. Did he get killed in the altercation or what?"

"You kidding? Everyone was too fucking scared."

"Still. I imagine Rick's pals will take him apart as soon as they get the chance."

"I wouldn't bet on it. Rick wasn't exactly warm, you know? Loyalties to him did not run deep. And your friend just took down the toughest bastard in Kingston. So in fact I'd say he's going to be sitting pretty. Once he gets out of solitary, of course."

"Right." Cardinal put the key in the ignition and started up. "Can I drop you anywhere?"

"Nah, that's okay, I got a rental right here." Kiki opened the back door. "I'm staying at the Birches Motel. Gimme a call if you hear of any openings, okay?"

"Minute I hear of anything suitable, I'll be on that phone, Kiki."

"Take care driving, now. Road's slippery as a bitch."

THE THREAT WAS GONE. And yet, Cardinal could not quite muster up a feeling of wholesale relief. As he drove home, he thought of Wudky, who, owing to his loyalty to Cardinal, would probably get another twenty years tacked onto his sentence. Others had paid for the mistake he had made so many years before, as he had not—and probably now never would.

When Cardinal got home, Catherine was at the woodstove in the living room, stirring a huge pot of stew. The power was off, and the flames behind the stove window lit the room with a deep orange flicker. Sally and the two girls were on the couch, peeling potatoes. Old Mrs. Potipher was asleep in Catherine's chair, her mouth hanging open. Beside her on the floor, Totsy, her miniature gray poodle, eyed Cardinal with instant dislike and started to tremble from head to tail. Two kitchen chairs had been brought out to accommodate the capacious behinds of Mr. and Mrs. Walcott, neighbors from across the road. They were sitting erect like a pair of matched dolls, each with a paperback balanced on the belly and eyeglasses secured by a length of cord.

"Power's off all over this side of town," Mr. Walcott said to Cardinal when he came in.

"I know. Highway's pitch dark. Judging by the rain, it isn't going to get better anytime soon."

"We stuck it out for as long as we could," Mrs. Walcott added, then turned to her husband. "I told you last year we should get a woodstove. But no, you had other ideas."

"What I said was, 'They're too expensive. You can't take a vacation in the Dominican Republic and buy a woodstove in the same year.' "

"That isn't what you said. You said, 'Let's think about it. We should wait for the sales.' Then of course you never got around to it."

"Go ahead. Make me out to be the jerk. That's fine. If it makes you feel better."

Cardinal unbuttoned his coat but then thought better of it. The living room was hot, but the rest of the house was the same temperature as outdoors. "Shouldn't we keep that open for now?" He pointed toward the front of the room where Catherine had strung up a curtain on a clothesline, separating the former porch area from the rest of the living room. "It'll cut the heat off in front."

"Go take a look," Catherine said.

Cardinal picked his way past the outstretched legs of Mr. and Mrs. Walcott, ignored an exaggerated growl from Totsy, and stepped beyond the curtain.

"Satisfied?" His father looked up at him from the depths of Cardinal's La-Z-Boy chair, which was draped with a bright red sleeping bag. "You got your way, now. I hope you feel proud of yourself."

Cardinal smiled. "I'm just glad to see you, Dad. I didn't want you freezing up there all alone. This curtain's blocking a lot of your heat, though. Maybe I should open it for a while."

"Don't touch it. Frankly, I don't see why I can't be allowed to die in my own home."

"Dad, it's not forever. Just stay till the ice storm is over."

"See how you like it when you get old. I don't even think of myself as old. I go past Leisure Home in summer and see the little old ladies sitting outside and I think, 'Look at the little old ladies.' Doesn't occur to me that I'm the same age as them. To me I'm the same age I always was, only I have this stupid heart problem that's not letting me do what I want."

"Have you got everything you need? Can I bring you anything?"

"What else could I need? I got my book, sleeping bag, catheter . . ."

"What?"

"That was a joke, John."

"Why don't we put you in Kelly's room?"

"Let someone else have it. I'm better off here. I can breathe better sitting up. Funny how history repeats itself."

Cardinal gave him a quizzical look.

"My dad. Had the exact same problem. Didn't have the drugs for it back then. But I remember how he used to sleep in the living room, sitting up. Now I know why."

"All right. But let me know if you want Kelly's room."

Cardinal was about to leave, but his father raised a hand to stop him. "This Dr. Cates thing, John. It's terrible. She was just starting out. You're going to get the guy who killed her, I hope."

"Well, we're working on it."

"She was a smart cookie, I think. Good doctor, too."

"What are you talking about, Dad? You were mad as hell at Dr. Cates."

"I know, I know. So sometimes I'm not too bright."

LATER THERE WAS A campfire feeling to the night as they all—except for Stan Cardinal—sat around the woodstove and reminisced about strange weather experiences of the past. The Walcotts argued about a storm that had kept them socked in at O'Hare for three solid days one winter, or was it two days at La Guardia? Mrs. Potipher remembered a hideous storm in the North Atlantic when she was crossing sometime in the fifties.

The shifting firelight lit their faces in shades of brown and amber. Catherine looked beautiful in her layers of sweaters and a long plaid scarf. As she tended to their unexpected guests, her face had a look of utter absorption, and Cardinal knew she was happy. All evening their talk was punctuated by the throaty hiss of the stove whenever Cardinal opened it to add wood. There was the drumming of freezing rain against the windows, and every so often there would be a terrific crash as a branch came down outside, and they would all jump and exclaim as if at a sporting event.

Cardinal and Catherine had to sleep with the bedroom door open to get as much warmth as possible from the living room. Even so, Cardinal was wearing long johns. Catherine fell asleep curled against him, but he lay awake for a long time, thinking about his father, and about Paul Laroche. He was now certain that Laroche was Yves Grenelle, and whether or not he had killed the minister Raoul Duquette, he had certainly killed Madeleine Ferrier to keep his past a secret. And Miles Shackley. And Winter Cates. He remembered the photograph in Laroche's office of him and the premier in hunting gear; that might connect him to Bressard. Proving any of this in a court of law, however, would be another matter.

Sometime later he was awakened by a sound, but he didn't know what it was he had heard. Another branch? A transformer blowing? He lay still, waiting. Someone cried out from the other room, a strange high-pitched sound—half shout, half moan. Cardinal got out of bed and threw on his dressing gown. He grabbed the flashlight from the dresser and went out to the living room.

The fire in the woodstove had burned down to coals, casting a dull red glow on the sleeping faces of Sally and her little girls, sharing a gigantic sleeping bag on one side of the room, and on Mr. and Mrs. Walcott on the other. Mrs. Potipher was in Kelly's room with the kerosene heater. It was his father who cried out—a choked call to Cardinal, who stepped swiftly around the sleeping forms and past the curtain.

His father had half fallen out of the chair, and hung draped over one side. He was drenched in sweat when Cardinal righted him, his face slick and white.

"Where are your pills?" Cardinal said, swinging the flashlight around. "Dad, where are your pills?"

His father moaned, his head lolling against the back of the chair. There was a rattling sound in his lungs.

Cardinal found the pills on a small side table. He tipped out one of the capsules into his palm. Pulling his father forward in the chair, he cradled his head in the crook of his elbow, and put the capsule into his mouth. He called out for Catherine.

"It's my leg," his father said. "My leg hurts." Translating from Stan Cardinal's stoic tongue, that meant he was entering previously unknown territories of pain.

"Catherine!"

Catherine appeared at the edge of the curtain, untangling her hair with one hand, holding her robe together with the other. "Call an ambulance," Cardinal said.

Catherine picked up the phone and dialed. Then she handed the phone to Cardinal. "They might respond quicker to a cop."

She knelt beside the chair. "How you doing, Stan? How can we help?"

He grabbed at his thigh and groaned. His face was utterly white.

"John's getting the ambulance now. They'll be here soon."

"My leg's killing me," Stan said. "Not literally, I hope."

Cardinal spoke his address into the phone.

"Sir, we'll get someone there as fast as we can. But the roads are impossible tonight."

Cardinal hung up and dialed the emergency room at City Hospital. The nurse on the other end asked him to describe the symptoms carefully. "All right," she said. "With a history of heart failure, most likely he's thrown a clot in his leg. It's painful but treatable with blood-thinning drugs."

"John! I think he's having a heart attack!"

Cardinal dropped the phone. His father sat erect clutching as if at an arrow in his chest, then collapsed backward, unconscious.

"Help me get him onto the floor."

Cardinal lifted his father under the armpits; Catherine took hold of his feet. "He's ice cold," she said. "Both his legs are ice cold."

They laid him on the floor, and Cardinal started chest compressions. Every six compressions, he leaned forward and gave his father mouth-to-mouth.

"Take the phone, Catherine. Ask them what we do next."

He continued pressing his father's chest while Catherine asked for instruction. "They say to keep doing just what you're doing," she said. "Keep it up till the ambulance gets here."

"He's not breathing, for God's sake. Maybe we shouldn't wait for the ambulance. Maybe we should drive. Ask her how long it's going to take."

"With luck, ten or fifteen minutes."

"Catherine, go outside and start the car."

"Is there anything I can do?" Sally was standing by the curtain now.

"Help Catherine scrape the car off."

Catherine and Sally went out. A few moments later Cardinal heard the raw sound of scrapers attacking hard ice.

His father groaned and opened his eyes.

Cardinal stopped the compressions and pressed one ear to his father's chest. There was a steady thud, but the lungs sounded full of fluid.

"Dad," he said softly. He placed a hand on his father's cheek. "Dad, can you hear me?"

"Yes."

"Which one of your pills is the diuretic? We need to get some of this fluid out of your lungs."

"Orange ones." His voice was a whisper; his eyes seemed to look somewhere beyond the ceiling of the room.

Cardinal selected the pills from several bottles on the little table. He shook two into his hand and started to raise his father's head.

"No," his father whispered. "No more pills."

"Your lungs are filled with fluid. They'll help you breathe."

"No more pills."

"Dad, it's just so you can breathe."

"No more pills." The eyes still scanned the ceiling, the breath came in short, static-filled gulps.

Catherine came back in, soaking wet. A cloud of frigid air blew in with her and occupied the room. "The ice is impossible," she said. "We can't even get the car door open."

There was a sound of a distant siren.

"It's okay. That'll be the ambulance. Dad won't take his pills."

Catherine came over and knelt on the other side of his father. "What's this I hear? You're not taking your pills now?"

Stan Cardinal's slack wet lips twitched into the slightest of smiles. "You going to give me hell?"

Catherine shook her head. Her eyes filled, but she blinked back the tears. She found the old man's hand and took it in both of hers. Cardinal gripped his father's forearm.

"Only thing you ever did right," Mr. Cardinal said. The words came out slowly, like notes so separate all sense of melody is lost.

"What's that?" Cardinal said. He did not want to cry in front of his father.

"Cathy."

"I know." Cardinal squeezed his father's arm. "Dad, listen. I know it's been a long time since you went to church, but—"

"No priest."

"Are you sure? We can call Corpus Christi, if you want."

"No priest."

Cardinal heard the wail of the siren pass by, behind the house. They had missed the turnoff. He didn't think there was much a paramedic could do at this point. Or a doctor for that matter.

"John."

"What, Dad?"

"John."

"Go ahead, Dad. I'm here."

"I thought we did all right, don't you?"

Cardinal swallowed. His Adam's apple felt three times its normal size. "We did fine."

Cardinal wasn't sure what his father said next. The siren was coming back toward Madonna Road.

"I'm sorry for anything I did. You know . . ."

"Dad, you don't have to apologize for anything."

"Anything, you know . . ."

"I know. I'm sorry too."

"Well, what are you sorry for?" The question seemed to hang in the air between them like a mobile.

"For not making sure you got what you wanted—you know—so you could go through all this at home, instead of . . ."

"No, no." His father coughed then. His hands shot out as if to catch a heavy object toppling over him, then fell back against the floor.

"Dad?" Cardinal rubbed his arm vigorously, as if stimulating circulation there might revive the entire dying body. "Dad?"

His father was struggling to say something. Cardinal and Catherine leaned forward to hear, but the words disintegrated into meager, breathy vowels, ahs and ohs without meaning. Then the last of his breath left the body, and almost instantly his eyes grayed over. Catherine leaned forward and wept. Cardinal sat back on his heels, stunned.

Lights flashed in the windows and there was the sound of car doors and heavy boots on the ice. Then the paramedics were inside, checking for vital signs and confirming that Stan Cardinal was dead.

"I'm sorry we didn't get here sooner," one of them said. "Roads are a real problem tonight. There's lines down all along Trout Lake."

"I know," Cardinal said.

"I gotta get on the phone. Coroner'll have to come out and confirm death."

"Okay."

The medic had already flipped open his cell phone. "Yes, we're at the Madonna Road cardiac? We got full arrest here, no vitals. Can you have the coroner out here right away? Thanks."

Cardinal was aware of Catherine moving in the firelight—someone must have thrown another log into the woodstove, he couldn't remember doing it himself. Somehow she had gotten the kids moved into Kelly's room without waking Mrs. Potipher. She boiled water and made tea for Sally and the ambulance men. They drifted in and out of Cardinal's vision, faceless silhouettes in a netherworld where all distances were vast, all voices echoes. Cardinal took a sip of tea and burned his tongue.

There was a blast of cold air and much bustle as Dr. Barnhouse swept in, clutching his black bag. He knelt beside Stan Cardinal, listening for a long time with his stethoscope. Finally, he said, "There's no heartbeat. And no respiration." He consulted his watch. "Time of death: two fifty-seven."

Barnhouse packed away his stethoscope and closed his black bag with a staccato snap. Then he was standing before Cardinal with his hand out. Cardinal reached out and felt the doctor's dry white palm squeeze his hand.

"I'm very sorry for your loss, Detective Cardinal."

There was a pleading in the doctor's eyes, as if to say, Help me! I'm no good at this! As he saw him to the door, Cardinal almost wanted to offer comfort, tell him it was all right.

The ambulance men moved toward the body.

Cardinal said, "Can you give us a few minutes?"

Catherine was beside his father, looking limp and exhausted. Cardinal knelt once more across from her and looked at his father. He was amazed at the vastness of his pain. "What was he trying to say?" he said. "Just before he went. He was trying to say something, but I couldn't make it out."

"He was responding to what you said."

"What did I say?"

"You said you were sorry. You were sorry that he didn't get to die at home."

"What did he say?"

"He said, 'I am home.'"

27

ALL THAT NIGHT and into the morning
the rain continued to fall in great heavy drops that hit every surface with
an audible smack. Perhaps "fall" is not the right word. The rain hurled
itself in a fury at every car, every house, and every road. It stung where
it struck the skin, and one could see the ice crystals inside each drop,
watch them graft themselves instantly to every icy windshield and sidewalk.

Salt spreaders were out in force until every street that wasn't a sheet of
black glass crunched like cinders underfoot. Snow tires crackled on the
few cars that prowled the city streets in slow motion. Power lines sagged
lower and lower under the weight of ice. Along the highways, hydro poles
tilted at crazy angles as if a mass crucifixion had taken place.

By nine A.M. the power was out across the city. The police and fire de-
partments had backup generators, but the one at police headquarters kept
shutting itself down, and a couple of overworked mechanics came and
went from the roof, muttering expletives in French.

By mid-morning the skies had cleared, and the sun was dazzling. A
cold front had finally pushed out the warm front, and while this drove the
rain away, it sent the temperatures plunging toward minus twenty degrees
Celsius. Without power, without heat, the residents of Algonquin Bay
were now in real danger. Schools were closed and turned into makeshift
dormitories.

Two people died. A man who had barbecued his dinner indoors was
killed by carbon monoxide. And there was a fire on Christie Street that
started when a kerosene heater was knocked over.

At the police station, all leave was canceled. The entire force was mobilized to go door-to-door evacuating children and the elderly to the schools. McLeod's howls of protest could be heard from Chouinard's office on the third floor to the weight room in the basement. "I'm an investigator, for God's sake, not a boy scout. What are we going to be doing next—getting cats out of trees?"

Cardinal woke up late. At first he thought there was a large dog sleeping on his chest, but then he realized it was the weight of his father's death. He called Chouinard and told him his father had died. Chouinard was sympathetic and told him to take as long as he needed; it was a time for family now. As if that were something that might have escaped Cardinal's notice.

So Cardinal resolved to stay home. He called the funeral home and made preliminary arrangements, then called his brother out in British Columbia. Catherine called Kelly.

The Walcotts had somehow managed to sleep through the events of the past night, even the coming and going of the ambulance. Once Catherine told them, they promptly took out their books and began reading. The others were kind, Mrs. Potipher in particular, and even the little girls were appropriately somber. But after an hour of this, Cardinal began to feel he was just a death's head in the room and he might be more use elsewhere. His thoughts turned to Paul Laroche and the mountain of files that was due to arrive by helicopter that morning.

Delorme gave Cardinal a big hug when he arrived at the squad room. "I'm so sorry," she said. "Promise me you'll let me know if I can help in any way."

Her sympathy made Cardinal choke up a little, but he managed a nod.

Chouinard was surprised to see Cardinal turn up, but having him there, he was determined to put him and Delorme to work. He tried to assign them to the house-to-house detail, but Cardinal would have none of it. He brought Chouinard down to the conference room they had commandeered for the files. The OPP had helicoptered in five crates of files from the CAT Squad's investigation of the FLQ kidnappings. Now the boxes were arrayed like opened drawers in the conference room.

"Okay, so you've got a mountain of stuff to go through. Do it as fast as you can and then we're going to need you on the streets with every-body else."

R. J. Kendall stuck his head in. "I want everybody downstairs, now. Why are you still up here?"

Chouinard stepped in. "Er, Chief—something you may not be aware of. Cardinal's father died last night."

R. J. looked at Chouinard as if he had just landed in a spaceship. Then he looked back at Cardinal. "Is that true?"

"Yes, sir."

"My sympathies," said R. J., conveying none. "But if you're not going home, I want you downstairs. We've got a full-scale emergency here." Then he seemed to relent a little. "Sorry about your old man," he said, and placed a hand on Cardinal's shoulder. "You take as much time off as you need. Losing your father, that's a real blow."

"Thanks, Chief. For now I'd just as soon work on this."

"Fine. You work on what you want. Right now I want everyone in muster," Kendall said, and left the doorway.

"Ontario Hydro's here to tell us what's what," Chouinard said. "It's not so bad. At least there's doughnuts."

"Why is it always doughnuts?" Delorme said on their way downstairs. "Do I look like I eat doughnuts? Promise me you'll shoot me, if I do."

Cardinal helped himself to a black coffee and parked himself nearest the exit.

The hydro man was Paul Stancek, a former high-school classmate: Cardinal's single memory of Stancek was that he could do a perfect imita-tion of their history teacher, Mr. Elkin, right down to the Aussie accent. That had been when Stancek—and Cardinal himself, he supposed—had been a reed-thin youth without the slightest trace of peach fuzz on his cheeks. Now he was a six-footer, with a walrus mustache that would have looked good on a Wild West sheriff.

"I know you're busy," Stancek said. "So I'll get right to it. The Ontario hydro system is built to withstand anything up to a hundred-year event. Right now, in Algonquin Bay, this ice storm is that event.

"Algonquin Bay gets its power from two separate sources. In order for the entire city to go dark, both those sources have to be disrupted. You've all seen the towers that come in from the east. They come in from the hills along Highway Seventeen over near Corbeil. Those are bringing power from the Ottawa River and the Mattawa River.

"The other source is up toward Sudbury. Those are the towers that come in along the bypass from the other direction. The likelihood of both those systems going down simultaneously more than once in a century is just about nil.

"So, welcome to the year one hundred. Normally when there's a severe ice storm we can simply up the amperage along the wires. That heats them up enough to melt the ice. This time, however, it isn't working. Those lines are bearing three times the weight they're built to withstand, and some of them are going to snap. Here's what to do if you are in the vicinity when one comes down."

McLeod shouted loud enough to make everyone jump. "Why don't you just shut the damn things down till it's over? The power's going off every ten minutes anyway."

Stancek didn't even blink. "We don't shut down the main transfer lines for three reasons. One, because if they're not carrying any load we can't tell where the breach is; so how can we fix it? Two, because switching the power back on would be far more dangerous than just letting it flow. You could kill people you didn't even know were in danger. And three: That's just the way we do it."

"Good one," McLeod said. "You should be a cop."

Stancek went on. "Each of the towers carries six lines. Each line carries forty-four thousand volts. That's *forty-four thousand* volts. Yes, it will kill you. It will kill you ten times over."

One of the first accidents Cardinal had covered when he had moved back to Algonquin Bay: A teenage boy, on a dare, had climbed onto a transformer at the relay station. By the time emergency crews got to the scene, the boy was a cinder. As they had pried him from the metal, his charred head had fallen off and rolled to Cardinal's feet.

"Forty-four thousand volts," Stancek said again. "But even if one of those lines comes down within twenty yards of where you're standing, it doesn't necessarily have to do you in. Not if you know what you're doing. So, pay attention.

"If a wire comes down on your car, you don't move. Just stay in the car, unless there's an even more compelling reason—it's on fire, say—to get out. If you must get out, do not step out. Jump out. What will kill you is the difference in voltage between the car and the ground. If you want to become a conductor, move to Toronto and study at the Royal Conservatory. Don't do it by stepping out of a live car.

"A more likely scenario? A wire comes down somewhere nearby." Stancek stepped to a flip chart and uncorked a marker pen. Red circles and arrows appeared as he spoke.

"Now, there's two things you have to understand. The first is ground radiance. Like any source of power, the voltage from a live wire diminishes over distance. And when the earth is the conductor, it diminishes quickly. In other words, if a wire comes down five feet away from a person, that person will probably get killed. Someone else fifty feet away may be totally unharmed.

"So obviously you walk away, right? Wrong. Did you get that? That is a negative. You do not walk away. You stay exactly where you are. And remember this, because what I'm about to tell you has saved many a lineman from an early grave. If a line comes down anywhere near you, keep your feet together. Do not take a step in any direction. Once again, it's the difference in voltage between point A and point B that will kill you. When you're that close to a power line shooting forty-four thousand volts into the ground, there can be a lethal variation in as small a distance as two feet. That's the dark side of ground radiance. So keep your feet together.

"If no one is coming to the rescue, the only way to get away from a live wire is to have only one foot on the ground at a time. That way you're not conducting any energy through your body. But we're in an ice storm, here. The chances of you being able to run without falling and landing on all fours and turning to one barbecued cop are very, very slim. So my best advice is: Stay where you are, keep your feet together, and don't move.

"And one last thing you must know before I take questions. Those power lines have a limit. If one comes down near you and you've got blue lightning all around you, know that that is going to happen only three times. The fuses are set so that when they short for the third time they don't reset again. They stay dead."

True to his word, Stancek kept things brief. When the question period started, Cardinal and Delorme went back upstairs. Cardinal had a message waiting for him from Toronto Forensics. He dialed from the conference room and switched on the speakerphone.

Len Weisman put it in his usual sympathetic way: "You got nothing, my friend. On the car? Nothing. No hair, no fiber, nothing. Water washed it away."

"It doesn't even seem possible," Delorme said. "You'd think just by the law of averages . . ."

"Forget the law of averages. Law of averages says no one should ever win the lottery. Law of averages says no one should get struck by lightning. There's a little thing called luck involved in this business, and your killer is getting all of it."

CARDINAL AND DELORME sorted the files into preliminary piles—those most likely to bear fruit concerning Grenelle.

"I'm not optimistic about this," Delorme said, "the way things are going."

They found a trove of informant reports—but Grenelle had not been informing for the police, he had been informing for the CIA—or at least Miles Shackley's personal interpretation of the CIA—and there wasn't a single report from him. Dozens of reports cited him as "also present," simply one among those enumerated, acknowledged to be at a particular place at a particular time.

"This isn't getting us anywhere," Delorme said. "None of these reports treats Grenelle/Laroche as an informant, or even as dangerous—he's just another guy at the meetings."

"Listen," Cardinal said. "If you're trying to make the point that I don't know what I'm looking for, don't bother. I may not know what we're looking for, but I'll know it when we see it. Is that all right with you, or would you rather go door-to-door helping little old ladies save their budgies from the ice storm?"

Delorme's brown eyes veered away from his gaze, and Cardinal regretted his show of temper.

She turned to him again, her voice soft. "Maybe you should just go home, John. Your father died. It's not something you can ignore."

"I'm not ignoring it. I have a house full of refugees at home right now and I'd rather be here with you." He felt himself coloring slightly and bent his head once more to the files.

Easily eighty percent of the paper before them was irrelevant, and most of the remainder contained the same information duplicated over and over again under different headings.

Their interest perked up when Cardinal found a file labeled 5367 REED STREET, the address where Duquette had been held and murdered. He pulled out a history of ownership from the Montreal city registry. There was even a floor plan and a small stack of photos from the police raid.

"This is interesting," Delorme said. She held a faded carbon of a rental agreement with a copy of the lease attached. "Hundred a month. My, how times change. And look at the signature."

Cardinal took the carbon from her. In the space provided for current address the applicant had given a street number in the town of St. Antoine. Occupation: Cab driver, Lasalle Taxi Company. It was signed Daniel Lemoyne.

"Lemoyne," Cardinal said. "That's right. They used a cab to kidnap Duquette, but I think it was a different company."

There was a flurry of excitement when Cardinal found the files labeled COQUETTE—source number 16790/B as she had been known. It was clear she had been invaluable to the CAT Squad; her reports were extremely detailed. In Simone Rouault's almost novelistic reports, Grenelle began to emerge as a real character. She described his clothes (much more style than the other *felquistes*), his manner (passionate, egotistical, wild). At one meeting he proposed a car bomb at City Hall, at another a series of nail bombs at rush hour. Then there was the scuba attack on the waterfront. In June 1970, just four months before the actual kidnappings, Grenelle had proposed kidnapping an American executive of the Pepsi-Cola company. Then in July, an Israeli ambassador.

By the time Cardinal looked at his watch, two hours had gone by. Delorme tossed her last file into their "done" box.

"There's nothing," Cardinal said.

Delorme stretched, yawning. "All that paper. And not a single useful item. It's practically supernatural."

"So there's nothing in the files. Fine. But Shackley came up here to blackmail Paul Laroche. He sets up a meeting and Laroche is scared enough to kill him."

"Can we connect Laroche to Bressard?"

"Laroche is a hunter—he'd know about Bressard. And everyone remembers Bressard's trial. It was the first time the papers admitted the mafia might exist in Algonquin Bay. All Laroche had to do was pretend to be Petrucci—not hard, since he communicated by note."

"What worries me more," Delorme said, "is that Shackley had to have something more convincing than that group photograph to threaten Laroche with. It had to be something good."

"I agree. It had to be something that absolutely nailed Laroche to the wall. He had to have it with him to show Laroche. And I wish we had it in our hands right now."

"But you know what happened to it," Delorme said. "Whatever it was, Laroche by now has burned it to ashes."

"I know."

"We went over that cabin with a fine-tooth comb. There was nothing in there, John."

"I know. And I didn't see anything at Shackley's apartment, either.

Probably because he brought it with him up here. To use. It was his main weapon."

"He probably hid it in the car."

"Exactly. The car."

"Which the ident guys have been all over. Forensics has been all over it too. There's nothing there. Nothing left."

"I know."

"You know what's happening, don't you?"

Cardinal shook his head. "I can't accept it. We need fingerprints, we need eyewitnesses, we need DNA. There are no witnesses. Not to Cates, not to Shackley. We've got no hair, no prints, no DNA. Not in the car. Not in Shackley's cabin. The only thing we have is the blood from Dr. Cates's office that matches the blood in the car."

"When we get the DNA back, maybe we can match it to Paul Laroche."

"The only way we can do that is if he volunteers a sample—and he won't—or if we get a warrant. Also not likely." Cardinal slammed his hand on the table. "I can't believe it. The guy kills four people and he's going to get away with it."

"It's like you told me. Talent, persistence, and luck. We just haven't had any luck. Not this time."

"I know." Cardinal closed the last file. "And doesn't that just make you sick?"

The lights flickered and went out. A silence stuffed itself like cotton into the room. The conference room got plenty of light from its large windows, but the hall was instantly filled with people hurrying this way and that. McLeod stuck his head in the doorway, flashlight in hand. "I hate this place," he said. "Have I told you that today? I hate this place."

JUSTICE WILLIAM WESTLY was a tall, bony man with a beaky face. His walk—a peculiar combination of a pronounced stoop and a bouncing step—was a source of amusement to most of the legal profession, and his voice, ponderous and plummy, much mimicked.

Westly looked up from the information Cardinal had filled out and signed.

"Do you have any idea who Paul Laroche happens to be?" Westly wanted to know.

"He's the chief suspect in a homicide investigation."

"Paul Laroche is not only a pillar of the community. Paul Laroche owns half the buildings in this town. Paul Laroche runs the local campaign for the premier of this province, in case that has escaped your notice. And also, in case it has escaped your notice, Paul Laroche happens to be the premier's golfing buddy and bosom pal."

"I know that, Your Worship," Cardinal said. "But look at what we've got."

Westly settled his bony chin into a bony hand and made a show of listening with great patience. The harder Cardinal tried to make the connections sound compelling, the hollower they rang.

"That's the entire sum total of your case? The evidence to the last tom-tittle?"

"Well, we're hoping more will turn up."

"Detective, I wouldn't give you a warrant to pick up a homeless person with that. Frankly it boggles the mind you even bothered to come down here."

"That's just me," Cardinal said. "Always the optimist."

"Convince me with some DNA, a fingerprint or two, some ballistic evidence."

"Give me a warrant for Laroche to submit a blood sample and you'll have your DNA."

"You don't have enough for such a warrant. You have a police artist's rendering of what a long-ago member of the FLQ might look like. I'm sorry, Detective. Bring me the slightest credible evidence that ties Paul Laroche to the murder of Winter Cates or the murder of Miles Shackley and I will hand you your warrant. So far, you have nothing."

"What about Madeleine Ferrier?" Cardinal tried to connect the dots from 1970 to the murder of Laroche's neighbor.

Westly didn't let him finish. "Believe it or not, Detective, I do under-stand the case you're trying to make. I'm just telling you you haven't made it. Not to my satisfaction and certainly not to the satisfaction of any court in Ontario."

"But we know he did this, Your Worship. Okay, he's a powerful man, but we know he did this."

"That's the way the cookie crumbles, I'm afraid. From what you've described to me, there's a reasonable chance that Yves Grenelle killed Raoul Duquette. What you cannot prove—correction: what you cannot come within a country mile of proving—is that Paul Laroche is Yves Grenelle."

"LET'S TAKE IT TO another judge," Delorme said, when Cardinal told her. "Gagnon would give us a warrant, I bet."

"I'd love to, believe me. But if we go judge-shopping, and it comes out at trial, we'd be thrown right out of court."

"Well, suppose we just happen to come across a glass Laroche drinks out of. A cigar he's smoked."

"Without a warrant? It's known as illegal search and seizure."

"No, but suppose we follow him. Sooner or later he's going to toss something away or leave something behind—in a restaurant, say—some-thing that we can test for DNA. A public place where there's no expecta-tion of privacy? We wouldn't need a warrant for that."

"Chouinard's not going to let us put surveillance on Laroche. Not with what we've got so far."

"I'm going to ask him."

Delorme went to Chouinard's office. When she came back a few min-utes later, her face was so transparent Cardinal didn't have the heart to ask what their detective sergeant had said.

After lunch, they spent the afternoon running down Laroche's history, trying to match it with Grenelle's. Following newspaper accounts and Laroche's social insurance number, they traced him all the way back to the

Société d'aide à l'enfance in Trois-Rivières. He had lived in an institutional group home until the age of sixteen, at which point the Society closed their file and lost track of the boy. No, they said in answer to Delorme's request, they had no photographs.

Cardinal's pulse began to quicken when he learned that the Society had also had in their care, and at the same group home, a slightly older youth named Yves Grenelle. Again, no photographs, no records after age sixteen. After fleeing the aftermath of October 1970, Yves Grenelle could have simply invited the young Laroche over to Paris, killed him, and taken over his identity; it would be as if Yves Grenelle had never lived. On the other hand, a third person who knew them both could have used both names. Without early photographs, the trail was a dead end.

BEACOM SECURITY WAS LOCATED over an empty storefront on Main Street. Whatever money Ed Beacom made from his post-police career, it hadn't gone toward décor. Aside from showcases full of various kinds of locks and alarms, the place was essentially an empty loft that had not been improved by the addition of cheap linoleum and bright fluorescent lighting.

Beacom showed Cardinal and Delorme into his office—same linoleum, same supermarket lighting—overlooking Main Street.

"How about this weather, huh? Oughta drive the crime rate down, let's hope." Beacom was a beefy man, fiftyish, and wide across the chest. His blue blazer had a strained look about the seams. He pulled two plastic chairs away from the wall. "Sorry about the accommodations; we can't all make the big bucks."

"Frankly," Cardinal said. "I'm not entirely sure why we're here. Covering the fund-raiser seems a pretty straightforward proposition."

"I agree. I don't know why you're here, either, but Paul Laroche is running this show, and what Paul Laroche wants Paul Laroche gets." Beacom reached into a drawer and pulled out a thin file. He opened it and leafed through the contents as he spoke. "I've been in contact with CSIS and frankly, they don't see this fund-raiser as a likely target for any terrorist groups they're interested in."

Cardinal laughed.

"Is that funny?" Beacom said. "If it's funny, let the rest of us in on the joke." He pulled out a floor plan of the Highlands Ski Club, and spread it on his desk, then proceeded to jab it with a thick finger. "I myself will be backstage. There's a good spot back there from where I can pretty much cover the room. Mantis will have a couple of bodyguards with him. And word is there'll be a former prime minister there, too; they'll have a couple of guys on him, too. I've already coordinated with their advance man."

"And how many people will you have?" Delorme said.

"Four, including me. I'm going to have men here, here, and here. At doorways, you notice, not at dinner tables. Not all of us get to hobnob with the rich and powerful."

"You think we want to be doing this damn dinner?" Cardinal said. "You think we don't have anything better to do?"

Delorme shot him a look that said "calm down."

"I don't really care what else you've got to do," Beacom said.

There was a long pause, during which Cardinal considered leaving.

"I think these should be your tables," Beacom said. He pointed to two corner tables on opposite sides at the front of the dining room. "They need me to tell them today where we're going to put you, so if you have any objections, speak up."

"Looks good to me," Delorme said.

Cardinal shrugged. "As long as we're facing the back."

"That's what I thought, too." Beacom said. He rolled up the floor plan. "I'll tell their coordinator and I'll let you know if there's any change. Personally I thought the two of you should have earpieces and wireless mics, but Laroche nixed that. Said it killed the whole advantage of having a couple of cops among the guests. He's got a point."

A few minutes later Beacom introduced them to the associates who would also be at the fund-raiser. One was a retired firefighter Cardinal had worked with many times; the other two were young men barely out of high school.

Delorme pretty much summed up his feelings when they were in the car heading back to the station.

"This job," she said. "Sometimes I wish I'd taken up something more satisfying—like, say, sanitation."

28

THE FRUSTRATIONS OF THE JOB, along with the loss of his father, had begun to tell on Cardinal. He didn't go in to work for the next couple of days, and dealt instead with the sad details of arranging the funeral. There were visiting hours at the funeral home, and there was the ceremony itself at the cathedral, followed by the crema-tion. Kelly had wanted to come home, and so had Cardinal's brother, but the ice storm had hit the airport hard, and there was nothing flying into or out of Algonquin Bay at this point. Despite the condolences of friends and colleagues, and the tender concern of his wife, Cardinal found him-self getting more and more depressed.

On Friday he went back to work, and Delorme filled him in on her progress on the case. That took about thirty seconds, because there was no progress. Forensics had had nothing more to report, a second canvassing of Dr. Cates's neighbors had turned up nothing new, nor had a micro-scopic examination of Shackley's personal effects.

"Okay, look," Delorme said. "We're not going to get him at this time. But something will happen—maybe a month from now, maybe a year from now—he'll make a mistake, or some witness we don't know about will come forward, and we'll get our break. But for now it's just not going to happen."

Cardinal closed his file; he felt like setting it on fire.

"The really grotesque thing," he said, "the thing that really drives me wild—is that we have to go to his damn fund-raiser, for God's sake."

"I know. I asked Chouinard if he could get us out of it, but he said no."

"Chouinard. I don't know what it is that happens to people when they become bureaucrats, but it sure happens fast." Cardinal put his file in the desk and slammed the drawer shut. "You know, even if Laroche wasn't our prime suspect I wouldn't want to help his bloody candidate. Thanks to Mantis and his cutbacks, my father spent his hospital stay stuck in a corridor."

Delorme laid a warm hand on his shoulder.

THAT NIGHT, as Cardinal and Delorme drove through the black, empty streets, they saw three separate transformers explode in beautiful blue flashes.

West of Sumner Street, the lights were still on. But the streetlights were severely weighed down. Several had snapped and lay like severed limbs across the highway, some still lit. Hydro crews were at work clearing them. The shopping malls and the businesses lining the highway were deserted, and the northbound lanes were empty. But a long line of cars snaked out toward Marshall Road. It looked like Laroche's fund-raiser would survive the storm intact.

"You have to wonder," Delorme said, "how many people would vote for the premier if they knew his local campaign manager was a murderer."

"Maybe quite a few. Some American politician once said, 'The only way I can lose this election is if I get caught in bed with a dead girl or a live boy.'"

"That's what I like about you, Cardinal. You always see the bright side."

The road out to the new ski lodge had been so thoroughly salted it was like driving on gravel. The line of taillights snaked over the hills and into the woods, the whole thing inching along like a rubescent worm.

Eventually they came to a set of traffic lights that had been knocked out by the ice, and a large sign announcing HIGHLANDS SKI CLUB. As Cardinal waited for the line of cars to move, he read the rest of the sign in the light from his headlights. There was a list of companies involved in the project, primary among them Laroche Development. Beneath the list of companies, in yet smaller print, was another notation: THIS PROJECT WAS PARTIALLY FUNDED BY A NORTHERN DEVELOPMENT GRANT.

Cardinal turned into the drive. He had to shift the car into low gear to make it up the grade. After about fifty yards, the birches cleared and the silvery expanse of the highlands came into view. The club was built in two sections: a five-story A-frame, set at right angles to a long, low lodge. Cedar cladding gave it the warm but rough-hewn country look favored by ski clubs, and the steeply pitched roof added an Alpine feel.

The parking lot was almost full. Clean-cut young men in earmuffs directed cars to the few remaining spaces. Cardinal parked a long way from the lodge doors.

Beyond the club, the Laurentian foothills flowed away in waves of ice that glowed like skim milk in the light from the club. A line of fifty-foot hydro towers stood at attention across the top of the ridge.

Inside the front door a large bearded man in a tuxedo stood by a velvet rope, checking invitations; Cardinal and Delorme showed their badges.

Delorme let out a low whistle as they entered the dining room.

Cardinal had to admit the place looked spectacular. The cathedral ceiling was hung with Canadian flags and Ontario ensigns. Three fireplaces blazed with the kind of fires that must have warmed medieval castles on such cold winter nights. On the far side of the room, a three-story glass wall gave a view of the icy hills. Cardinal scanned the crowd, particularly near the front tables, but could see no sign of Laroche.

Delorme moved up toward the front on the near side. She would be close to the stage steps and have a clear view into the wings on the far side. Cardinal headed for a table directly across the room.

He could feel the temperature drop as he moved toward the vast expanse of window. There was a sound like distant applause, and three hundred heads jerked around to see: It had started to rain again, and the icy droplets clamored against the glass. Cardinal recognized many faces in the crowd: aldermen, the mayor, several lawyers, a judge, the owner of a large construction firm, and at least five real-estate people. Toward the front he noted some old pols from Toronto, and a couple of Conservative federal MPs, and the former prime minister. Beacom's team, complete with earpieces, was posted at various exits.

A fanfare of trumpets split the air, courtesy of the Highlands' state-of-the-art sound system. Everyone faced the rear as the double doors swung open and Ontario Premier Geoff Mantis strode in, flanked by the usual cohort of men and women in suits, one of them Paul Laroche. They marched up the middle aisle, Mantis waving to everyone, smiling benefi-cently. The crowd rose to its feet, applauding wildly. There were scattered whistles.

Mantis shook hands with people at the front tables, then sat down. His wife, Cardinal noted, was nowhere to be seen. Charles Medina, one of the real-estate magnates and president of the local Conservative party, took the stage.

Medina thanked everyone for coming. He made a couple of jokes about the weather, and several more about the Liberals and the New Democrats. He praised Geoff Mantis, noting the benefits of his leader-ship: lower taxes, better investment climate, higher profits. Yeah, Cardinal thought, tell us about the closed schools or the growing hordes of home-less people, not to mention the crumbling health-care system.

Medina was interrupted several times by cheers. And when he finally introduced the premier himself, the crowd got to its feet again amid a roaring surf of applause as Mantis left his table and joined Medina on stage. They shook hands, grasping shoulders and apparently sharing an old-buddies joke. Mantis turned to the crowd, raised his hands in acknow-ledgment of his welcome, and made calming motions, grinning the whole time, until the audience quieted and sat down.

Cardinal was near the stage. He could see the place reserved for him at the third table, but he stayed by the wall.

Paul Laroche had now appeared in the wings on the far side. It oc-curred to Cardinal that Laroche might have a drink at some point and leave traces of his DNA on the glass. But Laroche showed no inclination to sit at a table. He was standing, feet apart, arms folded across his chest, a magician watching his sorcery unfold. At the microphone, Mantis posed a series of rhetorical questions: "How would you like a whole raft of higher taxes? How would you like to see more people get paid for doing nothing? How would you like to see our talented businessmen and technical wizards hampered by increased legislation?" Cardinal had heard it all before, so had everyone else in the place; everyone else in the place liked it.

Cardinal edged his way around the front tables. Delorme frowned at him as he passed by her toward the stage door.

"Where are you going?" she said, but Cardinal just waved her back.

Laroche was no longer in the wings. Nor was he at any of the front tables. Cardinal surveyed the crowd, all staring adoringly at their premier, the hometown boy who made good. Cardinal went out through a side door and into the lobby. Laroche was heading out the front door.

"You're not staying for your moment of triumph?"

Laroche turned, umbrella in hand. "It's not my moment, Detective. It's the premier's."

"Still, you pulled it off. Twisted the arms? Pulled the strings?"

"That's what a campaign manager does. So my job is done—for the moment, anyway. And I'm fully confident Mr. Mantis will handle the crowd like the professional he is. R. J. told me you'd be staying through the dinner."

"I don't think so. My appetite isn't what it should be."

"I'm sorry to hear it. And your investigation—are you making progress?"

"Oh, yes. We know quite a bit more than we did a week ago. For one thing, it turns out our two murders are connected. And in a way, it involves your line of work."

"Which one? Real estate or development?"

"Politics."

Laroche laughed. It was a big, easy laugh, the laugh of a man who knows he's too important for anyone to tell him he laughs too loud. "Of course, people who don't know much about politics are always accusing politicians of being rapacious. But they're not usually accused of actual rape."

"Dr. Cates wasn't raped."

"Really? The *Lode* had it wrong again?"

"Dr. Cates was murdered. And then the murderer went to some trouble to make it look like rape."

"That doesn't make sense. If you kill someone, how do you then improve your situation by making it also look like rape? You're compounding the offense."

"Possibly. You could also be disguising the motive."

"Of course. I hadn't thought of that. Chief Kendall did say you were good. And, silly me, I just put that down to esprit de corps." Laroche moved away from the front door and gestured toward the elevator. "I don't think you've seen the rest of the club. Shall I give you a private tour?"

Cardinal shrugged. "Sure."

They stepped into the elevator, which hoisted them soundlessly to the third floor.

"I'll show you the northeast corner. That's the best view—assuming the power doesn't fail." Laroche led him along a corridor. The cedar walls and rich red carpet gave a feeling of deep comfort, luxury combined with simplicity.

"We're taking bookings for two weeks from now. Believe me, nothing on heaven or earth is going to prevent this place from being open by the time the ice storm moves on. *Voilà*. Our prime run."

They were looking through a wall of glass. Lights on the tow line gave them a sweeping view of the hills, and to the south one could see all the way to Lake Nipissing. The far side of town was in complete darkness.

"Beautiful," Cardinal said. "I don't think you'll have any trouble filling the place."

"If I thought otherwise, I'd never have built it."

"And you managed to get a Northern Development grant. It was up on the board at the entrance."

"Oh, no question. This project falls squarely in their parameters: Will it employ people? Yes. Will it enhance tourism? Absolutely."

"I imagine having the premier of the province on your side doesn't hurt."

"Geoff Mantis is my friend, and I'll do anything—anything legal—to get him elected, but he isn't so stupid as to try and influence Ontario ministries in my favor."

"Of course not. Or CSIS, either."

"You've lost me."

"I doubt that," Cardinal said.

"Shall we go down? I promised my wife I'd be home to put the children to bed."

The elevator whisked them back to the ground floor. There was a burst of laughter from the auditorium, followed by applause.

When they were at the front door, Cardinal said. "You know, I was surprised Yves Grenelle wasn't mentioned on the project masthead."

"Who?" There wasn't a trace of nerves or fear in the thick, heavy face. The furry eyebrows knit together in consternation, nothing more.

"Yves Grenelle. He was in the FLQ cell that kidnapped Raoul Duquette. Excuse me, the FLQ cell that *killed* Raoul Duquette. Grenelle managed to escape just before the others got caught—no doubt assisted by his friend in the CIA, Miles Shackley."

"Detective, you have talent and you have persistence—two qualities I admire very much. But the stress of your job must be enormous, and frankly it seems to be getting to you. Making these disconnected remarks. I don't have the slightest idea what you're talking about."

"Shortly after he murdered Raoul Duquette—"

"Hah! That's a good one, Detective. You'll have your own grassy knoll, next."

"Shortly after he murdered Duquette, Yves Grenelle fled to Paris, where he stayed for approximately twenty years. He adopted a new identity. Lost a lot of those rough edges one might expect in a young man from Trois Rivières. Got himself an education, some surface gloss, and finally—probably sometime in the late eighties—he returned to Canada. Mind you, he wasn't so foolish as to return to Montreal. No, sir. He'd move where no one would be looking for a retired French Canadian terrorist: to Ontario. To Algonquin Bay, to be precise. The Willowbank Apartments to be even more precise. I know you've heard of the Willowbank Apartments."

"This is fascinating. Tell me while we walk to the car."

Laroche opened his umbrella and held it so it covered both of them. His car, a shiny black Lincoln Navigator, was only steps away, but the wind blew the rain sideways, and Cardinal's legs were getting soaked. Laroche pulled his car keys from his pocket and the door of his Lincoln popped open with a chirp.

"Get in! Get in! You'll catch a cold."

They got into the car, the interior of which was the size of a small apartment. The rain was loud on the roof. Laroche started the motor and switched on the wipers.

"Everything went fine for our newly respectable Monsieur Grenelle," Cardinal said. "He got a good job with Mason and Barnes Real Estate— people with political connections, the kind of people he liked. He was a young man on the make, and it looked like nothing could stop him. But then one day a terrible thing happened. An old lover showed up.

"She didn't look anything like a terrorist. Cute, petite, those good French bones. And she wasn't much of a terrorist, really—cooked the odd meal, carried the odd message, wouldn't hurt a fly. But she was crazy about Yves Grenelle. Or at least she had been, twenty years previously. By nineteen ninety, you'd think she'd have forgotten the guy, and maybe she would have, had she not moved into the same damn Willowbank Apartments. What are the chances of that, do you suppose?"

"Coincidences happen all the time. Where would we be if they didn't?"

"How did it happen? Did she bump into him in the elevator? That's what you told the police. 'I didn't know her. I saw her once or twice in the elevator. I didn't know her name, even.' That's what you told Detective Turgeon. 'Madeleine Ferrier? Was that her name? I never knew.'"

"I told your detective the truth. I didn't know her."

"Yves Grenelle did. It was Madeleine Ferrier, and he knew her very well. She'd been totally in love with him, and no doubt he had a good time playing to that hero worship. It must have been quite a moment in that elevator, when the two of you came face to face for the first time in twenty years. What did she say? 'Yves, my God! Where have you been all these decades?'

"Whatever her exact words may have been, you were absolutely certain that she recognized you. That was enough. You'd been so careful, so patient. And things were beginning to look secure. How could you risk your whole new identity? Not possible. So Madeleine Ferrier had to be killed. And she was: strangled with her scarf and then her clothing torn off to make it look like rape."

Laroche switched on the CD player. Classical music surrounded them.

"Poor Detective. You're really just not having any luck on this case, are you? Obviously you've got no prints, no DNA, none of those wonderful conclusive things that would make your job more satisfying. I mean, you seem to be accusing me of being this retired terrorist as you call him, this Yves Grenelle. But if you could prove such a thing, we wouldn't be having this conversation—not here, anyway. You'd have me down at the police station, waving your proof in front of my face. But you don't have anything to wave and so you're resorting to a kind of hysteria that's very unattractive."

"Dr. Cates lived in one of your buildings, too. When Miles Shackley threatened to expose you, you agreed to meet with him. Probably in his car. You shot him, but you were injured, too, almost certainly by a gunshot. Why else would you be afraid to go to a hospital? You tried to live with the wound for a couple of days, but you couldn't. You needed a doctor—a doctor you could force not to report the gunshot. And you knew where to find one. You met her the day she moved into one of your buildings."

"Hundreds of people live in my buildings. Maybe a thousand. Did you know your partner was once a tenant of mine?"

"But those names don't appear in two different murder cases. Both victims strangled, both made to appear raped? Miles Shackley liked to break the rules, didn't he? He broke them when he played his assassination scenario out for real. And he broke them when he showed up here thirty years later to blackmail his old associate in destabilization, Yves Grenelle. Because of course you never really were a left-leaning terrorist, you were a hard-right conservative, just as you are today."

"You think the CIA ran the FLQ? I thought you were more intelligent than that."

"They didn't run the FLQ; they ran you. Then you went your separate ways in the world. Shackley's was all downhill. He was out of the CIA and down on his luck and somehow—how? old intelligence contacts? the Internet?—after thirty years he found out where you were. He showed up with proof that you killed Raoul Duquette and demanded some outrageous amount of money in order to keep the lid on that little tidbit."

"Come on. I'll show you the view from the ridge. I wouldn't attempt it in any other vehicle, but I think this one can do it."

Laroche drove slowly round the edge of the parking lot and out past the sign. He made a right and drove uphill, keeping the Navigator in second gear. In a few minutes, the trees on either side cleared. Laroche pulled over and killed the lights. They were looking down toward the Highlands lodge, a yellow glow in the distance. Lights on the hydro towers blinked on and off, a warning to aircraft. One of the towers was less than thirty yards away. Even with the rain pelting the roof of the car, Cardinal could hear the throaty hum of the wires.

"It's a hell of a yarn you've concocted, Detective. Complete fiction, of course."

"You think this is fiction?" Cardinal pulled the photograph from his pocket.

Laroche looked at it without reaction. "Which one do you think is me? The girl? You think I had a sex change?"

"The girl is Madeleine Ferrier. You killed her, remember? That's you on the right, in the striped T-shirt."

Laroche handed it back. "It could be anyone."

"Really?" Cardinal pulled out a printout of Miriam Stead's work. "Here's a police artist version, thirty years later. Remove a little hair, lose the beard, add seventy pounds or so . . ."

"*Artist* is the operative word, Detective. It's work of the imagination, like your story."

"You know, the bullet exited Shackley's car by the passenger door handle. I figure he probably hit you just above the elbow. About here." Cardinal grasped Laroche's bicep and squeezed.

Laroche let out a cry, and pulled his arm away.

"I suppose that's my imagination, too," Cardinal said.

"You startled me, that's all. I don't like to be touched." Laroche regained his composure, but there was a fine sweat on his upper lip.

In the distance, transformers made tiny blue novas as they exploded with pops that sounded like gunfire. And there was another sound, a piglike shriek that Cardinal knew was tearing metal.

"I'd recommend we move the car," Cardinal said. "That tower could collapse any minute."

Laroche stared down at the silver hills, the line of hydro towers. "Two weeks from now, that state-of-the-art ski lift will be hoisting hundreds of people up those slopes. The hills will be full of the laughter of vacationers having a good time. Spending their hard-earned money in Algonquin Bay. Our studies suggest it'll be about a million each season."

"Like I said. I'm impressed."

"I don't know what you expect, laying out these accusations. Are you expecting me to bribe you?"

"You're too smart for that."

"Are you taping me? Hoping I'll break down and confess?"

"Why don't you? You'll feel better."

"I'm sure confession feels good for a lot of people. It wouldn't have become a cultural obsession otherwise. But I suspect that cleansing sensation is very short-lived. And I'm sure you feel the same."

"We're not talking about me."

"Aren't we? You seem fixated on the idea that men are not what they seem. I wonder why that is? Well, it's true, of course, men are often not what they seem. Geoff Mantis is an exception, and it's one of the reasons I admire him. Your father may have been another exception—my condolences by the way—a union man. A true believer in the dignity of labor, collective bargaining.

"Then take me: An orphan pulls himself up by his bootstraps. How likely is that? I almost don't blame you for wanting to pull such a preposterous story apart. But then, take you. You work for the city. I know exactly what you earn. It seems so unlikely that a local cop could put a daughter through Yale."

"I wanted to," Cardinal said. "Couldn't afford it in the end."

"And the Tamarind Clinic in Chicago. Best that money can buy for the treatment of depression. Particularly good with females, I understand. But medical care is not free in the United States. Even a short stay in such a place will run into the tens of thousands—American dollars, not Canadian. Are you getting this on tape, by the way?"

"I'd hardly tell you, if I were."

"And you could hardly use it, with what I've just said."

Cardinal opened the passenger door and got out. Freezing rain soaked him instantly. Laroche rolled down his window.

"You're planning to walk back in the rain?"

"I guess so. The only murderers I talk to are the ones I'm arresting. Maybe we'll talk another day."

Laroche shrugged. "How far do you think you'll get with that, Detective?"

"Probably not far. Like you said: If I had the proof, I'd put the cuffs on you now."

Metal screamed again, and with a slow, graceful gesture, the hydro tower tilted over on one side. A line snapped and cut through the air with enough speed to take a man's head off. It hit the ice with a sound that made Cardinal's guts liquefy, a colossal, intergalactic belch. It was maybe twenty yards away. Cardinal stood absolutely still, feet together.

"You sure you won't get back in the car?"

"Thanks. I think I prefer to stay here."

A stiff wind blew from the east. A crust of ice was forming in webs along Cardinal's sleeves.

"So here we are," Laroche said. "I didn't panic. I didn't break down and confess. What does that make me?"

"I wouldn't pretend to know. I don't understand you."

"You wouldn't. We're very different people. I mean, look at me: I'm building this place, I own more buildings than you own shirts, I've got enough money for thirty men. And I'm on excellent terms with your police chief and the Crown—not to mention the premier. And then . . ." He made a gesture toward Cardinal, as if pointing out a shoddy building he wouldn't even attempt to sell. "Look at you."

The hydro wire cracked again and hit the ice. Garlands of blue sparks danced toward Cardinal.

Laroche rolled up his window, and the Navigator pulled away. Cardinal watched the red lights descend the hill, throbbing now and then as Laroche tapped the brakes. Rain pounded his skin like marbles.

Three times, Stancek had said. A main wire would go dead after it shorted three times. Cardinal was already drenched, shivering from head to foot. He badly wanted to run. But he remembered that boy on the transformer years before. The power line slithered in rapid *S* patterns across the ice. Cardinal closed his eyes and tensed for the shock.

The power line came around again, whistling as it cut the air. It hit the ground with a roar and a spray of blue sparks. And then there was just the rain, and the creak and moan of metal.

29

IT WAS NEARLY NOON when Chouinard called Cardinal into his office the following Monday. "You're off the Shackley-Cates case," he said without preliminary. "You know why."

"No doubt because somebody told you to remove me."

"Talk to Kendall, if you want. It won't get you anywhere."

The chief was in an even worse mood than Chouinard.

"You completely ignore your assignment, a simple matter of augmenting security at a public function. You make wild accusations against a prominent businessman. You break so many rules of procedure I can't even begin to count them. And then you come to me wondering why you've been removed from the case?"

"Chief, have you looked at what we have against Laroche?"

"All I see is what we don't have. What we don't have is a serious case against Paul Laroche. In the first place, we cannot prove he's Yves Grenelle, therefore we have no motive. In the second place, nobody saw him at Dr. Cates's apartment or Loon Lodge, therefore we cannot show opportunity. In the third place, we have no murder weapon, therefore we cannot show he had means."

"There are no other suspects in this case, Chief. The DNA in the blood in Dr. Cates's office matches the DNA from the blood in the car. We know the man who killed Dr. Cates is the man who killed Shackley, and we know Laroche had a motive to kill him."

"No you don't. You know Yves Grenelle had a motive to kill him."

"All we need is a warrant to check Laroche's DNA. I know he's going to match. Delorme knows it. You know it."

"I know what the evidence tells me I know. And the Crown has already informed you we do not have enough for a DNA warrant. Apparently, you took this as a go-ahead to harass Paul Laroche."

"He's a killer, Chief. He should be behind bars."

"You're not going to put him there by ignoring reality. And the reality, now, is that you're off this case. Frankly, if it wasn't for the fact that your father just died, I'd consider putting you on suspension. We'll just say you were under stress and your judgment was clouded. What did you think, you'd rattle him into a confession?"

"Stranger things have happened. The whole Cates crime shows a certain degree of panic."

"Your judgment was clouded, Cardinal. Get out of here before I change my mind."

THE ICE STORM eventually departed. The clouds and the fog were trundled away like stage props, and the sun shone once more on the glittering woods. Gradually, the icy hills and roads were cleared of the fallen towers, the broken branches, the shattered trees. Winter soon returned with a more common run of snow and temperatures in the minus thirties. The people of Algonquin Bay huddled in their down parkas and turned their heat, once it was restored, up full.

Spring came early that year. The usual bets were placed on when the ice on Lake Nipissing would break up, but no one came close. By the middle of April the last miniature white islands had melted away. By May there was one last vestige of winter remaining. The bottom of Bradley Street, where it curves round a set of low-lying hills that embrace the northern shore of Lake Nipissing, is where the snow trucks of Algonquin Bay dump their dune-sized loads. By the end of the season, the dump is a flat-topped mountain of crystallized snow, dark on the outside with gravel, salt, and other debris, and on the inside, fretted with long white crystals. This man-made mountain is so dense it doesn't melt away until mid-July.

Cardinal and Catherine could see it from out on the lake, glittering in the sun where pieces of ice had fallen away. Along the shoreline, the buds on the birches and poplars were emerald green. Other trees Cardinal could not identify from out on the water were bursting with white blossoms.

The sun was warm on their faces and hands, but there was a crisp breeze that penetrated their windbreakers, and the Canadian flag on the stern of the boat set up a cheerful snapping.

Cardinal's boat was a small fiberglass outboard his father had bought when Cardinal was still in high school. The motor was just a 35 Evinrude, nothing that was going to tip any canoes in its wake, but it could get you across Lake Nipissing in no time. The odd thing about that lake, although it is the biggest body of water in Ontario outside of the Great Lakes, is that it is also one of the shallowest—no more than forty feet deep at its deepest points. Even a moderate breeze like the one that nipped at Cardinal's face this May morning could start a considerable chop. Waves kicked and slapped at the hull.

They had started out from the West Ferris dock and cruised slowly past the city. The limestone cathedral was bone white, and car windshields caught the sun and shone like mirrors. Joggers in colorful outfits moved in pairs along the waterfront.

"Look at the poor trees," Catherine said, pointing. Many of the maples and poplars had been sawed off flat at the top—a move necessitated by the split trunks and broken branches the ice storm had left in its wake. It would be years before they would recover their natural shapes.

"It's the buildings I'm looking at," Cardinal said. "There. There. And over there." He pointed to the red brick of the Twickenham complex, the white tower of the Balmoral. From out here, they could even see the main chalet of the Highlands ski club. "All of them owned by Paul Laroche, a guy who shouldn't even be walking the streets."

"Well, he isn't walking the streets anymore. At least not in Algonquin Bay."

"And we're not having any luck tracking him down. We think he's somewhere in France."

"Well you could count it as a partial victory, can't you? He's had to leave everything he's built up over the years."

"It's something," Cardinal said. "But it's not what I'd call a victory."

He swung the boat away from town and came about so that the bow was into the wind, then he eased back on the throttle.

"You want to do it here?" Catherine asked.

"It's as good a place as any, I guess. Can you take the wheel for a minute?"

The boat wobbled beneath them as they switched places. Cardinal pulled a dark canister from the cloth sack the funeral home had provided.

"I thought it was illegal to spread ashes on the lake," Catherine said. "Strictly speaking?"

"That's true," Cardinal said. "Strictly speaking." He was trying to figure out how to open the canister. It was a heavy black rhomboid object made of India rubber or something very similar. There was no handle or tab one could grab onto and pull. Nor did anything seem to twist off.

"What do you suppose they do if they catch you?"

"The cops? They make you pick them up again."

"No, seriously."

"It's probably a small fine," Cardinal said. "I think I'm going to need a can opener to open this."

"Want me to try?"

"Not to worry. I have the technology." Cardinal pulled out his penknife and set to work prying the lid off. A moment later it came away, revealing a clear plastic bag full of pale gray ashes about the size of a half-pound of flour. Most of the pieces were smaller than the nail on his little finger.

"I can't believe he's gone," Catherine said. "He was such a . . . vivid person."

Cardinal undid the little plastic tie and opened the bag, the canister still resting on his knees.

A moment ago they had had the lake to themselves. Now, there seemed to be boats everywhere. A sailboat fifty yards off. A motorboat cruising toward them at a good clip. Even a canoe, hugging the shore.

"I better wait for them to pass," Cardinal said.

"Are you going to say anything?" Catherine asked. "When you spread them?"

"I don't know. It seems like I should. I mean I want to. I'm just terrible at anything like that."

"Just say whatever you feel, John. You know he loved you."

Cardinal nodded. He took a few deep breaths to steady himself. The motorboat purred by. A family of four. The children in the back waved and yelled ahoy, ahoy. Catherine waved back.

"Well," Cardinal said finally. "Here goes." He turned around in his seat, kneeling on it. "I'm not going to drag this out, I'm just going to spread them and be done with it."

"Okay. I'll just keep it steady."

The wind had picked up. Cardinal had to keep low so the ashes wouldn't blow back all over the boat. As he leaned, the side wash from the motorboat caught them and rocked the boat. He had to clutch at the gunwale.

"That's all I need—to fall in. Dad would love that."

"Yes, he would."

Cardinal steadied himself and eased the bag from the canister. Then, using two hands, he shook the bag gently, as if he were seeding a garden. The ashes formed a swirling gray cumulus in the water. It took a minute or so to empty the bag, and by that time the boat had left a thick gray trail behind them. Many of the lighter flakes floated on the surface, and even finer particles blew away in the wind.

"I guess I just want to say . . . I want to say to the lake, I guess: Take these ashes, and you be kind. This was a good man." Cardinal had to take a deep breath. "This was a good husband and a good provider. A good man—I know I said that already. This was my father."

Cardinal turned and sat facing forward again, suddenly exhausted.

Catherine held his arm. She cut the motor, leaning over and resting her head on his shoulder in the silence. Cardinal felt her shake with tears.

The boat drifted in the wind, turning slightly so that once again they were looking at the sunlight glinting on Algonquin Bay. They drifted for perhaps a quarter of an hour, saying nothing. Then Catherine squeezed his arm and said, "I liked what you said."

Cardinal rinsed the plastic bag and the canister in the lake before putting them on the backseat.

"You want me to take the wheel again?"

"Nope," Catherine said. "I'm fine."

She started up the motor, and they cruised back toward West Ferris, the waves muttering against the hull. The wind caught Catherine's brown hair and tossed it every which way. Sunlight brought the color to her cheeks and she looked a lot like the young woman Cardinal had married nearly thirty years before.

He reached out and touched her shoulder.

Catherine looked over at him. "What?"

"Nothing," Cardinal said. "Head her for home, Captain."

Giles Blunt grew up in North Bay, Ontario, and lived for more than twenty years in New York City, where he wrote scripts for *Law and Order, Street Legal*, and *Night Heat*. He has recently moved back to Toronto, where he is at work on a new novel set in Algonquin Bay and featuring John Cardinal.

F